MW00480118

ELEMENT OF SECRECY

BOOK I

HEATHER SLAWECKI

Jeanne —
I look forward to taking
this adventure with you!
Heather Slawecki

g
Graylyn Press

ACKNOWLEDGEMENTS

Writing a trilogy in two years wouldn't have been possible without the support of some very special people. I'd like to start by thanking my mother, Carola, and my mother-in-law, Joan, for their involvement, encouragement, and enthusiasm. They read each chapter as I wrote them, helping me build momentum and the determination to cross the finish line. *As an aside, if one of your favorite characters lives or dies, it's possible they had something to do with it. True story.*

I would never have been able to juggle so many things if it weren't for my supportive husband, Adam, and our daughter, Lydia. Thank you for sacrificing time without me so I could pursue this goal, and for bringing me breakfast every Saturday and Sunday morning while I worked.

Big thanks to my editor, Becky Hamilton, for her contributions, great talks, and technical expertise. I'm equally thankful to Bill Sorg, Anthony Fusco, and Tom Whelan. Your feedback and encouragement (not to mention a little character inspiration) has meant so much.

The setting, I owe to the beautiful place I still consider home ... Bucks County. In this series, you'll find true depictions of Lake

Nockamixon, Tinicum and Tohickon Creeks, the Delaware River, New Hope, Peddler's Village, Doylestown, Van Sant Historical Airport, Ringing Rocks Park, Fonthill Castle, Mount Gilead, and Lambertville, New Jersey.

This trilogy is dedicated to my Bucks County Classmates from Tinicum Elementary, St. John the Baptist, and Central Bucks East, some are gone but not forgotten.

The many Ford references are in memory of the late and great Gary Buch, who owned McCafferty Ford, Langhorne from 1981 – 1999. The SOOOPER will always hold a special place in my heart, both for being my first feature story, and for being a great friend to our family.

Now, I invite you all to sit back and enjoy the wild ride.

1

ESCAPE

I heard them in the barn. They *still* don't know it, but I heard them. As a naïve 10-year-old little girl, it was so disturbing that I wet my pants.

My father, Sean O'Rourke, was once a well-respected and distinguished Manhattan attorney, a good dad, a dedicated husband, and a great provider. But that night I learned he had a dark side.

As I huddled in the corner of a stall, hoping desperately not to be discovered, I heard his gruff voice in the loft above me. Amid the chatter of strange voices, I heard him discuss plans to kill an enemy. At the end of the meeting, if that's what it was, he recited a Bible verse before all the voices joined together in a chant. I couldn't understand a lick of it, but I heard enough to be afraid. I wanted out of the stall and back into the comfort of my canopy bed. ASAP.

It turns out, that was just a sneak preview of things to come. It's time to shed some light on his dark secrets.

It's been a mentally exhausting day, one that has taken months of patience, plotting, and scheming to finally arrive. Getting caught could result in months, if not years, of seclusion or some other form of punishment.

I finally have somewhat of a life, so I'm really rolling the danger dice here. But it has to be done. My past has haunted me long enough, and I've come to the conclusion that the only way to get answers is to break the rules.

I'm absolutely forbidden to be sitting here in front of my childhood home. But here I am with two important mysteries to solve and a plethora of minor league ones. First, who killed my brother? And why? Second, who—and what—the hell is my father? I've narrowed it down to three possibilities: A secret agent of some sort, an organized crime leader, or a cult member. I'd love to rule out that last option, but I can't. It's bewildering to ponder, but I can't rule out the possibility that my own father is part of a cult. One without a name, as far as I know.

Aside from getting here alive, I don't have a solid plan. Probably because I didn't really expect to pull this off.

Before I cause an accident, I back up the Ford Escape, which I chose symbolically for its name, and park in the familiar spot across from the house. It's as inconspicuous as I'm going to get in a clearing before an old wooden one-way bridge.

I give myself a mental pep talk as I step out. It's an oppressively hot and humid day, and I was already sweating with the air cranked. I wipe my face with the bottom of my tank top and throw my long hair in a messy bun. I take a few steps forward to check out the creek and see dry exposed rocks and a slow-moving current. Not a whole lot of rain recently.

The familiar outdoorsy fragrance engulfs me. If someone blindfolded me and brought me here, I'd know exactly where I was, based on the smell alone. It's a blend of meadow, farm, and above all else, the creek. Some days the creek could smell kind of ripe, like something decomposing, others like a fragrance I wish I could bottle or find in a candle. I used to love watching its ever-changing motion and listening to it babble day and night. It was the only thing that soothed my soul during some of my darkest hours.

Before I attempt to play detective on the farm itself, I look straight up the dirt road perpendicular to the house and try to find a street sign. Nope! There still isn't one. The road is unnamed on maps, MapQuest, and navigation systems. We just always called it "the dirt road."

In the distance above the hill, I see the old windmill. It looks reconstructed, even larger than I remember. I count five large blades.

The hill itself brings back a memory of a day when my brother, Danny, and I were riding our bikes.

"Look, no hands!" I yelled and turned to make sure he was watching. The shift in position made the handlebars wobble and I lost my balance.

"The agony of defeat!" he hollered and began humming the Olympic theme. The fall knocked the wind out of me and left me with some sizable brush burns, but he made me laugh on the way down. He was always good at that. I glance at my elbow and can still see a faint scar, but I love it because it reminds me of him.

My mother reluctantly helped clean the wounds and remove all the tiny bits of gravel. "I swear you have a death wish, Jennifer," she said. My mother had no patience for this kind of thing. And by *thing*, I mean kids. I've often wondered how soon she regretted having us. Danny comforted me with a smirk and a rub on my back as she over-blasted my scrapes with antiseptic spray.

I can't help but smile at the memory. There really wasn't anything I wouldn't try. I liked to push the limits and consume whatever attention I'd get from it, even if it was negative. The result of this little excursion will certainly test my aptitude for that mentality again.

I flash back to our last night on the farm. The night we fled for our lives. I suppose I should consider myself lucky, because I'm standing here with air in my lungs and blood in my veins. My brother wasn't as lucky in that regard. I would do anything to reverse the situation, if only I had the chance.

Within days of our escape, at the tender age of twelve, I was sent to a private all-girls boarding school tucked away in Sun Valley, Idaho. I was miserably inconsolable and downright unlovable. My "sisters," as they called themselves, tried to friend me, but I wanted nothing to do with artificial family. I ached for the company of my brother and would accept no substitutes.

I haven't seen my parents since that day. That reality pales, though, in comparison to the pain of losing Danny. Eventually, I hardened on the inside and blossomed on the outside. I missed out on what should have been joyous milestones in my life, and I'm pretty pissed about it. Recklessly pissed off.

Since that night, I've been told that my parents split up. My mother moved to Italy with my grandmother, and I'm not allowed to have direct contact with either of my parents. Despite my father watching my every move, I know nothing of his whereabouts. I understand he moves frequently to avoid danger. Danger he likely perpetuated. He keeps track of me through one person, Ryan Burk. And they would both be very displeased to know where I am right now.

2

THE ROOSTER

No one has spotted me yet, thankfully, or there would be mayhem. I allow myself to relax a little and remind myself that there are no bad men after me, at least not today. I turn away from the dirt road and look back at my old house. There's a large tree masking my view, so I have to walk around to find a clearing. Everything's overgrown, compared to the way it used to look.

I trudge my way through tall grass across the street from the house, scratching and swatting at a few relentless horseflies along the way. As the house comes into view, I forget the flies. I'm mesmerized.

It's a very strange feeling to be on the outside looking in at your past life. I feel like a ghost, and I almost wish I could spy on my family as it was back then to witness the truth. See what I missed so I could put it all together. But someone seems to have started a new, much happier, life here.

There are some noticeable differences from how the farm used to look. Most obvious are the live animals. The only domestic animals to set foot on our property were a dog and a cat. I still miss my old tabby, Sherlock, and our barky old beagle, Daisy. Now, there's at least one sheep, a goat, and, in my opinion, far too many chickens running around. But maybe this is just how the whole free-range chicken thing works. Seems a bit much.

The chickens remind me of the rooster weathervane we had atop the barn. I shift my gaze and see that it's still there. My father told me that at one time roosters were placed on top of church steeples as a symbol of Peter's betrayal of Christ. He said Peter denied knowing Jesus three times before the rooster crowed. I don't recall which pope made the symbolic weathervanes a rule, but it eventually fell by the wayside and shifted to a tradition on barns instead. My father told me if I ever betrayed him, the rooster would crow. I would stare at the rooster when I got in trouble to see what happened. Luckily it was an idle threat, but I was very superstitious about it.

Before hitting the road, I did a little digging on the history and construction of this house. The two-story home was built in a Pennsylvania Dutch style. The exterior is completely covered by stone pulled from the creek bed, probably by the original owner. The roof is steep, and the windows aren't very wide, but they're quite long. I can see the chimney where our fireplace sat in the central part of our home. It, too, was made of stone and took up almost the whole wall.

There's a covered porch framed in dark oak spindles at the front of the house overlooking the creek. When my grandmother came for visits, she'd plop herself down on one of our wooden rocking chairs and take it all in. Visiting was like a vacation to her. "Potrei sedermi qui per sempre," (I could sit here forever) she'd say with a chuckle. It certainly is eye candy, and the type of home with surroundings so often captured on canvas.

We had a traditional bank barn constructed so the lower level could house livestock and the upper level provide storage for tractors and farm tools. It's still beautiful but much of the red paint has faded over the years. I assume the loft and ladder are still there—perhaps storing straw and hay now.

Before the weird meetings up there, it was empty except for a rope that Danny and I turned into a swing. We would disappear for hours, swinging and playing Tarzan and Jane. We'd glide from the loft over the center part of the barn and almost to the far end. That was probably a little dangerous, now that I think of it. We were crushed the day my father told us we weren't allowed in the barn again, "or else."

The top level of the barn overlaps the bottom, providing extra coverage near the stalls. I see a few more sheep have gathered in the shade beneath it, but the area and stalls were eerily empty when I was a child. I really wanted a pony like most of my friends had on their farms. The only creatures that occupied our barn were mice and barn swallows.

My mother was not a fan of mice. I smirk at another memory. One night when we were watching the news, the only thing allowed on our TV, a cute little mouse ran halfway across the room and then stopped. It stood up on its hind legs, wiggled its nose, and looked around. Danny and I thought he was adorable, but I'm surprised my mother didn't shatter glass with her shriek. She threatened to move out right then and there. My dad's solution was to get the cat. It worked most of the time. Sherlock brought us lots of "gifts." But there was still a decent amount of scratching coming from the walls at night. My dad convinced my mom that it was just an old house making old sounds. I don't think she bought it, but I know she wanted to believe it.

I see the chicken coop now. It's a bit dilapidated and definitely the original. There were two at first. My father got rid of one but kept this one for storage. I don't know what he stored inside because he kept a big lock on it and even boarded up the windows, but that didn't stop us from getting on the roof.

The chicken coop roof is high at the top, but slopes to about a foot or two off the ground in the back. I cringe remembering the day I convinced Danny that it was safe to ride our Big Wheels down it. I was even kind enough to *allow* him the privilege of going first. The ride down was amusement park fun but the landing ... let's just say, he didn't stick it. The wheels were spinning upside down as he shot up and through the air a good six feet away. I frantically ran into the house to get my mother, convinced he was dead. Thankfully, he was just a bit banged up.

It was his turn to endure the antiseptic spray, and I got a good ass whooping. My parents weren't afraid of corporal punishment. My mother preferred the wooden spoon method ... if she could catch me. My dad was the master of snapping the belt right before whipping us. My strategy was to make sure my behind was ready, or the belt would lash a shoulder, leg, or even my face. He always whipped us five times, no matter what the crime, but never told us why. Instead, he'd say things like "This is going to hurt me more than it's going to hurt you." I still don't buy that expression.

Because I was such a daredevil, I got in trouble the most and had my share of beatings. My brother was smart—he watched and learned. He'd lay low and out of my dad's way. I would gauge each situation and decide if it was worth the punishment. Most of the time it was, at least up until the exact moment when my father reached for the belt. Then I'd second-guess my actions. The harsh punishment, or abuse I should call it, began after we moved to the farm. My dad was softer and kinder when I was very young.

At this point, I've pretty much seen all I can from where I'm standing. Overall, I think it looked a heck of a lot better when we owned it. It's not that it looks run-down, it's just not pristine like my parents kept it. I think they were going for a *Better Homes and Gardens* look. Perfectly landscaped at all times. Not by them. I'm sure they paid big bucks for that kind of manicuring.

The current owners look like they're either in over their heads with maintenance work, or simply aren't obsessed with curb appeal. In addition to general disarray, I see spindles missing from the porch railing, and the once-adorable, red-handled well pump is trying to peek out from a bush or weed.

I shake my head and wonder why I care so much. I'm getting sentimental for absolutely no good reason. I have to remind myself that I'm not here on a nostalgia tour.

3

BRANDTVILLE, PENNSYLVANIA

The farm sits in the middle of Brandtville, a small town in Upper Bucks County, Pennsylvania. The county is one of the most well-known counties in the country, but virtually no one has heard of Brandtville, and that's the way they like it. I didn't find a lot of history about it online, but I did read that Brandtville was formally known as Red Bank because of the large ridge of red shale rock where the village sits. It's why the main road is called Red Rock Road and why the original owners named our farm Red Rock Farm.

By the early 1920s, some of the local farmers in the surrounding villages sold out for what they considered small fortunes to wealthy actors, screen writers, painters, and authors who wanted the ultimate place to relax on weekends or to spend their retirement. Some turned old dairy farms into beautiful horse farms. Architects and artsy types fixed up old barns and turned them into deluxe cottage homes. However, the land in Brandtville, along with some of the surrounding villages, is very regulated. There are tight commercial and residential building restrictions, so there are no strip malls and very few cookie-cutter homes.

The area is still connected mainly by dirt roads and covered bridges. Tinicum and Tohickon Creeks wind through the territory, eventually dumping their waters into the Delaware River or Lake Nockamixon. On summer days, locals and tourists tube down the Delaware River, many with Styrofoam coolers of beer floating along behind them. Some take their fishing rods and cast out while they're drifting.

Twice I got permission to go with my friend Karen and her family, who lived near the river. We tied our tubes together for a three-hour journey. I loved hitting the rapids and pretending we were on a wild adventure down the Amazon, looking out for hippos. I also remember fixating on the idea that my bottom was sitting in the river as we floated. I was convinced something was going to come up and bite me.

My father became enamored with the small town after visiting one of his old law firm partners, William (Billy) Weber. Billy's second home was in Brandtville, his first in Manhattan. He inherited the house from his parents, and they from theirs. One day Billy announced that he was selling his share of the firm so that he could "disappear."

The firm was famous for taking on high-profile cases and represented some of the most powerful and influential clients in New York City. They helped celebrities out of pinches and got greedy embezzlers off without time. But, hands down, defending organized crime leaders with their dangerous connections was the most unnerving part of their caseload. Their enemies had enemies. Nearly all the members of the firm received death threats at one time or another. But they beefed up home security and still enjoyed the exposure and limelight. Their wives enjoyed the life of luxury. Billy was an exception. Unlike many of the large egos in the practice, he hated the media attention. The pressure eventually got to him, and Brandtville seemed like the perfect place to disappear. He eased his way out, commuting to the city to finish some big cases, and then he was done.

Once he moved for good, Billy renovated the farmhouse, which stood secluded by trees on top of a hill just above Tinicum Creek on Deep Creek Road. About halfway down the road was a very deep swimming hole.

The villagers and surrounding residents knew about Deep Creek and spent the hottest days of summer with their families cooling off. It was way more fun and adventurous than a swimming pool. You could climb the red rocks and jump right into the middle of the deep end or skip rocks in the shallow end. The kids would gather to exchange tales about the creek, some saying a sea monster lived under the rocks. Some claimed they'd seen children dunked into the center by cults. It became a fun but very mysterious pastime.

Billy poured money into the house and property, adding a tennis court and a lagoon-style pool with a waterfall. The home itself had top-of-the-line everything, even a home theater in the finished basement. We'd never seen one of those before.

Still good buddies, my father made a point of visiting him more frequently than my mother cared for. Billy's kids were grown, and he and his wife were barely on speaking terms. He was lonely and liked my dad's company—at least that's what he told us.

My father and Billy started enjoying fishing and hunting together. We always had guns in the house once my father learned how to hunt. He built a special unit into a large closet on the main floor, which housed at least a dozen, including handguns, shotguns, and a bow and arrow set. He kept it locked to make sure we didn't get into it—probably a good idea with my unquenchable curiosity around.

After my father nabbed his first twelve-pointer, he had it stuffed and mounted above our gas fireplace in the finished basement. Danny and I didn't care for it. We could feel its eyes following us no matter where we were in the large room. We were bitter that he was turning our playroom space into some kind of primitive man cave.

Even stranger, Billy seemed to spark a passion for history in my father. Bucks County history exclusively. He sat us down on many occasions to tell us about the Delaware River Lenape Indians, including the peace treaty between Chief Tamanend and William Penn. Our eyes would glaze over with boredom. As time went on, he collected Indian artifacts like pottery and arrowheads. My mother put her foot down the day he brought home an authentic headdress, feathers and all.

"What the hell is wrong with you, Sean? This isn't normal. We don't have a single cell of Native American blood in us!" she scolded. "I don't understand."

"You buy shoes, Angela, and I'll buy what I want. It's a fun hobby," he said, but promised to rein it in a little.

On one of our visits to Billy's house, Danny and I took off to play our favorite game of hide and seek. We ended up deep into the woods and stumbled upon a clearing. There were "Danger" signs and barbed wire beyond it, probably going around the perimeter of his property, at least in the woods. Within the clearing, we discovered a small wooden podium and five chairs. Each chair had unique symbolic carvings. I wish like hell I could recall what they were now. At the time, we were too interested in the hollowed-out oak tree near the podium. We peered inside to find a secret safe. We were nervous about the consequences, but we decided to open it anyway. It was unlocked after all.

On top was a curious stack of papers. I took a look at the first page and saw the mugshot of a man who looked familiar from the news. There was also a chart with multiple lines drawn to the names of other people. In bold letters was the word "Enemies." We hightailed it out of there before getting caught and splashed in the pool instead, never saying a word to either of my parents.

I know now that the mugshot was no other than Dominick D'Angelo, the last man Billy defended in court. I also know that he disappeared before he could be sentenced. The news led with stories about his escape for weeks. Everyone assumed that he fled the country to avoid the death penalty.

They had Dominick on surveillance cameras fleeing the scene of a massacre in the Hamptons. He was on trial for the murder of

Dennis Alderman, the Chief Financial Officer of a financial firm in New York City, and his entire family. No matter how good Billy was at his job, the District Attorney was going to win the case.

Danny and I never came up with a single good reason why Billy would've been hiding secrets in the woods, but we were wary of him after that.

Not long after our visit, my father announced that he was heading back to Brandtville to check out a big beautiful farm for sale at the bottom of Red Rock Road, right around the corner from Billy's private property on Deep Creek.

"Not gonna happen," my mother told him on his way out the door.

When he returned to our home in Parsippany, New Jersey, later that night, he called for us to join him for a family meeting.

He grabbed me first and said, "Jenny, how would you like to move to the country?"

I looked from him to my mom, knowing my opinion didn't really matter. She rolled her eyes like I knew she would. She was raised in New York City before being spoiled by my father in North Jersey and wasn't even pretending to humor him with such a thought.

"And what're you going to do about the firm? That's quite a commute from Manhattan," she said sarcastically.

"I thought about that. There's a town not far with a big County Seat courthouse." He was referring to Doylestown. "Angela, I'm tired of the city. I'm tired of the traffic. I'm tired of the horrible people I represent, who literally get away with murder. I see how Billy's living, and that's the lifestyle I want for you and the kids. Life is too short. I want out of the firm."

I thought my mom was going to pass out. The firm had been his life for ten years, and he worked hard to become a partner. "I'll start up my own practice in Bucks County. There are plenty of opportunities there, I promise."

Let the negotiations begin. My father was one of the top defense attorneys in the city, known for his dramatic courtroom showdowns.

His approach stirred emotion and almost always left jurors with the reasonable doubt he needed to win. But Angela O'Rourke, attorney at home, could give him a run for his money, and she did a lot of winning herself.

My mother was not big on change, and this was rocking her world something awful. She was content with her network of hoity-toity friends, able to hit the clubhouse any time she wanted. And the spa treatments were part of her weekly routine, not an occasional indulgence.

My dad was in for a battle that night, but we all knew he would win.

4

THE SHOWING

The day we all drove to see the farm is etched in my mind. My mom reluctantly got in the car wearing white pants, a designer peach halter top with sequins, and a pair of heels. Her hair seemed extra high that day too, but it was the 80s after all.

"Really, Angela? We're going to be touring a farm. You'll be walking through a meadow to see the property and a barn. You look like we're heading into the city for dinner."

"We haven't even seen the house yet and you want me to change the way I dress? Dream on, cowboy. Or should I say, Indian?"

Danny and I leaned as far back as we could into the leather seats of the Mercedes, waiting for an explosion. My dad's face got red, but he surprised us and let it go.

My mom continued to sit through the two-hour ride with a bad attitude and resting bitch face. She was in a foul mood. My dad, quite to the contrary. He played and replayed "Spirit in the Sky" by Norman Greenbaum. I can still hear him singing along in my head.

"When I die and they lay me to rest, Gonna go to the place that's the best. When they lay me down to die, Goin' up to the spirit in the sky."

My mom tried to turn off the radio, but my father gave her a look I'd never seen before. She didn't touch the dial again.

It was 1984. I was seven and Danny was six. "Irish twins" we were called. We were close in age and always played very well together. When we weren't swimming in our pool or playing hide and seek, we occupied ourselves playing games like "Santa." We'd wrap up our own toys in towels and give them to each other as presents. We made Christmas happen any time of the day or year. Scavenger hunts were our absolute favorite. We'd leave each other notes, sometimes very complex, with clues to find the next item.

Once we got off the I-95 exit, things got very rural. We spotted a few deer, which made me think of the one stuffed in the basement. I couldn't imagine how my father enjoyed a sport that involved killing animals. Danny and I were ecstatic to see them grazing and looking down at us from the hilltops. My mom's first reaction was to lecture us about deer ticks and Lyme Disease. She was on all of our nerves at that point and sucking the fun right out of the trip.

"Welcome to Brandtville," my dad shouted, reading the wooden sign. "We're almost there. When we get to the bottom of this hill, you'll see the farm around the bend and in the distance." The road was steep and ran alongside a cliff overlooking the creek. Finally, my dad pointed to a house and said, "There it is."

The real estate agent was waiting in the long driveway next to an antique Rolls Royce. He opened the door for my mom, held out a hand, and introduced himself. "Please call me Thomas," he insisted.

He was a man in his late sixties perhaps, very gentlemanly and dapper in a grey summer suit. Danny and I were shy in his presence, so he worked to win us over. He bent down to our level and said, "Well, would you look at the two of you. Handsome children, Sean."

My father thanked him and shook his hand. Thomas announced that Ms. Aada had baked an apple pie from fruit she'd picked that morning. He pointed to the apple tree. Danny and I were impressed and wondered if Nonna could bake them too. As much as we wanted pie, though, Danny and I were much more interested in the creek.

My father gave us permission to explore, so we took off through the meadow and plunged in fully dressed, much to our mother's dismay. We saw frogs and crayfish while we splashed around and could smell the wildflowers from the meadow. The woods were both enchanting and ominous in every direction.

The home we had in New Jersey was beautiful, but our pool took up the whole back yard. There were so many possibilities running through our little heads. We were sold right then and there. My mom had her hands folded defensively, but even she seemed to perk up a little in the beautiful surroundings.

We were told the house was built in the mid-1800s by one of the wealthiest German immigrant farmers in the village, John Betzler. The second-generation owners, Ms. Aada and Mr. Alex, as they preferred us to call them, had lived in the home for over sixty years. They were too old to manage the farm at that point and needed to sell it. We could tell by looking at them that it was a difficult decision. They were very attached to the house, but they greeted us warmly and made a fuss over us, telling us they were never able to have children of their own.

Everything needed updating, especially the kitchen. My mom didn't cook, but my grandmother did, and we all encouraged her as often as possible. She made the best "gravy" on the planet and eggplant and chicken parm. There really was no end to what she could make well. She loved cooking, even when we devoured our meals within minutes after it took her all day to prepare them.

My grandfather passed away at a young age, very soon after they moved from Italy to New York City. Being a single parent, and learning a new language at the same time, was very difficult for her. My mom and grandmother leaned on each other for support for many years. It's part of why they were so close.

My father promised he'd make the kitchen his first project, just for Nonna, and make a spare room for her too. The four bedrooms were a decent size, but the closets were small. That's the way they made them back then, but my mother acted personally offended just looking at them.

For the next hour or so, Danny and I played hide and seek in the barn. There were lots of hiding places, which made it much harder for us to find each other than we were used to. By the time my dad told us to get back in the car, he'd won his biggest battle, successfully convincing my mom that it was the right move. The agent helped by describing nearby New Hope where there were plenty of spas, lots of action, and great restaurants. It was a hand well-played. We were moving to Brandtville.

5

SAL ROSSI

I 'm lost in vivid memories crashing over me in waves. The sound of a car coming around the bend transports me back to my present situation. I look away as a middle-aged woman, driving an ultra-expensive Jag convertible, creeps by me very slowly. She takes her time looking me over, which is both odd and unnerving. I only catch a glimpse, but from what I see, she's very exotic-looking, with long, wavy black hair. I get a shiver from the dark energy she's expelling and feel self-conscious standing here. Maybe it's the over-protective way she glanced at me that's making me uncomfortable, or maybe I'm being paranoid. Despite the old farm being my home for almost five years, I'm a total trespasser now. But I shake it off because I drove a good three hours from my townhouse in Baltimore to try and put my past together.

I suddenly wish Sal were here with me. He didn't like the idea of me coming alone, but I insisted. After boarding school, I was allowed out of my cage and permitted—technically, forced—to attend a very small private business and law school outside of Baltimore, Maryland. So small, in fact, that only about a hundred students graduate per year. Most are the children of politicians, celebrities, and other high-profile families for whom privacy is of the utmost importance.

Sal Rossi is my best friend and my rock. We met my sophomore year, and even though he was a freshman, we still had a few classes together. We hit it off right away by making fun of our economics professor, who was an uptight SOB. He would frazzle and lose his patience at the drop of a hat. So, Sal and I would take turns asking him really stupid questions and get the giggles as we watched him try to control his rage. We were terribly immature and still can be when we get each other going.

Much to the dismay of my protectors, I let loose during those college years. After what I endured in my adolescence, I deserved it. I was tough to keep track of and became the master of disappearing acts, reappearing at clubs in the city with Sal and other male friends in tow. I liked a few of the girls but never hung out with them. I found some to be too prissy and others pathetically needy around their boyfriends. Watching them dote and hang all over them seemed pitiful.

Not all of my guy friends were just friends. I had my share of lovers. The intimacy was therapeutic, but I bailed out of relationships before an "I love you." I didn't want to feel anything, so I built an impenetrable wall around myself. The fear of losing someone I cared for again was too much to bear. A defense mechanism.

Sal always tells me I'm gorgeous, non-judgmental, and can talk and hang like one of the guys. We learned over beers and lots of clubbing that we had some things in common. Not exactly apples-to-apples things, but we both grew up with instability. He comes from a tight Italian family, thick as thieves. His father, Anthony Rossi, spent some time in jail for racketeering, among other things. I told him it was a shame my father no longer practiced law, because he could have gotten him off in a heartbeat.

He also has an uncle currently standing trial for a big-time jewelry heist, which is ironic considering his own brother owns a jewelry store. I've asked him many times if his family is connected to the mob.

"Stop watching *The Sopranos*. It's not like that. You think just 'cause we're Italian, we're mafia?" He busts on me, but I get the feeling there's more to it. I stopped asking questions a long time ago because Sal doesn't like talking about it. He says it's embarrassing. Neither of us is like our families.

He got into real estate after college and owns several apartment buildings, as well as three very nice restaurants in the Little Italy section of Philadelphia where he was born and raised. The chefs are amazing, and I think of Nonna every time I take a bite, knowing how much she would have loved the food. He's done well for himself.

Sal is very close to his mom, who has always been protective of him. She speaks Italian almost exclusively in the house, just like my grandmother did. Sal can keep up, but I'm not very good at it.

And, yes, we've always been attracted to each other, but we know what sex can do to a good friendship. Sal's very handsome, well-built, and always dressed to kill in his Armani suits. I love hugging him and wearing his cologne for the rest of the day.

Over the years, we've had the best times simply confiding in each other, gossiping, drinking, and generally leaning on each other. We're committed to our friendship and have vowed to be forever "just friends."

"You're one smoking hot best friend," he tells me. I admit that I'm attractive, but these days I find it more of a burden than a blessing. Who wants to be stared at all the time? I really just want to blend. When I'm not out to impress, I skip the makeup, toss my hair up, and cover the bod, which thankfully I don't have to work very hard to keep fit. I enjoy a long run several times a week and eat healthy because it makes me feel good. I think what captivates most people about me are my eyes. They're emerald green without the fake lenses, but people still inevitably ask if I wear colored contacts. They're really that green.

There are advantages to being smart and attractive. I find it rather easy to manipulate men. Women fall prey to men so easily, but really, it's men with their raging testosterone, who are the easy ones to play. I can have them eating out of my hand after one conversation. Sal always asks me to remind him never to get on my bad side.

These days, I'm doing what I love, at least professionally. Despite dual law degrees in criminal and civil, I jumped ship. I passed the bar, gave defense a shot for a big firm in Baltimore, and had immediate regrets. I learned very quickly that our system is broken—or maybe it never really worked that well to begin with.

My last case, only the third I ever took, was defending Danbury Pharmaceutical Company, located a few blocks from Johns Hopkins Hospital. It was a small class action suit against the company for wrongful death, post-consumption of a new broad-spectrum antibiotic. No one was more surprised than I was when I won. But it was bittersweet and heartbreaking for the families who lost. I decided I never wanted to see grief-stricken faces in a courtroom like that ever again.

But Danbury loved me so much that they offered me a job anywhere I wanted it, assuming it would be in their law and compliance department. I asked, "Anywhere?" And they agreed, *anywhere*. I pulled off my most rebellious stunt ever, at least until now, and took a job as a pharma rep. Their case drew me to medicine, and I figured if I educated enough doctors about the side effects of some of these drugs, maybe things like that wouldn't happen again. It isn't something I plan on doing for very long, just long enough to figure out what I really want to do. One thing I know for sure, I don't want to follow in my father's footsteps as an attorney, and suffice to say, that decision hasn't gone over very well. My father threw an absolute shitfit but couldn't come out of hiding to do anything about it. Every few months, I get a message ordering me to start practicing again and to stop wasting my talent.

Who says I'm wasting my talent? Pharma sales is working out for me. I'm convincing as hell with my law background, and I know my shit. There isn't a drug we make that I can't sell, once I get beyond the gatekeepers in the office.

Another downfall to the looks, which may have more to do with my "issues," is my compulsion for men. I still like a variety, as my ex-husband found out. I disappointed him on so many levels.

6

ROAD TRIP

With my busy job and the inability to go anywhere without checking in, it's been difficult to pull off this road trip. I was patient and well-behaved for almost a year, waiting for an opportunity when no one was paying close attention. When a window cracked open, I slipped through.

I'm on guard twenty-four seven with both personal and government-issued security. The entire team has been getting complacent and bored with the dull routine and my lack of defiance.

This morning, I threw a pair of shorts and a tank top in my bag, along with a pair of sandals, but walked out looking like a million bucks in a Ralph Lauren classic navy suit, white shirt, heels, full makeup, the works.

I left in my Mercedes as usual and pulled into the Hopkins garage. Today is Saturday, so I'm sure whoever followed me was confused because I don't make calls very often on the weekend. I pulled in and made my way up the ramp at epic speed, barely missing the wall at one point. I had the advantage of knowing there were a few cars moving slowly behind me, buying me some time. I found the spot saved for me, hopped out, and slipped right into my other car, the Ford Escape. It was parked almost a whole flight up, but I nailed the timing, snuck through the back seat, and pulled the privacy panel closed to block their view. I waited about fifteen minutes before emerging, shifting out of the back and into the driver's seat.

"They" also still haven't figured out that I have a black Ford Escape. It's in Sal's name and he drops it off for me when and where I need it, which hasn't been very often. But I still like knowing it's there.

Sal is also the only one who knows I'm under such scrutiny, and my scrutinizers know Sal is aware. They weren't happy to find out that I confided in him. I didn't give him everything, mostly because I don't know everything. That's exactly why I'm here today, staring at my old farmhouse.

As a result of my big mouth, they keep tabs on Sal too. The last thing either of us wants, however, is for our unstable families to ever collide. We're both usually very careful and talk about them as little as possible because they don't matter anyway.

It was quite the workout stripping out of my suit and into my more appropriate summer wear. My hair was all over the place, but I straightened it out with my hands the best I could and got on the road. As I started the car, I found a note from Sal telling me to be careful. I'm so lucky to have him for a friend. Really, I consider Sal the only family I've got at this point.

The drive wasn't too bad. I got tied up a bit on the turnpike, but completely expected that. Once I got to Doylestown, I knew I was getting close. I couldn't believe how many new buildings, homes, and shops opened since we left.

But as I headed north on Route 611, it all looked almost exactly the same. Time has seemingly stood still in Upper Bucks County. It's a bit too rural for me now. Having to drive a half hour to get to the grocery store isn't my cup of tea, but it's just as beautiful as I remembered.

The quaint town I grew up in is a blessing to most, but it was a nightmare for me. There were things I saw that I can't explain. There were things I heard that I never dared to repeat. My innocence was taken from me here with abuse, lies, and traumatic experiences. My father tells me I've been shielded from the hard stuff. If that's true, I can handle it now. In addition to finding out what happened to my brother, I want to find out how and why Billy was found murdered in our favorite swimming hole in the middle of Deep Creek.

7

THE DORCYS

I 'm staring back at the farm, completely insecure and contemplating my next step, when I see movement. A man appears from behind the barn with his hands full of hay, attending to the farm animals. He's thin with salt and pepper hair, wearing what looks like a good old-fashioned pair of Levis and a tattered red T-shirt. Two adorable golden retrievers follow him around while he works.

I panic for a minute and consider hiding, which I realize would look pretty odd and suspicious. I have no idea if I should approach him or how I would even go about doing that. I certainly don't expect the new owners to know much, if anything, about the past life of the farm. If I could convince him to let me walk around the property, or better yet get in the house, maybe I could recall some important things. Things that will buy me a few leads or help me find the right people to talk to without completely blowing my identity. That would be very bad.

I watch the man as he goes from stall to stall, patting a goat here, a sheep there. I was so worried about him seeing me that I almost missed the woman coming out of the side door. *Shit!* His wife, I assume, is wearing a cute little yellow sundress and carrying a laundry basket. I realize the clothesline is directly in front of me, and she's coming at it.

She looks up, and I'm busted staring at her like a total stalker. As it should, my presence startles her, and she abruptly halts. She's pretty for a woman her age. She has long, wavy red hair with grey highlights, probably blonde highlights not so long ago. She's curvy in all the right places.

"Can I help you?" she asks.

I regain my composure and with my warmest smile, cross the street and gesture to her. She looks back to see where her husband is and cautiously inches toward me.

I introduce myself and reveal that I used to live on the farm as a child. I realize I'm playing with fire doing so, but it just came out. Luckily, she relaxes and lights up.

"Oh my gosh, how neat! We searched everywhere but couldn't find any records about previous owners after 1988." *Not surprising.*

"Really? Well we lived here for about three years," I minimize. "I had some time today, so I decided to take a road trip and sneak a peek at the house. Sorry for the intrusion. I didn't mean to bother you."

"Oh, no, not at all. When we purchased the farm, it was vacant for at least ten years, probably more. It was a mess, but we're working on it. The good part about the condition is that my husband worked a phenomenal deal with the bank. They told us there had been auctions before, but no takers. They just wanted to dump it. Were you the last owners?"

"No. I think my parents sold it to a family, but I don't remember their names."

"Oh, I see. I heard a family with two children lived here last and there was some sort of ugly divorce or something. Or maybe something even more tragic." She eyes me up curiously to see if I have any details to offer.

"Yeah, that must've been the family. My parents are still happily married and I'm an only child."

She yells for her husband to join us at the end of the driveway. Reluctantly, he follows her request. The dogs start barking and race to investigate me. The man tells them to settle down. I let them sniff my hand, and they lose interest pretty quick and lie down.

He lights up too when he sees me, but for different reasons I suspect. The woman throws her husband the hairy eyeball as he looks me up and down.

"Well, hello there! What brings you here?"

I meet Jack and Katie Dorcy, the current owners of Red Rock Farm. They're in their mid-fifties and have two daughters in their twenties who still live in their hometown city of Boston. They've only lived in Brandtville for about three years and purchased the farm to fill their empty nest syndrome and to keep busy and active. They admit they're still adjusting to country life but love it.

I look back at the animals going about their business. I can't help but notice the odor they're emitting but suppress the urge to make a face. I'm no primadonna, but it's a little rank. Time to lay it on without giving away how I really feel.

"I just love that you have so many animals. Do you mind if I pet the goat?"

"Miss Mable? No, not at all, she's a sweetheart," Jack says.

I walk closer to the barn area and open a little gate where the animals are fenced in. The sheep stay where they are, but the goat moves in fast. I've never been this close to one before and am not really sure what to do. She's studying me back, waiting for some attention or maybe a treat. I give her an awkward pat on the head and exclaim that she's precious, while strategically edging myself deeper into the property.

Jack and Katie are just as interested in what I have to tell them as I am to ask questions. I start with the true-story fun things I used to do, like sledding down the big hill on the side of the barn.

I point to the patio my father built with his own two hands. I'm happy to see it's still there, because that job nearly killed him. It was the only home improvement project he ever did on his own. I guess he was trying to prove that he was capable of creating something from the natural surroundings like most of the locals and early settlers did. He brought up big stones from the creek to form a retaining wall. The patio itself he designed with stone-colored pavers, which he purchased from a local landscaper. I notice grass and weeds coming up through the cracks, and it sort of annoys me, maybe because it's one of the few good memories I have of him here. But I keep it to myself and remain pleasant because I'm on a mission.

As if reading my mind, Katie invites me inside.

"Tricia, the house isn't very clean and I'm kind of embarrassed, but why don't you come in so you can see your childhood home."

I had to give them the name I go by now, Tricia Keller. I wish the Witness Protection Program had let me choose my own name. Although at the time, I probably would have given myself a far-out name like Starlene. I really just want to be Jenny again. Sal calls me Jen when no one's around, but absolutely no one else does. It's in the vault.

"Thank you, Katie. Are you sure? I don't want to intrude."

"No, no, please, you've come all the way from where?"

"Maryland. And to tell you the truth, I really need to use a restroom."

"Oh my gosh, please, come in then," she says with a laugh. Katie walks me in through the side entrance and shows me to the restroom, exactly as I remember, while Jack goes back outside to finish his chores.

After washing the goat smell off my hands, I reemerge and listen as Katie tells me more about the condition of the home when they moved in. "The pool was in ruins, so we had to almost entirely rebuild it. None of the radiators worked. We had to put in new windows because half of them were broken. Oh, and replace the hardwood floors completely."

"Sounds like a total mess! What a shame. I'm so glad you bought it and saved it."

"Thank you, Tricia. You're very kind. People had been breaking in for years and vandalizing. We found some weird stuff and drawings."

"Oh, really, of what?"

"Curious symbols. Pyramids with eyes. Crosses. Some sort of ancient Egyptian writing, which Jack had decoded."

"What did it say?"

"Something relating to judgement. I couldn't wait to paint over them. I'm sure it was just kids, but it was kind of scary."

"That is very strange! You said stuff too. Like what?"

"In the barn, we found a bucket with a rope tied to it, like a well bucket." I look at her, waiting for the weird part. Could have just been a well bucket. Maybe they don't know they have one because of the weeds. "There was a bowl, some silverware, and a thermos inside."

"Eww? Did you check your well for dead bodies?" I laugh. She doesn't.

"Actually, yes we did. Water was clear. Thank God."

"Do you still have them?" *This is kind of huge!*

"No. We burned them in our first big bonfire after we moved in. Anyway, thankfully the main structure of the home was intact, and none of the pipes burst over the winters, or there'd be no way Jack would have talked me into this farm."

Kudos to Jack! He must have made one heck of a sales pitch. My mom never would have considered buying this house in such condi-tion. It's tour time! Much to my surprise again, Katie invites me to look around on my own.

"You go ahead. I'm going to hang up the sheets," she says. Was this really happening? I'm so grateful. I go from one room to the next and can't believe how much smaller the living room looks. I remember it being so big that I could do cartwheels across the floor without hitting anything. It looks like they're working on the library, which was my father's office. It's where he kept his law books, among other things. It was off-limits to anyone but him, including my mother.

31

The Dorcys are refurbishing the large built-in mahogany book-shelves. The walls used to be hunter green with burgundy accents. They're a trendy grey now. I also remember two original foxhunt paintings that hung on the wall. Once my father got his practice going in Doylestown, he spent about half his time here and half his time at his small office in town, which he shared with an accountant.

One thing is for certain ... I'm not going down into the basement. It was partially finished with dark wood paneling. My father kept his ever-growing collection of taxidermied animals and artifacts down there, including a new set of Indian drums. Every now and then, he played them. I get a shiver thinking of it. Nope. No way.

Instead, I make my way upstairs and smile when I see they still have our old clawfoot sunken bathtub. I don't want to be too intru-sive, so I stay out of the bedrooms, except for mine. It's a good size, like I remember. I can visualize where my Barbie house was on the other side of my bed. Now the room is used as a home office, probably until they finish refurbishing the library. There are stacks of paper and a desk with a rather impressive workstation. Someone must work from home. There's a large-screen iMac plus a printer, scanner, and overflowing bookshelves. Maybe Jack is a writer.

When I have nothing left to scan, I take a deep breath and turn my attention to the closet. My heart sinks and I feel raw emotion for the first time in a very long time. I open the door slowly and look for the semi-hidden panel that leads to a large, open crawlspace. It's still there. My eyes get watery as I remember the day.

The crawlspace saved my life, but my brother had no time to hide. I heard gunshots and my mother screaming, so I found my way into our secret hiding place, but Danny couldn't escape. He'd been outside riding his bike. I'm not exactly sure how yet, but I'm going to find out who killed my playmate and best friend. Even more than finding closure, I'm looking for justice and revenge.

8

A HUGE OPPORTUNITY

I dab at my eyes and join Katie in the kitchen. She's smiling and looking for feedback.

"Well?" she asks.

I put on the charm and a bright smile. "I just can't thank you enough, Katie. Walking through the house has brought back so many wonderful memories. Not much has changed, really. You and your husband have done a wonderful job fixing it up. It looks absolutely great." She's flattered and pleased with my response. "Can I ask you a few questions while I'm here?"

"You sure can," she replies pleasantly.

I'm very interested to know if some of the neighbors are still here, one in particular who lived in the only house you could see from ours. The adults were hippie types, always smoking pot, and had a child with some "mental problems." That's how my mom described her. But I never thought of her that way. At first, I didn't know why they kept her so locked up. She would stare at Danny and me from her bedroom window when we played in the creek. I made eye contact with her frequently and always made a point of waving. She'd wave back with sadness in her eyes and a big frown on her face.

"Do the Bergers still live around the corner?" I point in the direction, just beyond the bridge where I parked.

"Yes, they do," Katie says with disdain. "Well, Rob died a few years ago. They have a daughter around your age. Did you play with her?"

"No. I didn't," I say, hoping my nose won't grow.

"Well, she's been in and out of psych wards since we moved here. Kathy seems to get her under control, and then she goes off her meds and the bizarre behavior starts again. One morning, I found her sleeping in the barn in just her nightgown. Scared me to death. Another time the dogs chased her out of the meadow. She said she was following a man. What the heck is that, Tricia? I don't like her on the property and think she's very disturbed. As far as I know though, she's never hurt anyone except herself. She cut her wrists and was admitted a few months ago. I hope she stays there. Does that sound harsh? I hope I'm not coming across as mean."

"No, not at all. I'm so sorry to hear that though. That's sad." I'm not contributing as much as I could to this gossip session. I have more than my share of Jodi stories but keep them to myself. "The only thing I remember about Jodi is that she didn't go to school with the other children. I hope they can help her." And then I change the subject.

"How do you like living here? It must've been quite an adjustment coming from Boston."

She smiles. "You can say that again! It was exciting at first, but I feel like we're in over our heads." *I knew it.* "I'm honestly getting burned out."

I can tell by looking at her that she's fried. She has big bags under her eyes and looks like she hasn't had a good night's sleep in months.

"Jack does his best to keep after the animals, but I feel like we're losing control. I keep telling him to get rid of some of the chickens, and why do we need sheep? Lord have mercy! Tricia, we must get a dozen eggs a day. I make egg salad, deviled eggs, and egg casseroles. I'm getting really tired of them. In fact, before you leave, I'm going to give you what's just been laid." I laugh and accept. "Maybe we just need a vacation."

I suddenly get the craziest idea. "You know what? I have the perfect solution for you. Why don't you take a vacation and let me watch the farm?" *How the hell was I going to do that?* But the words keep coming. "I mean, I know the house well and I love animals. It would be great for both of us. You wouldn't have to worry about a thing. Take a break. It's a win-win."

Katie looks surprised by the offer, but her expression tells me she thinks it's a great idea. She may even be getting a little misty.

"Tricia, that's a wonderful idea! Your little road trip is turning into a blessing for me. Our girls are too busy, and quite frankly, they don't like it here very much. They never offer to help. I would love to go to Maine and visit my sister in August. It's her sixtieth birthday."

Now she's pacing like she doesn't know what to do with herself. "Are you sure? There's a decent amount of work that needs to happen on a daily basis. Did I mention the eggs?" We both laugh.

"I'm one hundred percent sure or I wouldn't have offered. I only have one request. Please don't tell anyone *who* your housesitter is." She looks surprised, so I quickly explain. "I still have some very good friends, and even some family in the area, and they would never let me live it down to find out that I'm in town and didn't tell them. As much as I'd love to see them, I kind of want an experience like this to be all mine."

"Oh, I totally understand. Your secret is safe with me. To tell you the truth, I haven't even introduced myself to the other neighbors yet. Jack has met a few. How do you go about introducing yourself to neighbors you can't even see?" She laughs. "I feel very isolated sometimes. Plus, it's been so hectic and all work around here. Let me talk to him and get back to you."

We exchange information. I give her one of my burner phone numbers as well as an email that I'm hoping is still off the grid.

She escorts me out through the side door again, right over the patio my father built. Jack is sitting down on the stone retaining wall having a beer. I assume this is how he rewards himself after farm chores. I make a mental note that if I pull this off, I'm going to need a lot of wine.

"How was your chat, ladies?" We look at each other and smile.

"It was great," we say simultaneously, as if rehearsed.

"Jack, how about getting Tricia some eggs to take home with her," Katie suggests.

"Good idea." He grabs a carton from the kitchen and makes his way to the coop. It doesn't take long before he has a full dozen, just like she said he would. I accept them graciously and reach out with the other hand to thank them both for their hospitality. Katie reaches in for a hug instead. It surprises me, considering we just met, but I really like her and give her a squeeze back. I bet she's a great mom, very warm and easy to talk to. Her daughters don't know how lucky they are, and it reminds me of how much I'm missing not knowing my own.

But I'm not sure about Jack yet, and don't care for the way he's looking down my tank top. I give him a handshake instead to send him a message.

I climb in the car and give them both a final wave. Before I head home, I have one more stop to make. I want to check out Deep Creek where Billy's body was found.

9

DEEP CREEK

I make a K-turn by the bridge and get back onto Red Rock Road. Before long, I see the covered bridge ahead and can't help but light up. I'm happy to see how well preserved it is. From what I understand, there aren't many covered bridges left in the area.

I remember Mrs. Charles, my second-grade teacher, telling us that they built covered bridges to calm skittish horses as they crossed water. Another reason was to keep snow off the deck so it wouldn't get slippery. Even in the winter, I'd roll down the window to hear the noise the wheels made on the wood planks as they echoed through the enclosure.

On any given day, you could find local artist Judith Kamp with her canvas and easel. She's captured the most scenic places in Bucks County and sells her work in her own gallery in New Hope. She painted the original foxhunt artwork in my father's office. I bet she has stories to tell and consider looking her up if I get the chance.

Deep Creek Road is directly on the other side of the bridge and still unpaved. It's a mix of earth and gravel with some of the deepest potholes I've ever tried to navigate. Despite my best efforts to avoid them, I hit a few big ones, which rock the small SUV pretty hard.

I pass Billy's old house and quietly pay my respects. The current owners have cleared some of the trees away, so you can see it better from the road.

Then I see it. It's still a thing! There are a few cars parked alongside the road, which bums me out on one hand and relieves me on the other. The road is very secluded and downright spooky to venture out on your own. In fact, most of the roads are spooky, especially at night. It gets pitch black except for the light beaming down from the moon and stars. There are no streetlights and very few homes to offer light for guidance.

I pull up behind a red Ford pickup truck with an NRA bumper sticker. I'm personally not afraid of guns, just some of the people who carry them, so I'm going to have to eye-up the driver before getting too comfortable.

I hear children splashing in the creek as I get out of the car. I find myself feeling like a trespasser again. I certainly don't look like I'm here for a swim and hope I don't have to explain myself. I brush off the insecurities and decide to stay as elusive as possible as I make my way down the short path toward the water.

"Hello," says one of the cutest little boys I've ever seen. He's about five, I'd guess, with summer blonde hair and a very serious, inquisitive expression.

"The water's really warm today. Are you going to swim?"

"Oh, honey, I don't think so, not today. But I plan on getting my feet wet for sure."

He looks disappointed and goes back to his spot in the shallow end. I assume his parents are the ones sitting along the side of the creek in beach chairs smoking and downing cans of Bud. They look harmless enough and say hi with a friendly wave. I walk to the furthest side of the swimming hole, opposite where they're sitting. I take a seat on one of the larger red rocks along the bank to reflect.

It's just like I remember. There's an area of the creek above the deep end with shallow rolling falls. The center is almost completely still, with only small trickles heading further down the stream. It's about the size of our old in-ground pool. I wonder if I could touch the bottom today or if I'd still be afraid of sea monsters. There's a rather steep cliff on the other side of the creek with natural stairs made from the rock. An older boy, the little boy's brother from the looks of him, is climbing them and contemplating how to perform his next jump. He chooses a cannonball. *Shit!* I'm drenched.

"Robert, you just got this young lady all wet. Apologize!"

He looks at me and I give him an instant smile even though I want to throw a rock at him. *What a terrible thought.*

"I'm sorry, ma'am."

"It's okay, pal. I used to do the same thing when I was your age."

What do I expect to learn here? I see the general location where Billy's body was found. It was a gruesome discovery by a young family innocently coming to swim. He was floating face down. Took a bullet to the head. Everyone said it looked like the work of a professional.

Why and by whom? I walk many yards beyond the pool, where no one ever ventures. It's slippery and dangerous and certainly not ideal for swimming, fishing, or anything else for that matter. There are jagged chunks of exposed rock, making it nearly impossible to walk or wade through.

I find a rare opening in the water, with small pebbles between big rocks, and sit by the bank. The water's very clear and still. I see a few beer bottles and a hubcap, not surprising considering the potholes. Then I spot something shiny and grab a stick to poke at it. The motion stirs up the water, so I have to wait until the murky cloud dissipates to find it again. I stare at the particles as they sink back into the creek bed until I see it. I plunge my hand into the water all the way up to my shoulder. I would've gone under if I had to. It's a gold charm or something.

I wipe off the creek grime with my hands and splash it around at the top of the water. Hmm, more like a lapel pin without its backing. I can't quite make out all the details, but it's circular in shape. There are letters and a number four in the middle, plus two swords forming an X. Could be some kind of pledge pin, like a fraternity or something. Or a cult pin? I can't help but think it. I flip it over and make out the initials MJB inscribed, and the year 1996. That's over twenty years ago, but it couldn't have been here very long. It's in great condition, so I can probably eliminate it as a clue from Billy's murder. Still, it's very curious.

I let my mind wander. What if it *does* belong to one of his killers? And what if there have been more murders here? Is this a lucky find or a random find? It's not like this town is full of people who would wear expensive lapel pins while swimming in the creek. I put it in my pocket and wonder if it's possible to find the owner.

I'm tired of watching reruns of *Unsolved Mysteries* sharing Billy's story. "Who murdered William Weber?" The hour-long episode describes Billy as a loving father, spouse, and friend, with no known enemies. He was active in his church and would do anything for anyone. I know a little better than that. But I certainly can't call the number at the bottom of the screen.

As much as I want to know the truth about Billy's murder, I'm much more desperate to find out what happened to my brother. I was told he was murdered the night I hid and was later buried by my parents. Where? No one will tell me, and I have scoured the Internet for articles about his death and get nothing. I'm not that stupid though. I know there'd be plenty of articles written about the terrifying death of a child in a small town, especially one with a well-publicized murder on record. Someone made the story disappear. Or, maybe he's still alive like I've always hoped.

It's getting late. I have to get out of here or there will be an all-out manhunt for me. I give a little wave to the family at Deep Creek and tell the boys to have fun. I pull the car out of sight and put my Ralph Lauren suit back on. It's pretty wrinkled. Oh well. I have three hours to come up with an explanation, and I'm going to need a good one.

10

AN EXPLANATION

I'm starving by the time I get back on the road. Out of desperation, I opt for a McDonald's drive-through. It's been a long time since I've had a quarter pounder with cheese and it's messier than I remembered.

There's no way I'm going be able to get my car out of the Hopkins's garage at this point, so I'll have to be sneaky. I pull the car into the Harbor Sheraton Hotel parking lot and call an Uber, hoping Sal will take care of the SUV tomorrow.

Ryan, my main security guard, and the only one I am allowed to converse with, or in this case be lectured by, is waiting for me. He storms out of the house in a foul mood.

"Tricia, what the fuck! I was just about to call Sean." Ryan knows my birth name, and probably knows more about me than I do, but calls me by my alt name as a precaution. "Where. Have. You. Been? And don't insult me. You weren't working."

"Don't you dare call my father unless you find me dead! And for your information, I actually did do some work and then bumped into a colleague on the way out. We decided to go for lunch and then back to his house for drinks. A girl needs a little privacy sometimes." I wink at him. Is that a look of anger *and* jealousy?

"Where's the car?"

"I had too much to drink, so I called an Uber. You should be proud of me."

"Why didn't your *colleague* take you home?"

"He fell asleep and I slipped out. I wasn't in the mood for pillow talk, not my thing." I'm already tired of the twenty-question routine and attempt to dismiss him.

"Do you have any idea how stressed out I am now, or do you really only think of yourself one hundred percent of the time? If you die, I'm as good as dead too." He's told me this before, and I believe him.

I would be incredibly upset if something ever happened to Ryan. I don't like lying to him at all. Having life under constant surveillance has destroyed any sense of normalcy for me, but I do sleep better knowing he's next door. Ryan has lived in the townhouse next to mine for over two years now, since my divorce. Before then, he worked in the shadows. This is way more convenient for both of us.

How the hell am I going to get away from him for an extended period of time? Of course, the Dorcys haven't officially asked me to housesit, so maybe it won't happen.

Ryan is thirty-five years old with no kids, no wife, and no commitments—except keeping a close eye on me. He has sandy blonde hair and olive skin that tans easily. I can always tell when he's been golfing or just got back from the beach. It's a good look. He's in good shape, but not "muscle head" shape, just very toned with a firm upper body. He's hot, and I can't help thinking about having sex with him on a regular basis. However, he's the one man I've mentally identified as off-limits. I need him to stick around because he's been the only constant in my life besides Sal. Having a crush on him has been difficult, and I often wonder if he has feelings for me too. I see the stares when he thinks I'm not looking.

He's allowed me next door a few times to check out the operation.

It's very sophisticated and not my area of expertise. Cameras monitor the entire complex from every angle. I'm also followed everywhere. His people, or my father's people, must be bored to death most of the time.

I throw my bag on the counter and put the eggs in the fridge.

"You stopped for a dozen eggs?"

"Yep."

"With an Uber?" He's winding up to verbally clock me when the phone rings. Saved by the bell. It's my ex-husband, John Keller, MD.

"What's up, John?"

He apologizes for calling on a Saturday night but has a work-related favor. I'm still his pharma rep, and he's looking for samples. Thankfully, John has forgiven me. I probably wouldn't have if I were him. "No problem. I'll get them to you on Monday." He's such a great guy. I'm the one who royally screwed up.

We met after I made a sales call to his busy practice. He's a brilliant surgeon, making America's Top Doc list every single year for as long as I can remember. We both thought it was love at first sight, so after a whirlwind romance, we exchanged vows at a small chapel in Annapolis. He still has no inkling of my real identity or the fact that we were constantly monitored.

The pressure of keeping so many secrets is bad for a relationship, let alone a marriage, and I behaved terribly. I turned to the one thing that took me away from the constant gnawing in the pit of my stomach. Sex.

One night when I was alone, I seduced a new and young security guard named Jacob. He was good looking. Tall. Dark. Handsome. Great hair. All the prerequisites. I pushed my alert button and he was at the door in five seconds flat. I told him I heard a noise in the house, so he thoroughly searched the home and gave the all clear when he was done to however many people were on the other end of his watch. "You're safe, Tricia." *He wasn't.*

He neglected to see one detail in his initial search. My new sheer white shirt. He looked at the door—his way out—then back at me.

Decisions, decisions. He took the risk and chose me, which I gambled on.

I should've stopped with that one impulsive and sinful moment but there was no way I was letting Jacob go after one round. We enjoyed each other as much as we could without getting caught. But we got sloppy. Maybe I subliminally wanted to get caught. John walked in and found us one afternoon and was completely devastated.

I only had a half-assed apology to offer, so he left baffled on top of hurt. Shortly after, he served me with divorce papers, and soon after that, Jacob was let go. I assume by Ryan. I haven't heard from Jacob since. I'm glad both relationships are over and know, without a doubt, I have no business ever getting married again.

11

A WARNING

It's Sunday, and I wake up with another adrenaline rush. I hope it's not too early because I can never go back to sleep after a big one. I roll over, look at the clock, and am a bit surprised to see it's 11:00 a.m. I guess the stress of the previous day must've really knocked me out. The last thing I remember was having a glass of wine and watching *The Haunting on Hill House* on Netflix. I double-checked the locks a few times because it was wigging me out.

I hear rain, so I get up, shut off the TV, and look out the window. It's pouring all right. I ask Alexa for the forecast and she tells me it's going to rain all day. That's probably a good thing because I have my own chores to do. I need to prep a bit for work tomorrow and remember to bring the samples John wants. Then it's all about laundry and shopping. At least my daily chores don't include feeding and cleaning up after farm animals. I can't imagine doing that every day.

Coffee first. I grab an umbrella, slip on a pair of khaki shorts, a T-shirt and my Sperrys, and walk over to Starbucks. I need to call Sal but certainly not from the house. He's glad to hear my voice and listens intently as I tell him some of the details of my day. He's astonished to hear I made my way into the house and very glad I made it home safe and sound.

"I'll take care of the SUV."

"Thank you, darling, and thanks for the note! How was *your* day?"

"I met someone last night."

"Nice! Where? Another blonde?" He laughs.

"Champagne bar on Front. And no, you big smartass! A brunette."

"You and your champagne. That would give me such a migraine. Anyway, I can't wait to hear about this one." We wrap up and plan to get together later in the week for complete details.

Next off to Whole Foods. I grab all organic, feeling guilty about my fast food binge from the night before. It's still pouring when I get back, and I'm struggling with my umbrella and bags. Ryan steps out of his house and helps me like he always does. I thank him and promise to make him some eggplant soon. That's one recipe Nonna taught me and my mom that I still remember and have mastered. He nods and only manages a semi-smile. He's still upset with me, and I'm probably about to make it worse.

"Before you leave, can I talk to you?"

"What's up?" he asks coldly.

"I just want to apologize for yesterday. I'm sorry. I really want you to trust me and that was unfair." He looks at my eyes for sincerity and shrugs. He's tired of my excuses. I'm attempting to suck up as much as possible and get some intel out of him at the same time. Any future shenanigans are going to be tough to pull off and I may be about to pull off my biggest one ever. I wish Ryan were my true ally here, *my* partner, not my father's. I feel so alone and wish we could confide in each other and work together. But, because he's so unwavering, he leaves me no choice but to rock the boat. I don't understand why I'm not more in the loop when it comes to my own family.

"I want to talk about my parents. You know more about them

than I do. I'm thirty-three years old and have the right to know at least as much as you do, don't you think?"

"Oh, come on, Tricia! You know I can't do that. What makes you think I know that much anyway?" I ignore him.

"And I want to know what happened to my brother." I have a not-taking-no-for-an-answer look, with the body language to match. This has gotten me nowhere in the past, but I have to keep trying. Someday Ryan has to spill it, doesn't he?

"No, you don't!" He raises his voice and points a finger right in my face, which I hate. I slap it away and throw him a dagger. I'm tired and vulnerable and begin to tear up, which is not like me at all.

"Jenny, look at this goddam place." I'm taken aback hearing my birth name, so he means business. "You're under one of the most sophisticated surveillance systems run by one of the best surveillance teams on the planet. Why? For your protection! And I'm personally protecting you on behalf of your father, as well as *from* your father." I can tell he wished he hadn't said that.

"What does that mean?"

"Nothing. I'm just saying, I'm risking a lot here and you have the nerve to run around gallivanting like a child. Don't be so fucking selfish." I start to feel the beginnings of shame, but I'm not giving up.

"I'm going to ask you this for the tenth time, why do I still need so much protection? What is my father part of?" He's clenching his jaw which means I'm getting under his skin.

"Don't you get it? What you don't know hopefully can't hurt you. Now assume the opposite. And Jenny, I'm on a need-to-know with Sean. I don't have all the answers. My job is to protect you, and you don't make it easy." I call bullshit, and he retreats from my kitchen towards the door.

I'm beyond angry and frustrated, and yell after him, "I'm going to find out with or without your help, Ryan, so be prepared for the slip again." He stops in his tracks and turns to face me very slowly. I'm a little nervous because I've never seen him this mad before.

"You give me the slip again and I'll make sure you're locked away.

No life. No fulfilling job. No Whole Foods. No fucking any guy you want! Nothing!" He yells louder with each example.

Ouch. That kinda hurt, but he was just as disgusted as John after my affair with Jacob, and every now and then he throws it in my face. I get a shiver wondering if he really has the power to take away what little life I have. It's an unpleasant thought and one I never considered. I go at it one more time.

"How long have you known my father? How did you get this job anyway?"

"That doesn't matter! I give you as much freedom as I can while protecting you, and you thank me by putting us both in danger. Don't you ever fucking do that again!" He's scolding me like a child and I suddenly feel like one.

"I'm sorry, Ryan, okay?" I grab his arm and turn him around so he can look at me. I'm exhausted and confused and give in to my emotions, letting a tear flow down my cheek again. He eases up a bit and wipes it with the back of his hand while letting out a sigh.

"I know it's hard. I try to make it easy on you. Don't you see that? If you only knew how much worse it could be. Please don't make it so hard for me. I care about you. Just make the most of this situation for now because there's nothing you can do about it."

I don't like that. I'm an adult and there's nothing I can do about it? This is why I am the way I am. I'm gonna do something about it at some point and there's nothing *he* can do about it. I should probably quit with Ryan now, but I'm becoming more convinced that our families are connected in a way that goes beyond home security.

"Have you ever been to our farm?" He exaggerates his denial, so I know he's lying. I can see it in his eyes. He pulls away to avoid my stare down.

"I know you used to live on one, but I've certainly never been there." I retreat with hands in the air. He turns to leave but gives me one last glare, a final warning.

Not five minutes later, one of my burner phones rings. I jump. *Jesus!* They're getting hard to keep track of, and I realize how careless

I've been with them. I have two right in the bag next to me. I knee-jerk react when I see the incoming number and quickly answer.

"Hello? Tricia? It's Katie Dorcy. How are you?"

I hang up abruptly. There's no way I can talk in here. I grab the phone and tuck it into my bra and head back to Whole Foods, hoping they'll think I just forgot something. I call from the front of the store and apologize. I explain that I'm in a grocery store and the reception is terrible. It's partially true at the moment.

"Katie, thanks again for yesterday."

"You're quite welcome. Listen, I spoke with Jack and we'd both like to take you up on your offer. Are you still interested?"

"Heck, yes, I'm interested!"

"How is August 16 through the 20? We can be home in the afternoon on Sunday."

"It's perfect." I do the math and realize that's only a few weeks away. We discuss timeframes and a little detail about chores. "I'll get there early enough on Wednesday so you can give me the full drill on the animals."

"Sounds terrific. Thank you, Tricia. Give me a ring if anything changes, and let's chat again the day before you arrive."

"Sounds like a plan. See you soon, Katie." *God help me.* I shove the phone back in my bra and grab a few more things before checking out. Despite the constant stream of rain, Ryan doesn't help me with my bags this time, even though I can see him staring out at me.

Back in the house, I towel off, grab a pile of laundry and remember the lapel pin in my shorts. I pull it out and try to come up with names that fit the first initial from the inscription, MJB. Mark, Mike, Mick, Manny, Mason, or Melvin. They're all decent guesses. I plop the pin into my jewelry cleaner, and it comes out shining like brand new. I examine it closely. The letters on the front read "ignis." I don't know what it means for certain, and I can't look it up from here because everything I do is monitored, but I can make an educated guess that it's Latin for fire. The flames behind the word are pretty telling. I can see the swords better now behind the flames too.

There's a lot going on, and I've never seen anything quite like it. I flip it back over to see what looks like a tiny emblem on the back. If I'm not mistaken, it bears the resemblance of a paw print. I remember most high-end jewelry stores have emblems to identify their work, kind of like a hidden logo. Sal's uncle has a shop on Jeweler's Row in Philadelphia. I'll give it to him to see if he can identify the designer.

I spend the rest of the day keeping myself as busy as possible to get out of my own head. Dusting. Vacuuming. But the thoughts just keep swirling around, especially how I'm going to pull off a five-day retreat to the country. I don't have much time, and I'm worried about the wrath of Ryan.

12

THE PIN

I kick off the workweek very off my game. My mind is reeling, and I'm having trouble focusing. First thing in the morning, I head over to John's office to give him some samples. I park the car in the Hopkins garage as usual and head to the GI wing.

John J. Keller, MD. The gold plate on his door makes my heart heavy. I pause for a moment and think of our wedding day. It was beautiful, very intimate with just a few guests, his parents, and his sister. As far as they knew, I was an only child, and both of my parents were deceased. They adored me and always went out of their way to treat me like part of the family.

I knock and John yells for me to come in. I open the door and immediately trip over my own feet. I catch myself from falling, but half of my paperwork and a bunch of samples spill out of my briefcase. *Ugh.* John gets up to help me and we lock eyes for a moment. It's been two years, but the look hasn't changed. He's still hurting.

"Well, that was very graceful. You okay, Trish?"

"Yeah, I'm fine. I just haven't gotten a lot of sleep lately."

"Maybe you should see one of our internists for a checkup. When's the last time you had a physical?"

"No, Johnny, really, I'm fine. Thank you though. I'm just tired." There he goes. He can't help himself and starts casually examining me for signs of illness, checking my eyes and looking over my skin. I even catch him looking at my nails. It amazes me what he can see with a quick look. He seems satisfied enough.

"Alrighty then. What do you have for me?"

I hand him dozens of the samples he asked for. They're technically in the clinical trial stages, so I go over the potential side effects very carefully with him. One of John's patients isn't responding to traditional drug therapy, so he wants to give it a try. I give him almost every last one, and he thanks me profusely. I'm ready to leave, but he's not finished talking.

"What have you been up to, Trish?"

"Not much. Same old, same old. Living the dream." I use every lame cliché I can think of for "nothing." Then he blurts it out.

"I'm getting engaged."

"Oh my gosh! I'm so happy for you."

I rush to his side and give him a big hug. I'm sincerely happy for him and relieved because it eases some of my never-ending guilt, but I'm also a little sad because I messed things up so badly. John was probably the best thing that ever happened to me. He was stable, honest, supportive, and smart as hell. He's going to make this lucky lady very happy and be a great father someday.

"Are you?" he asks.

"Am I what?" I have no idea what I'd just said.

"Happy for me?"

"Absolutely!"

He looks a little disappointed, so I remind him of what a bridezaster I was after such a short time. I tell him he's going to have the happily ever after he deserves. He pulls me closer, and we melt into one another.

"I will always love you, Trish."

"I will always love you too, John." And I mean it, in a way. We pull away and meet eye to eye. He's easy to read and I fear, despite this joyous news, he will never truly be over me—all because of what I did to us. I feel like a terrible person.

Before leaving the hospital, I call Sal from the ER phone to see what his availability is like.

"For you? Wide open. But we have a problem."

"What?"

"Your boy, Ryan, paid me a little visit and threatened me. He said even though he can't prove it, he knows I helped you fly under the radar on Saturday. I don't like being threatened, Jen. I almost popped him one. He said if something ever happens to you, something's going to happen to me. I told him I would never put you in harm's way and that if he threatens me again, he's gonna get hurt." Oh boy. A pissing contest is not what I need.

"Calm down, Sal. Let's meet at your mom's, then I want to head over to Jeweler's Row. I'll explain that later."

"To Elio's? Why?"

"Like I said, I'll explain later."

We're all set, and he promises to try and keep his temper under control, but it worries me.

I head home and do my best to stay out of Ryan's way. I meal prep, freak myself out watching more *Hill House* and manage to get a solid two hours of sleep. I'm blowing off work completely today except for a few phone calls.

Usually I announce where I'm going, but I don't feel like a lecture. They'll just follow me anyway. So, I hop in the car and begin the trek. On my way to Philly, I stop and buy Sal's mom a gift at the Hallmark Store. They wrap it extra pretty with a big pink bow. I love surprising her with gifts. Plus, it gives me a good excuse for the road trip. Shane, one of Ryan's top guys, follows me. It takes me a good two hours with traffic, so I'm sure he's thrilled and reporting hateful things back to Ryan.

I walk in and give Mrs. Rossi a huge hug and offer her the gift. "Per me?" She's pleasantly surprised. In broken English she tells me Sal will be right back. "Bellissimo!" she says and holds it up. It's a

Vera Bradley scarf with a pink and green paisley pattern. Mrs. Rossi is undergoing treatment for breast cancer, so I thought it would be a nice picker-upper. While we chat, she plays around with different ways to wear it.

We talk some about what's left of her chemo and radiation. She's been lethargic and sick to her stomach but hanging in there, knowing she's almost finished. We've all been very worried about her, and I'm so glad to hear that her prognosis is good. John helped me find a doctor at the Hospital of the University of Pennsylvania who turned out to be just the right guy. The whole family is incredibly grateful.

Sal returns, gives his mom a kiss, and guides me into the back room. I tell him more about my visit to the country and the fact that the Dorcys just called me to farmsit. He's all ears but very concerned and squeezes my shoulder in a protective way.

"I don't like this, Jen. No fucking way you're going to that place by yourself. I'll go with you."

"Are you out of your mind? That'll completely blow the whole thing. No way! You can't, but I promise to keep you posted every single day. The dude has a nice computer system, so we can keep in touch easily, assuming I get the passwords."

"I don't know."

He's worried about me, but I think he's worried about the wrath of Ryan a bit too. We negotiate some more, until he realizes he can stay close by shuffling his schedule. He's got a big real estate project emerging in Doylestown and can put in some time there while I'm at the farm.

"So, what's with this new girlfriend?" I probe.

"Girlfriend's a little strong," he says with a laugh.

It turns out that Sal has known Sophia since grade school and really likes her. I'm not jealous, but I'm a bit concerned that she'll take him away from my "me time." I need him right now and I don't want to worry about him screwing her all over town and being hard to get a hold of. I guess I really can be selfish, just like Ryan accused.

On the way to the jewelry store, Sal tells me more about Sophia, but I'm barely listening. We arrive on Walnut Street and pull behind the shop. "Elio's Diamonds since 1952," the sign reads. Sal and I walk hand in hand just to torment my tailgate. Let Shane report to Ryan that we're jewelry shopping. I suddenly want him to be jealous.

"Uncle Elio!"

"Salvatore!" There are big Italian hugs and cheek-to-cheek kisses.

"How's everything? How's your mom?"

"She only has a few treatments left."

"Oh, thank God," he says as he makes the sign of the cross. "Your mother is a saint."

"No shit!"

"What brings you here?"

I pull out the pin and hand it to Elio.

"I was wondering if you could help me find out who the designer is and maybe tell me what it means."

He grabs his special opticals for a closer look.

"Here's something you don't see every day. Well, it's solid gold and twenty-four karat at that. It's got quite the interesting symbolism, doesn't it? Maybe some sort of religious thing? Did you try and Google it?"

"I did. I couldn't find anything like it. Do you know if the number four over the Latin word, fire, is symbolic for anything?"

"I'm not into that shit. I make engagement rings," he laughs sarcastically.

"But can you tell who made it?"

"I don't recognize the work, no. Where'd you find it?"

"At the beach." I hate lying to him. "I thought I'd try to find the owners. Maybe it's sentimental or something."

"I'd give Steinbach a try. Fred keeps records of emblems and rare pieces. He's a jewelry geek."

"Where's that?"

"In Trenton, Jersey. Tell him I said hello," he says and laughs sarcastically again. I must be missing his own private jokes. Sal cuts in.

"Thanks so much, Uncle Elio. Give my love to Aunt Theresa."

"I will and give my love to your mom. Oh, and tell my asshole brother he owes me money from poker the other night." We laugh and give each other the same cheek-to-cheek good-bye kisses.

Once we're back in the car, I remind Sal that we're only an hour from Trenton and that it'll be a lot less suspicious if we go to another jewelry store *today*. I can't take another road trip like this or Ryan will lock me up and throw away the key.

"Done. Let's go."

It's a short drive, but I'm ready to stretch my legs by the time we arrive. We enter the store and are greeted by a matronly, middle-aged woman. She's got a coffee stain on the front of her white blouse and buttons straining to escape their holes. Great first impression. Sal asks if Mr. Steinbach is available to look at a piece of jewelry for us. She looks bothered but disappears into a back room. I eye up some of the jewelry in a case while we wait and point to a two-karat princess cut diamond that Sophia would love. "Very funny," Sal says.

We look up as Fred Steinbach approaches, greeting us warmly. He's a sweet-looking, older gentlemen wearing a sharp but outdated suit.

"What can I do you for?" he asks with a smile. I watch him closely as Sal hands him the pin. He loses the grin in point five seconds flat and looks up at me. I tell him the whole story about wanting to find the owners and how I found it at the beach. He doesn't really look like he's buying it.

"You cops?"

"Cops? No why?" Sal and I stare at each other. He looks it over quickly again and hands it back to Sal.

"I'm sorry. I have no idea who created this piece or what it means."

"But you hardly even looked at it," I say. "And why would you think we were cops? What kind of a pin is it?"

"Yeah, take a closer look there, Fred. My uncle said you keep records of this kind of thing," Sal retorts.

"Who's your uncle?"

"Elio Rossi. And he told me to tell you that he says hi."

"Oh, Jesus Christ," he curses.

Sal and I are perplexed by both his reaction to the pin and to Elio.

"You know something, don't you?" I press. He flips the pin over and nods.

"I have a suspicion."

Sal pulls out his wallet, and I roll my eyes. He's not going to take a bribe.

"Don't insult me," Fred responds immediately.

Sal pulls out about a thousand dollars in hundreds and Fred snatches them up. He looks over the pin one more time and grabs a piece of paper and a pen. When he's finished writing, he folds it up and hands it to Sal.

"You didn't get this from me, understand? And tell Elio I don't appreciate the shit he tells people about my business. I'm a damn good designer."

Whoa! I don't know what's happening here, but I've learned that money really does talk. I throw Sal a look that says, *I can't believe you*, and he throws me a mischievous grin in return. A quick scan of the store indicates they're not doing great. Inventory is pretty sparse, so maybe he's just desperate to make a few bucks.

"Do *me* a favor though, never mention this to anyone, okay? Make up another story of how you found out," he requests and points to the door.

Sal motions for me to go ahead of him. I start but turn to see what he's doing. He's whispering something in Fred's ear. Something that puts a frightened look on the man's face. We've clearly ruined Fred's day. Sal catches up to me and grabs my arm.

"What'd you say to him?"

"I just made it clear that he's not to give away our visit either."

"It looks like you scared him."

"Nah."

I don't push because I'm too interested in seeing what the note says. The only thing written is "Michael Brandt." I was hoping for more details than that, but I consider it significant. It's vague, but potentially important, especially knowing it belongs to an ancestor of the actual town of Brandtville. There are dozens of Brandts in the area, even one family I believe who lived pretty close to us.

If we did find a name, I was irrationally hoping we'd find the name of an enemy connected to Billy from a case in New York, but I guess a local makes more sense. I wonder if Mr. Brandt is in trouble with the law. The Brandts are affluent, but I don't know much else about them. And I can't think of a single *good* reason the pin would be in the water at Deep Creek unless maybe he was robbed? I suppose it's possible a burglar could have dumped any unwanted contents in the creek. Maybe that's why Mr. Steinbach inquired about us being cops. Perhaps it's a very valuable stolen piece.

And of course, I can't help but wonder if Michael Brandt was a friend of my father's and if he was one of the men who met for meetings in our barn. I never saw a pin like this on my dad, but I wonder if he had one too. Maybe they were part of an elite group—or one as innocent as the Knights of Columbus. The only thing I know for sure is that I'm more determined than ever to get to the bottom of it all.

13

THE WITNESS PROTECTION PROGRAM

I t's the weekend, and I'm officially on Operation Red Rock Farm. It's time to plan this near-impossible mission out. I'm not going to get away with the same Ford Escape switcheroo routine again, so I need something really good. I wish I had a few female friends who I could confide in instead of all of these men. Why am I so hard on women? Maybe my irrational feelings stem from how I view myself. I have to lie constantly and disappoint the people I love and care about the most. Or, maybe it's how badly my mother has emotionally scarred me. I don't just blame my father for my miseries.

My mom was tough, but I still think of her often and wonder if she thinks about me. Sometimes I can't even remember what she looks like, and I have no family photos to recreate her in my mind. It's very hard knowing that she hasn't found a way to contact me, so I have to believe she's put me last. That puts her at the bottom of my own priority list. I don't need her. Besides, I like the feeling of empowerment I'm getting from doing this on my own. I just hope it's worth it.

The only real opportunity I would take if I saw her again would be to ask her how she could abandon a child at such a young age with a broken heart. I had just lost my brother, and she washed her hands of me. I don't blame her for leaving my father, but I'm her only child now.

Within days of leaving Brandtville, I was given a new identity, Patricia Lakefield, under what is officially called the Witness Security Program. U.S. Marshals were assigned to my case and escorted me to boarding school in Idaho. I received a new social security number and birth certificate, as well as fake transcripts from a school in Delaware. Sun Valley was beautiful but even boonier than Brandtville. I stayed with my full-time marshal, Harold Dixon, and his wife Tammy during downtime. They had a beautiful log cabin near a stream. It was picturesque, but I wouldn't go near the water because it reminded me way too much of home. They tried to reason with me, telling me it could help me heal and move on. But I refused and would lock myself in their spare room.

The Dixons were nice enough, but I didn't allow myself to form a bond with them. In hindsight, I could have been kinder, especially to Tammy, who tried so hard to reach me. I imagine she agreed to the lifestyle thinking she could do something rewarding, like fix a broken child, but I never let her in, choosing instead to internalize it all.

I was told I could never reveal my true identity to anyone. Sal knows I've changed my name and am under paternal surveillance, but he has no idea that I'm also in the program. Even I know that would be extremely dangerous to share—or maybe that doesn't matter either.

For some, the program is temporary and protects witnesses during big trials from criminal harm or attempted jury bribes. Others, like me, must remain in the program for life. Personally, I think the agency is enough to keep me safe and hope to shake my father's crew completely once I put this puzzle together. My feelings for Ryan have kept me from going completely AWOL. I suppose I could easily tell the agency more about my father and let them go after him, but I want my own shot at this—and him—first.

Mr. Dixon proudly told me over and over that they had never lost anyone in the program, but warned me that if I broke the rules, I would put myself in danger. He told me of a story about a woman who wanted to take a small leave to attend her best friend's funeral. They warned her about the risks but didn't forbid her from going, since the program is technically optional. When she returned, her house was blown to pieces and she with it. "She blew her cover," he said, getting a warped kick out of the punchline. I never forgot that story, but yet, here I am about to do something potentially as dangerous.

Going back to my old house goes against the number one rule: You can never go back. The farm is even more off-limits because crimes were committed on the premises. I check in with the agency pretty rarely these days, mostly through technology and a few scheduled visits. I don't think they monitor me as closely as they used to, given all the private security I have. It's overkill, and I suspect they do it less for me and more in an effort to track my father. Every meeting starts the same way, asking if I know of his whereabouts.

My story never changes, telling them I never want to see him again. They've followed me long enough to know I've had no personal contact, but I grill them wanting answers. He's a wanted man for reasons I want to know. But they won't tell either. They advise me that what little they know is classified, so around and around we go getting absolutely nowhere.

My father has taken security to a beyond-paranoid level, and I don't understand why he wants to remain this connected to me. I'm ready to cut the damn cord. He obviously has ulterior motives that have nothing to do with fatherly love and obligation. I'll bet he's protecting himself, along with another operation. Maybe a very criminal operation, and I'm after it. Maybe that's what he fears the most, or he wouldn't be watching me this closely. His crimes are the reason I'm in this virtual prison, and I resent the hell out of him for it.

I have to force myself to concentrate again on planning. I'll never have another chance like this under such unbelievably perfect conditions. I can't blow my cover, as Mr. Dixon would say. The first step will hopefully be the hardest, just getting back to the farm.

I have a few ideas. John has a colleague who owns a personal jet. I could ask for a ride to the Doylestown airport and then grab an Uber. It's risky though, and John would be all over me wanting to know what's happening. Plus, I absolutely need a car.

I have one final plan and go over it again and again with Sal. I'm going to need a few of his buddies to help me. But I think we've got this.

14

A DESIRE FOR TRUTH

Tomorrow is the big day, Wednesday, August 16. I call Katie from my new burner phone with California area code and explain that it's my work phone when she inquires.

We confirm plans and I gush about how excited I am to go "home." She's so happy to have a reprieve and can't wait to see her sister. I'm aiming to get there before noon. She gives me a few tidbits about the drippy faucet and the special diets the aging dogs are on now. Their names are Sonny and Cher, chosen by their daughters when they were younger. A little corny, but I like them.

We're about to hang up when Katie drops a bomb.

"Oh, Tricia, I almost forgot to tell you that Jodi is back home. Please keep an eye out for her, and if she ends up on the property, just call the police." This is actually great news to me.

"No worries, Katie. Everything'll be just fine. I promise. See you tomorrow."

Knowing full-well I can't just walk out of the house with a packed suitcase, I've been slowly ordering things off the Internet, using one of the hospital computers designated for reps, and having them delivered to Sal's cousin, Antonio Rossi, in South Philly. I really hate bringing this guy into the mix because he's a shady asshole, but I need him. As long as Sal trusts him, I'm making an effort to do the same, but my natural instincts give me reason to doubt.

Sal also gave Antonio money to buy an old Ford Thunderbird he found on Craig's List with zero bells and whistles. No power windows, no air conditioning, and no technology that could track me. It was smart thinking, but it's God-awful looking. Sal and Antonio took selfies with it and sent it to my office email. It's baby blue and monstrous. I stopped laughing when I realized I was going to need an explanation for Jack and Katie.

There are going to be lots of car exchanges before I get behind the wheel of that bad boy, but I'm ready. I think.

I make some business calls early in the day and then one to my manager, telling her I'm not feeling well and need to rearrange my schedule. Luckily, it's not a problem, or I'd have to quit. I get home, grab a bite to eat, and go over the plan again and again in my mind, praying it works because I have no room for error.

It's now 7:00 p.m., and I'm antsy as hell. Before I attempt to sleep, I need to take a shower, and then I want to see Ryan. I feel the need to give him sort of a pre-apology and hope he doesn't catch on.

The shower is soothing, so I wait until the hot water completely runs out before stepping out. I towel off and sit at my vanity and stare at myself in the mirror. Despite being the smallest, it's my favorite space in the house, just a little passageway between my bedroom and the bathroom. That's how easy I am to please. I bought a plush, pink satin ottoman and a mini crystal chandelier with dangly details to fancy it up even more. I keep a sachet of lavender and a glowing crystal salt rock on the vanity, which help me start the day relaxed.

I'm lost in thought as I study myself. I'm having more of an identity crisis than usual. I wonder if my life will ever be normal, if I'll ever get married again. I can't help but think of Ryan. I've been trying to suppress my feelings for him, but I don't know if I can for much longer. What would it be like with him? My off-limits guy. I don't know much about him. The few times we've engaged in long conversations, it's always been about me. I want to know more about him and how he paired up with my father. I mean, did my father put an ad in the paper? "Double secret agent needed"?

I wonder if Ryan even likes me, or if he hates my guts and just does his job to collect the paycheck. That wouldn't surprise me one bit. I've been a royal pain in the ass at times.

Well, no need to overthink, because the chances that he'll ever talk to me again after tomorrow are probably nil. It saddens me because I can't think of another living soul I'd like to know more on both an emotional and physical level. I'm being truthful with myself for the first time in a long time. It's why I haven't been with anyone since Jacob. It's why Sal and I rarely sneak out anymore. I don't want to be with anyone but him. But I'm committed to this plan and won't turn back now no matter what. Seeing Ryan tonight may be goodbye forever, and I'll just have to accept it.

I put a little makeup on, just enough though to enhance my natural features. I want him to remember me at my best. My eyes are popping tonight. I put on a coral romper, which accentuates everything. It's sexy but casual and cinches at the waist. I'm thankful for my God-given shape at this moment. I hope this is how he remembers me. I look good.

I knock on the door and Ryan opens it in khaki cargo shorts, shirtless. His hair is still wet from his own recent shower, and I have to bite my lip at the sight of him. He's chiseled and I'm horny, a bad combo for me. He does a double-take, eying me up suspiciously. I can see the *what's-she-up-to* look on his face and consider turning back. I realize this looks bad. I never stop by his house at night. I think of the Jacob situation and worry he's assuming I'm here to seduce him too. Am I? I question my own motives. He sees my hesitation and opens the door wider.

"What can I do for you, Tricia?"

"Just a quick talk? I'm bored."

"Beer?"

"Yes, please."

We're in the kitchen and the lights are dimmed. As he reaches into the fridge, his muscles light up from the glow. *Kill me.* I'm gawking and he knows it. He hands me an IPA and gestures for me to follow him.

We have to pass through a maze of monitoring on the way. He dashes ahead and turns off two that look different from the others and punches in a code.

"What are those? I hope they aren't cameras to my bathroom or something."

"Very funny. Even we have limits."

"Well, that's a relief." I check a few screens for geographical gaps but don't find any. They have every square inch covered.

"Shane's tapping into the system tonight. We can go downstairs."

"What's downstairs?"

He lights up a little and gives me a "gotcha" kind of look. "It's *my* escape." Uh oh. He knows about my Ford Escape. I bet he caught Sal with it when he went to pick it up the next day. Time to sell it.

It's a finished basement. I have space envy, as I don't have one of these. It's really cool, contemporary with a hint of man cave. The walls are painted a light grey, which makes the white crown molding pop. He has the largest wide-screen TV I've ever seen with a golf tournament in full swing. His black leather sofa and love seat are plush and inviting with lots of extra pillows.

"You ever have a woman down here?"

"Now how would I manage that with this operation?" he asks smiling.

"What a waste!"

"Actually, I kind of like it to myself. It's where I unwind. You're the first woman I've had down here. Aren't you lucky!" He gives me a sexy smile that makes my knees weak. I continue scanning the room and notice a few acoustic guitars.

"You play?"

He nods and smiles. "Yep. Not professionally of course. My mother gave me a choice. Piano or guitar."

"Really? Was she one of those moms who wanted a well-rounded and cultured kid?" He smiles and nods.

"Yeah, you could say that."

"Play something?"

"No way. I'd need to tune one up and I'm really rusty."

"Please? Do you sing?"

"Not well."

"Oh, come on. What do you like to play?"

"Classic rock mostly."

"Okay, then how about some Pink Floyd?" I've worn him down. He walks over, picks up a guitar, and starts fussing with the strings. He takes a seat on a wooden chair and starts playing "Wish You Were Here."

Oh no. I should have asked him to play "Comfortably Numb." Every note, every chord of this one digs deep into my heart. It makes me think of my brother and mom and grandmother. I have to fight back tears. I don't want him to see how emotional I'm getting, but I definitely don't want him to stop. I fight and concentrate on the sheer talent before me. He finally looks up at me as the song winds down. I give him a standing ovation. He bows and rejoins me, taking a swig of his beer.

"Ryan, I'm so impressed. That was incredible. You almost made me cry."

"Really? Yeah, that song gets me too. You all right?"

"Yeah, I'm fine. Thank you so much for playing."

"Sure. I never get an audience, so I must admit that was kind of fun." He turns his attention right back to the golf game as I attempt to cool off.

"Ryan, do you have a girlfriend?" He almost spits out his beer at the question.

"What? Why do you want to know?"

"I'm just curious. I've never seen you with anyone and you're pretty freaking hot." He blushes but shifts to look straight at me.

"You think I'm hot?"

"Yes. Every inch of you. And talented to boot." He looks beyond flattered but taken off guard by my forwardness. I get a little flushed by it too.

"I get around. But no, I don't want a girlfriend." *Is that directed at me?* "Not in this business."

"Someday you're going to want a family, right? And kids? You can't do this forever." He shakes his head.

"Hell, no, to the kids. I'm not bringing kids into this fucked up world."

Wow! Quite a strong reaction to that one. I agree with him but look away because it makes me sad. Deep down, I hope that someday I can have it all and wonder what kind of mom I would be.

With my eyes off of him, he takes the opportunity to look me over. I can feel his gaze, and it gives me intense butterflies. While he's staring, I imagine his touch. He breaks the silence but not the sexual tension. Softly, sensually, he says my name. "Jenny."

"What?" I look back at him and into his sexy eyes. He purposefully wants me to follow them and starts scanning my body slowly from the bottom up. He bites his lip and clenches his jaw, and I'm done.

"You're absolutely beautiful."

"Aww. Thank you." I'm blushing and unsure of what to do. Despite the compliment, he's not moving like I would expect a man to do. In fact, I think the longing in my eyes is making him uncomfortable. I watch him push aside any affection he's feeling and give himself a reality check.

"But you know this already, don't you? You use people, Tricia. I've seen you."

"Wow!" I say, stunned. That's one hell of a way to ruin a moment. I turn away, stung and flustered by the impression he has of me and feel the need to defend myself. "I take responsibility for my actions but give myself a pass every now and then because of my upbringing. I mean cut me a break! How many people live like this? Sex has been my escape in the past, but shit, I haven't been with anyone in years."

"What about your little afternoon delight the other day?"

"I lied. I wasn't with anyone."

"Then where were you?"

I shake my head, so he knows I'm not going to tell him anything.

"Where were you, Tricia?"

"You have secrets, Ryan. I'm going to keep one too." He doesn't like the response, so I figure I might as well start cross-examining him while I'm at it.

"Do you think I'm always going to need this level of protection, or will this mysterious high alert ever go down? I mean, has anyone ever actually come after me? I'm starting to think this whole operation is total bullshit." He looks insulted.

"Yes, it's necessary. And, yes, we've intersected on multiple occasions."

"You have?" I'm completely thrown off by this. "Give me an example." He thinks it over and decides to divulge.

"Before we bought all of the townhouses ..." I cut him off.

"Wait. How many townhouses do *we* have? More than these two?"

"Yes, we have one on the other side of you and one more on the other side of me." *What the heck?*

"Why didn't you tell me this before?"

"You never asked," he says with a smirk. This part is total bullshit, and he knows it.

"Well, how the hell am I supposed to know what questions you will or will not answer?" I give his naked torso a good shove and playfully punch his shoulder, which tenses. He's playful, too, and pushes me back.

"I like to keep you guessing!"

"You're a complete ass."

"I know," he admits. Then he gets more serious. "Look, we have multiple security operations overlapping at all times." I start thinking about the other townhouses.

"Wait! So, wait. Alicia Wilson next door? Is she part of the operation?"

"Yes."

"She's a spy? I go for my morning runs with Alicia. She's seriously like the only woman I ever talk to. Plus, I think she has a crush on you. I take that back! I know she does. You're all she talks about."

"Oh, please," he says with a grin. He sees the betrayal in my eyes and eases his way closer to me.

"She's not a spy, Jenny." *My real name again.* "She watches out for you, and she likes you too. Not all women are rotten, despite what you think."

I thought I was pretty slick, but I never suspected that my neighbor was in on the operation. We've had wine and a few good talks over the last two years. He eyes me up to see how the information is registering. I know he'll stop if he senses an overload, so I brush it off and ask him to go on. I want to know about an actual time when I was in danger. He double-checks my expression and continues.

"Remember the bar fight in Annapolis at your wedding reception?"

"Yes. That nearly ruined my night!"

"That was no ordinary fight."

"What happened?"

"Your identity was compromised, temporarily. An enemy of your family was in the right place at the right time. We took care of it."

"How? You didn't kill him or anything, did you?" I say and laugh out loud. Ryan gives me a serious look, so I repeat. "Ryan, the guy's still alive right?"

He looks concerned by what he's about to tell me but also deter-mined to drive home the point.

"I can't be certain. I'm not in charge of that department."

I stand up, pacing, and shake my head in disbelief.

"So, it's possible he's dead?" I'm trying to process the information and keep looking at him for a playful *just kidding*. But it doesn't happen. "Oh my God. What the hell." I'm quiet for a few minutes until it sinks in. I guess I do need protection. If someone was trying to kill me, maybe it's good if he's dead. I think of Danny. If it was the person who killed him, good. I cross my arms and sit back down.

"When else?"

"Well, when you and your buddy Sal were yucking it up in college bars, there were quite a few close calls, from what I've been told."

He's not a fan of Sal. Sometimes I think he's jealous, but other times I think he's just concerned about the added risk. In his defense, it's probably a valid concern.

"I wasn't part of the team at that time. I was living my own life of hell." He drifts off and takes a big gulp of beer.

"What do you mean?"

"Forget about it," he says, and takes another sip.

I'm studying him. Ryan doesn't typically show emotion unless he's mad at me, but I see pain in his eyes. He has his own story to tell. Without saying anything, I reach for his hand. He accepts it for an instant but pulls away, clearly not used to being consoled. We sit in silence again, both absorbed in thought.

"How often do you talk to my father?"

"You have a one-track mind." I give him a devilish grin. "Okay, a two-track mind." I laugh and shove him again. "Once a month or more if I need to."

"When will you talk to him again?"

"Tomorrow."

I'm disturbed and a little put off by this revelation. Tomorrow of all days. Plus, he gets to talk to my father, and I don't. I don't really want to talk to him, but still, all of the secrets are stacking up, and I'm bitter.

"Do me a favor? When you talk to him, tell him I hope he rots in hell for putting me in this situation." I let out a whimper and fight back tears, totally feeling sorry for myself.

"Oh, come on, Jenny, he loves you. He's not a monster."

"Ryan, I can't do this for much longer. I mean it. I'm not coping well." A tear streams down my cheek and he moves all the way in and wraps an arm around me. I lean in but don't find the comfort I need. He senses it, picks me up, and places me face forward, legs straddling his lap. I'm wide-eyed and surprised by the move. But he gives me a *it's-not-what-you-think* look and simply embraces me. I get the sense he needs one too and hold him close. He rubs my back and plays with my hair. I return the gesture and run my fingers through his. It's soft with curly blonde highlights from the summer sun.

We're both trying not to move too much, but I'm getting turned on despite my best efforts to keep it platonic. I'm guessing he's trying to figure out how to transition me back to my place on the sofa. I don't want to let go, so I squeeze him back in as he tries to let go. He tries again, but I plant my pelvis strategically close until I can feel him. He's aroused. I'm desperate for him and promise myself that I'll call off tomorrow if this happens.

But he's disciplined and remains in control. Any other man I know would have pounced, but he's strong. I take it as a challenge. I test his willpower and look him directly in the eyes. They're wilder than before. He's not in as much control as he wants to be, so I lean in and give him a kiss. He lets out a groan and gives in, grabbing the back of my hair with one hand and my jaw line with the other.

After waves of intense kissing, I'm ready to make love. I try unbuttoning his shorts, but he stops me.

"What's wrong?" I ask.

He shakes his head, picks me up, and plants me back on the ground. He's out of breath from our too-short of a make-out session but blurts, "Not gonna happen, Tricia. I'm sorry."

I'm stunned and stare at him for an explanation, but he doesn't offer one. Feeling deeply rejected, I'm at a complete loss for words. Maybe this is payback for hurting so many others. I'm upset, but way worse, I'm embarrassed. I turn to go upstairs.

"Get some sleep," he says, adding insult to injury. The suddenly cold exchange is killing me. I give him a glare but keep my mouth shut. Out of loyalty more than anything, he follows behind me and up the stairs. I'm tempted to turn around and slap him across the face. But I let him take the uncomfortable walk up with me.

I suddenly have the guilt of tomorrow's plans swirling around in my head again and give myself a much-needed reality check. As confused as I feel, I stifle any desire to lash out. Instead, I turn and smile at him as I near the door. He looks ashamed and utters a weak apology.

"I'm the one who should apologize. I'm so sorry for barging in here like this. I was out of line. Again, right? Have a good night, Ryan." He's clenching his jaw again and holding back. I let him off the hook but stop so he can see me in the light of the doorway one more time. "Thank you for everything you've done for me over the years. I promise nothing like this will ever happen again."

Now he looks a bit panicked as well as injured. He exhales loudly and rubs both hands through his hair. He takes a step toward me, but I shake my head and put up a hand. "Nope." I close his door, open mine, and plop down on my sectional and cry. I cry myself to sleep from the anguish of the evening and the fear of what's to come.

15

IT'S TIME

I wake up to the mother of all adrenaline rushes. This time at 3:33 a.m. to be exact, which is a number sequence I see everywhere. I see it in the middle of the night, on receipts, on gas station prices, and on everything in between. I'm trying to read it as a positive sign because I'm having a panic attack and second-guessing everything. To make it worse, the Ryan rejection is still fresh. I make the sign of the cross and pop an Ativan, one of the perks of pharma friendships. It takes a good thirty minutes, but the pill eventually kicks in. I manage a small nap before the alarm goes off.

I'm a bit shaky as I get dressed and ready for my run. Alicia Wilson is waiting for me. Until now, I thought she was *just* my friend and running partner, not a forced friend on the payroll. Ryan peeks out of the window as we warm up in front of the complex. He's trying to get my attention, but I can't face him. He opens the door, much to my chagrin, and I worry that he knows what I'm up to.

"Tricia, when you get back, please come over. We need to talk." He looks tired and stressed, but not on to me.

"Okay!" I holler back. I imagine what he wants to say. Probably something like, we can't be in a relationship. I have a job to do ... blah, blah, blah.

Alicia and I run through the harbor area, past the Rusty Scupper and into Fells Point. I look ahead and see my first ride. *Well, here goes nothing.*

I stop and pretend I'm having trouble breathing.

"What is it, Tricia?"

"I don't know. I'm just really short of breath."

Alicia holds up her wrist, ready to talk into a communication device, but I reassure her that I'm fine, just tired. "Let's just walk for a bit." She obliges but looks concerned. On cue, I fake collapse right next to a police cruiser. One of Sal's buddies, Steve Marino, is a Baltimore police officer and agreed to help me shake off my running partner. For what in return, I don't know. But I'm forever grateful to be able to tap into Sal's many resources. He's got a guy everywhere.

Steve gets out of the car, bends down, and checks my pulse. "Is she all right? Ma'am, can you hear me?" Alicia is on the talkie now, so he moves quick. "I'm going to take her to Hopkins." He sweeps me up and puts me in the back of the car. Alicia is panic-stricken and tries to climb in after me, but Steve shuts the door, locks it, and floors it. I stay down until we make it around the bend. I feel a little bad for her and hope she doesn't get in trouble, but then again, she's been lying to me, so whatever.

Time to ditch the cop car. We make our way to the projects, where Sal is waiting. Steve releases me from the back of the cruiser, and I climb into Sal's Porsche. They exchange nods, and we head north for Philly while Steve makes his way to the other side of town and on to his real shift.

I'm nervous as hell and quiet through the whole drive. We arrive at Antonio's rowhouse in South Philly around 8:00 a.m. Sal drops me off at the door and parks his car three blocks away in a garage. We all convene in the kitchen and Antonio hands me some coffee.

"So far, so good, kid."

Even though Ryan hurt me last night, I know he's freaking out right now. I don't want him to think I came up with this escape plan *because* of last night, or that I've been kidnapped by one of my enemies. I don't want him to worry, and I definitely don't want to hurt him. I left him a note in the fridge near the eggs, which he'll find soon enough when he looks for clues. I wrote:

Ryan—please don't worry about me. I meant what I said yesterday. I need a break. DO NOT tell my father. And in case you're oblivious, I'm also in love with you. I understand the position this puts you in. Decide if you want to be here when I get back. I will only be gone a few days. Love, Tricia

I came right out with it and meant it. Despite the hurt I feel, I'm pretty sure I'm in love with Ryan. It's not like it was with John. I only loved the idea of him. Tack on all the secrets and lies, and we never had a real chance. I don't typically have to lie to Ryan, and I feel like he knows me more than anyone else, the good and the bad.

Of course, he lies to me all the time, but I understand why. I also know these words are going to terrify him and buy me time. He'll be gone when I get home. I'm sure of it.

True to his word, Antonio did a great job with my bag. I thank him and get changed into one of my new outfits, a simple pair of denim shorts and a white T-shirt. He's growing on me a little.

"You ready, Trish?"

"As ready as I'll ever be."

Sal hands me the address where he'll be in Doylestown. He cradles my cheeks and chin with his hands so we're face-to-face. "I'm thirty minutes away, tops. Capeesh?"

"Capeesh. I promise you'll be the first to know if something isn't right." I'm trying to reassure both of us.

"The Thunderbird is ready for you. I even washed and shined it," Antonio says with a smirk. I roll my eyes and let out a groan but return the smile.

Sal brings me in so hard that he cracks my back. "Be safe, Tricia. I love you to the moon and back. Call me as soon as they leave." I promise and slide behind the wheel of the beast.

16

HOMEWARD BOUND

The lack of air conditioning makes my journey home less than comfortable. But it's still early enough that I'm not getting baked by the full effects of the sun yet. It's another hazy, hot, and humid day, typical of this time of year. As I fiddle with the radio, I catch the tail end of a stormy evening forecast. It was staticky, so I hope I heard wrong.

The Thunderbird drives like a boat, and I feel like I could lose control at any given moment. I've got a white-knuckled grip on the wheel, but I'm still drifting side to side without power steering. I can't wait to get out of this thing.

It's 11:00 a.m. when I pull in the driveway. If I make it through all of this, I may take John's advice and get a good workup. I wouldn't be surprised if I am getting high blood pressure.

I step out of the car and am greeted warmly by Jack and Katie, accepting hugs from both. Instinctively, I take a fresh breath of country air and smell the creek. I hear the unmistakable sounds of cicadas chirping and remember going tree to tree collecting their shells. Danny and I would leave them on each other's shoulders and wait to see how long before we found them. I left one on my mother's arm one day to test her aptitude for a good prank. Turns out, Angela's tolerance was low.

Jack is inquisitive seeing the car, just like I figured he would be. "What's with the car?"

I explain that an ill friend needed a car with air conditioning until the weather breaks, so I took hers.

"Aww, that's so kind of you," Katie gushes. Sonny and Cher are barking and jumping all over me. I feel a few scratches on my bare legs but give them some loving anyway. Jack settles them down with a "heel" and takes my bag into the house.

I follow Katie over to the barn for chore rehearsal, where I get a crash course in farming. I duck as a barn swallow swoops down, barely missing my head. They're relentless little creatures. Both Daisy and Sherlock steered clear of them, but funny how oblivious the sheep and goat seem to be around them.

Farm chores aren't very complicated, really. Hay at all times and some grain once a day. There's a big pitchfork propped up against a wheel barrel—my pooper scooper. I'm not totally looking forward to that, but I think I can handle it.

I find myself way more comfortable with the sheep and goat than with the chickens. Walking into the chicken coop makes me feel claustrophobic, even for someone who loves small spaces. There are an awful lot of them and just two of us—*one after today*. I hold my arms close to my sides, in fear of being pecked to death. Katie laughs hysterically, promising they won't hurt me. I do everything she tells me and proudly gather fresh eggs for the first time in my life.

"Yay! You did it!" she says with encouragement.

I can't help but think again what a wonderful mother she must be to her daughters.

Next stop, the pool. We go over cleaning and chlorine schedules. Now that I'm up close, I see they've added a waterfall feature. It looks very inviting, and I definitely plan on hitting the pool later with a glass of wine. Antonio put six bottles in the car for me, which may be the real reason he's growing on me.

In the house, she shows me that she's done a little grocery shopping. She's thought of everything. I thank her and ask if it's okay to use their computer. "Of course." She's more than happy to share the Wi-Fi and computer log-in with me. Next, she guides me up and into my old bedroom. I try to focus on what she's saying, but I have to fight to keep my eyes from drifting to the closet.

"Jack retired from the *Boston Herald* years ago but occupies his time as a feature writer for the *Bucks County Examiner*. He still needs to write, or he'd lose his mind. We should probably check with him on a few things. God forbid you delete some of the stories he's working on." Ah ha! Another good guess. This new piece of information is interesting but a little unsettling. I fear his journalism skills could create an even larger danger zone for me. I'll need to be extra careful.

Jack walks in as she's explaining. "You'll be fine. Just use the laptop and avoid this computer." He puts his hand on a big old iMac with a few metal boxes attached. One looks like an extra storage unit but the other looks like it could be some kind of server. "This one links to *The Examiner*."

"No problem. That whole thing looks very complicated." *This is huge!* Unless I literally can't find or break a code, I'm diving in for articles. What if there's some old stuff in there from Billy's murder or about my brother?

It's time to bid them farewell. Their car is all packed and they certainly look comfortable with me being there. If they only knew how uncomfortable they should feel. They provide me with every possible number to reach them, and I promise I'll call if anything pops up. I follow them to the end of the drive and wave as they take off up Red Rock Road.

That fast, I'm alone. I'm not used to being alone. Even when I think I am, there are eyes everywhere. I need to call Sal first so he doesn't worry. I use my new burner phone to call his new burner phone. What would we do without these things?

He picks up right away and breaks the news that Ryan called him at the office.

"I laid it on thick and said I had no idea where you were. I even told him I would help him track you down. He's a no bullshit kind of guy though. We both know that. He called me a fucking liar and every name in the book before literally threatening to kill me. So I threatened to kill him back. I'm a Rossi. Fuck him and his threats. I can have ten guys up his ass in twenty minutes."

He could? That's disturbing, and it's exactly what I don't want to happen. It's not like I didn't expect the shit to hit the fan at all, but this is more than a little shop of horrors. I imagine carnage and feel sick.

"Sal, maybe I should call him."

"From where?"

"I don't know. From here. I'll use the spare burner and then destroy it in case he can track it."

"Might be a good idea, Jen. Maybe you should call him. He was in such a rage—said he'd take drastic measures to find you. Plus, babe, I've got work to do. I can't be looking over my shoulder every ten minutes. Sophia's starting to ask questions, along with everyone else. I'll be the one blowing covers soon if I'm not careful." I feel terrible for putting him in this position and swear to never do it again. "He mentioned a letter, too. What's that about? You leave him a letter?"

"Please don't ask."

"All right, all right. Not my business."

"I'll call him and call you back later. I'm gonna need more burners though, Sal."

"Not a problem. I'll find a way to get you more. Be safe. I hope you find some answers."

"Thanks for everything."

I must be burning him out. And the reality that I have to call Ryan is unpleasant, firing up my stress and guilt levels. I grab the burner and notice my hands shaking. I'm having trouble pushing the numbers because I'm so nervous he's going to be furious. He picks up on the first ring as I stand here trembling in my old kitchen like a kid in trouble again.

"Tricia?"

"It's me," I say fearfully.

"Where are you?" He's calmer than I expected. I, on the other hand, am barely audible but manage to whisper, "Safe."

He's quiet, and I realize he's buying time to trace the call. I need to keep it together. I clear my voice and tell him again that I'm safe and I'll be home in a few days.

"Damn it! Come on. You know you can't do this."

I ignore him. "Will you still be there when I get back?"

"I will if you come back now," he says. Not exactly the answer I'm looking for.

"Your note, Tricia. If you really feel that way, you'll come home now so we can talk about it." He found it and is using it against me. Low blow.

"I can't. I need this break, don't you understand? I need a break from you and this whole unhealthy operation."

"Listen to me. You are one person who can't run away from your problems. In fact, when you run, it creates infinitely more problems."

I'm listening, but I don't care. I only care about one thing, and I will run home right now if he answers correctly.

"Ryan, do you have feelings for me too?" It's a tall order for a man to answer. I get it. I'm setting him up to fail, but I still want to hear it, one way or another. The silence is deafening. I decide it's the last time I'm going to put myself in an emotionally vulnerable position. He makes a loud clucking sound like he can't believe I asked the question. It hurts and angers me at the same time. Saying nothing is worse than telling me he has no feelings for me at all. I'm back in control. In fact, I feel so powerful it scares me a little.

"Two things, Ryan. If you ever lay a hand on Sal, I'll find a way to hurt you, maybe kill you. Or maybe I'll just kill myself. Second, I'll only come back if I know you're gone. So pack the fuck up and put someone else in charge." I hang up, walk out the side door, and bash the phone against the retaining wall. Goddamn that felt good! Screw him and this whole victim mentality. It's not who I am. At least it's not who I want to be any more. I pull myself together. I have way too much work to do.

17

JODI

I grab a fresh peach out of the fridge and plop down on a stool at the center island. Now that the clutter is organized, I'm pleased to see how nice the kitchen looks. The antique white cabinets offset and complement the exposed beams perfectly, and the black and white marbled granite countertops are sleek and beautiful. I dry the peach juice dripping down my hand and grab the pen and paper I found in the junk drawer. I need to prioritize and hope for no more drama over the next five days.

Most of my initial work involves a lot of research on the laptop, which I'm thrilled to have access to. I can finally Google freely. I'm generally pretty paranoid about doing it from home, knowing someone is keeping track of my searches. I catch a break every now and then in the office, but I'm too busy most days to spend the time I need. Now I can take my time and search for information about the Brandts, Billy, cases my father may have worked on, any murder cases in the general area. I start the list.

-Find MJB
-Visit Judith's Gallery

-Scour the property
-Tap into Jack's computer
-Talk to Jodi ...

I think about the last item on the list and it saddens me. Poor Jodi. I know what's wrong with her. Sure, everyone knows she suffers from depression, but I know why she suffers from it. I would be depressed, too, if I were her, and it has nothing to do with being crazy. Well, perhaps it does now. From what Katie told me, she's likely beyond help at this point. I'm quite convinced that Jodi has an incurable sleeping disorder.

The few times Jodi and I managed to spend time together, she confided in me about her family. Jodi was bright in her own way, but lacked a proper education, homeschooled by far-from-capable parents. They were too clueless to understand what was happening, so they kept her locked up. They claimed it was for her own protection. Ironically, that may have been true for more reasons than they considered. Or maybe they weren't as dumb as I thought and actually knew some of the dirty secrets in Brandtville.

Jodi got clever over the years and found a way to pick the lock to her room. It wasn't that hard at all. She just shoved a hairpin into the center and voilá. On occasion, she was able to sneak out for a few hours to play with me in the creek, usually after her parents finished a case of beer and a giant batch of weed. We'd chat and play while Danny spied on her parents through the window for movement. When they stirred, he'd alert us, and she'd sneak back upstairs. We'd lock the door from the outside again and run out. They never knew. Jodi was so bored, so we started giving her our books to read. She went through them quickly, wanting more every time we saw her. She had so much potential but was so neglected.

Jodi wasn't able to properly communicate her symptoms because much of them happened in her sleep, so she got worse. And her parents, who inherited their farm but never worked a day on it, were too ignorant to get her the right help. I'm technically a lawyer, not a doctor, but it's my job to research diseases, especially as they relate to the products we market. I need to be able to describe them both medically and metabolically. We have a new drug, just approved by the FDA, that I know would help her. It treats people who suffer from a rare combination of sleep disorders—narcolepsy followed by sleepwalking. It's very rare to have both and causes extreme hallucinations during the sleepwalking stage. I think that's exactly why Jodi looks deranged during episodes.

I think of Katie's story about finding Jodi curled up in the barn and force myself to recall one of the most horrid memories of my childhood. We, too, found Jodi curled up in the barn sleeping on more than one occasion.

When she came to, she always had the trippiest stories. One time, she said she made friends with a giant lizard from the creek and wanted to put him in a nice stall in our barn. When she woke up, she was distraught that he was gone and cried out for her new friend. It took a lot of convincing to prove to her that it was just a dream.

One day after she snuck out, she told me she had an episode but awoke in the middle. She insisted that she wasn't dreaming this time and that it was real, so I was all ears.

"If I tell you, you'll believe me, right, Jenny?"

"Pinky swear," I promised. "What was it about?" I imagined a cool story about a panda bear or a dragon. Sometimes her stories were even more adventurous than some of the books we read, so I couldn't wait to hear about them.

"I woke up in one of your barn stalls last week. I think because I heard voices. I sat down and listened while I tried to figure out how I got there. I heard men talking."

"What did they say?"

"Pinky swear again that you'll believe me, Jenny, because it's true." I pinky swore again and asked her to continue.

"I heard your dad talking about killing someone."

"It was a dream, Jodi. He would never kill anyone." I no longer believed her or was interested in this story.

"Please, Jenny, you promised," she pleaded. Aside from the preposterousness of my father being a killer, who would be in our barn in the middle of the night? It was a dream. But I did promise her after all, so I let her continue.

"He said, 'Billy, you fucked up. Two wrongs don't make a right, and I warned you to leave it alone. You left the city to leave the sins of modern society behind.' Sorry to curse, Jenny, I'm just repeating what your dad said."

"I don't care if you curse. Did you say, modern society?"

"Yes. Then he said, 'There's a price to pay for this. In the meantime, we'll all have to do our part to repent and take care of this situation.' Someone else asked where the body was, and the man said it was in the trunk of his car. Then another man said they'd burn him to ash and lay him with the land. I ran all the way home after that. It's the first chance I've had to tell you. Please believe me, Jenny. It wasn't like the other times. I swear."

My mouth hung wide open like a Venus flytrap, staring at her in disbelief. I told her I believed her because she was so distraught. I hugged her and told her not to tell anyone else and made her return the pinky promise. I wanted to believe this was just another one of her episodes, but it put me on high alert.

I read into everything that came out of my father's mouth after that, even something as simple as saying he was tired. Why would he be so tired unless he was out murdering people all night? I couldn't take the suspense anymore, so I started plotting a spy session. I had a plan and was ready to operate when given the right moment. I finally got it about two months later, just as I was starting to forget the whole thing.

I was about to fall asleep for the night when I overheard my father telling my mom that he was going to meet the guys in the barn to talk about their next hunting trip.

"We'll just go out there, Ang, and have a few beers so we won't wake up the kids."

"Fine by me, Sean. I don't give a rat's ass!" She was slurring her words, so I assumed she was drunk again and would pass out any minute.

My mother started drinking heavily about a year after we moved. I overheard her tell Nonna that it was the only thing that kept her sane. She drank straight out of the bottle when she thought no one was watching and would pass out cold soon after. I would put a blanket over her if she fell asleep on the sofa. I knew what was happening but protected Danny from her growing addiction. I didn't want him to worry and hoped she'd get better on her own.

Hearing a meeting was about to take place in our barn launched me into action. I was ready and in a rebellious mood. I already accepted any punishment that would come as a result of my snooping. I'd gladly take the belt to find out what in the world they were doing.

I pretended I was asleep when my dad came in to kiss me goodnight. He didn't do that very often, so it confirmed my suspicion that he was up to something. I waited in my dark room for hours, staring out the window. I peeked just enough to see out, and I hoped no one could see in. Finally, I heard whispers and looked out to see six men and a woman walking towards the barn, but not a car in sight. They seemed to appear from nowhere. They continued walking, quite familiar with the property, and went around the back and into the upper portion of the barn.

I stuck to my plan, tiptoed down the stairs and snuck out the back window furthest from the barn. I had dark clothes on for concealment and was having a little trouble seeing. I smashed my big toe into the wall of the well pump and had to suppress what would have been an ear-piercing shriek on any other day.

I watched from behind the house for a while until I decided all of my father's guests had probably arrived. The border above the house and barn is lined with dense forest, providing good coverage. As quietly as I could, I crept from tree to tree, hiding behind each along the way. I was hoping the barn doors would be open to see the men and hear what they were saying, but they were closed. I could only see slight movement through one tiny crack. It wasn't going to work.

I changed my plan and took off down the bank to the front of the barn. I opened one of the stall doors and froze as it creaked. My heart was pounding. Thankfully, the sound of the door went unnoticed, but I knew I couldn't afford to make any more noise. I sat down in the center of the dirt stall and practically held my breath. I could hear them perfectly.

I quickly realized that what I'd hoped was just one of Jodi's awful dreams was horrifyingly real.

My father was speaking. "Chuck, tell me where we are with the neophyte."

"We've taken action, with permission from the Masters, Sean. He'll no longer be able to hurt anyone. He confessed that a voice told him to do it."

"So, the reports are true? So senseless and devastating! Damn it! I'm so sorry, Fratres and Sorores."

"Where's he now?" a woman asked.

"The sinker," a man responded.

"Are my people watching him?" she asked.

"Yes. They're following orders."

"Good."

"I can't believe this has happened," a weary voice said. "Nothing will bring my boy back, but I will rest better knowing his killer will be punished in this life and by the wrath of God into his next. My son is now under the watchful and protective eye of God."

"Amen," said several of the men at once.

"Tomorrow we'll take our rightful positions and rid our sacred grounds of the evil among us. Unlike the all-too-pardoning laws written by our predecessors, we know true divine balance can only occur when evil is expelled. In order to protect, we must punish. Dunlap has finished his work and has brought in the animals. We must align to the traditional ways of our ancestors."

What was my father talking about? Nothing made any sense at all.

Chuck said, "Yes, it's merciful all things considered, Sean. I will have the prisoner ready at the Twenty-Fifth Acre at high noon."

"A quick prayer, shall we?" my father suggested.

"In you, Lord my God, I put my trust. I trust in you; do not let me be put to shame, nor let my enemies triumph over me. No one who hopes in you will ever be put to shame, but shame will come on those who are treacherous without cause."

"Amen!" they said in unison again. I didn't recall this verse from CYO and was surprised by how openly religious my father was behaving around this group of people. But with this bizarre behavior and talk of killers, I knew I had to get out of there before I was caught and punished more severely than I dared imagine.

As if prayers in my barn weren't creepy enough, there was strange chanting right before the members drank. I heard the clanking of glasses followed by random overlapping conversations after that.

I stood up and wanted to run, but my legs felt like cement. There was a prisoner locked up in a sinker, whatever that was, about to be slaughtered by wild animals? Fear had a grip on me, and I was frozen. I remember the warmth of urine as it ran down my leg. The sensation snapped me back to my senses long enough to put one foot in front of the other. I couldn't process what I was hearing. I still can't, but I'm certainly more curious now about the lapel pin, remembering it all. I managed to sneak back in the house through the window. My mom was still out cold. I started running up the steps to my room, but the next thing I remembered, I was in a bed at Doylestown Hospital. My father was looking down at me.

"Hi, honey."

I let out a shrill shriek that must have startled the entire wing. It took my father very much by surprise, so he hollered for the nurse.

"Her vitals," I heard someone say. I was injected with something through my IV and knocked out again. The next time I awakened, my mother was asleep beside me in a reclining chair. I looked up at a nurse washing my face with a warm washcloth. She had kind eyes.

"Good morning, Jenny. My name is Lori. I'm your nurse."

"What happened?"

"You fell down the stairs and bumped your head pretty hard, sweetie. You have a concussion, but you're okay. Dr. Braun and I are taking very good care of you."

My mother popped up, hearing the conversation and practically jumped in bed with me.

"Oh, thank God, baby. How do you feel?"

"Okay, I think."

Then it hit me again. I remembered the conversation I heard in the barn. "How long have I been here?"

"Three long days," my mother answered. She was sniffling and looked tired, but very relieved. I reached out for her and she gave me the biggest, warmest hug I'd ever gotten from her.

I decided to keep quiet about the real reason I fell down the stairs. Thinking back on it now, I'm guessing I was in shock and passed out midflight. When I was released, I told myself it was a bad dream. I just hit my head. I didn't want to accept that such a sadistic conversation ever happened. But here I am, remembering it like it was yesterday. I still wonder what happened to their prisoner and what vision came to reality. I had trouble looking at my father the same way ever again.

18

THE CRAWLSPACE

Time to grab the laptop and see how far I can get with Google. I unplug the cords, planning to work downstairs, but freeze with technology in hand. I'm trying not to look at the closet again, but I give in to what feels like a gravitational pull. I open the door, kneel down, and search for the opening to the space. It's covered by some of Jack's research books. I push them aside, but the one on top catches my attention. It's a historical book about Bucks County. I toss it out the door to bring downstairs with me later.

The panel is exposed now. I lift the small latch and am surprised how easily it opens. The latch is new. Someone has replaced it. I wonder if Jack and Katie know about the second panel and the depth of the space. I kind of doubt it. But I'm not feeling brave enough, or emotionally strong enough, to find out what is or isn't still in there, so I close the door and put the books back in front of it.

I found the small opening one day when Danny and I were playing hide and seek. I was crouched down in the closet as I heard my brother counting. 25 ... 24 ... 23 ... Something was sticking out and poking me in the back, so I turned and found the small latch. It was obviously meant to be hidden, but I was surprised I hadn't seen it before. Danny and I thought we'd investigated every part of the house.

The closet backs up against an inward wall between rooms on the second floor. The attic stairs are in the middle of the space. On the other side of the stairs is the bathroom. It's the only closet like it in the house. The others all have traditional sliding doors.

When my brother got to about 15 ... 14 ... 13 ... I opened the door panel, which was about the size of a large pet door. I thought maybe it was meant to be a safe, like the one we had in Parsippany. It wasn't huge, but I was definitely going to fit. I went in sideways, knees up in the air, and leaned against the back. I was pretty excited because there was no way he was going to find me. Without warning, the wall behind me gave out and I landed in the big open space. It scared the hell out of me, and I screamed, afraid I was going to drop down through the wall and be trapped. Danny heard me and ran into my room.

"Jenny? Are you okay?" he asked.

"Danny, come here! Quick!" I popped my head out of the side of the first panel.

"What the heck?"

"You have to promise not to tell mom and dad about this." He pinky swore. I told him to close the panel until I got a flashlight. My dad was working that day at his new firm, and as I passed my mother on the way to the utility room, it was obvious she had been drinking. She was out. I assumed that meant we were going to be fending for ourselves at dinner again that night. She was starting to remind me of Jodi's parents. I didn't like it, but I also didn't care at that moment. This was the greatest gift two hide-and-seekers and scavenger hunt detectives could ever ask for.

I went in first with an industrial-sized flashlight and Danny followed with a regular-sized one. Mine lit the area perfectly. We were both completely mystified but enamored by our discovery. We could stand on opposite sides of the back of the attic stairs. There were multiple shelves on the other side of the room. A small, very old mattress was on the floor. We wondered what the old owners did or hid in there. "Maybe they hid treasure in here, Jenny! We should look for some. Or maybe money?"

"Yeah, maybe."

Our minds were creating all kinds of exciting and mysterious scenarios. I know now that it was likely built during the prohibition when they hid alcohol, money, and guns. We found an old Bible on one of the shelves too, which was odd. There was some writing on the inside cover. The only words I can recall were "Find the hidden truths."

I pictured Ms. Aada lying down and praying in the room. Maybe it was a prayer room. Too hard to tell. Looking at the Bible made us feel like we were doing something wrong, so we hid it in the corner out of sight.

Over what became our last year at the farmhouse, Danny and I turned the space into our own secret hideout. Every chance we got, we cleaned the cobwebs, dusted the shelves, and decorated it with our own pictures. We covered the old mattress with some sheets and blankets and used it like a sofa. To make it homier, we added our favorite stuffed animals and my Cabbage Patch Kid, which I really just wanted out of my room—I never really liked it.

I got it from the previous owners one Christmas not long before they passed away. They put the doll in an unusual outfit with wings, like an angel. I tried to take it off, but it was sewn on. It was one of a kind, that's for sure. I suspect Ms. Aada was deep in dementia by the time she did that.

When we played inside, one of us would take turns listening for my parents. We used a code phrase if we heard either of them coming up the stairs. It was "What's for dinner?" It worked like a charm. Those were the last words my mom wanted to hear.

One day we scored some carpet remnants being tossed for a redo of the hardwood floors. The contractor used a box cutter to tear it into pieces for disposal. It was perfect. Danny and I grabbed some we knew would fit. I liked the shaggy green carpet at the time. The hardwood floors were too squeaky.

Seeing wasn't always easy in the dark room, so we started hoarding batteries for our flashlights. We hung them from the ceiling like lights. When they went out, we had to be patient until our parents bought more. We would tell them our remote-control cars and other toys died. They were disgusted by how quickly they went. If only they knew. We were becoming good little liars, just like they were.

The crawlspace became our sanctuary. My parents weren't in the same room together very often, but when they were, they were usually fighting. When they really got into it, my mother would tell us to go to our rooms. We would look at each other and smile. Their time of misery was our secret playtime. Every now and then, I would try to make out what they were saying. Danny tuned them out completely, I think. But I heard bits and pieces. "I hate you for bringing me here," my mom would say.

"Then go back home to the city where you belong," my father would reply. It was rough. My parents seemed to change overnight.

19

THE DOUGLAS BRANDT FOUNDATION

I t doesn't take long to drum up information on Michael and Denise Brandt. I found Denise's obituary. That's unfortunate, but maybe it will give me clues about the family. I click the link.

Denise (Long) Brandt of Brandtville, Pennsylvania, passed away suddenly on Thursday, July 15, 1997. She was 54 years old and the loving wife of Michael J. Brandt II, the great grandson of the late Joseph Brandt after whom the town was named. Denise graduated from Pleasant Valley High School and was a registered nurse. She was passionate about helping others, and her children were her pride and joy. She enjoyed gardening and was active in her church. She helped found the Douglas Brandt Foundation in memory of her son, Douglas Brandt. In addition to her husband, Denise is survived by her daughter, Jacqueline Brandt, and her oldest son, Michael J. Brandt III. A private ceremony will be held at Mission Church. In lieu of Flowers, donations can be made to the Douglas Brandt Foundation. PO Box 81, Brandtville, PA 18978.

That was the church my father started attending. My mother kept us in the Catholic Church. No way was my Italian Catholic mother switching to a non-denominational church. She called it a cult, which made my father snap. Mission Church had a very small congregation—invitation only. It was an honor to be accepted.

"Any house of God should be open to anyone," my mother would say. It was out of the question that we'd attend. He let her win that battle easily, saying he preferred to enjoy services alone anyway. If it were up to my brother and me, we wouldn't have attended any service. But the Catholic Mass was only an hour and sometimes my father would be at Mission Church all day. We didn't complain too much, fearing we could lose half of our weekend if we weren't careful.

How terrible. Mr. Brandt lost a son and a wife? I search again and find a link to the foundation. It provides resources and funding for families of missing and exploited children. There are multiple other links, including one that describes how the Amber Alert Program works, how to locate sex offenders, and a bigger link to the National Center for Missing and Exploited Children. I click into it. There are several profiles of missing children. I see one who looks similar to Danny, and I have to turn away.

I click back to the foundation page and find small details about Douglas. He was born in 1984 and went missing in 1995. Doug was a straight A student and had a passion for art. He loved sports and played soccer and hockey. He would've been just a few years younger than me. His brother and sister are likely closer to my age. I wonder if they're on Facebook. I hope Katie has an account I can get into.

I search again to see if I can find Michael Brandt's address. The lapel pin absolutely has to be his. The initials are a perfect match. "MJB." Michael J. Brandt. I find a website telling me for just nineteen

97

dollars and ninety-nine cents, I can get it all: Address, phone number, and criminal history—all one hundred percent confidential." I grab my Visa Gift Card, which I loaded with five thousand dollars in anticipation of needing non-traceable funds and plug in the numbers. I get a pop-up telling me it's searching. *Oh, come on already.* I finally get an address, but the number is unlisted. Good grief! What did I just pay for? It lists his criminal history as "none." Well, at least I got an address.

I Google it and find the location. It's only two miles from the house. I've never noticed it before, but that's not surprising because the driveways around here are very long, and most of the homes are hidden. It looks pretty sizable, based on the aerial view. I can see a pool and gardens. I'm bummed I can't zoom in closer, but I can make out some details—like the fact that it's very iron-gated. I'll bet there's a ton of security as well.

I'm suddenly struggling with the notion that Michael Brandt could be a murderer. He lost a son. He's invested a great deal in helping others. I just can't imagine that he would've been the one to kill Billy. But what's with his mysterious pin and why was it in the water? And Denise's death—a sudden death could be a heart attack or a car accident, I suppose. I can't find anything else about her. The foundation was set up for Doug as a missing person, which means they haven't solved the murder. If that's true, it couldn't have been the boy they were talking about in the barn that night, could it? And I'm still not confident that I heard everything correctly.

I wonder if Jack's connection to *The Examiner* holds clues. I waste no more time with the laptop and try hacking into the iMac. I fire it up and hope he's the type of guy who writes his passwords down. I look under the desk, in the drawers, and under the keyboard, but find nothing. I get the prompt to enter a password. *Crap. Crap. Crap.* I could be so close to something. It's tempting to guess the password, thinking maybe it's Miss Mable or one of the dog's names, but I'm worried I'll get completely locked out. I'll have to give my patience a try, but I absolutely have to log into that thing at some point, even if I have to call Jack.

I'm forced back to the laptop and psyched to see Katie left her Facebook page open. Score! I search for the Brandt children but come up empty-handed. The foundation, however, has its own Facebook page. There are quite a few random posts from do-gooders and well-wishers. Some have attached links to articles about missing children, hoping the foundation can help. None of the children are from the area.

As I'm scrolling, a new post pops up. It's a reminder about an event. I click on the link provided. There's a private event this Saturday at the country club where we used to belong. I know that place inside and out. The proceeds will benefit the foundation. How do I get in on that? There's a phone number listed, so I use the landline and dial. A nice woman answers.

"Good afternoon. Douglas Brandt Foundation. How can I help you?"

"Yes, hello, my name is Katie Dorcy. I understand there's an event this weekend, and I would very much like to attend. Any possible way for me to get a ticket?" She pauses longer than I expected.

"So, you'd like your ticket back? Your husband said you couldn't attend due to a conflict. He said you were going to be away."

"Oh, right. Well, we are, but I will be back on Saturday. He won't be home until Sunday. I'm sorry for the confusion." I'm not sure if she's buying it and feel my hands start to shake. I want into this thing, but I'm worried about getting caught.

"Well, Mr. Dorcy was invited to cover the event for *The Examiner*. We've already replaced him with another reporter."

"I understand, but I would still very much like to attend. It's a cause that's very close to my heart. When I was a child, I lost my best friend. After all these years, she's still considered a missing person." I whimper a little, thinking of Danny.

"I'm so sorry. Let me see what I can do. I'm going to have to speak to Mr. Brandt, but I'll get back to you. Where can I reach you?" I read her the landline number.

"I really appreciate it. I'll be happy to donate extra funds in the amount of one thousand dollars." I'm having a what-would-Sal-do moment.

"Oh, that's very generous of you. I'll be sure to mention that. Hopefully we can work something out."

"I hope so. Thank you again and I look forward to your call back."

Still shaking, I think to myself how twisted this could get. I hope Michael Brandt isn't good buddies with Jack or something. I need wine.

20

A TICKET

It's 4:00 p.m. already and I realize I haven't eaten anything except the peach. First things first. I walk out to the car and grab the wine Antonio left for me. *Ugh!* The bottles are warm. I probably should have thought of this sooner. The dogs follow me out and do their business. I make note of the pissing and shitting zones, so I don't step in them later.

I put one bottle in the freezer and two in the fridge. As I do, I see a note on a container that says, "For Tricia." It's homemade lasagna, enough for days. Oh, this woman is my hero. The last thing I want to think about is cooking, or how to find the nearest grocery store. I scarf down a generous portion and feel very satisfied.

Even though the wine is still kind of warm, I'm ready for my well-earned private happy hour. The cork pops at the same time as the phone rings.

"Hello? Dorcy residence," I say for good measure.

"Hi, Mrs. Dorcy, this is Jill from the foundation returning your call."

"Yes, hello, Jill."

"Mr. Brandt is happy to accommodate you but will not accept additional money. He's simply glad you'll be able to join."

"Oh. Are you sure? I'd be more than happy to contribute."

"He said perhaps one day you could do some volunteer work instead."

Gulp. "That would be wonderful."

"Hopefully you'll have a chance to talk to him at the event. You're all set. Would you like us to leave your ticket for you when you arrive, or do you want to pick it up beforehand?"

"I'll be away, but I can have my daughter pick it up for me if that's all right?"

"That's fine. I'll be here tomorrow from 9:00 a.m. until noon. Will that work?"

"I'll make sure it does. Thank you. This means a lot to me."

"You're quite welcome. Have a good day, Katie."

Katie? Now we're on a name-to-name? Shit! Are Katie and Jill friends? I'm getting paranoid again. This is nuts. I try not to think too much about the admission I may have to make when Jack and Katie return.

With wine in hand, I head back outside and make myself comfortable at the patio table. It's cheap, just a simple glass table with tan plastic chairs. My mother had impeccable taste. This never would have worked for her. Our table was wrought iron with matching chairs, and the patio was blooming with flowers. Not so much now. I pick at some of the grass growing between the pavers. I'm being too hard on them. This farm does look like a lot of work.

I feel the tense muscles around my neck relax for the first time today. What a day it's been. The animals are quiet and laying down. The farm is peaceful. I pretend that I'm younger and at home, with Nonna in the kitchen fixing dinner. I look in the distance and can visualize Danny riding his bike up and down the driveway. A cool breeze blows through my hair and I hear the rustling of leaves. I notice the leaves are blowing sideways and look up to see heavy clouds forming. I remember they were calling for thunderstorms this evening. I'm not crazy about thunderstorms to begin with, so the thought of them while I'm staying here alone is a frightful one. I chug my wine and get ready for farm duty.

I race inside, put on a pair of jeans and sneakers, and head over to the barn. The animals are eager to greet me. The goat is a little too eager, and I have to fight to keep my balance. "Chill out, Miss Mable." I pat her on the head and run my hand over one of the cleaner looking sheep. "You must be hot, little buddy." I grab the pitchfork and muck the enclosed area. I've just gotten everything perfectly clean when Miss Mable goes number two again. I can't help but laugh.

I hear a rumble in the distance. The storm's coming, whether I like it or not. I quickly put the animals in their stalls, just like Katie showed me. I give them all fresh water, their share of grains and hay, then close the stall doors.

Off to the coop. I give it a quick cleaning and am thankful I don't need to gather eggs right now. Katie specifically told me to collect them in the morning. They're clucking away and walking all around my feet. Why am I so freaked out by chickens? I can't get this job finished soon enough.

As I'm sweeping over the far end of the aging planks, I feel one of them wobble. I crouch down for a better look. Katie warned me to be careful, saying she hurt herself a few times on it. They plan on tearing down the coop altogether and putting up a new one soon. It's definitely seen better days.

For the heck of it, I pick up the plank and take a look down. I don't see anything except a bunch of debris mostly. But my level of curiosity is heightened, remembering how my father turned the coop into Fort Knox. I dash off to the utility room and find a flashlight. It's even windier when I get back outside, so I quicken my pace. It's gross, but I lie down and look as far as I can into the opening. I don't really expect to see anything but think, *leave no stone unturned*. This is my one and only chance.

Much to my surprise, I spot a small mason jar. I can't reach it though, so I run back to the barn and head upstairs to where Jack keeps the tools. None of them look like they'll work. On the way back, I scan the ground and see a decent-sized branch with a curved end. This may do it! The rumbling is getting closer, so I sprint the rest of the way back to the coop and reach into the hole. I'm able to loop the jar and move it slowly until I'm able to reach it. It's covered in nasty gunk, but I hear something clank.

My heart nearly stops as huge clap of thunder shakes the coop. What chickens were left outside, dart inside. It's gonna pour! I replace the plank and throw down some feed. Katie said a fox would get them if they're not locked up properly. Not on my watch.

Just as I have the door locked, the sky opens up. There's no dodging the giant raindrops. I'm soaked from head to toe within seconds as I head for the house. Sonny and Cher are pacing as I open the door, seemingly glad to have me safe inside. I look back out the window to see sheets of rain, the heaviest rain I've ever seen. I put the jar down and strip out of my wet clothes. Butt naked, I head to the kitchen sink and run the jar under hot water, trying to get years of muck off. It's no easy task, but I can see enough to make out a key and a piece of paper. The lid is completely rusted and not budging. I only have one choice and that's to break it. I crack it like an egg against the counter, and it does the trick. I carefully pull the key and paper out and clean up the shards of glass left behind.

It's a key all right, but to what? I'll probably never know. The only thing the note says is "Oh dear." What on earth does that mean? Is that code for something?

It would be stupid to keep a key to the actual coop under the coop, so I can cross that out. And there's no way we would have needed a spare key to the house in a jar under it, would we? It's strange and confusing, but I consider it a decent find and put the key in the side zipper of my purse. Every lock I see, I'll be checking. I start thinking about all the scavenger hunts Danny and I used to plan together. That's kind of what I'm doing here over this long weekend. It's an adult version of "scavenger hunt" but with no elaborate clues to help guide me—unless this *is* one meant just for me. But I don't want to get my hopes up.

A bolt of lightning catches my eye. I head into the living room near the fireplace and look out the window. Another huge bolt flashes, followed by a crash that literally shakes the house. I'm hating every second of this, and so are the dogs. They're whining and looking at me for support. "It's okay, guys." I'm trying to convince myself as much as them. Another big bolt lights up the sky and then silence consumes the house as the power goes out. Oh, Mary, Mother of God.

21

THE STORM

I'm standing in a dark room, completely naked, with no power. I can't take a shower now, not during a storm. At least that's what I've always been told. I grab an afghan and wrap it around myself.

And for Mother Nature's next act, I hear hail rattling on the roof and against the window. It's quarter-sized, some bigger. All I can do is sit and stare and pray that it'll be over soon and that nothing is damaged. The hail is bouncing off the ground, the coop, and the car. There's one loud boom after another. I squeal with each and put my hands over my ears.

I find the flashlight I used earlier and look for a phone book. I need to call the electric company because me, in this house at night with no lights, is not going to happen. I find the Yellow Pages and pick up the landline to call. *Shit!* It's dead too. Time to play my last card. I grab my burner with the California area code and call Katie.

"Tricia? Is everything okay?" The reception sucks, but I manage to tell her what's happening. She tells me not to worry and that she'll make the proper calls.

"Do you have candles, Katie?"

"We have lots of candles. Check the armoire in the living room. I have a whole cabinet full of them. There should be matches there too."

"Yes, I see them."

"You poor thing. Are you okay?"

"I'm fine really." I laugh to settle her and tell her I'm being silly. "I'm just glad I have candles now and really glad I got the animals in the barn when I did."

"Oh, smart thinking! How'd it go?"

"It went great! The goat, Miss Mable, is it? She was very happy to see me." Katie laughs.

"She always is. She just loves attention."

We exchange goodbyes for now, and I start lighting candles like I'm in St. Patrick's Cathedral. I get about a dozen lit and notice the hail has stopped. The rain is coming down lighter, and I see some of the clouds breaking up. I take a deep breath and feel safe enough to head upstairs, flashlight under my arm and a candle in each hand. I *was* going to get into the bathtub, like old times, but now I just want to get in and out of the shower as quickly as possible.

I'm done and back into clean clothes, tossing back another glass of wine. I scan the property for signs of damage or downed trees. There are a few small branches down, but they don't concern me. What does, however, is the sight of the creek over the bank and road. I'm not sure how deep it is, but this isn't good. I would've loved the sight as a kid, but not now. I hope the electric company can make its way through. Or, I hope I can make my way out of here if I have to.

Something catches my eye as I continue looking out over the property. I see movement near the chicken coop. The dogs must sense something too and start barking. I'm officially spooked and wish Sal were here. Maybe it's a fox or something.

Suddenly, a figure steps out from behind the coop and turns toward the house. It's a woman. I let out a gasp but stifle an all-out horror movie scream. My heart is pounding again, this time so hard I can barely catch my breath.

She looks ghostly. Am I seeing a ghost? Is this house haunted? I'm totally superstitious of such things. She's pale and soaked from the storm, her pants barely clinging to her waist. They're way too big, as is her tattered T-shirt. She looks disoriented, and that's when I realize it has to be Jodi.

She looks terrible. I command the dogs to stay, with a "heel." They stop barking but are still wound up. I open the door and slowly walk toward her. She's definitely sleepwalking and hallucinating. This makes no sense, based on my research. Water is one of the few things that can bring people out of sleep and sleepwalking. It's why in so many movies people splash water on faces to wake up deep sleepers. I wonder what's going on in her terrible world. Even though the research I did isn't matching her current state of mind, I came prepared to help her if I got the opportunity.

"Jodi?" I call to her. She looks at me, but her eyes move right through me. She's only partially aware that another human being is present. I place one arm gently on her shoulder. She flinches and gives me a look like something out of *The Exorcist*. I can see why Katie's afraid of her now. She has dark circles under her eyes and her hair has thinned. She's terrifying to view, and I start to wonder if I'm half as ready for this situation as I'd hoped. I take a deep breath and a leap of faith. I remind myself that she's gotten this dysfunctional due to exhaustion and nothing more. She's still the sweet and fun person she used to be. *I hope.*

"Jodi, honey? What do you see?"

"A man."

Katie told me she said the same thing to her. She must think she's following someone or being followed.

"What does he look like?"

"He's very handsome."

"Is it your boyfriend?"

"No. I don't have a boyfriend."

"Can you describe anything else about him?"

"He's tall now."

"Oh, that's nice. Was he short before?" I add for humor.

"Yes, he was just a little boy," she says with a schoolgirl laugh.

"Does he have a name?"

"It's Danny."

I take a step back. "What did you say?"

"It's Danny. He's my friend."

A jolt runs through my body upon hearing my brother's name. She must be remembering Danny from when we were younger. She must be hallucinating about him and placing him in a future scenario, but it's really freaking me out. I take another deep breath, knowing what I'm supposed to do now. I just hope I don't lose it.

"Jodi? Let's go find Danny."

"Okay," she says with a big smile. Her eyes are still glazed over and ghostly. I can see the cuts on her wrists now. They're several inches long on both sides, with thick scarring. She sure did a number on herself. I find myself pitying her more than I've ever pitied another person in my life. Well, except for myself. But that pity party is over.

I guide her in through the door, not knowing exactly what could happen. I'm pretty sure I can handle any scenario, even violence, because she looks terribly weak.

"Danny?" she calls out loudly, giving my willies, the willies.

"He's in his room. Let's go upstairs," I suggest.

I'm tearing up now, wishing it were true. She follows me as I guide her, one hand in hers, into Danny's old room. There's a daybed in here now, and an antique desk and dresser. She allows me to direct her to the bed and onto her back. I kneel by her side and gently rub her forehead and hair. If the water didn't work, I'm hoping gentle touches will wake her up.

"Danny and I are here with you. You can go back to sleep now."

"Okay. Good night, Jenny."

With that, she falls into a deep sleep. But I'm left with my mouth hanging open and the hair on the back of my neck and arms standing straight up in the air. I always thought that was just an expression. But I can literally see the hairs standing up on my arms above the goosebumps.

What the fuck. I say it over and over in my head. I'm not leaving her side until she wakes up and out of this hallucination. I hope it doesn't take all night and fear her mother will come looking for her. I put a towel gently over her then a sheet, hoping to soak up some of the rain saturating her nightgown. She's starting to shiver.

I stare out of my brother's old window and see the sun poking out from the clouds on the horizon as it starts to go down. Thank God. I sprint downstairs and grab a bottle of water to sober up, then run back up the stairs and sit on the floor beside her and stare at her, bewildered. She's been through so much. Even if I have to stick her in the trunk of that beast of a car, I'm committed to getting her over to Hopkins for a complete analysis.

I've made it to the bottom of the bottle when she looks up. She's aware now, and even more freaked out than I am.

"Where the hell am I?" she yells in a panic.

"It's okay, Jodi. I helped you out of the storm." She looks at her clothes and sees and feels that they're wet. I continue using a soothing tone. "You're fine now, Jodi. Let's get some tea." It's working. She's fixated on my voice and face. She's studying me. I can tell by her expression that it's familiar to her. It takes her a few more seconds, but that's all.

"Jenny? Is that really you or am I still dreaming? She's tearing up, which makes me tear up more.

"It's me, Jodi."

She pounces on me for a hug. We're both blubbering but looking at each other in between with smiles.

"I didn't think I'd ever see you again," she whimpers. "You and

Danny were the only friends I've ever had. It was so lonely after you left."

"I know. I've missed you too. You can't tell anyone I'm here though. Do you understand?"

"Yes, I understand. I've kept the same secret for Danny."

"What do you mean?" I'm studying her face.

"Danny. He's been here too."

22

SLEEP WALKING

"When was Danny here, Jodi?" I'm no longer gentle, practically shaking her for information, my stomach in knots.

"He was here a bunch of times before the Dorcys bought the farm. He said he left you a note in case you ever came back. They told him you died, but he didn't believe it.

My nervous system is being tapped like never before. I'm dizzy and the world is starting to go dark. I put my head down between my legs and my hands over my face. *Don't hyperventilate.* I concentrate on my breathing while Jodi rubs my back. I can't speak. But I'm suddenly seeing red. I'm outraged at my lying parents and at Ryan. He must know. I don't know how, but I'm going to make them all suffer for this.

I switch gears for my own sake, allowing myself to feel hope and joy by the idea that my brother may still be alive. I don't trust Jodi one hundred percent because of her long track record of hallucinations, but I really want it to be true.

"Tell me more. Please."

"We only spoke once, but I saw him a few times from my house. I saw him and another man come in through the door with some kind of supplies. I also saw him near the barn, near the chicken coop, and in the meadow. Then nothing once the Dorcys moved in."

"Supplies? What was he doing? Did the owners know?"

"No. He was definitely discreet. I heard some drilling and hammering in the middle of the night. He hid his truck behind the barn. But otherwise, I don't know. He didn't want me to know."

"When you spoke, did he say where he was living?"

"He told me he couldn't say anything. Not to say anything to anyone. I haven't. Although I can't be sure what I say when I sleep-walk. Where've you been, Jenny?"

"I can't say either, for your own protection. There are very bad men who could hurt us both if they find out."

"I figured. I remember the bad men in your barn."

This is a torturous conversation for me. And as much as I love the catch-up session, I want her out of the house. I'm itching to start looking for a note Danny may have left. But how could a note still be here after the Dorcys moved in? They would've seen it. I'll ask them later if they found one, if I don't find it. It's getting dark, and I still don't have electricity. I can barely see Jodi at all in the room. I'm frustrated, knowing this situation is going to slow me way down.

I guess I was never truly prepared to hear the words that Danny may be alive. I'm so grateful that Jodi is here and not still stuck in some mental health facility. I would never have known. I'm selfishly chomping at the bit to learn more about Danny but follow through with my original plans to help Jodi. I stop asking questions she can't answer and bring the conversation back around to her.

"Jodi, I think I can help you. That's one of the reasons I came back."

"You did? How?" she asks meekly.

"I did some research for you."

"For me?"

"Yes, for you. Jodi, I never stopped thinking about you." She smiles with tears in her eyes, touched that someone has cared. It makes my heart ache. "I think I know why you're having these episodes, and I have a prescription that should help you. What medications have they given you?" She doesn't look hopeful but rattles off a few that she remembers.

"They mostly give me anti-depressants and anti-anxiety medication. But they don't work."

"I know they don't. They're making you worse because they complicate the sleep cycle even more. Let's go downstairs. I have some new medicine in my bag."

She looks confused but follows me with the flashlight. I give her a month's worth and promise her more if it works. I keep my explanation short, knowing that too much jargon will confuse her.

"Basically, it's going to help you sleep better at night without interrupting the REM cycle sleep that you need. You'll probably always have narcolepsy and small episodes, but with the proper sleep, you'll have far fewer. And the sleepwalking, especially in the middle of the night, should stop. Our studies have shown that it can work in just a few days when the body catches up on sleep. Please try it, will you? Just take one every night."

"Are you a doctor?" *I wish.*

"No, but I work with some of the best doctors in the country and have access to the latest and greatest medical breakthroughs."

"Wow, Jenny! I'm so impressed. Should I still take the anti-depressants?" She raises her wrists to show me. I can't help but give her a big hug.

"I'm glad it didn't work. Please keep taking them. I'll be here for a few days housesitting, and I'll check on you to see how you're feeling."

"That's why you're here?"

"Yeah, don't ask. It's such a long story."

"I won't ask any questions, Jenny. I'm just glad you're here. I better head home or my mom will worry. She stopped drinking you know?"

"That's terrific news."

"She got herself together after my dad died of alcoholism."

"I'm so sorry. All right. Get home and take one tablet before bed. Or now. You look exhausted."

"I am. You have no idea."

I follow her to the edge of the property to make sure she gets home safely. As she crosses the road, Jodi sinks ankle-deep in floodwater. She looks back at me and smiles, wanting me to see how deep it goes. I smile back as she drags her leg across the top, creating a wake just like we used to do. I shake my head and hope the medicine works. I feel a bit nervous about complicating her state even more. Maybe I don't know what the heck I'm talking about.

I sit blankly staring into space for a good hour just trying to digest what Jodi told me. I keep coming back to the same question. Why? I have no answer. I finally get up and look outside with a flashlight. The flooding has receded even more, so I'm hoping the power company will be out soon. It's very dark in the country and my skin is crawling. I'm thankful for Sonny and Cher at the moment.

I make myself a cup of tea, grab the pen and paper again, and try to remember all the places Danny and I would hide things: The crawlspace, the barn stalls, the woods, the coop, the rocks by the creek.

With all the rain and flooding, the rocks would be tough to preserve an old note, so I can probably scratch that off.

(*Bang. Bang. Bang.*) The dogs bark and dash for the door. I jump right out of my chair and almost out of my skin. I'm definitely going to need blood pressure medicine. I peek out and see the PECO truck and open the door.

"Ma'am, there's a tree down over the wires up the street, which is also blocking the main road. But we're working on it. Should be a few more hours though."

We're both eyeing each other up with a sense of familiarity.

Oh no! It's Eddie Smithfield, one of my old classmates.

"Jenny?"

"I'm sorry?"

"Pardon me, but you look so much like a friend of mine who actually used to live here."

"Stop it. Really? No, I'm Jessica Dorcy. My parents live here."

"Oh, that's flipping weird. Felt like I saw a ghost."

"What ever happened to that family anyway?" I can't help but ask, despite the risk to my cover.

"Don't know. They disappeared one night. There are plenty of rumors though. Some think they were all murdered."

"Oh, good heavens!"

"Well, I'm going to get back to work, so you'll have light soon. Have a good night, ma'am." He looks me up and down one more time and shakes his head. "Uncanny." I hope it ends there. I can't have Eddie running his mouth.

23

THE RETAINING WALL

I need a break. My adrenal glands have crashed, and the drugs and wine have put me in a stupor. It's hard to believe that just this morning, I fled my townhouse in Baltimore. Oh well. No electricity equals no more searching for me. All I can do is just wait for tomorrow and see what the new day brings.

Before I conk out, I grab my burner and call Sal. I need to hear his voice.

"Hey! How's it going?" He picks up right away. I feel bad that it's so late.

"It's going pretty well, except I lost power." He starts laughing, knowing how much I hate thunderstorms.

"Big storm, huh?"

"Yes! It was awful. I was trying to feed the chickens and the lightning was everywhere. Did you get hail? We got huge hail. I was so close to calling you to stay with me. You have no idea."

"I would have. Are you getting anywhere?"

"Yes! I've actually made a lot of progress."

"Tell me."

"I'm so tired. I don't even know where to start."

"Try me."

I'm not used to this tone. It's much shorter than usual. But I don't blame him. He went through a lot to get me here. I decide spontaneously to minimize any findings and protect what I know. It's just a gut instinct. But it's also Sal, so I have to give him something.

"Well, remember my old neighbor? The one I told you about who sleepwalks?"

"The crazy one, right?"

"She's not crazy." I sigh. "Anyway, she was on the property today."

"No shit! What did she say?"

"She was having an episode. I helped calm her and get her home. I really think I might be able to help her."

"Did she say anything about Danny or your parents?"

"Danny?" I'm getting even more protective. "No, why?"

"Jesus, just checking. That's why you're there right?"

"Yes, of course. I'm definitely here to find out everything I can. You're right, but she doesn't know anything about that. She's too sick and lives in another dimension completely. There's no past or future." I start rambling off some medical mumbo jumbo, which I'm not just stretching, I'm downright making it up at this point. "It's terrible."

"Stop. Listen, Jen. I have no idea what you're talking about. You lost me at another dimension."

I'm glad I lost him, and glad he could care less about the rest of my Jodi story. I change topics.

"Any word from Ryan?"

"Nope. Nothing."

"Well, that's good! Maybe he'll give me some space."

"I wouldn't give him that much credit. Nothing else at all? Did you find anything on the property?"

"Like what?"

"Jen, you said you hoped there'd be clues to some of the shit that went down there. Nothing?"

"No, nothing yet. But I just got here, and the power is out."

"Oh, right." Sal sounds agitated and it's not sitting well with me. I want off the phone. Maybe he's just had a bad day.

"Is something wrong? You don't sound like yourself."

"I'm sorry. I'm on edge. I just want you safe and out of there as soon as possible." I get it now. He's just worried. "Do you want me to come and stay with you?"

"I'm fine. Really. Just exhausted and ready to pass out. I hope the power comes back on by the morning."

"Me too. Oh, and I overnighted you some new burners. You should get them in the morning."

"Awesome! Thank you so much. I don't know what I would do without you."

"Call me if you need me, or if you find anything, got it?"

I agree and we hang up, but I decide that no matter what I find out, I'm not sharing. Not even with my best friend. Maybe I'm being selfish Jenny again, but this trip is about *me*. I don't care how much trouble he went through to get me here. I'll give him nuggets of boring details, but that's it.

The dogs are staring at me and pacing. I realize I haven't fed them yet. Poor Sonny and Cher. I head back into the kitchen, bumping into things along the way. I fill up their water and give them an extra-big scoop of food. They're sweet dogs, and I find myself wondering if I should get one when I get back to Baltimore. Maybe that would fill the void I've had for so long. Or, maybe my own brother will fill it again. What an incredible, but unlikely thought.

I sit down on the sofa, exhausted. I hate how dark it is. The candles help, but I'm not a terribly big fan of sleeping with lit candles, especially with the dogs wagging their clumsy tails, knocking things over. I blow out the last candle and pass out cold on the sofa.

The sound of the power coming back on wakes me up. (*Beep. Swoosh. Zap. Ding.*) It sounds like an arcade. I'm totally disoriented. I check my watch to see it's 3:33 a.m. *Really?* That's the time? I debate whether to move upstairs to the bedroom or stay where I am. There's something comforting about sleeping on the sofa. I look down and see the dogs have been sleeping right next to me, so I decide it's the perfect spot and plan to sleep here for the rest of the weekend. I don't want to be on the second floor at night anyway.

I'm still worn out, but I can't help but think of yesterday's events. I'm also fighting the urge to call Ryan and give him a piece of my mind. He better be gone when I get back. Or, maybe I want him to stay so I can confront him. He knows how hard it's been on me. Even if he told me nothing, other than the fact that my brother was still alive, I would've led a much happier life up to this point. I wouldn't have worried myself sick every day. Why wouldn't he give me that much? Is it possible that he doesn't know? I want so badly to give him the benefit of the doubt, but it seems unlikely.

I drift in and out of sleep for a few more hours before getting up. The dogs need to go out. I scan the property before opening the door, not wanting any surprises. I watch through the kitchen window to make sure they don't go too far, then put on a giant pot of coffee. I'm gonna need it.

I prep myself for morning egg collection. I grab two containers and join the dogs outside. The sun's coming up, and the dewy meadow shimmers in its light. It's so serene. The creek is running fast and high after the storm, but the roads are clear.

I collect a total of ten eggs rather effortlessly and let the chickens out for their organic free-roaming exercise. I'm getting good at this already. I put the eggs in the fridge beside the dozen or so already in there. How does Katie keep up with this?

Time to head over to the barn. It's eerie for a hundred reasons, so I open the stall doors as quickly as possible. Miss Mable is looking for some attention, and rubbing her neck slowly calms my nerves. She presses her head up against me so hard that I have to take a few steps back. I'm starting to see the appeal of farm life. But if it were my farm again, I would replace all of these cute but rather useless animals with horses.

My morning chores are complete, so I wash up, pour myself a hefty cup of coffee, and wander back out to sit on the patio to mentally prepare. I look over my father's hard work. The retaining wall is still lovely despite some loose stones. I wonder why this was such an important project for him. He paid top dollar for everything else. It makes me a little suspicious. Maybe there was more to it than a home improvement project.

I inspect the wall more closely, examining the stones and structure. I pick up a loose stone. Aside from it being heavy as all get out, there's nothing special about it. I scan the wall methodically from top to bottom, but nothing looks dodgy.

I make my way over to the very far end of the wall and I see a section with multiple loose stones. I wonder how far down it goes before there's solid foundation. I start picking one up after another. It's a bit peculiar having so many loose in one section, but I would imagine time and the elements would have eroded the end adhesions first.

I get all the way to the base and see a hollowing. I can't budge the rest of the stones on my own, so I run up to the barn and grab a sledgehammer. If I tear this sucker up, I'm going to have more explaining to do, but this is a once-in-a-lifetime opportunity. With a strong upward swing, I come up underneath the largest stone and dislodge it. I can now make out what appears to be a safe. An outdoor safe on our property? Now that's kind of a big deal.

It has to be the work of my father—he was obsessed with safes. I can't help but hope there's a message inside for me from Danny. Now I have to find a way to open it without a pipe bomb or something. I'll never be able to remove it from the wall itself. It's cemented to the ground and to the rocks surrounding it. Unlike the other stones, not even a sledgehammer is going to help my cause.

I try a crowbar, but that's a waste of energy. I head back into the utility room and grab sandpaper and a toothbrush to remove some of the rock fragments from around the lock itself. On impulse, I grab some WD-40. That stuff is magic. You never know.

After ten minutes of hand-aching scrubbing, it looks pretty clear, so I give the black dial a good squirt. Much to my amazement, it starts spinning. *Yes!* The best thing about these old locks is that I can't get locked out after trying too many wrong combinations. I sit for thirty frustrating minutes trying formulas. I try our birthdays, house numbers, codes for pet names, everything.

I only have two more numbers going through my mind. The number twenty-five. The Twenty-Fifth Acre like I heard in the barn. What does it mean? I still remember some of the Bible verse my father was reciting that night, but I have no clue what book it was from. I go back into the house and grab the laptop. I Google, "Shame will come on those who are treacherous without cause." I get a match.

Psalm 25. There are twenty-two verses, but I scan the first three because those were the exact words I heard in the barn.

> [1] In you, LORD my God, I put my trust.
> [2] I trust in you; do not let me be put to shame, nor let
> my enemies triumph over me.
> [3] No one who hopes in you will ever be put to shame,
> but shame will come on those who are
> treacherous without cause.

I shudder. Is it a coincidence that the Twenty-Fifth Acre coincides with Psalm 25? Maybe I'm on to something. If I am, two and five are likely the first two numbers, but it's a three-code system. I start from the beginning. It's not 2-5-1, but it clicks at 2-5-2. That's the combination. What the hell was my father into? And what, or where, is the Twenty-Fifth Acre?

24

THE SAFE

I start pulling out the contents of the safe one at a time. There's a loaded revolver, eight hundred dollars in a plastic storage container, and an envelope sealed in a plastic bag. I pull the envelope out of the bag. The front is addressed to Chuck. I remember that name all too well. I look around again to make sure I'm alone, then open it.

We need to protect the village at all costs. Punishment is not an option. It's a duty. Once Johnny is captured, we must follow through with a hunt. This enemy must be stopped in our sacred way, to establish peace once again. Johnny must pay for Billy's death. He's made the connection to Dominick's disappearance. It's time for the D'Angelo brothers to be reunited. We cannot allow our enemies to triumph. Newushkinkw Newa Newushkink.

Light the fire. I leave you with some extra money and a weapon in case you or one of our brothers or sisters needs them. But the sacred way is first. If something goes wrong, I'll do what is just and flee. I've already put my family in grave danger, and I will not risk harm to our way of life. We must protect our children at all costs. Keep our secrets from them for now. They cannot expose that which they do not know. We will initiate them once this is over. Do not stop the progress that we have made. May the eye of the Great Spirit watch over you, today and always.

There it is! My father was—or is—into something super twisted. I don't know which sentence to dissect first. One of my mysteries is solved though. I'm guessing Johnny D'Angelo killed Billy, my father's best friend, for revenge. Johnny was Dominick's brother. *Real brother.* What's with this brother and sister talk?

As much as I hate to admit it, I hope my father's crew killed Johnny D'Angelo, too, or he may be one of the men after me. If he's still alive, he's likely the reason I'm under such guardianship. If he's dead, there must be more out there just like him. Along with Dominick, Johnny was one of the names on the list Danny and I found in the hidden tree safe behind Billy's house. I wish to hell we had cell phones back then, so I could have snapped a picture of it. What's with open, but hidden safes? Access. It's about access for the others.

I think back at the words Jodi told me that she overheard in the barn. "Billy fucked up." I wonder if Billy screwed up and got sloppy after he killed Dominick. He must have gotten caught by Dominick's very connected family and was tracked back to Brandtville. "Light the fire. May the Great Spirit watch over you." This weird speak reinforces the fact that I didn't know my father. Not at all. And what the hell is this about initiating the children later? Is that why my father keeps in touch and tracks me everywhere? Does he think I'm going to be a part of whatever this insanity is some day? Guess again. I plan on getting out of here as soon as I have my answers. I would never move back here, let alone get initiated into some twisted secret society.

What's also disturbing is this whole modern-day vigilante thing.

My father was a defense attorney. He knew his clients were bad people, especially those who went to *that* firm. No one forced him to get into that line of work. It's why I stopped practicing after three cases. But he must have made a ton of money doing it. The questions keep coming.

Was he playing judge after some of his cases settled and then becoming a punisher? Did he get paid for it too? Maybe he made more money being a ritualistic hitman. I don't know what to think, but I get a shiver considering the range of possibilities. Maybe he and Billy got caught at their game, and that's why my father has to hide both from the authorities and from his enemies. What a predicament he's gotten us all into.

"Your father loves you. He's not a monster." Ryan's words are in my head. Based on what I've read, I'm not so sure. And all of this weird hunting talk. These are human beings. What kind of punishment was this?

I think of the money my father earned and must still be earning. Is it about greed? My mother was relentless, always driving my dad to make more, buy more. It was never enough. I remember some of his clients. They were some of the wealthiest people in the country, and my father lightened their pockets considerably with his liberal billing. If my father invested well, he's worth millions today.

Now there's no doubt in my mind that he's doing more than hiding. He's still working hard at something, certainly not reading AARP magazine and playing Bingo, that's for sure. Is he involved in something even worse than anything I've considered? Could it even *be* worse?

Despite being trapped in an expensive surveillance operation, I've refused all money from my father. I pay the mortgage on my townhouse and all my own bills. I even refused alimony from John, mostly out of guilt. I'm on a massive independence streak here. That's all I really want—independence and freedom. It shouldn't be too much to ask!

I look back at the note. What's with the long foreign words? They look Native American, and my father was an enthusiast. Is there some sort of Indian ritual behind this? I Google it and find nothing of the sort. I bracket the words in quotation marks and get a message saying my search did not match any documents. I wonder if it's a code or something. I don't think I'll be able to crack this one without a little help.

I do a quick mental recap. My father is, or at least was, involved in some sort of cult-related ritual murder that incorporated bizarre language and biblical quotes. It just seems so unlikely. Present mystery aside, my image of him is still clear. He was very distinguished, well respected, and highly educated.

This letter does explain the extreme chaos during our last night in the house, though. Something must have gone terribly wrong.

I add, "identify and locate Chuck" to my growing list of action items.

I wonder what to do with the contents found in the retaining wall safe. They've been here a long time. I decide to put them all back, but I take a snapshot of the letter with my digital camera before closing everything up again. I think it looks straight. Not perfect, but good enough.

I'm making progress but have more questions than ever. When I finally agree to speak to my father, I'm going to squeeze him for answers and use this stuff as blackmail if he refuses to cooperate.

25

WHAT'S FOR DINNER?

I've put off getting into the crawlspace long enough. *If* there are clues from Danny, they'll probably start there. Before I go in though, I need to grab my event ticket for Saturday. I don't want any interruptions once I get started. I throw on a denim skirt and casual white blouse and put a little makeup on, so I don't look as exhausted as I feel, and get in the car. I wonder if the county club still looks the same as I remember.

I'm embarrassed to pull up in the clunker, so I park as far away from the entrance as possible. The building is as impressive as I recall. The outside has a plantation feel, with beautiful white columns and a large porch for sitting. There's still a golf course beyond the clubhouse and an outdoor pool for members.

I walk through the main entrance and step up to a smiling receptionist.

"Hello. I'm here to see Jill."

"I'm sorry. She just sat down with Mr. Brandt to go through some of the event details. Can I help you with something?"

"Yes, of course. Please don't interrupt them. I'm simply here to pick up a ticket for my mother, Katie Dorcy."

"Oh, hello. She told me to expect you." The woman opens the top file cabinet and pulls out my ticket and a note from Mr. Brandt himself that says, "We look forward to finally meeting you." Alarming! But, Phew. They haven't actually met yet.

"Thank you so much." Even though I know the answer, I ask anyway. "Is there a restroom I could use real quick?"

"Sure. Turn right at the top of the stairs and it'll be on your left."

I thank her and make my way up the curved, elaborate staircase and past the bathroom. The club has a two-story dining room, so I can see straight down at Jill and Mr. Brandt. Jill is trophy-wife gorgeous, with blonde hair and big boobs. I wonder if they're a couple. Mr. Brandt actually looks familiar to me—maybe from all the time we spent here.

MJB is an attractive man, likely in his late sixties, with a full head of hair. He's just a tad grey around the temples and has a deep tan, probably from hours on the golf course. He's wearing a very expensive-looking suit, maybe a Stanley Korshak. It all combines to lend him a distinguished air, much like my father's. I wonder what he does for a living. I assume some of his wealth has been passed down through generations, as the Brandts own most of the land in the area. But he's got that sharp, CEO look about it him that suggests he wouldn't be satisfied just living off family money.

Jill is joined by three more women making a fuss over the floor plans for the event. They seem fixated on the head table. I plan on sitting as far away as possible from that table on Saturday night. I'm skipping cocktail hour, too, to avoid as many introductions as I can.

Somewhat satisfied to put faces to the names, I head back downstairs, out into the summer sun and casually step back into the car. I prepare myself mentally along the way home to spend some time in the crawlspace.

I imagine it's dingy and dusty from years of disuse. If my custom-made, angel Cabbage Patch Kid is still in there, I'm going to be truly shook. And I'm not in the mood for cobwebs, spiders, mice, or whatever else may be inside. I hope if Danny's been there, he left his message close to the door. I'm not as adventurous as I was when I was nine.

I pull into the driveway just as the FedEx truck is leaving. That was close! I climb out, sign for the phones, and let the dogs out. I watch them as I open the package. Sal has outdone himself. There are five burners. What *would* I do without him?

I grab two flashlights from the utility room and take my time going upstairs. Why am I dreading this so much? Maybe Danny's alive! But I don't want to get my hopes up, and I don't totally trust Jodi's story.

I slide back into my yoga pants and put on a tattered T-shirt that I found in Jack's drawer. In addition to rifling through Jack's stuff, I'm going to need to rummage through Katie's closet later for the proper attire for Saturday night. I hope she has a decent dress in my size.

I'm ready. Deep breath. I head into my old room and push the books away from the first panel in the closet. The door opens easily. I gently push on the inside wall, which should collapse easily too, but it doesn't budge. It feels like someone has replaced the dry wall with some kind of heavy metal then painted over it to match the rest of the cubby. *Now what?* I run my hands up and down, hoping for another latch, but find nothing. I lie on my back, stick my head in, and see words scrawled in pencil on the ceiling.

What did we say to alert each other when mom and dad were coming? Say it out loud.

I can't believe what I'm seeing. I have a huge lump in my throat. It's true. It has to be true. Danny *is* alive and this is his message. There's not another living soul who would know the answer to this question. My shoulders heave up and down as tears fall from my eyes. With total confidence, I say, "What's for dinner?"

I hear a clicking sound before the solid door pops open into the space. Simultaneously, the whole room lights up. Lots and lots of lights—the exact opposite of what we had to work with when we were kids. With a sense of urgency, I slide in and find the room transformed from a child's imaginary palace into a real one.

The bare floor is now covered with shaggy, cream-colored carpet. Strands of Christmas lights crisscross the room and line the freshly painted white walls. On the largest wall in the space is a framed picture of our farm from about the time we lived there, signed by Judith Kamp. I was right to consider Judith a person of interest.

Some of our old toys, including my creepy Cabbage Patch Kid, sit atop brightly painted shelves. I feel like I'm having an out of body experience and pray that I'm not dreaming.

I continue admiring Danny's work. He put a pink beanbag chair in the furthest section, with a package in front of it. As I sit down for a closer look, the suspense of what's inside has me just as excited as when we were kids. It's a towel folded like wrapping paper covering a Christmas present—just like the way we played "Santa."

With a huge smile on my face, I unfold the sections slowly until my present is revealed. It's a picture of Danny.

I gasp and shed more tears. Happy tears. I love the picture, but all I want to do is hug him. He's not here, so I hug the picture and then look back at it again. He's so handsome. His eyes are almost as green as mine. There's no mistaking that we are siblings. What I like most is that it's a selfie, not a portrait. I can see his personality, and it doesn't look like it's changed. I look around again. Yep. Definitely creative. I guess I know now what Danny was discreetly working on when Jodi found him. I still can't believe my eyes.

I turn the picture over and see a note taped to the back. It's a little dusty so I know he hasn't placed it there very recently. I mean, how could he?

Jenny,

I hope you're looking at me, if only in a photograph for now. I have so much to tell you. I hid just a few clues around the farm. If I thought it was safe, I would have left you everything here. But I couldn't take that chance. And really, why not scavenge a little for old times' sake? I can't stress this enough ... don't trust anyone. Even though Jodi is our friend, you can't tell her much either. Be careful. I don't know where you are or what you've been doing since we left. You were still hiding when I was taken away by marshals from the Witness Protection Program.

I was told you were murdered, but over the years I stopped believing it. I made you this safe room in case you found your way back here. It's even safer than before. The room is lined with a thin but almost indestructible material. There's emergency food and water that will last you at least a week if you need it.

Behind your cabbage patch kid is a loaded Glock. You have ventilation and a peephole that looks out on the side yard in front of the barn. If you found your way in, Jenny, I will get pinged. I will know you're here and be on my way. I may be far away, though, so be patient. It could take me a few days. But I promise you, I'm coming so please don't move.

To lock yourself in from the inside, just close the door. To get back out, just turn the lever. No need to repeat the password. Also, erase the note from the wall now that you're in. You can't be too careful. The new owners make settlement tomorrow. No more coming in and out of here for me. Hopefully they won't find this room before you do. All the clues I left you on the farm will catch you up on what I know. Which isn't much. Hopefully the two of us together will be able to fill in the missing pieces. I can't wait to see you.

Love, Danny

P.S. Your next clue is a little trickier, but you'll get it, just like you always have.

You just can't BEAT RICE.

26

COPPERHEADS

I read the note over and over again. Even with the evidence in front of me, it feels so unreal. My brother is really alive! As I'm struggling to pull myself together, I search the space for everything he mentioned. Yep, there's the food, at least ten brown bags lined up on the top shelf labeled U.S. Government Property. I've seen these at the gun shop. It's becoming more and more popular to buy survival supplies. He chose cheese tortellini and spaghetti and meatballs. The water and some sterilization tablets are also here. *Too bad he didn't include wine.* I snicker to myself. It would have aged quite nicely in here.

Everything's here just like he said, so I'm very confident that I'm the only one who's discovered it. I look through the peephole and it gives me just the right aerial view of the property in front of the barn and chicken coop. This is amazing! He's thought of everything.

It's a little dusty, but still so cozy. I consider sleeping in here. I could use a solid night's sleep without having to keep one eye open.

Knowing Danny's on his way makes this the happiest day of my life. I look back at his picture and wonder where he's coming from.

Days to get here. I know one thing, once he gets here, we'll never be apart again, even if he lives in Iceland.

I'm ready for my next clue. *You just can't BEAT RICE.* I don't like rice very much, so the phrase itself is off. What about my mom and her cooking or lack thereof? She *tried* to make rice but never *beat* me with the wooden spoon for not eating it. I shake my head remembering how she always either burned it or undercooked it. What happens when you beat rice? Do you get rice milk? Nah.

I see it by putting the words together. BEATRICE. It's the name of my spooky Cabbage Patch Kid. Well, she's good for something now at least.

I grab her by her stringy yellow hair and look for another clue. *Really, Danny? It's in her underwear?* I laugh out loud. If this weren't such a serious situation, it could qualify as one of the most fun days of my life. Really, it still may be. That's how pathetic my life's been. I catch the self-pity and brush it off. My new message awaits.

Jenny,

There's a loose board in the chicken coop at the far end. Depending on when you find this, it's possible the board has been replaced or nailed down, so you'll have to get a crowbar to lift it back up again. I put a key and another note inside a jar I found hidden under a rock by the barn. I have no idea what it goes to. I tried everything on the property, but I think it's worth keeping and investigating more. I don't know what dad was up to, and we can't change the past, but we can take control of our future. I hope this will all be over soon.

Found this one already. I have the key and the clue. It may be the literal key to unlocking answers. Danny's last few lines bring me renewed faith. There's hope? I have trouble imagining a world without protectors. A world without monitors and check-ins. What must it be like to be free? It's a strange concept that will take some getting used to.

Rebellion got me here, but I think *caution* should be my watch-word for the next few days. I've been a little careless so far. I worry about Jodi and Eddie and the event I'm attending. I don't care *how* careless that is though, I'm going. Plus, it'll be my last night, so I can afford to be a little reckless.

I head back out of the space and into my old room. I can't move forward without protecting how far I've already come. I grab a burner phone and write a number on it that leads to another one of my burn-ers. I hope Sal doesn't call the one I'm hiding.

Hmm. What shall my scavenger hunt clue be for Danny? I go outside and scan the property. I'm a tad concerned about the barn. What if the men come back and want to reconvene in there? Doubt-ful, but I still worry. I head into the woods behind the barn instead. We had lots of hiding places there too. The dogs follow, which makes me feel safe. I assume they'll know what to do if there are trespassers.

So many things are different. Trees are gone that used to be here, including some of my big old favorite climbing trees. New, skinny ones are growing in their place. This is going to be tricky. I'm directly behind the barn now and can see the cavernous rock formation. I almost forgot about it. There are lots of huge rocks scattered across the land and forest but not like this one. This one has always been big enough to hide in.

We never actually tried to hide in it though, because we were afraid of snakes. My father warned us about copperheads in particu-lar. I take a good look around to make sure there aren't any where I'm stepping. My father was bitten by one as a child, so he went out of his way to show us pictures of what they looked like. He showed us a faint scar on his ankle to prove it.

Copperheads have a distinctive hourglass pattern and copper red heads, hence the name. The water and dense forest make it the perfect habitat. Danny and I used to get the heebie-jeebies sticking our bodies or hands into anything that could resemble a nesting space for them. We saw plenty of other snakes by the creek and weren't terribly afraid. Rat snakes and garter snakes were aplenty, but not to be feared. Copperheads though? We didn't want to find out what a venomous bite felt like.

I think this is the place. I grab the freezer bag holding the phone and note with my phone number on it and place it carefully inside the mouth of the little cavern.

I make my way back up to the closet and erase the message he left for me, replacing it with one of my own. This is where he would start too. It just says, "Copperheads." He'll know. It makes me feel so much better knowing he'll have a phone to reach me when he arrives just in case I'm not here.

Back to the house and on to *my* next clue. "Oh dear."

Now that I know it's from Danny, I know what it means. He's talking about the deer dad used to have above the fireplace. He's going to make me go into the basement. That's just wrong.

27

THE BASEMENT

I would have made my way down into the basement eventually, seeing as it's the only room in the house I haven't searched, but at least now I know it will be worth it. I open the wrought iron latch and the wooden door opens. It smells musty, just like it did when we lived here. I flip on the light switch and head down slowly. I peek around the room and sigh with relief. No Indian drums or taxidermied creatures in sight. There's a little water damage and recent dampness from the storm and some stains around the edges, but, Katie's right, the overall foundation looks pretty solid.

Jack and Katie have a workout station going. There's an elliptical, a set of weights, and a treadmill. No dead animals or anything unusual. I have to assume Danny wants me to check my father's large walk-in hunting safe, but it's gone. It certainly should still be here though—it was bolted to the foundation. If a tornado ripped through the house, it would be the last thing standing.

I realize something's off. I look from one wall to the next. Son of a gun! The wall that used to be paneled is now exposed stone, and the wall with the safe is now paneled. I grab a corner and try to pull the paneling away from the wall. It's not really budging, so I hope it's not glued. I go back upstairs and grab a hammer, crowbar, sledgehammer, and screwdriver trying to cover all my bases. I'm going to have some explaining to do though, if I need all of these.

I find a few nails and yank them out with the claw of the hammer. The paneling's not glued, and I can peel it back a little now. As I pull, more nails pop out of the wall.

Within a few minutes, one panel is off, revealing my father's safe. The rest of the paneling is glued to the remaining wall. My brother is good at this. I hope I can put it back together well enough when I'm finished. Maybe I'll just tell Jack and Katie it's here. They may want to use it. I would.

Combination time. We all knew the combination to the lock on this one. My father was teaching us gun safety and how to shoot. He'd line up tin cans on top of bales of straw out in the meadow and let us take turns trying to hit them. We both had good aim. I still hit the range every now and then with some of my security staff to blow off steam.

My father wanted us to have access to the contents of the safe in case there was ever an emergency. So much for that! The combination is 9-1-3-4. No rhyme or reason to it. *I don't think.*

It opens, and I walk in. The guns are all gone, but a bow and several arrows remain. At some point, he, or maybe Danny, took the rest. No matter how many people broke in during its abandonment, they would've needed a tank to open it without the combination. Waiting for me on a small table inside is a plastic bag.

I pull out the contents. There's another note for me on top and a stack of articles Danny must have researched and printed from microfiche. Maybe I won't need to hack into Jack's computer after all.

There are multiple articles about Billy's death, an article about Denise Brandt's suicide, and several missing person articles. A sudden death. Denise's sudden death was a suicide. I never considered that. I really thought maybe she was in a car accident.

Before I dive into all the articles, I want to read my note.

Jenny,

Sorry if you're disappointed by such a small hunt. This is your last stop. If you end up in here first, search more (wink). I hit a wall after finding the articles. I don't know how to put all the pieces together and am hoping you know more than I do.

The marshals who took me couldn't wait any longer for you. I didn't know they were actually trying to protect us, or I would have given up your hiding spot. Maybe we could have stayed together. I want to know more about what you saw that night. I want to know what Dad or Mom did to put us in the program.

When we left, there were men coming and I heard gunshots. I heard mom scream from the house and then my driver took off. I have so many questions.

I found the painting of our house in here, too, but thought it was a nice touch elsewhere! I can't wait to see you again.

Love, Danny

He really can't get here soon enough. This sucks! I understand why he can't say more about himself, because if someone found his notes before I did, they'd be hot on his trail. Once he gets here, I know we'll be better together at solving this.

I think back again to that last night. I wasn't planning on coming out of hiding, ever. But after I heard gunshots, my father's tone was intensely commanding, and there was no ignoring it. I came out, ran downstairs, and jumped into his arms. We went down into the basement and out through the Bilco doors. I heard voices and instructions, but I was too afraid to look at who was ordering them. I just kept my head tucked down into my father's shoulder.

The next thing I knew, we were driving. I fell asleep at some point, and when I awoke, it was daybreak. My mother was crying and probably had been all night. She looked back at me and tried to look reassuring. I attempted to ask questions, but my father told me to keep quiet.

A few hours later, I was whisked away with no explanation other than the fake details of my brother's death. I was placed in the hands of marshals and then sent off to boarding school. Our family unit was completely splintered. I have to assume Danny ended up in boarding school somewhere too.

I grab the stack of articles, close the vault, and head back upstairs. Perched on the edge of the sofa, I pull the top article and start reading. The first few are all about Billy and about the day he was found, sparing no grisly detail. Unfortunately, none of it offers me any new insight beyond the *Unsolved Mysteries* episode about the murder. I'll bet the guys from the barn just love that story airing over and over in reruns, drawing constant attention. The next one is from a few days later, describing Billy's line of work and the last case he worked on as a defense attorney. Nothing new there either. I knew his last case was with Dominick D'Angelo and that he disappeared in the middle of the trial.

The next one is almost exclusively about Dominick. *Here's something new.* He was one of four children raised by Rosa and Dominick D'Angelo, Sr. There's a picture of his childhood home on Prince Street in the Little Italy section of New York City. His parents were first generation immigrants from Sicily who ran a bakery on Mulberry Street for twenty-nine years.

Dominick was one hell of a badass. Early in his criminal career, he sold cocaine to the wealthy. Big time stuff, not like street punks. Then he partnered with a few crooked finance guys and began money laundering through dry cleaners, sending the funds to a bank in Italy. There was one problem though. The money was disappearing into thin air after the wire transfers. Dominick assumed that Dennis Alderman, from the financial firm in the city, was stealing from him and killed the whole family. As far as the DA's office was concerned, it was a brutal revenge killing. Case closed.

Mr. Alderman was probably part of Dominick's ring, but was he really the one taking the money? I think it was Billy. It makes sense. As Dominick's attorney, he probably had access to just about everything. He knew Dominick was going to jail and probably figured, why not take the crook's money? Dominick must have eventually figured out Billy was the one taking the money. Billy was as good as dead, and he knew it. He had to beat him to the punch. Kill or be killed. He must've found a way to knock him out and drag him home to Brandtville. That's the only reasonable explanation. Not that any of this is reasonable. So, he got caught stealing then killing, before being killed himself. *I just solved your mystery, Unsolved Mysteries.*

So why were my dad and the rest of his clan helping him? What's the connection?

The next article has a bunch of pictures of Dominick during the early days of his trial. His family is there, supporting him. I can make out what must be siblings, maybe a wife, and his parents, in a packed courtroom. One woman catches my eye. It can't be. How can it be? It looks like Sal's mother. I laugh. It can't be. That's ridiculous. I take the picture and move into the light by the window.

I'm not laughing any more. It's Maria Rossi.

What the hell?

What's her connection to the D'Angelo family? She's sitting next to what looks like Dominick's aging parents. I flip back to the article about Dominick's childhood. He had three siblings. Sal's mother is Dominick's sister. She was Maria D'Angelo before Maria Rossi. A chill runs up my spine and I collapse back onto the couch feeling like the wind has been knocked out of me. I'm absolutely flabbergasted by what this means.

28

ENEMIES

"Keep your friends close and your enemies closer." It was one of Sal's favorite sayings. I just didn't realize I was the enemy. My rock, and my best friend, has been using me since we met. I'm putting it all together now and can't believe how stupid I've been! I'm literally here finding the answers *he's* looking for so he can do justice on behalf of his family. His family must have made the connection between Billy and my father. They know I'm Sean O'Rourke's daughter. For all I know, they were the men who came shooting the night I disappeared. In fact, I'm certain of it now. Our families are enemies. *How about a head's up, Dad?*

I feel bile rising in my throat. Sal has set me up since day one. His family planted him in my school. The whole "besties" thing was just to keep tabs on me. Well, until now, I haven't known jack shit. That's the point Ryan has been trying to make over and over. "The less you know, the better." I wonder if he knows about Sal. He must. I'm the monkey in the middle of how they keep tabs on each other. So much for street smarts. I feel so dumb.

I hope, for my sake, they're paying attention to Sal now. Everyone's been waiting and watching. Sal's family has been waiting for me to screw up and shake my father out of hiding for over a decade.

I'm trembling, in utter disbelief, and at the same time mourning the loss of the man I trusted more than anyone in the world.

Maybe I'm getting used to my emotions coming full circle, because the hurt is quickly being replaced with hatred. I feel vengeance coursing through my veins and want Sal dead.

Sal doesn't know I've figured this out. He does, however, know that the pin belongs to Michael Brandt. He'll do his own research and find out about the foundation and the event on Saturday. He'll either go or send someone in his place.

I should call Ryan. I should call my father. I should call the Protection Program. But I can't. Danny's in transit and I still don't know a damn thing about the warped crap my father was into. Even though my gut instinct is to run, I need to stay just where I am, try to turn the tables on them all. I hope I have it in me.

The pieces are starting to come together. The men from our barn took care of Dominick and Johnny. That would leave one more male sibling and Mrs. Rossi. Then there's Sal's dad and his brothers, including Elio, and all of their sons—Sal and Antonio included. I hope Uncle Elio isn't part of it. I'm not totally sure how many there are, but no matter how I do the math, I come up with an awful lot of them and just one of me, at least for now.

It boggles my mind. John and I helped Mrs. Rossi so much. Maybe that's the only reason I'm still alive. I suddenly want to know exactly what Sal said to Fred Steinbach at his jewelry store. I grab the phone and call the shop.

"Hello. Steinbach Jewelers."

"Mr. Steinbach?"

"Speaking. How may I help you?"

"My name is Tricia Keller. I was in your store a few weeks ago with my friend. We were asking about the lapel pin." I hear a click. "Hello? Mr. Steinbach?" I call right back. He picks up but doesn't say anything. "I need to ask you something, please, just listen. What did my friend say to you? I could tell by your expression that he frightened you. I'm scared now too. Please?"

"Miss, you should be scared."

"What did he say?"

"He told me if I said anything about your visit, he would kill me and my whole family."

"What?" I feel bile rise in the back of my throat again.

"You best stay far away from that man. And from his whole family. They're not good people. And please, never come here again. You've put my safety in severe jeopardy." With that, he hangs up again.

WTF! I need to focus. I'm losing it. My brain is trying to make sense of all the angles but falling very short. To make matter worse, I'm running out of daylight. I need to attend to the animals, but I really don't want to go outside. I hit the crawlspace and grab the Glock. I'm gonna make this fast as hell. With Wonder Woman speed, I race up to the barn. Wishing I had eyes in the back of my head, I pick up animal waste with the shovel and wheel it into the manure pile. Dirty work done, I usher the animals into their stalls and practically throw the feed at them. I close their doors and give the goat a quick pat.

I hear something. An animal sound, like a howl. Do foxes howl? It sounds close. But then again, with the creek and rocks, things do echo. It could be far away. I freeze in place and listen. I hear it again. It's a howl. Are there wolves around here? I need to Google that. It's possible, I guess, and bears for sure. I don't remember my father telling us to watch out for wolves.

"Jenny?" I nearly have a heart attack hearing my name. I turn to see Jodi. "Jesus, Mary, and Joseph. Jodi, you scared the crap out of me."

"I'm sorry," she says with a giggle. "I just wanted to tell you that I feel a tiny bit better today. I slept all the way through the night!"

"That's amazing!" If it were any other time, I would be clicking my heels and celebrating along with her, but I'm way too distracted. My eyes dart in every direction while she's talking.

"Jodi, are there wolves around here?"

"You heard the howling. Yes, that's been happening on and off for years, but we've never seen anything. My father used to tell us it was bloodhounds. Lots of hunters with 'em around here."

"Oh, okay." *Not buying that one.*

"Jodi, that church. Mission Church. Is it still active?"

"I don't think so, but we never go up that road. It creeps my mom out."

I hate to brush her off, but I want back inside. I haven't finished all the articles, and once I do, I want to put them back in the safe. I can't risk Sal showing up with them lying around. It's not safe for Jodi to be here either.

"Let's chat more tomorrow. I need to finish the chores and then I have some calls to make." She looks a little disappointed but catches the drift and turns back toward her house.

I'm no sooner done with farm duty when I remember the pool. To think I thought I would have time to relax by it for a while. I add chlorine and head back to the house for cover. I lock all the doors and windows as soon as I'm inside. I'm spooked as hell, and shiver when I remember that I have to check in with Sal. If he was impatient the last time we talked, I can't wait to hear how he sounds today.

I open up a bottle of wine and put the other two bottles in the fridge. I need a glass to calm my nerves before I call. I may need rehab after this week. I hold my breath and dial.

"Hey, gorgeous."

"Hey! How was your day?" I ask.

"I think the question is, how was *your* day?"

"It was good. I just got back from relaxing by the pool. I guess I fell asleep. It was so nice to get some rest, Sal." He's quiet at first.

"You're only there for three more days and you chose to relax by the pool?"

"Well, no, I worked around the farm for a few hours in the morning too." He's quiet, confused by my lack of motivation.

"Well, it seems I've done more homework than you. Come on, Jen, pick up the pace. I mean, do you want answers or not?"

"Of course, I do. I've been looking all over the farm while I work. It's not like I'm just sitting on my ass. Geez. So, what did you find out?" He lets out a disgusted-sounding sigh.

"Michael Brandt lost a son and has a foundation. They're having an event on Saturday night. I got us both tickets." *Damn it.*

"A foundation? What kind of event? That's probably not a good idea. I mean, we can't go together. What if someone recognizes me?"

"Who's gonna recognize you? Dye your hair or something, I don't know. And obviously we can't go together. We'll sit apart. Divide and conquer. I'll FedEx your ticket."

"Sal, if the guy lost a son and has a foundation, don't you think that eliminates him from any criminal activity? It's probably a fluke that his college pledge pin, or whatever, was in the water. I feel like that rules him out as a suspect."

"Jen, what is wrong with you? This is the perfect opportunity to get a look at this guy. And we can see who else is in the room. You're not thinking!"

"I *am* thinking. I just don't think Mr. Brandt is a person of interest. I have a few other leads that I'm working on. I want to visit some art galleries in New Hope. I found a painting of our house in the basement."

"Did I just hear you right? You want to go to an art gallery?"

I'm really starting to get irritated by his tone and, as much as he scares me, I'm done with it.

"Sal, what the hell is your problem? Why don't you leave me alone and let me do this my way? This is about *me*. What's with your badgering? Your only responsibility is to make sure I check in once a day and that I'm not dead. Why are you so interested?"

"Excuse me? My badgering? I risked a lot to get you there and cater to your every wish."

"I don't want your help anymore." I absolutely mean it. I want him to go away forever. I hear him suck in a deep breath.

"Okay, look, I'm sorry. You're right. I need to back off. This is your thing."

I feel some of the tension in my muscles release. Even though I'm probably on his hit list, he still needs me. I've bought myself a little more time.

"Thank you. I don't want to argue, Sal. You're my best friend."

"I know. I'm sorry. Get some sleep and check in earlier tomorrow."

"Will do. Love ya."

"Love ya back."

"Rot in hell," I say out loud as I hang up the phone. I'm glad the crawlspace is there if I need it. I have some more reading to do before I decide if I want to sleep in there tonight. I sit on the sofa with my wine and grab the missing person articles, forcing myself to push aside my anger and focus again.

There are three more articles, each about grown men missing from the area. The first was a man in his mid-twenties of Native American decent. That's kind of interesting. I pause to let his name swirl around in my head. It's not familiar. The only thing I heard in the barn was something about a neophyte. I do a quick Google search and get a lesson on the word. Neophytes are early students, especially of esoteric orders. Secret societies. *Awesome!* The article lists a number for the local police if he's seen.

The next two are similar. Grown men missing from the area. The scenarios that the articles lay out about what happened to these men rattle my imagination and give me gruesome thoughts. I have a hunch these men met their dooms courtesy of the barn clan. What did they do to earn it? Whatever it was, I'm guessing they deserved punishment, but by our laws, not this anarchy.

Next, I read the article about Denise Brandt. She was found at Mission Church hanging lifeless from a rope attached to one of the beams. All the usual language is there. "The Brandt family would like privacy at this time." It was a big loss for the community as well as the foundation.

Why would she kill herself? Maybe the grief and misery of never really knowing what happened to her son was finally unbearable. I can understand that completely. How terribly sad.

I'm trying to keep track of everything and do my best to compartmentalize so I don't lose focus of any one particular problem area. There are almost too many to count. I can't let the Rossi situation make me lose sight of the odd happenings on the farm. It's still why I'm here, first and foremost. The church thing is mysterious too. I grab the laptop and look for the Bible search link I used before. It's quite possible my father had more than one biblical code he was using for secretive purposes. People hide behind religion all the time to look holy on the outside as they cover up evil doings. Maybe that was his MO too.

Since my father went with Psalms before, I use the first two digits '9-1' and hit enter.

Psalm 91. The Protection of the Most High

³ He Himself will deliver you from the hunter's net,
    from the destructive plague.
⁴ He will cover you with his feathers; you will take
    refuge under His wings. His faithfulness will be a
    protective shield.
⁵ You will not fear the terror of the night, the arrow
    that flies by day,
⁶ The plague that stalks in darkness, or the pestilence
    that ravages at noon.

I focus on the second set of numbers from the lock, 3-4, but am equally intrigued by verses five and six. There's hunting. Protecting. Not fearing the night. And what about the reference to noon? The men said they'd hunt at "high noon."

Bizarre. Being raised Catholic, we didn't really study the Bible, much less take it literally. And my mom stopped taking us to Mass once we made our First Holy Communions, so my knowledge of religion *at all* is at a bare minimum. I've always had faith, though, even during some of my darkest hours at boarding school. I believe in God and need Him now more than ever.

I've organized my list of things that I need to accomplish tomorrow. Visit Judith's gallery, get into that weird church, and find the Twenty-Fifth Acre. Something big may be there, and I would love the company of my brother when we find it.

I'm exhausted. It's nearly impossible to concentrate, but I do my best. Acres. There are hundreds of them. But acres are square, not linear. How would I find the distance in yards, miles, or whatever to an acre? And in which direction would I even start looking? I recall the hunter tags on the trees and think I remember numbers on them. I also remember lots of signs, which, ironically, all say, "No hunting." Figuring out where the Twenty-Fifth Acre is, and whether it even exists, may be an impossible task.

My eyes are heavy. I'm too tired to move upstairs and sleep in the crawlspace. And besides, it feels cozy and safe in here, with reruns of *Friends* playing on Netflix, the dogs at my feet, and the Glock on the end table. I close my eyes and nearly instantly drift into a deep sleep.

29

JUDITH KAMP

When I wake up, I'm pleasantly surprised to see I've gotten a solid eight hours of sleep. How's that even possible? My body must have won the battle with my mind. I get the coffee going, put on my now designated-as-farm-clothes, and cautiously head out the door, Glock in pocket. I let the dogs roam ahead of me to see if they sense any danger. I scan the property and don't see anything off. It looks clear, but I know as well as anyone how many hiding places there are around here.

I cautiously work my way up to the barn to let the animals out for the day and clean up a bit. Boy, did I make a mess last night. I straighten up and make my way back to the house to grab a carton for morning egg collection. I can hear the chickens clucking away, scratching at the pen's gate to be let out. I wonder if something's got them all wound up, or if this is what they always do. I look at the dogs to see if this seems normal to them. Sonny is eating grass and Cher is rolling in something. They don't seem fazed, so I open the coop door. Like bats out of hell, the chickens frantically pour out, trampling on each other's backs in their haste to escape. All except for one. There's a hen with its head chopped off right in the middle of the coop. I stagger back, both afraid and repulsed.

Gaining my wits, I scan the edges of the property again. This time, I see a black Volvo in the exact spot I parked the Ford Escape just a few weeks ago. I pause for a moment and wonder what to do. Instead of taking shelter in the house, I decide to go on the offense. I crouch down, gun in hand, and creep toward the car. I feel powerful, ready for battle. I'm within ten feet when the engine roars to life. The wheels spit gravel and carry the car off over the bridge and up the hill. There's no license plate.

I don't care for this sick intimidation tactic, and quite frankly, I think it lacks creativity. But it worked. I feel like someone's closing in on me. But who? If this was their first attempt to scare me, what's next? I'm rattled and know the blood has drained from my face, but I'm not going to let it derail my plans. Even though I'm trembling, I need to look in control.

I grab the carton I dropped and head back to the coop, looking away from the dead bird as I collect the eggs. I put them in the fridge and grab some rubber gloves. The dogs are fired up now. They're pacing and barking, lunging at the gate for the remains of the bird. I have to kick them out of my way to grab the carcass and put it in a plastic bag. I plan to chuck it in the woods on my way to New Hope. This day is starting off just great. Maybe I'll tell Sal about it later to gauge his reaction. I wouldn't be surprised if he did it just to light a fire under my ass and get me moving.

I pour myself a hearty cup of coffee and step back out onto the patio to try to make sense of it. I grab the laptop to check the gallery hours. Judith's art gallery is open from 10:00 a.m. until 8:00 p.m. today. That gives me a little time.

I do a search on the missing men from the articles Danny left me. I Google Paul Poanto, the missing Native American man from the article, as well as the town name. For nineteen dollars and ninety-nine cents, I can get all the information I want. Here we go again. I grab my card and punch in the numbers. This time I get a criminal record. Three counts of child endangerment, one count of domestic abuse, and a DUI.

"It won't bring my son back." I'm recalling the mysterious voice from the barn. This Poanto guy could have done something to a different child and the vigilantes took it out on him, giving him a giant dose of his own medicine. I think about the Douglas Brandt Foundation again. It can't be the Brandt boy because his body was never found. He's an active missing person. Well, if Poanto was from the area and put down like a dog by my father and friends, it means they did more than hunt down big city criminals. They had a broad range of targets. No one is safe from their form of justice.

I look up the other two missing men. I get a bunch of free hits on Donald Spar. He went missing while hunting, but he was a well-respected business owner from Quakertown. He was a churchgoer and left a heart-broken family.

Next, I look up Rusty Hanes. More free hits. This guy was an animal, wanted for rape and murder. I think I remember this story. He allegedly raped and murdered his girlfriend's daughter not far from here. My father lectured me after the story aired, about being aware of my surroundings. "There are predators everywhere, Jenny. You can't trust anyone." Like Dominick D'Angelo, Paul also disappeared before his trial. I would love to see a pattern forming here, but Mr. Spar doesn't fit. I'm also finding myself in a moral struggle. I'm glad that rapists and killers were ashed. The world is a better place without them.

I make my way upstairs, take a quick shower, and look through Katie's closet. I pick out the yellow sundress she was wearing the day we met and slip it on.

Next, I grab the painting of our house, lock the door, and meander outside, taking a good look around for anything unusual. Jack's car is suddenly much more appealing to me than the clunker. He's got a sporty red Mazda Miata. It shouldn't be a big deal if I borrow it. I dig around for keys in the junk drawer and find them.

I hit the ignition and the stereo goes off like I'm front row at a concert. *Stairway to Heaven* is playing on 93.3. Good tune but good grief, he likes it loud. I visualize Jack driving around in the sports car. Mr. Cool Breeze, I nickname him to myself. He must be going through a late mid-life crisis or something.

Once I'm on the road, I toss the chicken carcass out the window near some overgrowth of weeds and try to relax and enjoy the scenic drive. The sun is shining, and the humidity is low. The hum of the engine echoes as I go through two covered bridges along the way.

Main Street isn't hopping yet, but it will be later. It's Friday. New Hope is super artsy and quaint, with a Playhouse on the edge of the Delaware River. There are lots of shops, clubs, spas, restaurants, and cute boutiques with unique gifts and clothing. What I wouldn't give to just be a tourist today.

I find a parking place close to the gallery. Painting in hand, I enter the shop, which smells like a mix of fresh paint and turpentine. I'm probably earlier than her usual traffic, so I find myself alone. I take the time to look around and admire her work. There are covered bridges, old farmhouses, foxhunts, barns, and horses. She's very talented. Judith emerges from the back a few minutes later and apologizes for not hearing me. She hasn't changed, except for a few wrinkles. Her hair is in a tight blonde bun, and she's wearing a cute black halter dress. I'm not worried about her recognizing me. I was so young, and we never formally met. I mostly saw *her* from the car when we were driving here and there.

"Is there something I can help you with?" she asks.

"Yes, please. I'm hoping you can tell me more about this painting." I place it down on the granite countertop near the register. Her smile is replaced with a pucker, like she just ate a raw lemon. She clears her throat.

"Where did you find that?"

"In the actual house you painted. My parents live there now. I found it in the basement. It's beautiful." My explanation is realistic enough, but she looks like she's seen a ghost.

"What is it you'd like to know about it?" she asks, attempting to recover.

"I don't know. I guess I'm curious about the owners at the time. The house was abandoned for years before my parents bought it. The painting is very detailed, so you must have spent a decent amount of time there. The house looks well-manicured. I hope my parents can get it back to its original form. They're working very hard."

She nods and shifts uncomfortably. "Yes, I've seen them. I'm glad someone finally bought it. It was sad to see it empty. I dare say it was once one of the most beautiful homes in Brandtville. But unfortunately, I don't know anything about the owners. In fact, I have a secret for you. Most of the time, I just take pictures and work from the comfort of my studio."

She's lying. She was known to paint on sight to capture her subjects in real-time. I saw her with my own two eyes. I would buy her studio story if it were a foxhunt painting, but not a farm. I give her a look that says, *I'm not buying it.* She looks back at the painting, lost in thought, eying up the corner where there's a pile of supplies.

"What is it?" I ask.

"Pardon?"

"Were the owners working on some kind of construction project at the time? What was in the pile? Looks like wood and big rocks."

"I'd like to buy the painting back," she abruptly announces.

"Excuse me?"

"How much do you want for it?"

"There's no amount of money I'd take. I'm sorry." I grab her elbow gently and look desperately in her eyes. "Judith, please tell me what you saw when you were painting."

"Who are you?" she asks.

"Please, Judith. I need to know." She's studying me. As it registers, she places her hand over her mouth, and her eyes get wide.

"You're Jenny O'Rourke, aren't you?" I don't say anything, nor do I blink.

"Please tell me what you saw."

"Hold on a minute." She walks to the front of the shop, flips the sign over to "Closed," then turns off the lights. I follow her to the back of the studio and into an office.

"I cannot be honest with you unless I know I can trust you. Can I? No one can know about this painting. In fact, you need to destroy this, Jenny."

"I didn't say my name was Jenny." Now she looks at me like, *really?*

"How do I know I can trust *you*, Judith?" She places a hand over mine and promises.

"You can trust me. I'm more worried for your sake than mine," she half-whispers.

"How so?"

"I never put this painting up for sale."

"Then how did it get in the house?"

"Your father spotted me across the street while I was painting. I thought I was completely concealed behind the brush near the creek. I was there for a few weeks, off and on. Long enough to almost finish it. See here, I didn't get to finish the details of the pines behind the barn or that pile."

"What happened?"

"Your father marched across the street and grabbed the painting. Most people are flattered to discover I'm painting their property. But not him. He was very angry. He snatched it off my easel and told me in not-so-friendly words to get off the property. I attempted a short rebuttal, and even tried to snatch the painting back, but he was too tall and held it out of my reach. He threatened that if he ever saw me anywhere near the house again, he'd sue me. I wasn't really all that concerned about being sued. I was sure he didn't stand a chance of winning. But the way he said it, and the look on his face, scared me. I didn't go near the area again until recently. Now that it's being renovated, I've been by it a few times. I was thinking about giving it another try. What are you doing here, child?"

"Judith, that's one hell of a story. Let's just say I got lucky. Please, you cannot tell anyone that I'm in town. I go by a different name now for a reason. Do you understand? I'm here to find out what happened when I lived there. I haven't seen my family since we left. I want to know more about my father. Have you seen him here since?"

"No, I haven't. No one has, as far as I know. I don't know much, but I can describe what I saw over the two weeks I was painting. Nothing seemed out of the ordinary at first. I figured your family was working on some sort of construction project myself."

"When was this?"

"It was July of 1985. No, 1986." I think back to that time period. We spent a month at Nonna's in North Jersey that summer. My father had given her our family home. But we did not have a construction project going on at that time or I would have known about it.

"Each day, several men moved the piles into the woods somewhere. It took them a long time to get back from each trip."

"What kind of materials? I see wood and stone in your painting. Is that cement?"

"Yes, there was lots of wood and stone. Later windows and material for a roof. But I believe what you're seeing is clay from the area."

"Clay?"

"The area is rich with it. It's better than cement for some projects. I've done plenty of pottery with it myself."

"I see. Do you know who the men were?"

"Most of them, yes. Michael Brandt, Ray Myers, Chuck Burton ..." I cut her off.

"Who's Chuck Burton?"

"He was the sheriff at the time."

"Where's he now?"

"Jenny, you don't know this?"

"Know what?"

"He was killed on your property the night your family fled." I feel dizzy and look for a chair.

"Do you have any water?" I ask and sit on a stool. Judith jumps up and grabs me a water bottle.

"Here." I take a sip. Well, this makes perfect sense. That's why Chuck never grabbed the note, money, and gun my father left for him. He didn't escape the gunshots I heard either. That's three murders that I know of near the farm, not to mention the others I'm starting to suspect.

"What happened that night?" she asks.

"Your guess is as good as mine, Judith. That's why I'm here."

"I'm so sorry."

"What direction were the men walking with the construction stuff?"

"They were moving to my left away from the barn and up into the woods. I could see them for a little while, then they'd disappear."

I push the painting toward her. "Here. Take it and destroy it. The new owners haven't seen it. My father had it in a safe. Ironically, he loved your work and kept two of your foxhunt paintings in his office." We smile at each other over the irony.

"What's with Michael Brandt? Beside his work with the foundation, what does he do?"

"That's kind of what the whole town wants to know. He keeps a tight-knit group of friends and doesn't socialize much unless there's an event. He's very mysterious, and he has looks, money, and a widower status. So, as you can imagine, all the single ladies my age are infatuated. But unless you work for him, there's no getting near him. I've circled the area before. Between the physical presence of security and the security systems, it's quite intimidating. Don't even try to ask him questions, unless you want to get caught. I'm glad you found me first. Be careful! When you find out what you're looking for, get out of here."

"Could he and my father have been part of a cult?"

"A cult?" she asks, giving me a long look to see if I'm serious. "Why do you ask? Oh, let me guess. Because they belonged to Mission Church?"

"What is with that church, Judith?" I ask, hoping she has some good details.

"Not much really. I've been in there before with permission to take pictures, hoping it would be interesting. I think it's less of a church and more of an old boys' club. Very uninspiring. No, I believe your father had trouble with the law, but I doubt he was mixed up in a cult. The only cults people talk about around here are like a few Rosicrucian Orders. But they're not really cults. They're more like an ancient fraternity or something. They're harmless and peaceful. All about spiritual growth and living clean lives."

"I can honestly say I've never heard of them. Rosa what?"

"Rosicrucian. There are variations of Rosicrucian Orders. Mostly interested in mysticism and learning how to better one's self through esoteric wisdom. Oh, and they're not very materialistic. Wealth comes from within," she says with a smile.

"They're not just a local thing? Would they by chance have Native American roots?"

She cocks her head and gives me an inquisitive look. "Not that I know of. German originally, then brought to America. I think Ben Franklin was a Rosicrucian."

"Really? I thought he was a Mason."

"Probably that too. Or even more likely, it's all a bunch of horseshit."

Horseshit maybe, but it's worth noting. I think of my father's passion for history, including the peace treaty between William Penn and Chief Tamanend. But peaceful and spiritual is not how I remember my father's group sounding. They sounded like a group very much to be feared.

I think I've pressed my new artist friend enough for now, so I rise and thank her. My shakes have finally died down.

"Listen, you take care of yourself," she says, and gives me a firm handshake. We both promise to never speak of this meeting.

She unlocks the door, flips the sign back around, and gives me a little wave. I've got the car door open when I hear one of my burner phones ringing. I'm so not in the mood to talk to Sal. I open my bag and look at the number. It's not Sal. It's the burner that goes to the one I left Danny.

"Danny? Is that you?"

"Hey, sis! Copperheads, huh? Good one."

30

DANNY

I slam the car door shut and prepare to speak to my brother for the first time in a very long, painful time. "Danny, you're here. I can't believe it." I start sniveling immediately, and he sounds choked up too.

"I got here and couldn't find you, so I went to our hideout."

"I'm in New Hope. I just left Judith Kamp's gallery. That painting you found in the basement was chock full of information. I have so much to tell you." I quickly mention the dead chicken I had to toss on the way here.

"That's sick."

"Yeah, so stay in the house. Someone is lurking around."

"How the heck did you find yourself here? What'd you do, break in while the owners are away?"

"No. Can you believe I actually talked them into letting me housesit."

"No way! You didn't tell them who you are, did you?"

"No, not exactly. Stay put. I'm on my way. And Danny ... I can't wait to see you."

"Same here." He sounds choked up again. "See you soon."

I try to take the lead out of my foot but find myself going way over the speed limit. I have to constantly check the speedometer, because the last thing I need is to get pulled over. I take a short cut down Deep Creek Road. I slow down, seeing cars in front of the swimming hole.

There's a group of people, fully dressed, standing in a circle in the middle of the creek, hands outstretched to touch a man in the center of the ring. I guess it's some sort of baptism. Maybe the man in the middle is becoming a born-again Christian. Although I don't see him among the group, maybe this is how Mr. Brandt lost his pin. A few eyes turn to look at me, making sure I'm aware that I'm not invited or welcome to view this special moment.

I've never seen anything quite like the scene before, beautiful on one hand, and bizarre on the other. I speed up again. The covered bridge is just ahead, when I spot the Volvo again. I'm about a mile from the farm. I pull up behind the car and don't see any movement, so I pull out the gun and slowly approach. Whoever it is parked further away and is likely spying on our old property right now. *Game on, asshole.*

I try the doors, but they're locked. I see the license plate in the back seat, but it's upside down. If I'm going to figure out who the Volvo belongs to, I'm gonna need that. No time for second-guessing what could be a bad decision. I grab a large rock and swiftly shatter the glass. I've got instant access, but the alarm is blaring, so I move fast and grab the plate. While I'm at it, I flip the button to open the trunk and find a telescope, hunting knife, and some camouflage clothing. This is an enemy. I take the knife and slash all four tires, sending whoever it is a warning of my own.

I climb back into Jack's sports car and tear out, gravel spitting. I'm feeling more confident knowing Danny's here. I also know that with one call to the agency I could have a hundred Feds here. That card hasn't slipped my mind at all, and I'm so glad I never told Sal about the program. It may be my one saving grace.

I pull into Red Rock Farm and look around excitedly, but don't see another car. Dread starts to build in the pit of my stomach. Maybe something has already gone wrong. I repark the Mazda and sprint toward the house. Danny opens the door with tears in his eyes and open arms. "Oh, thank God!" I jump on him, knocking us both straight to the ground. We embrace and look at each other and embrace and look at each other. Tears stream down both our cheeks.

"Jenny, look how beautiful you are. You're gorgeous."

"You're very handsome yourself. Oh, and my name is Tricia Keller by the way. What's *your* name?"

"You got lucky. My name is Alfred Boyton"

"Alfred?" We're both laughing, on the verge of hysteria.

"Everyone just calls me Al."

"Doesn't Paul Simon sing a song that goes like that?" It makes us laugh harder.

Are you married? Do you have kids? Where do you live? Where have you been?" I'm pelting him with a hundred questions at once.

"I'm not married, and I don't have kids. I'm an architect and have been working on a project in Rome on and off for the last five years."

"An architect! No wonder you did such a good job with the crawlspace. And you always made the best forts! I should have known. Rome? What an exciting place to work. Have you seen Mother in Italy?"

"Italy? I was told she was living in Hawaii with Nonna."

"Hawaii? I'm guessing she's in neither place. They're a pack of liars."

We don't have too much time to catch up on the past, so I bring him as far into the present as possible. I go over everything I know. He's impressed by how far I've gotten, but a bit shell-shocked.

"This is like something out of a horror flick, Jenny."

"I know, right?"

He's shaken over the Rossi and D'Angelo situation, as well as by the cryptic Bible verses our dad has been coding out. He wants to run a few searches on the design of Mr. Brandt's pin. Working near Vatican City, he knows a thing or two about symbolism.

First things first. I remember the license plate and run back outside for it. Danny calls a friend, who's a policeman, and asks for a favor. Danny smiles at me as he reads his friend the plate. "He's looking it up now," he whispers. There's a pause while we wait, so Danny puts the phone on speaker.

"Dude, I got it. It's a New York plate belonging to Ben Grover." We both look at each other.

"As in the actor?" Danny asks.

"Yes. No warrants. Let me do a little more digging, and if I find anything else, I'll give you a call back."

"I appreciate it, James. I owe you."

"Not a problem."

Ben Grover? What the heck would Ben Grover be doing spying on me? He's one of my favorite actors on a spooky new series I just started watching. We're both utterly perplexed. And I'm a bit mortified thinking I just slashed all of his tires and on two occasions was prepared to kill him. Would Ben Grover chop off a chicken's head? Maybe the poor guy is just out here looking at property like all the rest of the New Yorkers. We both laugh at my paranoia. That's at least one less famous person likely to buy a farm around here. It doesn't explain all of his combat gear though. I don't trust him.

"I'm starving. What do they have to eat? And where are they, anyway?"

"There's some lasagna in there, and they're in Maine for her sister's birthday." Danny scarfs down the whole thing.

"This is fantastic! Is she Italian?"

"No. I'm guessing a little Irish with the red hair."

While we wait to see if his friend calls back, we start planning our venture into the woods. I tell him about the Twenty-Fifth Acre anomaly and the howling I heard yesterday. He agrees with me that it's all more than a little bizarre. We Google "wolves in Pennsylvania" and find a few things. They did start a wolf-release program in a park in Lancaster, but that's kind of far from here. There's also a link to a story describing sightings of "coywolves" in Bucks County. They think they're some kind of coyote but resemble the size of a wolf.

To think I was afraid of chickens when I got here. Now I have to consider the possibility of a hybrid wolf situation.

"How many guns did you bring? And where's your car?"

"I brought two. And no car. I borrowed a Harley and put it in the barn up top and threw a tarp over it."

"Oh, smart, bro!" It feels so good to call him that. We're smiling at each other as his iPhone rings with an updated report.

Apparently, Ben Grover has two addresses, one in Manhattan and one in Brandtville. Danny writes it down. "Thanks again. I owe you, buddy!"

We realize he owns a home up the hill, probably the farm past Jodi's with the windmill. Turns out the road actually has a name, Mill Road. Amazing how the roads are so literal in these parts. But why was he stalking me and the property? Maybe he wasn't. I feel like a total ass all of a sudden.

Danny's burner rings. The one I gave him. I grab it before he can pick it up. It's Sal.

"What's up, Jen?"

"Just having lunch. What's up with you?"

"You haven't called. How was the art gallery?"

"It was excellent. I bought a painting just for you." *I'm done with him.*

"A painting? Of what?"

"A covered bridge," I say sarcastically.

"You listen to me. You're playing fucking games with me. You've found something important and I want to know what it is. You owe me." I'm calm and collected and not going to let Sal bully me.

"I found a chicken with its head cut off in the coop this morning."

"What do you make of that?"

"Someone just trying to scare me."

"And are you scared?"

"No. I called Ryan and he's sending the troops."

"You fucking bitch! You're lying. You wouldn't. That would ruin everything."

Wow! Sal just called me a fucking bitch in a tone that makes me realize I don't know him at all.

"Never call me again, Sal. Ever. And don't you dare show up here or at that foundation event. I'll make sure you pay for it if you do."

I hang up and imagine the look on Sal's face. I've completely turned the tables on him. Danny's looking at me like he hopes I know what I'm doing. I make the decision to call Ryan. He answers on the first ring.

"Jenny, where are you? I'm losing my mind. I haven't slept since you disappeared. I'm not going anywhere, by the way." He starts unloading, but I cut him off.

"I'm sorry for my outburst. I'm absolutely fine and very relaxed. I needed this getaway. I can't talk long because I'm going kayaking, but I'll be home on Sunday."

"Okay, good. We need to talk. Jenny, I have feelings for you too. I realize it now more than ever since you left. All I can think about is getting you back. But we need to start fresh with no secrets. That's why I couldn't be with you the other night. It's definitely not because I didn't want you."

My stomach flutters and I feel a blush come over me. His words catch me off guard, and I don't know what to say. Without knowing his role in any of this, I can't make any promises about how I'll feel. I'm going to scrutinize whatever truth he has to offer and thoroughly cross-check it with my own findings. We'll see how honest he is before I can allow myself to get too involved.

"Jenny?"

"We'll talk on Sunday. I need you to do me a favor. Keep an extra close eye on Sal. I no longer trust him."

"Jenny?"

I hang up and smash the burner to smithereens. I'm down to three. He'll have guys swarming all around Sal and his family. Time. We just need a little time.

31

THE MEMORIAL

We flip a coin. Heads for the church and tails for the Twenty-Fifth Acre hunt. Tails it is—*our* hunt is on. It's 3:00 p.m., so we have a good five hours of light. Even though I like having them near, I decide not to bring the dogs because I'm worried that they'll get lost or hurt. But I'm also concerned about leaving the other animals out in the open. I would be mortified to come home and find Miss Mable with her head chopped off. I put the animals away and lock them in using padlocks and keys. Katie said they don't usually use them, but I'm not taking any chances.

Before heading out, Danny and I do our best to estimate the linear version of twenty-five acres to find a logical course. We calculate that a quarter of a square acre is 208 feet. Then we multiply it by twenty-five. It comes out to 5,200 feet, just short of a mile. We may be way the heck off, but it's a start. We're both glad the math didn't come out to five miles, because one mile is challenging enough through dense forest and rocky terrain.

We've got jeans on, as well as Jack and Katie's hiking boots. Mine are a little snug and Danny's are a little big, but they're better than sneaks. We're packing heat, rope, a compass, and water canisters. We were looking pretty tough until I whipped out the bug spray. I don't like bugs. I also have a couple of thick, red Sharpies to mark our way so we don't get lost. There are thousands of acres surrounding the farms in the area.

"Judith said they went to her left, which is our right, away from the barn. Let's start behind it in the woods." I look straight back and see a familiar orange ribbon. My dad and his hunting buddies would mark their trails with those. "Let's see if that one has a number on it."

It's pretty tattered, but I can make out the number three. What are the odds that they'll lead us right to the number twenty-five? We decide to try it. We look ahead and see the next one. It's even more faded, but I can still make out the number three again. So much for that theory. But now I'm curious. There's one more, which also has the number three. *333, again?* The ribbons form a triangle, and we realize there aren't any others in sight. "Danny, do you think this is another Bible code or something?"

"I can look it up." He's lucky to have access to an iPhone. All he has to do is turn off his location services. I wish it were that easy for me. He doesn't have to check in as often as I do, only occasionally with the agency. We both come to the conclusion that I'm more heavily scrutinized because of my track record of rebellion and the fact that I'm in the U.S.

"I don't see anything specific to the Bible but the numbers 333 are symbolic, representing the Trinity: Father, Son, and Holy Spirit."

"Danny, this is going to sound weird, but I wake up in the middle of the night all the time at exactly 3:33 a.m. This is giving me the heebie jeebies."

"I see the same recurring numbers. And 11:11 too. Hold on, Jenny, this is where I found the key that I hid for you in the coop. There was a line of rocks around here somewhere at the time. They formed a pattern. I remember thinking it was odd so, I started flipping some of them over. I found the key under one of the larger rocks in the very center."

"Seriously?"

"Yeah. Did you bring the key?"

"Yep! Got it."

"Good." It's all so strange that we shake our heads in unison before looking toward our intended direction. I mark where we are with the letter A. There are twenty-six letters in the alphabet, so we decide to use that approach for now. Every 208 feet, we decide to mark them up to the length of a mile. I haven't had to do this much math since college and can't help but wonder if we're over-thinking it.

We walk and mark. As we get to the letter, T, a packed trail begins to form. There are multiple deer stands. I spot a really tall one and wonder why a hunter would want to be up that high.

"Danny, I'm gonna climb up that," I say, and point to it.

"Why don't you let me do that?"

"No. I need you on the ground. Watch my back, will ya?"

It's a red oak tree. The biggest one I've ever seen. The ladder of two by fours is still in great condition, so someone close by is still hunting. About halfway up, one of the boards wobbles and I nearly lose my grip. Danny lets out a gasp. To reassure him, I give him a thumbs-up, but I pay closer attention to what I'm doing. I reach the top and feel the tree sway. It's just a simple wood platform with wood railings. I sit down and look it over but don't get any weird impressions or vibes. I stand back up and look out as far as I can. I just see more dense forest at first, then notice a clearing about a football field away and something else, maybe a rock formation, standing tall in the middle. Maybe that's the infamous Twenty-Fifth Acre.

Going back down the ladder is much more nerve racking then going up, and I'm grateful when my feet are back on the ground.

"Did you see anything?" Danny asks.

"Yeah, there's a clearing up ahead with some sort of big rock or something."

"Let's check it out."

The path continues to widen, guiding us to the location I saw from the deer stand. It's no ordinary clearing. It's some kind of memorial area. The grounds are well-manicured and there's a large obelisk monument dead-center and facing east. There are red rock stone benches on either side. And on either side of the benches are large torches that still have plenty of fuel. Beautiful red rose bushes surround the area. The monument reads:

In Loving Memory
of
Douglas Michael Brandt
March 2, 1984 – July 5, 1993

The benches each have engravings. The one to the left reads: *Dear Michael, Archangel. With God-power bright, we pledge to uphold every child of the light.*

The one to the right reads: *Dear Michael, Archangel. We call unto you. Protect us, defend us in circles of blue.*

There's a blue slate stone not far from the memorial. I make my way over and give it a read too. *Beware of false prophets, which come to you in sheep's clothing; inwardly they are ravening wolves.*

We're back to Bible study class and prayers to Archangel, Michael. Everything we've seen is so random, with no pattern to help us bring it together. At the very least, we're now keenly aware that Douglas is not an active missing person. His body lies right here beneath us. He died at the young age of nine at the hands of Paul Poanto, a felon with a track record of abuse and, I suspect, mental illness. I recall now what they said in the barn about him hearing voices. And my father sounded almost empathetic. Like he knew the man. Maybe he was once part of their click.

It was Michael Brandt's son after all, and MJB was the one in the barn who sadly thanked the men for helping him get justice.

"Michael Brandt is keeping his foundation running with false claims that his child is still a missing person. Why?" I ask Danny for theories.

"He probably wanted to keep it a secret so he could kill the guy himself before a forensics team found him and locked the guy up.

This group wants justice their way. The sure way. Instant resolution. No juries. No judges."

I have the key in my hand and fear it leads to a cell. Is that what they were building? Maybe a place to hold their captives in some sort of jail cell?

"Getting back to Dominick and Johnny D'Angelo. They're both dead. They have to be. You said, Dominick was dead in the trunk according to Jodi, right?"

"Yes. Maybe *they* decide who's punished and how. They seem to have their own judicial system working here. Billy and Dad were defense attorneys but sickened by the system at the same time. They'd be shocked to win cases and see murderers set free."

"And how on earth do you remember that?"

"That's what Mom said sometimes when Dad was in a really bad mood."

"Where the hell was I?"

"Busy trying to have fun and building forts." I give him wink. "Anyway, it makes sense that Michael Brandt joined this group after losing a son and Chuck, the Sheriff, was probably happy to help out too. Take it from me, there's nothing more frustrating to law enforcement than seeing their hard work end in mistrials and not-guiltys by dim-witted jurors."

"You're good at this," Danny says.

"Yeah, we'll see. I'm not sure about this Twenty-Fifth Acre thing. And there are plenty of unanswered questions about the weird hunting references and expelling evil. If there was a release and catch scenario, I don't think they'd drop criminals off at the sight of a beautiful memorial. And we haven't even touched upon the meaning behind all the symbolism."

I look back at the slate again. "A wolf in sheep's clothing." It's a phrase I've heard many times—it's how I'm thinking of Sal.

Our conspiracy theories are abruptly halted as Danny and I hear the unmistakable sound of a shotgun cocking. "Do you mind telling me who the fuck you are and what you're doing on private property?"

32

MR. DENNIS

We instinctively put our hands in the air. A deep stern voice tells us to turn around slowly. We have no choice but to abide. The stranger is a middle-aged man wearing military fatigues. In addition to a communication system, he has a drop leg holster with a pistol. He looks legit militia. This guy looks like the type to chop off a chicken's head.

"We were hiking, sir," I offer as an explanation.

"From where?"

"I'm Jessica Dorcy. My family owns Red Rock Farm. Who are you? Why are you pointing a shotgun at me and my boyfriend?"

"You both have guns. Why?"

"For protection, sir. We both have licenses. Whose property is this? I was under the impression it was *our* private property. Why are you on it?"

"It's the property of Michael Brandt. You crossed over."

"Where?"

"There." He points back the way we came.

"Well, how far can we hike? We've only gone a mile and we were hoping to get a few hours in," Danny adds.

"You can hike it right back where you came from and as far as you want in the other direction. This whole perimeter is off-limits."

I look further beyond the memorial. There's an expensive iron fence on either side, but with barbed rings. An effective but ugly way to keep trespassers out. However, the space on our side is wide-open.

"Why doesn't the fence go right across? How could we have known?"

"You know now. Any more fucking questions?" His flippant and vulgar tongue irritates me, so I decide to push him.

"Actually, I do have one more question. Who should my mom tell Mr. Brandt, when she sees him tomorrow night, that I had the pleasure of speaking with today? I understand she will be doing some volunteering for the foundation in the future. We were just on the phone with her a few minutes ago telling her about our hike."

I want him to think someone knows where we are, in case he's tempted to make us disappear. It works. His tone shifts slightly.

"Before your family moved in, we had an agreement with the previous owners. The land right here is the exact location that divides the property."

"One mile?"

"Approximately." He turns his head slightly to the right, giving away what might be the real area we're seeking.

"Well, our apologies then. It's a beautiful memorial. It's a shame there's never been real closure for the family. I understand Douglas was never found. So sad."

"Yes, it's a terrible thing not knowing, and this is a private place for the family to grieve. Mr. Brandt would definitely appreciate keeping it that way. Understood?"

"Of course. My mother lost a friend when she was young. She has never gotten over it." Danny's head tilts and he looks at me inquisitively. I'm thinking fast and recalling the reason I was probably able to get the ticket in the first place. The story I gave Jill about Katie losing her friend. "She's hoping the Douglas Brandt Foundation can help, even after all these years. She and her best friend's family have dreamt of learning who may have killed her, and then making them pay. They'd do anything for justice."

I have his full attention now. I can't help but wonder if Jack and Katie ever found this place, and if this guy knows anything about them. I feel like they would've warned me not to wander if they knew there was a memorial with a militia guard practically in their backyard. I guess that's why their hiking boots still look like new. Too busy on the farm to meander.

"What do you consider justice?" I put my hand on my Glock.

"Personally, I'd have no trouble putting a bullet in his head. But that's just me. I always say, an eye for an eye. Our legal system is set up to give criminals every opportunity to walk. It's bullshit. Anyway, sorry for trespassing. It won't happen again." I grab Danny's hand, like a good girlfriend would, and start walking back the way we came. Danny looks pale and squeezes my hand.

"Jessica?" I turn and look back at him.

"You never know what can be arranged. Will you be joining your mother?"

"I don't have another ticket."

"I'll put one in your mailbox."

"Thank you very much, Mr. ..."

"Dennis. You can just call me Mr. Dennis."

"Thank you, Mr. Dennis."

"Have a good day, now. Stay out of trouble," he says rather seriously. On eggshells, we follow the path back the way we came.

"What was that all about?" I whisper.

"Damn! You're quick on your feet, Jenny."

"Just call me Miss Jenny." We both laugh. "Now we have two tickets at least. You're going too, Danny. We'll figure it all out tomorrow."

"Yeah, I'm pretty pumped about that part, but what the fuck?"

We stop when we're far enough away that Mr. Dennis hopefully won't be able to see or hear us. "I think the Twenty-Fifth Acre is just to the left of where we were. Did you see how he glanced in that direction? When we get back to the house, let's get an aerial view. I should have thought about that before. Maybe Google Maps can enlighten us, although I wouldn't be surprised if the Brandts are powerful enough to find a way to get that kind of imaging off the grid."

"Shh!" Danny grabs my shoulder. "What was that?"

"That's the weird howling I was telling you about." We stay still and listen.

"Let's get the hell out of here."

We jog back to the farm and catch our breaths once we reach the patio. "Seriously, Danny. What's going on around here? We're dodging Dad's enemies from the city, there's a movie star stalking me, Bible stuff, a howling wolf or something, and weird symbolism. What does it all mean? Judith mentioned something about a Rosachrist."

"Rosicrucian?" he asks with a laugh.

"Yes. That's it. You've heard of them?"

"Yeah. They're an esoteric order. Philosophical and mystical. They go way back. Plenty of them in Italy. There's a very old ruin that's always intrigued me called Porta Alchemica. Rosicrucian Orders claim it as part of their historical past, but so do a handful of other ancient orders, including alchemists. It's known as the magic door."

"Are Rosicrucians tied to a specific religion?"

"No. I think some even frown upon religion altogether. But originally, they had ties to Christianity. Personally, I think they're just a bunch of nerdy misfits who need to feel part of something special to give them purpose in life. No way Dad is one. They're very against violence and believe it's up to a Higher Power, or the universe, to punish. And big on karma and symbolism. The rosy cross in particular. I never got a chance to look at that pin. Maybe we can try to match it up to some sort of esoteric order though just in case. Let's see what Google has to offer in an aerial view first."

We go back inside, grab the laptop, and plug in the location. I see the Brandt Estate as I had seen it before and scan back to check out the view of our house too. I get the general idea of where we were, but there's nothing in the blurry image to reveal a clearing. I look in the direction Mr. Dennis was eyeing and think I see a small building. It's too unsafe for us to go back there tonight, but we agree on a very early morning hike. The man has to sleep at some point, doesn't he?

"We should check out the church before the day's over," Danny suggests.

"Yeah, we'll run out of time if we don't do it now." We're on our way back out the door when the landline rings.

"Dorcy residence," I answer.

"Tricia. How's it going?"

"Oh, hey, Jack! Everything's going great. I'm enjoying my stay very much. Are you having a good trip?"

"Yes. Everything's just fine. Katie's relaxing for a change. Listen, I just got a call on my cell from the Douglas Brandt Foundation."

Bloody hell.

33

JACK

I'm frozen as I wait for Jack to put the kibosh on all of my plans, or worse, call the police on me. "They wanted to personally thank Katie and me for offering up a one-thousand-dollar donation and to volunteer. Oh, and discuss Katie's missing friend?"

"Oh, Jack! Please tell me you didn't say anything."

"Hold on, Tricia, I'm going to go into the other room." There's a pause and I hear a door shut. My heart's beating a mile a minute. "Listen, I didn't say anything to Katie, but, kiddo, I'm a writer and a researcher. Never underestimate the power of a reporter to investigate who's staying in his own house. I know who you are, Jennifer, but there's an awful lot that I don't know. There are secrets in this town, and people are protective of them. So, here's the deal. Your identity is safe with me if you give me a story or two for *The Examiner*. I'd go pretty global with this shit. We can all win here. In fact, I encourage you to get out there and keep digging. Think of yourself as my researcher."

"Jack, I'll give you what I can, but you might not be safe knowing some of it."

"I'm not worried."

"You didn't tell the Brandts, did you? What did you say to the people at the foundation?"

"The Brandts. They are a dark and mysterious bunch. I've been trying to dig up dirt on them for years. Nope. I didn't say a damn word. They're interested in Katie's supposed lost friend though now, that's for sure. The man I spoke to, Mr. Dennis, said he could possibly help find the murderer and bring us justice. He said he met you and understands the pain. I played along, not knowing what you said."

"Jack, you don't understand the magnitude of the situation. I'm not safe if they know my true identity. On any level."

"I'm not going to say anything. I wouldn't put a young lady who reminds me of my own daughters in harm's way."

"Thank you, and I promise, Jack, I'll give you everything I find out."

"You can tap into *The Examiner* computer if you think that'll help. The code is downstairs in the drawer all the way in the back. It's in a leather notepad."

"I can't thank you enough. What will you tell Katie?"

"I'll throw her a story. She's much more gullible than I am."

"I really like Katie. I wouldn't want her to think any less of me."

"She adores you too. It'll all work out. Enjoy the event. I can't wait for some details, and we'll see you on Sunday, Tricia."

"Sounds good. And Jack?"

"Yeah?"

"You may as well call me Jenny."

"The name fits you much better. Jenny it is. Talk soon."

I hang up and look across the kitchen. Danny is staring at me with hands on hips.

"What was that all about?" he asks.

"It seems that I've underestimated Mr. Cool Breeze."

"Mr. Cool Breeze?" he asks with a laugh.

I fill him in on my own little private joke and the conversation. We're both surprised how quickly Mr. Dennis got in touch with Jack.

We figure it was a test to see if my story was real and to measure Jack's appetite for vengeance. I bet they'd love to have a journalist on their side. That would really take the pressure off.

"Let's get moving, sis. It's getting a little dark."

"Yep, let's go! I want a ride on that Harley."

"You got it."

I've never been on a motorcycle before. I thought I'd be afraid, but I'm not. Danny's a good driver and takes his time. We turn onto Church Road from Red Rock. It's barely wide enough for one car and impossible for two cars to pass each other. An umbrella of trees overhangs the road from the turn-off all the way up to the church. There's an overgrown path beyond the church leading to an old, abandoned Indian Reservation. Trespassing is forbidden. Between my father's obsession with historical Native America and my imagination, I always heeded the warnings.

We make our way up the steep, rocky hill. The church sits atop, isolated, with a minimalist sort of grandeur. It's been a long time since I've seen it, and it turns out to be much less interesting in person than it was in my memories. There's a small cross but no steeple or church bell. The outside walls are built of stone, just like many of the original farmhouses in the village. The roof is made of Spanish ceramic tiles. The gothic style windows are simply framed with no stained glass. I find nothing inviting or prestigious about the church. Judith is right, boring. Danny has his phone out and is reading.

"What?"

"Mission Church was once a missionary church. That's how it got its name. Spanish priests settled here and converted the Lenape Indians to Christianity. I don't recall that tale, but apparently, it's a well-known historical fact about the area. It's right here on the Brandtville Historical Society site."

"Easy to buy," I acknowledge. "And right near the reservation. Makes total sense."

There's an angel above the doorway. Otherwise, it's very basic. A little too basic. Judith said it was a glorified old boys' club. She could be right. But I haven't forgotten the folklore. My classmates told tales of people being boiled or skinned alive by the Indians, and there were stories of the church being haunted. Some said they saw images of ghostly children playing outside. Others heard the sounds of adults screaming. I also haven't forgotten the stories of human sacrifices that were supposedly made at the altar on special evenings. I asked my father about that once. His answer didn't make me feel better. "Not as far as I know, pumpkin, but there were sacrifices made in the Bible, don't forget."

We appear to be alone, so we casually stroll and snoop. Neither of us has ever before set foot inside the church. We climb the old wooden steps, which brings us up to a solid oak door. There are words above the angel. They read, *"Love that knoweth no fear, protect all who are near."* There's no window at the door, and the windows around the church are covered from the inside. It's impossible to see in. We circle the building and end up staring back at the front again.

"Can I help you?" I jump and pivot toward the voice. "Sorry to startle you," the old man says with a chuckle.

"Jesus," I say, and hold my hand over my heart. Danny has a hand on his pistol. I recognize the old man as the owner of the farm just before the turn onto Church Road. I went to school with his grandson, David. Explanation time.

"It's all right. Sorry to be jumpy. I'm new to Brandtville and looking into churches."

"Oh, I see."

"Do you know anything about this one? It's very quaint. I like the intimacy of a small church. You really get to know everyone." Danny nods along with me and the man chuckles again.

"Well, you might want to keep looking. This one here is so small that only a handful of people belong. It's exclusive, I guess you could say."

"Oh, that's a shame."

He looks at his watch. "You have pretty good timing. Aside from Sundays, this so-called church only comes alive Friday nights around nine o'clock. You have a half hour before the members arrive. I'm not a church-goer myself, but this is the last one I'd join if I were a believer. The people who attend are real jackasses. Well, enjoy the rest of your evening. Doc says I need to exercise the new hip, but I think I've walked far the hell enough. I'm ready for some scotch."

"Thank you and have a good night. Be careful," Danny says. We watch him walk, grunting in pain with each step, until he's out of sight. Danny and I look at each other and know damn well we're staying.

"Let's move the bike." Danny puts it in neutral and we push it as quietly as possible into the woods. There are "No Trespassing" signs everywhere. I trudge through at least three giant spider webs, which wig me way out. There are sticky strands of web in my hair, but all I really want to know is, where are the spiders? Danny is laughing and watching me wrestle with an imaginary tarantula.

"Are they on me? Are they?" Danny uses both hands to pat me down.

"You're safe. Let me see if there's a way in."

We're behind the church, which is overrun with weeds and thick patches of ivy along the back wall. There's a small round window facing east. Danny wiggles it to see how solid it is, but it's not budging. There'd be no place to hide even if we got in, so we're just going to have to wait. We slip back into the cover of the brush and wooded border. It's pitch-black. I can't see my hand in front of me, let alone my brother. In hushed tones, we take the time to catch up a little. I tell Danny more about Ryan. He's a good listener.

"It sounds like the two of you have something special. I hope when you get back you can find a way to make it happen."

"Me too. But it's going to be so complicated."

"Shh!" Danny whispers. "Cars." I look at my watch. It's 9:00 p.m. on the money. They're all lined up in a tight row, like a funeral procession, instead of coming in spurts. They file in in what looks like assigned positions. It's ritualistic, for sure.

Danny and I each have a big tree to hide behind. We're far enough away that I don't think we can be seen, but it's possible a headlight could capture our profiles. I decide to lie down on the ground, even though there are spiders and maybe snakes. I'd rather chance it than get caught. Danny follows my lead. I recognize the first woman as Jill from the Douglas Brandt Foundation. She's the one with the key. She opens the door and flips on the outside light, providing us a much better view.

Next, I see Mr. Brandt with two bodyguard-types, one on each side of him. A few more women and men make their way in, so nope, not a good old boys' club. Behind them is a tall man with several bodyguards of his own in tow. Danny's trying to get my attention, but I'm trying to zero-in on his face.

I whisper, "What?"

He's pointing feverishly at him. My jaw drops as I see who he's pointing to now. It's our father. And he's seen better days. He's limping and looks beyond weathered. I guess I imagined when I saw him again, he'd look the same, handsome and distinguished. But he looks very far from it.

34

MISSION CHURCH

The doors close, but one security guard remains. We can't speak to each other without giving away our hiding spot, so we just keep giving each other *what the fuck* looks. Now what do we do? My mind races, remembering childhood confusion, adolescent angst, adult anger. Seeing him again is drumming up so many emotions.

We wait in silence for a good hour, both of us trying to figure out what he's doing back in this town, the town we've been forbidden to speak of or return to.

With an impatience bordering on mania, I know I won't be able to stay still for much longer. There are unidentified bugs crawling all over me. If that's not bad enough, I also remember my mother's fear of deer ticks, which she has apparently passed on to me. Just as I've diagnosed myself with Lyme disease, the guard gets a call. He walks toward the road and looks down, as if waiting for an arrival. Headlights appear, and a van pulls in front of the church. The guard opens the door and forcefully removes someone by the arm. He's handcuffed, with a black sack over his head. The guard and driver drag him into the church.

Danny and I look at each and move as one. We run around the unlit side of the church where there's no parking. We're beneath a window and can make out only bits and pieces. We hear the captive demanding to know where he is. I hear a loud sound and nearly jump out of my skin. I wonder if they're beating him. I whisper to Danny, "What if we just march right in? Dad isn't going to kill us."

"I swear I knew you were thinking that. No, we can't. Let's wait until they leave and then try to get in. I'll kick the door in if I have to."

"I can't take it."

"I know. I'd love to walk in and punch Dad right in the face. But we can't get caught. We have virtually no real answers and exposing ourselves would end our search right here and now."

"True. Fine, we'll wait."

We wait. And wait. Finally, the church doors open, and people file out and head back to their cars. The prisoner is escorted back into the van and everyone drives away in the order in which they arrived. Jill is the last one remaining, maybe cleaning or locking up. Much to Danny's dismay, I break for the front steps and look inside. She's at the far end. I motion to Danny, who's shaking his head. There are a few pews, but the church is mostly filled with long tables. I see one at the back of the room that we can hide behind. Danny's still shaking his head as I move inside. I haven't left him much choice except to follow. We crouch down under the table and hope she doesn't walk back our way.

"Hello? Michael?" She heard us.

We're as still as can be as she listens. I breathe again as she gets back to business. Once her work is complete, she shuts off the lights and exits through the front door, locking us in.

"You're crazy, Jenny. Jesus, no wonder you have security up your ass."

My heart is pounding out of my chest, but I'm pretty satisfied by how this went down. We're in. We wait until we hear the car roll out of the parking lot and stand up. I smack my head against the side of the table as I do, and Danny covers his mouth to keep from laughing.

There are a few little red lights flickering near the front of the church, so we suspect there's some kind of security. Danny turns on his iPhone flashlight to look for cameras. He spots two—one in the front and one behind us. Damn!

A full moon shines through the windows, giving us enough light to spot a path that's hopefully out of view of the cameras. We army-crawl up the center aisle, keeping our heads below the armrests of the pews, and hope there's not a motion detector that we haven't noticed.

We make it to the front of the altar. Eight chairs stand in two rows beside it. If there's been a sacrifice tonight, I'm probably going to wet myself like I did as a child. I'm feeling the ground for anything moist, but thankfully only feel dry wood floors. Behind the altar is a large chair. I've never heard of a chair being directly behind an altar, not in the Catholic Church or any other.

I turn around to see what Danny's doing. He's fussing with some sort of app on his phone. I look up in time to see the little security lights go from red to green. "I turned the alarm system off but not the cameras. I'm working on it though. Until then, stay low. Don't show your face in case they have an infrared system."

"Ugh, okay." I put my head down. Without looking up, I reach my hand up around the altar and feel something familiar. It's a gavel. That's the noise I heard.

"Danny, this isn't an altar."

"Yeah, it's a judge's stand and those chairs are meant for jurors."

"I think we're good." He shines his flashlight app around the room. It's very boring. Almost too boring. There are no papers, no Bibles and not a trace of anyone having been here. They must do their thing and get out.

Danny keeps looking. He opens a door, which turns out to be an empty closet. We give it a good once-over, but there's no hidden panel that we can find.

Still crawling, I get closer to the judge's bench and push the chair away.

"Danny, bring the flashlight over here." He shines it under the desk, and we can make out creases in the wood. "You think it's a safe?"

"I wouldn't be surprised." He scans under the desk. Behind the drawer he feels something and ducks further inside. "It's a thumbprint scanner, Jenny."

"Well, that sucks." We'd need the person it belongs to in order to open the door. "Now what?" Danny gets a big smile on his face. "What? This is impossible. There's no biblical code to open something like this!"

"I've got an app for almost everything. Some of them are illegal, but that's what friends are for. Whoever the thumbprint belongs to probably has it all over the gavel and the desk." His phone goes from flashlight to black light.

"What kind of architect are you?"

"Got one." He snaps a pic, looks for a few more, and projects the light over the thumbprint zone. I hear a noise just before the door gives out underneath me. Danny grabs my arm, before I fall down the stairs and into a basement.

"Unfucking believable," I whisper.

"My work near the Vatican requires lots of specialties, my dear sister."

"Well, that explains even more about the safe space you made me." We both look down into the dark basement.

"Danny?"

"Yeah?"

"I'm gonna let you go first."

35

THE PRISONER

I'm coping with a level of anxiety I didn't know was possible. It's part fear of the unknown and part wondering if I really want to know. Fortunately, Danny accepts the challenge to go down the basement first. His phone battery is running low though, so we can't waste time. That part isn't very comforting. He cautiously steps down, as my imagination runs wild. What if there are dead people down here? Or haunted children? I check to make sure I still have my Glock, and Danny reaches out for my hand. I'm tempted to run, but the drive to find answers is stronger than my fear.

"You think it's okay if we just turn on the light? I see a switch."

He decides it's probably safe now that we're below the main level and flips it on. Rooms light up in two directions but are brighter to the right. We reach the earthy bottom and take a look around. The room extends way beyond the length of either side of the church. We've definitely stumbled upon some sort of underground sanctuary —or dungeon. The very bright lights to the right look less terrifying, so we go that way first. We enter through a curved, Mediterranean-style archway and find ourselves in a large chamber made of concrete, or perhaps clay. Gallery lighting shines on plaques mounted on walls with stone benches facing them. They're similar to the benches in front of Douglas Brandt's memorial. The floor is covered in terra cotta tiles, with a colorful mosaic centerpiece in the middle of the room. It forms a circular pattern and looks symbolic. We simultaneously start to decipher its meaning.

"Um, Danny. Is that a pentagram?"

"Not exactly, it's a pentacle. See the circle?"

"What's the difference? And what's in the middle? Is that a wolf?" I answer my own question. There's no mistaking it. There's writing at the bottom of the rather docile depiction. It reads, "Niša Nalan." I think I just had my first heart palpitation. "Mom was right, wasn't she? This is a cult! Aren't these symbols of witchcraft, Danny?"

"Maybe in horror movies, but historically, for pagans, like our ancestors, it can be a symbol of protection and balance. The five points of the star represent the elements, earth, air, fire, water, and spirit. Plus, there's a feather at the top. They're very symbolic to Natives Americans. We can look it up when we get back to the house, but I think we're dealing with something quite original here."

"Do you think the words at the bottom are tribal?"

He takes a picture of the room and the symbol with his phone. "Yeah, probably."

"And what the hell is that?" I point to another mosaic on the wall. It's a pyramid with an eye in the middle.

"That's the Eye of Providence. It's a Christian symbol. The eye of God watching over us. Haven't you ever seen it on the dollar bill?"

"Well, I know what it is but what does it mean down here? Isn't it a symbol associated with Freemasonry? I don't know how to put it all together." The idea of protection and God watching over us isn't such a bad thought. If I didn't witness a prisoner interrogation, I'd think this was just some traditional fraternity, or even a one-off Freemason society. After all, my father is way too sophisticated to be a Wiccan or something fantastical like that.

At the front of the room is a traditional altar with a purple silk cloth draped horizontally. There are dozens of candles for memorial lighting on either side, which I remember from Mass. My mom would give Danny and me a dollar per candle to light for people who were sick and for my dearly departed, Nonno. Behind the altar is a wooden cross with a rose in the center.

"Is that the rosy cross? Maybe they are Rosicrucian?"

"No. That rose is black. Purposefully maybe. Rosicrucian Orders are all about the light. The rose would be red. There's a certain opposition represented here. Everywhere. There's a darkness, yet there are also examples of faith in God. It's confusing."

I start reading the plaques on the wall, which have tiny built-ins beside them. The color drains from my face as I realize they're housing tiny urns. There are dozens of them. I start at one end and start reading.

Justice was served in
loving memory of
George Michael Brown
March 19, 1982

"Lord have mercy! Are these urns filled with the ashes of children?"

"I don't think they're all children, but I'm willing to guess they're filled with ashes, yes. I think they're remains being housed down here for remembrance and maybe to protect them in eternal life."

We keep reading. We find Douglas Brandt's plaque closest to the altar. *Justice* was served around the time I recall the conversation in the barn.

"I'm not sure I want to be down here anymore, Danny. I'm scared."

"Let's look at the other side of this place, then we'll get out of here and get a few drinks."

My hands are shaking. I show Danny. He gives me a quick hug. "Come on. You're the brave one."

I take a deep breath as we cross over to the left side of the room. It's cold and dingy, with no tiled flooring, just earth. There's another door, which is locked. Otherwise, the room is empty.

"I'm not sure I want to know what's in there."

"Do you have that key?"

I fumble through my pocket and find it. The key fits. On three, we open the door together, and even though I want to scream, I trap the sound in my lungs. The walls are splattered with symbolism and there are five holding cells. One is filled. A trembling and terrified man wearing a grey prison uniform is sitting, chained to a bench in his cell. There's only enough room to make it about a foot away to a bucket—by the smell of it, his bathroom. The man tries to jump up but doesn't get far. Inside his cell, he's surrounded by pictures of a child. I look away when I see them.

"Help me!" the man yells. "Get me out of here. They're coming back soon."

Danny leaves my side and stands in front of his cell. "What did you do?"

"It was an accident. He's my son. I didn't know he was in the car. He must've crawled in when I wasn't looking. I went to work and found him when I got back. The heat killed him."

I edge a few inches closer and ask him his name.

"Bart Wheeler," he responds.

Danny does a search. "I see it. He may be telling the truth. There's a news article about a little boy from the area. The father found him at the end of his workday in the back seat of his car unresponsive. He called an ambulance, but he was already gone. The same child in the picture."

"Yes. That's my son." He puts his hands over his face and weeps. My heart hurts for this man.

"How'd you get here?" I ask.

"I was set for a hearing, even though they told me it was a formality. The police believed me. Everyone knows it was an accident. I fell asleep in my own bed a few nights ago, and I don't remember anything except waking up in here surrounded by pictures of my baby."

"We have to get him out of here!"

"Please!" he begs. "It was an accident."

"To where? He won't be safe back in his home," Danny points out.

He knows what I'm thinking, the crawlspace, but before I can say it out loud, he shuts me up with one look. He's right. We can't be certain of anything. This vigilante group obviously has a long reach and plenty of secrets we have yet to uncover. We can't give away this find.

"What did they say to you?"

"They said they'd be back soon and justice would be served."

"When was that?"

"Two days ago, and again tonight."

"Who's been down here?"

"A blonde woman. She doesn't say anything, just leaves the food and goes. I heard more people tonight. I yelled, but no one came."

It has to be Jill. What's that Barbie doll's connection to all of this? Danny and I go back into the other room to talk in private. We decide he needs to stay even if he's innocent, which breaks my heart.

Bart is upset by the decision but agrees to let me send his captors a message. Nothing too outrageous, just enough to make them paranoid. I find the key to Bart's cell hanging from a nail on the far end of the room. I remove all of the pictures of his son. He can't reach me from his position chained to the bench, or there's no way I'd do it. I turn them over and find my Sharpie. I write on the back of three and leave them in a line in front of his cell.

GOD. WILL. JUDGE.

I tell the man we'll get to the truth and protect him the best we can. But if he gives our identity away, we won't be able to help him. He nods. There's something about the look on his face that makes me leery of him. Maybe it wasn't an accident, just a good excuse. We shut off the light, returning him to the darkness, and lock the door.

"I can't decide if we'll regret your little message to Dad or not," Danny says with a smirk. "But I like your style. Let's get the hell out of here."

We climb up the steps and use our shirts to erase as many fingerprints as possible. We flip the switch off, and Danny attempts to use his phone to lock the door with the fingerprint code, but it's dead. There's no way to lock it properly. Breaking the fingerprint code, leaving a note, plus leaving their secret door hanging wide open is going to make them frantic.

Forgetting that we crawled our way to the front of the room, I stand up and trigger an alarm. Bright lights illuminate the room and the buttons on the security system turn red. The cameras are rolling. "Cover your face!" I pull my shirt up over my face and flash them something good. Danny grabs the gavel and tries to break the glass window. It's a lot stronger than a standard window, more like hurricane glass. We look at each other simultaneously and grab our Glocks. Danny shoots the lock and releases us from our own prison.

Already, we hear cars in the distance, so we race into the woods toward the bike. Our arms and legs are scratched by thorns and branches, but thankfully it's right where we left it. No sooner am I on, Danny guns it, and I almost fly off the back. On our way out, I faintly see a path leading to a cemetery. *For another day.* We forge our own path through the woods, right to Deep Creek Road. There are cars lined up again, heading toward the church. Danny has the lights off as we roll down the bank and into a shallow part of the creek. He shuts off the engine and lets them fly by us.

I remind Danny to stay in the meadow on the other side of the creek like we used to do as kids. It'll take us right to the house. We need to get back as soon as possible to have the upper hand if, more like when, someone decides to pay us a visit. We decide to ditch the bike in the woods behind Jodi's house and dash home and through the front door. It's midnight and the dogs are barking their tails off. I let them out and feed them, then join Danny upstairs to wash the mud and blood off best we can before we change into the Dorcys' pajamas. I need to feed the other animals, but my hands are tied for tonight.

We turn on Jimmy Fallon and cuddle. We're going to have to put on the act of a lifetime. I duck under the windows and grab us some wine to make it look good. The dogs are calmer now that they've done their business and have full bellies. They take their places next to the sofa as if they're part of the act too.

Not two minutes later, we're rolling. There's a loud knock on the door. "Be ready for the space, Jenny, okay?"

"You be ready too. I'm not hiding in there alone this time." With wine in hand, Danny walks to the front door and asks who it is, while I do my best to look groggy.

"Open the door. County police." We look at each other and I shrug. I stay where I am under the blankets. The dogs are barking again. I command them to stop with a "Heel!" and they actually abide. The officer looks very confused, convinced he had a gotcha moment.

"We're looking for two people who broke into Mission Church this evening. Would you happen to know anything about it?" Danny shakes his head, but I speak for us.

"Where's Mission Church? Is that the vacant one up on the hill? Should we be afraid?"

"You're Jack and Katie's daughter, correct?"

"Yes, sir."

"Can I see some ID?"

Those are the last words I want to hear right now.

36

THE CLASSIFIED AD

Hoping he doesn't see the stress radiating from my body, I give the officer a bit of a hard time. "Sir, it's after midnight. Is this really necessary? My things are all over the place."

"What about you? You're the boyfriend, right? Let's see some ID."

"No problem." Danny's calm, but I'm in a cold sweat. Maybe the message was too much. Danny pulls out his wallet and hands him an ID.

"Military, huh?" Danny nods.

"Yes, sir. Army. Served two tours in Iraq." He embellishes with a long-winded description of his duties and continues with a conspiracy about terrorists trying to enter our country. The cop looks at me again and back at Danny.

"When do your parents get home? Jessica, is it?"

"Yes, how did you know my name?"

"It's a small town."

"Not soon enough, sir. I expect my mom tomorrow and my dad some time on Sunday." I'm aiming for solid consistency here.

"Well, here's my card. If you hear anything suspicious, call me immediately and no one else." Danny takes the card. I yawn and take a sip of wine, acting as bored as possible. His name is Sergeant Christopher Brandt. Another Brandt.

"Will do, Sergeant Brandt. I'll keep a sharp eye out, don't you worry." The officer looks confused, but nods and leaves. Danny locks the doors and settles back to the sofa, wrapping an arm around me. "I think he bought it."

"Where'd you get the ID?"

"From a buddy in the Protection Program."

"Oh. Hmm. I could've used a friend like that. Now what?"

"I say we finish this bottle and get some sleep." We decide to go upstairs and sleep as close to the crawlspace as possible in case of a forced entry situation. We leave the dogs downstairs to be our ears. Danny opens and enters the safe room, coming out with a rope fire ladder. He says we can use it if there really is a fire or toss it out the window to make it look like we've escaped if someone breaks in. He's so smart and I'm so happy he's with me. I can't believe it's only been a day since we've been reunited. We make our way into the master bedroom. I lay flat on my stomach across the bed and pass out.

It's still dark, but I hear typing. I get up to find Danny on Jack's computer. "What time is it?" I see it's 5:00 a.m. from the computer screen. "Have you been up all night?"

"No. I nodded off a few times."

"Find anything interesting?"

"Some stuff, yeah."

"The words Niša Nalan at the base of the pentacle translates to the numbers two and five in Lenape language."

"Oh, come on, really?"

"The Lenape Indians, or Delaware Indians, occupied the land all around the area way before immigrant farmers."

"Two and five. More symbolism for the Twenty-Fifth Acre, don't you think?"

"No doubt. Do you still have the picture of the note you found in the retaining wall?" I grab my camera and find the image. *Newushkinkw Newa Newushkink.* Danny's on the site where he found the translation.

"I see why you didn't find anything when you Googled it before. Dad didn't add the accents. "Nëwùshkinkw" means eye and "Newa" means four in Lenape. Put it together and get *an eye for an eye.* Just like you told Mr. Dennis."

"Hold on." I run downstairs and grab the Bucks County book I found in the closet earlier. We flip through some interesting facts about Washington's crossing and William Penn before landing on a section about the Lenape Indians. They were thought to be extinct at one time, driven out West to Oklahoma. But there are potentially thousands of descendants living in the area. I also find a very limited vocabulary list and see the same words. I take a mental note that "tëme" stands for wolf.

"What does it mean when you put it together? Do you think there's been some sort of native agreement over the centuries?"

"No idea. I suppose they could've formed a complex group and worked together for the greater good or something."

"What else?"

Danny found a bunch of articles from around the same time Billy was murdered. Almost all of them have entire sections blacked-out. No wonder Jack isn't getting anywhere. Someone with power is doing a great job of covering darker historical facts. There's one article about Jill Stevenson Grover. She's Ben's wife.

Apparently, they're both originally from Brandtville, but Jill moved to Prague, Czech Republic, with her family when she was in grade school. Her father was a history professor and researcher. They moved back later, and she reunited with Ben. There's not much else about her.

Ben's story is that he moved to New York on his eighteenth

birthday and started modeling and acting. He was close to his single mother, who was also a model. Then one day she disappeared, and Ben inherited the three-generation family farm. He met Jill at their grade school class reunion, and they've been together since. He's also a pilot, which is kind of interesting. He frequently commutes on his private jet to the Doylestown Airport.

Danny reads a published interview dating back a few years ago. It goes on and on about how losing his mother affected him. Their permanent address is on the Upper East Side of Manhattan, but Jill stays in Brandtville most of the time to help run the foundation. She's quoted as saying she feels like it's her calling. Ben stays in New York and other locations to film, coming home in between.

"What about this Mr. Dennis guy? What's his last name? Or, maybe Dennis is his last name. In that case, what's his first name?" Danny starts searching, but dead-ends. "Look up Dad," I tell him.

"I did. But let's try again."

There are a few articles. He made the paper representing some high-profile cases in the Bucks County area. There's nothing about the happenings of our last night on the farm—obviously that's been covered up, since a family's disappearance and a murder on the property should have made at least local, if not national, news. He keeps typing.

"Wait a minute."

"What?"

"Here's something in the classified section around the time we went missing. It's in Italian." It's a simple message, translating to, "Nonna misses you," and then a number, 201 555 8910.

I think I just heard my own heart crack. She must have left it there for us, hoping we'd find it someday. We take a minute to internalize it, both wondering if our mother and grandmother have been searching for us all of this time and what they've been told. I suddenly regret some of the hostility I've been harboring toward my mom. She's probably the biggest victim in all of this. She was a tough mom, but she loved us. I remember her sleeping by my side in the hospital. I'm overcome with emotion, as is Danny.

"What are the odds that she still has the number?" I ask.

"There's only one way to find out," Danny exclaims.

"It's pretty early."

"I don't think they'll care." We use one of my remaining burners and put it on speaker. A sleepy woman answers with an Italian accent. Danny and I look at each other, both our faces now ashen. I can't speak. Danny manages only to say, "Nonna." There's silence.

"Nonna?" I repeat her name but am barely audible.

"Who is this?" she demands.

"Nonna, it's Danny and Jenny."

We hear a wail, followed by a bunch of loud words in Italian. Much to my amazement, Danny starts speaking fluent Italian in return. The only thing I understand in the midst of the conversation is "Angela." And then the *Hail Mary*, which she's reciting loudly.

"It's okay, Nonna," I comfort. She puts our mother on the phone.

"Who is this? This isn't funny."

"Mom, this isn't a joke. I would never do that to you. It's Danny, and I'm with Jenny."

She's quiet for a minute. "What was the name of our cat?"

Simultaneously, we say, "Sherlock." She lets out sounds only a tormented mother could make. Nonna is making them as well. Danny cuts in, afraid of staying on the line too long.

"Mom, listen. Tell me where you are." Her voice is still shaky, but she manages to say, "Washington, D.C."

"Why there, Mom?" Danny asks.

"To stay as close to the Federal Bureau of Investigation as possible. Your father is very dangerous." She's having trouble speaking, and I feel bad because the Bureau is half the reason we've been apart.

"We know, Mom. We're gonna find you. Just stay where you are and please don't tell the Bureau we called, or we'll have to go back into hiding."

"No, you don't understand." Her voice gets stronger and more controlled. "Sean got into law because of his father. His father was a serial killer. His name was Timothy Engel. I didn't know it until after we all separated. I hired a very good private investigator, who's now missing. Your father told me his parents died when he was young but he's a goddam liar." Danny's Googling. He finds a link that verifies what she's saying. We see our grandfather's mugshot and there's no denying the resemblance. Sure enough, he appears to have been a notorious serial killer—of cult leaders no less. He pled not guilty to every charge and never spoke during his trial, and so had no defense. It also meant no insight, no motive, and no rationale. He was sentenced to life in prison but spared the death penalty, probably in the hope that he'd provide intelligence to the Bureau. He never once gave an interview or spoke to the media. He's a modern-day mystery and we never knew he existed. They found small shreds of evidence that he may have been into satanism, but that was never proven.

"What happened to Timothy, Mom?" I ask.

"He was murdered in prison before your father had a chance to appeal his case. Billy was going to be his lead defense attorney. It's around the same time your father started acting strangely and moved us to Brandtville. He was never the same again. Kids, he's unstable and paranoid. He started performing weird rituals with some of the men in town. Please, stay away from him and don't do anything crazy. I want to see you both again unharmed," she says and starts crying again.

"Why O'Rourke, if his surname is Engel?"

"I can only assume he changed it to escape the stigma of being related to his father. I believe O'Rourke was his late mother's maiden name. I don't know," she says through more tears.

There's bombshell after bombshell going off here. Why would my father insist I go to law school if his old man was already dead? Unless he wanted me to go into law, knowing he'd need the defense someday. Killing other cult leaders reeks of either protecting his own cult or having a vendetta against another. Pleading the Fifth means we'll never know for sure, but I bet my father knows. In a million years, I wouldn't have expected that my search for the truth would lead down this dark, twisted path. I honestly thought this was a case of greed and power or organized crime. Nothing like this. Now I wonder if my father's been protecting me from revenge cults or if he is actually the leader of one. I'm confused and frightened.

"I love you both so much. I never gave up hope," my mom continues.

This conversation is almost more than either of us can handle. We both sniffle and tell her that we love her and promise to find her as soon as possible. We hang up, both of us rattled, and quite frankly, feeling a little stupid that neither of us thought to dig into our family tree. We've been lied to so many times though that I'm not sure we ever would've believed a tale such as this. Danny turns to me, tormented and distraught.

"I'm worried that I may have it in me to kill him, Jenny."

"I'll bury the body."

37

COOPED UP

After the emotional phone reunion with our mom, and the bombshell that we're descended from at least one serial killer, we're more determined than ever to find the whole truth. The information about our paternal side of the family is distressing and humiliating.

Danny closely examines Mr. Brandt's pin and runs a search, trying every cult and secret society he can think of to find a match. He gets close a few times but continues to hit brick walls. For certain, we know that "ignis" is Latin for fire, one of the elements that makes up a traditional, philosophical pentacle. It's possible that there are five main members who represent each element. The design on the floor of Mission Church could be their group's logo, and each leader could have a similar pin. The number four has no significance yet, unless it refers to the fourth place in the star. The feather is a nod to any Native American aspects, and swords generally symbolize strength and protection. The paw print on the back of the pin throws a wrench in the whole thing. It's more whimsical than you'd expect from a wolf print, unless the artist had a sense of humor. Our search leaves us without a match or a name—just more puzzle pieces.

The dogs are up and pacing, more than ready to go out. It's also time to feed the other animals, so we head downstairs and cautiously open the door. I watch the dogs to see if they pick up on any unwanted scents, but they just seem obsessed as usual with emptying their systems. I give Danny a rundown of what needs to happen, and we decide he'll watch while I concentrate on the chores. *One more day of this.*

With pajamas still on, we step out into the humid morning air. We check for the Volvo, or any other vehicle that's not ours, and cautiously work our way to the barn. I unlock the padlocks and free the animals, who are thankfully all accounted for and in one piece. Danny has a hand on his Glock and is scanning and searching as I clean and hand out breakfast. I'm giving Miss Mable lots of attention this morning. Danny notices and smiles. I introduce him as he walks backward toward us and gives the goat a little rub.

"Isn't she the cutest?"

"She's really sweet. It's a shame we never had animals."

"I know, right?"

"Would have loved a pony or something."

"Same!" I exhale a little stress and ask Danny how we're supposed to process all the information we've just acquired. I'm feeling weighed down.

"We do nothing for now," Danny says. "We'll have time to work it out." He's way more patient than I am.

Danny brings up our father's condition as we saw him enter the church last night. We both noticed the limp, but Danny thought he saw scars on his face. I thought they were deep wrinkles, but it was dark. I assume he's right and wonder how he got them. Whoever gave them to him didn't win, because Sean Engel is still here.

We suddenly hear a strangled noise from inside the chicken coop. Danny and I both freeze. *Oh, no. Not again.* I hate that chicken coop. I lock the gate to the pen and pull out my Glock. We separate and walk all the way around the coop on opposite sides. No one's hiding around it, but we hear quite the ruckus on the inside.

Nope! I can't do it. Danny opens the door and the chickens run out. Tied up and gagged, lying in the middle of the floor, is Jodi.

I shriek and rush in. This is probably my worst nightmare, and she just lived it. Danny backs out, scanning the property with his gun out. I ungag her and hold my breath as she catches her own. Danny gives me the all-clear, so I help her up, lead her into the house, and sit her down at the kitchen counter. I soak a washcloth and start cleaning the coop filfth off of her. Whoever did this is sick. She's shivering but doesn't seem to be in shock.

"What the fuck happened, Jodi?"

"I'm sorry, Jenny."

"Sorry? I'm sorry! What happened?"

"My mom was asleep, but I was still awake around midnight. I heard the sound of a motorcycle and came outside. I saw you and Danny come out of the woods and run toward the house. I wanted to make sure everything was all right."

"No! Come on, Jodi. No matter what you see us doing, you cannot investigate. It's horribly dangerous."

"I know. I should have known better. So anyway, I got dressed and snuck around the side of the house. Then I saw a cop pull in the driveway, so I figured I'd wait until he left. As he did, I saw some movement near the barn. I watched a man try to open the barn stalls, but they were locked."

I'm ready to have a nervous breakdown over this story. To think we were sipping wine and I was passing out while all of this was happening. I didn't realize there was anyone else on the property. *So much for guard dogs.* "Then someone came up behind me and threw something over my head and tied me up," she says.

"I'm so sorry. Did the other man join? Did he say anything to you?"

"No. The one who grabbed me whispered for me to keep quiet. He told me that when you found me, to stay away. He didn't want me to wake up my mom and call the police. I got the feeling he didn't want to really hurt me either. But he gagged me and shut the door. I tried to get out, but couldn't, so I decided to stay calm and wait. Hey, I've woken up in stranger places," she bravely admits.

"Jodi, do you think it was my father?"

"No, he sounded younger. And, no offense, nicer."

"None taken. Who could've had a key?"

"It was in the lock, Jenny," Danny says over my shoulder.

"Crap. It's my fault. I forgot to pull the key out yesterday." I apologize profusely, but she's adamant that it's not my fault and that being locked in could have even saved her life from whoever else was prowling around.

Danny asks if the person had an accent—even a local accent, Philly or otherwise, but she shakes her head. I finish helping her get cleaned up and start wondering what to do with her. She's so vulnerable. On top of the unidentifiable threat, there could be anarchy tonight after the event. It makes the decision to get Jodi out of town a no-brainer. I ask her if there's anywhere for her and her mother to go, but she shakes her head. "Nobody wants us for company."

I wish I could send her to my townhouse in Baltimore, but that's not going to happen. I have another idea and grab my bag and Visa gift card.

"Jodi, you've been through enough, between your sleep deprivation and this sick shit. How about if I find you and your mom a nice little place to go for the weekend?" I start brainstorming. "How about down the shore? Do you think you can convince your mom to go? Say you won a sweepstakes or something in Atlantic City."

Jodi starts to get excited by the idea, never having been to Atlantic City. She's been through so much, but still has her unbridled enthusiasm. It says a lot about her character and inner strength. I still can't imagine someone so cruel as to lock her in a chicken coop with hens prancing over her all night long.

"Is it possible for you to keep your little stay in the coop a secret from your mother?"

"Yes. She's probably still asleep. She likes to sleep in on the weekends. I'll go right up to my room and put my pajamas back on."

"I'm going to make some calls. Does your mom have a car? It's about a two-hour drive."

"Yes, she does."

I stare at her in disbelief and protective concern. "Jodi, are you sure you're all right?"

"I'm okay. I knew you'd find me in the morning and rescue me. Mom just got a new car and has been working again. We could both use a few days out of this God-forsaken town. Thanks, Jenny." She's about as resilient as they come.

We hug, and I tell her that I'll be in touch with the details and ask her to leave the keys to the house in case we need them. She agrees to hide them under a rock near the back door. Danny rejoins to check up on us and escorts her home while I stand guard, making sure nothing happens to either of them.

I feel better when he and the dogs are back in the house. In my mind, despite everything we've learned over the past twenty-four hours, I believe this is the work of one of Sal's family members. I'm so tempted to call him, but Danny won't let me. I'm assuming whoever chopped the chicken's head off is probably the same prick who pulled this stunt. I feel such hatred toward the man I loved just days ago. I wonder if Ben Grover saw the whole thing from his Volvo. Or maybe it *was* Ben Grover. And around and around I go again.

Time to play Santa for Jodi. I look up the number to Caesar's Palace and ask for a manager. I explain that a friend's been sick and before long we've reached a nice little package deal for Jodi and her mom. He's going to call them to give them the good news himself. I'll feel so much better with them out of here. I don't want them in the middle of whatever we've got brewing. They wouldn't be able to protect themselves, and I'd never forgive myself if something happened to Jodi.

Before we dare attempt to find the Twenty-Fifth Acre again, I grab the computer. I want to know more about this philosophical pentacle.

38

THE PENTACLE

D anny and I go to town on twenty ounces of coffee each and get back to business. I've got control of the laptop now and find lots of sites about witchcraft and pentagrams.

"See, I told you!"

Danny laughs and takes it back. He clicks through a few sites and finds one that satisfies his thought process. I'm happy to remove the idea of witchcraft again from the equation, although nothing would surprise me at this point. If I saw a bunch of people hovering around the symbol dressed in black robes, it wouldn't surprise me at all. He shows me the symbol with the elements surrounding it. It's a star with the circle around it like we saw in the church basement. The one on the screen is a simple diagram. The corners reflect the elements he was talking about in the church.

The top represents *spirit* and bears the symbol of an upright triangle with a dot in the center.

The right represents *water* and bears the symbol of an upside-down triangle.

The bottom right represents *fire* and bears the symbol of an upright triangle.

The bottom left represents *earth* and bears the symbol of an upside-down triangle with a line across the bottom portion.

The left represents *air* and bears the symbol of an upright triangle with a line across the top portion.

He takes the computer back and finds more links, which provide more details about what the elements stand for. Not all of the links describe them in the same way, but most are consistent in their descriptions.

Spirit represents things like infinity, pure energy, and unlimited potential.

Water represents things like turbulence, forgiveness, and purification.

Fire represents things like power, courage, and vindication.

Earth represents things like perseverance, solid foundation, and abundance.

Air represents things like freedom, trust, and optimism.

I think of how the pentacle relates to the lost souls in the sanctuary below Mission Church. I suppose it could be comforting to the families who lost their loved ones, but I never want to go down there again.

"What about the wolf and the feathers?" Danny looks for symbolic explanations. Symbols of the wolf vary. A wolf can mean freedom, the ability to pass through danger unharmed, or represent a clan. Ironically, feathers have similar symbolism in Native American culture. Power, protection, freedom, and unity.

"Hold on a minute. Hold on a minute!" Danny's animated and on to something. "Think about the elements and think about where we are right now. To the right we found the memorial with the big torches remember?" I'm following.

"And the church, Danny, that's diagonally ahead of us. The Grover's windmill is diagonally to the left."

"Yeah, and Deep Creek is to the right." He prints out a map of the area and grabs a pen. He connects each site. It almost forms a perfect star. The top one is a little off, so he uses the distance of the others to make the star align equally. The line touches the church, but the tip encompasses the old Indian reservation.

Each one now equals a straight linear mile to the center and two miles straight to each corner. We were right about the linear interpretation of the Twenty-Fifth Acre.

The reservation, and maybe the church, represent the spirit. The windmill, air. The creek, water. The memorial, fire. And our property represents the symbol for earth.

"The rock formation where I found the key. I remember now. It formed the symbol for earth. Dad hid the key in the middle. A solid foundation. Our farm represents the foundation for which this group likely originated."

"Do you think Dad started it and maybe followed in his father's footsteps, but tweaked it a bit?" Danny shrugs and points to the center of the star he's drawn on the map. It's where the image of a howling wolf was depicted in the mosaic.

"That's going to be the Twenty-Fifth Acre, and I don't think it's a coincidence that we've been hearing howling."

I was afraid to say that out loud, fearing it would come true. I stop and think about all the points and how they could relate to the key players: My father, Mr. Brandt, Ben Grover, maybe Billy at one time. I'm not sure. Obviously, they have a decent-sized congregation going too. I wonder if the actual windmill could offer clues. Even if it does, we agree there's no time to investigate that right now. The Twenty-Fifth Acre will hopefully answer everything. We start planning and realize it isn't going to be easy. We're one hundred percent sure we're being watched. One of us is going to have to create some sort of diversion to get at least half of the security team scrambling while the other goes in.

We play Rock, Paper, Scissors. Both tasks are risky. I can't decide which one scares me more, but I win the Twenty-Fifth Acre effort. He wins getting back into the church and releasing the prisoner. His release will be our big diversion and should scatter the hell out of them. It's going to be one chaotic, stressful day.

We decide to meet back at Jodi's house later instead of ours to get ready for the event. *Assuming we're still alive.* We go through the Dorcys' closet for clothes. I choose a cute black cocktail dress, and Danny finds a suit that fits perfectly.

"It's not exactly my style," he jokes. "But it'll do for Jessica's boyfriend." He folds them as gently as possible and places them in his backpack. I toss in the tickets, some makeup and our shoes. It's snug. We may look like something the cat dragged in when we finally get dressed.

We're going to leave the bike where it is for now, and he'll take the clunker and roam all over Bucks County for about an hour. His final destination will be near Deep Creek where he can cross and head up through the woods behind the church. He'll send the prisoner, who shouldn't be a threat to society in the near future, further up the hill in the other direction and make a run for it back to Jodi's.

If we didn't have to get ready for the event, we'd meet back in the space and do some hiding. Something tells us we're both going to need the crawlspace during the sleeping hours. We're also very prepared to call the agency if something goes horribly wrong. We estimate that they can get here with an entire task force of marshals and FBI within an hour or two.

My plan is to weave in and out of the woods using my compass. I can't just march through them in a straight line again. I'm going to try a zigzag approach and hope like hell I don't get lost because I don't know the woods in that direction. But if I'm followed, I can definitely lose a city-slicking D'Angelo or Rossi. The locals will be more difficult to manage, and I don't know what surprises I should prepare myself for along the way.

I grab my father's bow and arrows from the safe. Archery was one thing I enjoyed in boarding school. If I could do it then, I can do it now, even with this more elaborate compound bow. String and wheels are looking pretty good. If I need to defend myself, I'll start with the bow to avoid loud noise. If not, I have the loaded Glock and the revolver I pulled out of the retaining wall. I'm nervous as hell. My hands are sweating, and my blood pressure is up. Danny's pacing and talking to himself. He has a burner and his cell phone, and I have the other two burners.

"No time like the present, Jenny. Let's get this done and get back to Jodi's as quickly as possible. Maybe we'll have time to relax for a few minutes." We remain still, locked in a long embrace, saying how much we love each other. It would be devastating to lose each other now.

39

FIRE

Danny drives off in the clunker while I strategize. Judith said the men walked to the left with the equipment, but the only thing we found was the memorial. Mr. Dennis looked to the right when I inquired about the distance from our property. The center of the star, which we're counting on being the Twenty-Fifth Acre, is straight ahead. But that's not the direction he was eyeing. I have some time before Danny gets to the church, so I decide to investigate the area around the memorial again. I start off behind the barn and find my alphabetical coding system.

I'm as quiet as I can be, but inevitably snap a few twigs. Each time I snap a large one, I pause and check my surroundings. I haven't forgotten to look up at the deer stands either. The thought of being stared down at like a hunted deer puts me on edge.

I locate the stand I climbed before and scale it again. This time, I brought binoculars and zoom in for a better look. I see the memorial and the security fence, as well as several men standing guard. I can also make out some sort of cabin in the distance, likely the one we saw in the aerial view.

I find another stand that's probably too close, but I climb it and zoom in again. I can see the structure much better. It's no cabin. There are large stones stacked up to form a giant retaining wall in front of the entrance. The building itself is shaped like a pyramid. At the top, there's a pipe with a pillar of smoke coming out. In fact, the whole building is aglow. The men are working together and carrying wood, I assume to keep the fire going. Do they symbolically do this all day? How stupid and exhausting.

I focus the binoculars in on the material and can hardly believe my eyes. They're carrying a wooden coffin. It takes me a few moments to realize that the pyramid building must be a cremation chamber. That's about as symbolic as it gets for the element of fire. The torches by the memorial were a good guess, but not even close.

I'm only a little relieved to see that it's a large coffin and not one small enough to fit a child. I have to guess it's either holding the prisoner they interrogated or the one from the church basement. Or it could be someone else altogether. The workers seem pretty busy at the moment, so I'm contemplating sneaking around the fence and working my way onto the Brandt's property. It's dangerous but screw it! I decide to go for it. I leave the bulky bow and arrows and climb down. They won't hear me with all the commotion they're making.

Depending on how far the fence goes, I have to consider the possibility of getting trapped on the other side. There must be cameras too. I weigh the pros and cons and still decide to go for it. I duck down around the edges of the memorial behind the trees and inch my way toward the property. The two men carrying the coffin go right through the entrance, and I make a run for it. I dodge beyond the crematory and down the hill, staying close to the fence but deep enough into the woods for cover. At least that's what I'm hoping.

I'm officially in survival mode and stop every now and then to use all of my senses. I'm listening, looking, and smelling. I don't want to smell a burning body, so I keep moving. I have my eye on several more deer stands and climb the tallest one. This one is much more elaborate than the ones on our side. I realize I'm probably inside a watchtower from which the very men I'm trying to avoid scan the property. How soon before someone comes back?

I hate like hell to have to move because I have a great view up here. I can't see the Brandt Estate, but I can make out what, at least from the back, looks like a concrete mausoleum. I climb down before I get caught and hide behind the trees again. I work my way closer to the side building and see a Roman pillar as part of the architecture. Between the incinerator and this building, it covers the materials Judith was describing. I duck behind what I'm hoping will be my last tree before moving all the way to the front. I feel the familiar two by fours. It's a tree with another stand. I make my move but snap a large twig on my first step. It arouses a dog that starts barking its ass off. I quickly move out of view.

"What's the matter, girl?" I hear a man say. *Shit!* They must have been on guard in the front of the building.

Knowing I need even more cover now, I dart up the ladder and take a quick look from the top. There's a man in fatigues holding a leash connected to a very excited German shepherd. Her persistent barking is helping my cause, but the platform I'm standing on won't be safe for long. I look up and consider another possibility. I was an excellent tree climber as a child. I guess I'll find out if I've still got it. I start the climb and land on a large V-shaped joint, with my back to the building. I'm pleased to find myself almost completely shielded by branches full of large oak leaves. I'm about as camouflaged as I'm going to get. I sit tight and wait for my next opportunity.

The dog is still restless and carrying on, attracting more men who approach from different directions. "What's with her?" one asks.

As if the German shepherd weren't enough, I hear bloodhounds. I'm so screwed. Slowly, I turn to look at the dogs, who seem to have picked up my scent. They appear to be heading back toward the memorial. Some of the men stay and some follow the dogs. I'm scared, but at the same time I know if my true identity is revealed, at least my father's in town. He won't let them kill me and stuff me in the incinerator. I just have to be patient. I look at my watch. It's about the time Danny should be getting to the church. I'm really counting on losing these guys when they're alerted.

I hear twigs snapping behind me. Now what? Through the woods, I catch a glimpse of a man attempting to hide behind trees, but he's not very good at it. I have the binoculars ready and wait for him to expose himself again. He's out, and I zoom in. It's Antonio. I don't need this right now. He has no idea what he's up against here, and I'm in no position to warn him. The dogs are barking and gaining on him. He makes a run for it but is totally surrounded. *Welcome to Brandtville, Antonio.* I realize he was probably following me, but I lost him somewhere along the way.

A security guard throws a sack over his head and another cuffs him. I suddenly feel sick. Not because I feel bad for him, but because I realize I don't really care what they do to him. Apparently, I have a dark side. They can shove him right into the incinerator if they want. Antonio's destination is surprisingly close, right in the building in front of me. Now I'm really trapped, and even more worried about the time. This was a bad idea. A few of the men follow to interrogate him and the others go back to what they were doing. I try to keep track of them all.

I almost fall out of the tree as an ultra-loud, bone-chilling alarm system goes off, like the ones I've heard in war movies. It's definitely meant to reach more than just this property, so my guess is that Danny has reached his destination. I account for the men who went in with Antonio. They're out and moving with purpose closer to the estate. I say a quick prayer that we'll both be safe and start climbing down. The hounds are gone. I can't resist the temptation to creep up in front of the building.

Now I see what they've built. It's some sort of folly—designed with a portico entrance. I see four pillars and elaborate custom tiles with symbolic three-dimensional artwork. Lady Justice is represented, with her blindfold, sword, and traditional scales, but that's just the start. There are Egyptian and Native American depictions and symbolism. It's like a clash of cultures, but the same theme is implied—punishment and justice. Maybe this is where their prisoners come first. Or last, before they're burned. No one is standing guard, and I notice what appears to be a key on the ground. In their haste, they must have dropped it. I quickly unlock the padlock and enter.

"Who the fuck is there?" Antonio shouts.

I'm quiet and too busy looking around to reply. He's tied up and cuffed to a chair that's meant to hold someone captive. There are more tiles and mosaics depicting stories. There's a lone wolf, feathers, and another pentacle, this one with the elements represented. Behind Antonio is a larger scale version of Mr. Brandt's pin. There's fire, the swords and the word, *ignis*. No number four is represented, however.

"Hello? What the fuck? Where am I?"

It's tempting to surprise him, but I decide to leave him and lock up the building with my new key. I scan every angle of the area and seem to be irresponsibly alone. They're all too busy putting out fires. I run back out and through the memorial toward my alphabetical trail. I'm about to make my way up the stand to grab the bow and arrows when I hear him.

"Jen. Stop." I don't have to turn around to know who it is. It's Sal.

40

A TRUCE

I draw my gun and aim it right in the middle of Sal's forehead. "No, don't. We need to talk. I don't have a weapon."

"Prove it." I make him strip down to his skivvies and let him put his jeans and dirty white polo back on only when I'm satisfied. But I have no intention of taking the gun off of him.

"This has gotten out of control."

"You think?"

He sits down on a boulder, puts his hands over his face, then runs them through his hair, looking exhausted. "If you want to talk, now's your chance. Or, I can probably get you a nice little spot next to Antonio."

"What do you mean?"

"Oh, come on, Sal! You were both following me."

"I didn't know he was here, or that he was following you. Where is he?"

"You're a horrible actor, Sal. But if you must know, he's probably locked up somewhere for now. They won't kill him right away. Everyone gets a chance to be heard around here. At least I think they do." He looks both genuinely surprised and scared, so I start wondering if maybe he didn't realize Antonio was here. *Nah. He knew.* "Okay, Sal. Spill it. Spill every detail from day one."

"Okay, okay."

Sal admits that he was sent to school to friend me. He flatters me and tells me it was easy, and that he loved spending time with me. He even professes that he'd been in love with me but was forbidden by his family to become intimate. "You don't say no to my family, Jen." I'm not in the least bit moved and doubt it.

"You were my best friend, but you lied to me every day. How could you do that to me?"

"I didn't really. I may not have told you everything. As time went on, my mother grew attached to you too. She's grateful to you for everything and forbade the family to ever hurt you. So, in a way, yes, I was betraying you, but I was also protecting you. Hell, so many years went by with no talk about our families at all. I started to forget that we were on opposite sides. It wasn't until you wanted to dig into your past that I had to alert my family. I shouldn't have. I should have let you do your thing and decide later. Your dad and friends did our family dirty, Jen. They're out for blood."

"How many people are after my family? And where are they?" I want to know.

He shakes his head. "I don't know. I was to be the only one in contact with you and the only one getting information. Now you tell me Antonio is here. And I've seen others. They're betraying me as well."

"Well, how many do you suspect?"

"My Uncle Paul, for sure. I saw him near the property."

"Who's that? Your mother's remaining brother?"

"Yes. I've been watching out for you when I can. I didn't want anything to happen to you. That's the honest-to-God truth."

Sal's confusing me. "Have you seen Ryan?" He rolls his eyes.

"You're in love with that guy, aren't you? Oh yeah, I've seen him. He followed me everywhere after you called him. We kind of had an altercation."

"What happened?"

"We went at it. Had ourselves a good old-fashioned fistfight. He's a lot tougher than I thought he'd be." I see the bruises on his face now. They're yellowing. "Antonio came up behind him and pistol whipped him."

"What? Sal, please. Is he okay? Give me your phone." He hands it to me, and I call Ryan just to hear his voice. Once I do, I hang up.

"He's fine. Trust me, Antonio wanted to kill him, but I wouldn't let him. But that's when we were able to lose him. I've been here ever since. Slept in the barn last night," he confesses.

"Jodi said she saw someone trying to get into the barn stalls."

"Guilty. I was actually checking to make sure they were locked. If someone in my family chopped off a chicken's head, I assumed they wouldn't hesitate to take out one of the larger animals."

"Yeah, well, one of them locked Jodi in the fucking chicken coop."

"I swear I didn't know anything about that. But I looked out of the barn window this morning and saw you escort her out. I refuse to believe someone in my family would do that. It's not their style, but I'm so sorry. That's wrong on so many levels." I believe him on this one and flip to Grover as the one who put Jodi in the coop. He was trying to scare her and get her out of the way. But not harm her.

"So, let's try this again. Who am I dealing with here, aside from your Uncle Paul and your father? I don't think I have to worry about Antonio at the moment."

"My father, plus my late uncle's sons. I have one cousin from each of them. Maybe some of their buddies too. I don't know. But that's it. Uncle Elio would never be a part of such a thing, and my dad tells him nothing."

"Do they know about the event?"

"I didn't tell them, so I don't know for sure. But probably. You found Danny, huh? How?"

"He found me." I'm not giving him anything else.

"How about *your* father? You guys have been all over the damn place. I couldn't keep up."

"Sorry, Sal. If you're telling me the truth, I'm grateful. But you must know I'm not going to tell you anything."

"I know. I deserve that. Can we call some kind of truce here? My family has basically betrayed and abandoned me. Well, except my mother, who'll have a conniption if something happens to either one of us. My father may as well not come home if they hurt you. Not to take away from how you feel, but this is my own family, and they've been using me too. Whether you believe it or not, I've been trying to protect you. Let me help you at least. Maybe I can help stop them before they get to your father and this Michael Brandt guy."

I think about it for a minute, wondering how I can use him to my benefit. I want answers, but I want them straight from my father's mouth. I'm not sure if I care what happens to him after that.

I look at Sal and say, "Keep your friends close and your enemies closer." He looks down, ashamed. "Sal, I assume you're my enemy, so I'm going to keep you close for now. I'll need to ditch you later though, sorry."

"For the event?"

"Yes."

"I'm still going too."

"I figured you'd try, but I doubt you'll make it through the front door. Come on. You're going to help me find something. Stay about ten feet away from me at all times."

He agrees to my terms and asks where we're going. I admit that I don't know for sure, but I warn him there's definitely the potential for danger. We call a temporary truce. If he's telling me the truth, he's going to be valuable to me. And I want to believe him because I still care about the man that I've been friends with for all of these years. At the same time, I won't hesitate to shoot him if he betrays me again.

I climb up the tree stand and grab the bow and arrows. He watches in awe, then looks around as he discovers more. This is news to him? Clearly, he's never gone hunting. I begin disclosing some of the plan, but nothing about symbolism, the church, the incinerator, or

Antonio's iconic folly prison. I just tell him we're looking for some sort of potential hunting ground.

"You grew up here? This is more terrifying than the city."

"Tell me about it. And your family is making it ten times worse."

"Hey, if that Billy guy didn't steal my uncle's money and kill him, neither of us would be in this situation."

"I'm pretty sure your uncle stole the money first, Sal. Anyway, let's not talk about it for now." Both of our families are criminally insane. If he only knew just how deep the river flows in my family.

"At least I got to meet you," he says with a slight smirk.

"Too soon, Sal."

Knowing I have a bunch of Sal's family roaming the grounds, I need to find an alternate route off the beaten path. We trudge through the meadow and get to a point where we'll have to cross the creek. Sal starts taking off his shoes. "Really?"

"They're expensive."

"Don't be such a pussy." He rolls his eyes, but leaves them on and crosses the creek, almost falling a few times on slippery rocks. I'm already a good twenty feet ahead and watching him. He's so out of his element.

"What the hell is that?" he says, pointing at something. He high-tails it away from the area so fast he almost accidentally slips out of his shoes. I refrain from laughing and take a look.

"Son of a gun!" It's an actual copperhead, the first one I've ever actually seen. I'm too amused at his expression not to give in to a belly laugh. I can't help it. He looks at me and tells me to shut up, but he's laughing too. I get a little more cautious where I'm stepping, not wanting a real-life copperhead experience.

"Let me ask you this, Jen. Are there like coyotes or something around here?"

"Possibly," I reply.

"For real? I've been hearing them howl for two days now."

"I'm thinking they're likely coywolves. A cross between coyotes and wolves." I say it like I know what I'm talking about.

"How would that happen?"

"Shh. You're asking too many questions." We're heading into the woods through terrain I've never explored before. I ask him to slow it down and to stop bitching about his wet loafers.

I'm looking up and all around but don't see any tree stands. It's 11:30 a.m. I think about the term "high noon" and decide we better speed up.

There are large pine trees all around us, their needles completely covering the ground. It smells like Christmas. I'm allowing Sal to get a little closer to me, but I still have my guard way up. It's pretty spooky here. We both stop, hearing a haunting howl.

He looks at me and asks, "Coywolf?"

I shrug my shoulders. I really wish I knew for sure, but it's coming from the direction in front of us. I just hope whatever it is, it isn't roaming free. I stop and look at Sal. "What?"

"I don't know about this."

"Then let's get the hell out of here!"

"No, we can't. I'm running out of time here." I walk slowly with the gun still out, but the exploration is over for now. There's a fence. An electric fence no less. But there's a clearing in front of us in the shape of a pentagon, which makes up the center of the star. Right in the middle looks to be another stone folly—this one a bit gothic, with a look-out tower at the top. This is definitely it.

It's 11:50 a.m. now. I look around and spot two decent climbing trees. I shoo Sal over to climb one and I climb the other. They're a good thirty feet away from each other.

I get ten feet up in no time at all and look over at Sal. He's having trouble, slipping and sliding in his Allen Edmonds. I suppress a laugh that could've been loud enough to hear. Eventually he uses his upper body strength to get about seven feet up and onto a decent branch. He can see almost as well as I can.

It's noon and there's suddenly lots of commotion. A gate opens to the far right and four men and one woman emerge, each with a leash full of wolf yanking them toward their symbolic corners. These *are* wolves I've been hearing. They're not coywolves. They're purebred. They're huge and snarling, trying to break free from their masters. I hear drumming, which must indicate this ritual is about to begin. The wolves strain even harder against their leashes.

My father is closest, with his back to me. Michael Brandt is next to him, and to his right is a woman with long dark hair and a very muscular build. I can't see her face, but I wonder if she's the woman who stared me down on my first visit to Brandtville.

As I guessed, Ben Grover is to the far left. I can't see who the last person is because the stone folly is in my way, but I catch sight of some sort of headdress as he makes his way to his place. He's Native American for sure. This is unreal.

I look over at Sal. I've never seen his eyes so big. Five gates, behind each of the members, begin to open right into the forest. *Holy hell!* I wonder if the wolves can reach me from here.

When the gates open completely, a door opens from the front of the gothic building, and Jill pushes a man into the center. He's trying to get the sack off his head by lashing about. Jill is giving him orders, which I can't hear. She removes his handcuffs and then the sack. It's the man from the church prison. Danny never got to him. Where is he then? Sal is trying to get higher in the tree, but I motion for him to stay still. He's making too much noise. I should've left him where he was, back near the memorial.

There's more eerie drumming, followed by the sound of a trumpet, and suddenly the prisoner begins to run. He studies the five gates trying to decide which one to exit. He chooses "air," the one by Grover. I'm sure he's not aware of that, but I think it's a pretty good choice for all of us because it's in a direction with less danger. More importantly, it's the one furthest from me. Once he's out of the arena, neither Sal nor I can see where he goes. Much to my surprise, the gates begin to close. I don't understand. They're letting him go. I assumed if the men weren't hunting, the wolves were. I look again and realize Grover's gate, the gate he chose, is still open. Once the other gates are closed, Grover releases his wolf. The hunt is on.

41

THE TWENTY-FIFTH ACRE

S al looks like he's going to pass out, and I feel like I'm going to throw up. I don't like the suspense of not knowing what's going to happen, but we can't move now. And I'm having major anxiety worrying about Danny. No doubt he created the diversion, which helped me escape earlier, but I worry that he got caught. If he's locked in a prison somewhere, I need to find him.

Our heads pivot to the left at the same time as we watch the prisoner zoom past us, running for his life. The wolf is growling and closing in on him. Sal has a better view and puts his hands over his face, unable to watch. I look back into the arena and notice that the group has remained statuesque in their symbolic corners. "Ability to pass by danger. Freedom." Those were the words Danny and I found describing symbolism for the wolf. I wonder if this hunt is a chance for nature to decide his fate. Then the blood wouldn't necessarily be on their hands. If he makes it through the hunt alive, then what? They're not really giving him much of a chance. I don't know much about wolves but I'm quite sure if they're hungry and someone is running, their natural instinct is to devour.

I check one more time. The members are still, despite the wolves yanking at their chains, desperately wanting to be part of the action. I climb down and start running in the direction I saw the predator chasing its prey. If I didn't see him go by me, I wouldn't do anything, but I can't stand by and let this happen. I order Sal to get down and follow me. I hear the man scream, giving away his location. The wolf has him by the shoulder and is tearing flesh from bone. The man throws up his good arm to protect his throat and face.

I aim and shoot the arrow, hitting the wolf in the chest. The animal lets out a yelp and collapses. Bart Wheeler jumps to his feet and recognizes me. "Oh, God! Thank you. What the hell is this place?" He's trembling and looks close to shock.

"Your worst nightmare, Mr. Wheeler. To you, even worse than losing a child." He lets out a sob, followed by another.

"You know this guy?" Sal asks.

I don't feel sorry for him necessarily, but I have to get him out of here. I give him good directions outside of the range of the pentacle. His order from me is to confess or I'll bring him back. "You're safer in prison." He agrees and runs, holding his injured shoulder.

It's our turn. "Did you see the man at the far end?"

"You mean the freaking guy with feathers and shit?" I was right. He was wearing traditional Indian garb. "And there was another one who did the drumming."

"Sal, you need to go, or you'll be the next one running for your life in the woods, and I'm not sure I'll be able to protect you."

"What about you, Jen? I don't want to split up. Come on."

"I'm safer than you. Run. Get in your car and don't come back here." I give him a refresher to find his way out, but I can't be certain he won't get lost—or that he's smart enough to listen to me.

"Why can't I stay with you? I don't know what to do."

I raise my voice and insist he go. He hesitates, trying to read me. I let him peck me on the cheek then watch him go. He's running fast as hell in his loafers now. Amazing what you can do when you put your mind to it.

I look down at the wolf as it twitches in its final stage of death. I feel terrible for this beautiful animal that's been used for a game. I pull the arrow out, not wanting my father to identify it as his own.

Using the animal's blood, I mark a birch tree. I want to spook them. Make *them* God fearing. I use my imagination, since I don't know a single Bible verse.

"The wrath has begun."

Technically it may be true with Sal's family waiting to pounce. This could be Doomsday for us all.

Not soon after I finish my message, I hear a whistle blow. It must be for the wolf to return. No time for zigzagging. I B-line it towards Jodi's house. I hear the whistle in the distance blow two more times.

I'm behind the house and alone, as far as I can see. I find the key and open the back door. I'm in and safe for now, but what about Danny? I catch my breath and call the burner number I gave him. No answer. Damn it. I don't know what to do.

I look in the direction where we ditched the bike and think it's still there. Hopefully the key is still in the ignition. I consider taking off now, but know I've just started what will be hellish fury and probably mass confusion. It's a bad combination.

With any luck, I created a diversion for Danny to get back to me. I sit and pray for a few minutes, then decide to hide upstairs in the attic where I'll have a decent view of the farm. I climb up and look out the window. I'm horrified to see that my father has already arrived. He's pounding on the door right over the patio he built. Several other men are searching the property, rifles drawn. I wonder if he's figured it out yet and knows it's his own children tracking him down, or if he really thinks Jessica Dorcy and her boyfriend are meddling. I grab my burner and call Ryan.

"What the fuck is going on, Jenny?"

"I can't talk long. Did you tell my father I'm on vacation?"

"No, but he's called me about a hundred times for reassurance that I have eyes on you. I can't lie to him much longer. He's demanding to speak to you directly, but I told him *you* wouldn't talk to him. Jenny, he's beyond agitated, and he's called Shane and the other guys too. I can't believe he hasn't shown up here yet. We're all covering for you, but you have to come home. Jenny, what have you done?"

I don't like the sound of this, but I need to press on and worry about him later. "Ryan, just be prepared to tell me everything you know when I get home tomorrow. Okay?" He senses I'm going to disconnect again.

"Don't hang up. Stop doing that. I can't trace a burner phone, Jenny, or I would have found you by now."

"I'm safe. That's all I want you to know and all I want you to tell my father. Got it?" He lets out a big sigh.

"It's all about trust at this point, Ryan. I trust you. Please trust me."

"Trust?" he says with a laugh. "You want me to trust you after all of this?" He takes a deep breath. "What time should I expect you tomorrow?"

That's a good question. "Before dinner? Maybe we can have dinner together, and I'll explain everything."

"Please, don't do anything crazy. You've gotten Sean's feathers ruffled, and not knowing where you are makes it impossible for me to protect you or myself."

It scares me to think I've put Ryan in danger. "Then please hide out somewhere until I get home. Please? I don't want anything to happen to you." My voice quivers. "I'm sorry. I promise after tomorrow there'll be no more lying. Can you promise me the same?"

"I promise. And, Jenny, I'm in love with you too." I'm touched, but I can't return the words until this is over. Maybe tomorrow I'll be able to say them. If I'm still alive.

42

UNCLE ELIO

I look back out of the attic window and see they've made their way into the house. Sonny and Cher run outside and away from the house, tails between their legs. They linger beside the barn, crouched down and trembling. I feel a sense of dread. If they shoot those dogs or hurt them in any way, I'll have no choice but to run over there and accept my fate. I won't allow that.

I wonder if I left anything behind that could give away my identity. I have my ID on me, and Danny has all of his stuff and then some. Before we left, we shut off Jack's computer and deleted the history on Katie's laptop. I don't like that they're in there. It feels like they've invaded my territory.

I look down and see a few men approaching Jodi's front door. *Oh no.* They bang loudly. My father is gimping his way toward the house as well. I'm about to stroke out. I want to confront him, and maybe this is a good opportunity, but I really want into that event tonight by my brother's side. I want us to confront him together.

I need to hide, and fast. Luckily, Jodi and her mom are hoarders. There's stuff strewn everywhere. As long as they don't bring in a hound, I think I can pull it off. I see a crawlspace, but that's a dead giveaway. I hear the door burst open and quickly bury myself under a stack of old clothes. They're in and looking.

"Jessica. I know you're here. I just want to talk to you." My father is either lying, or he truly believes he's looking for Jack's daughter. "I think we both have some explaining to do." They've finished searching the downstairs and are on the bedroom level. I hear the attic door open and footsteps coming up. I'm trying not to shake the clothing above me. "Jessica? I will find you." His voice is putrid and evil, not the father I once knew. Not the father that would wrestle with me and read me stories at night, at least when we lived in New Jersey.

I hear him open the crawlspace. It must be quite cluttered, because it takes him what seems like an eternity to move things around.

Gunshots. I hear gunshots. My father abandons his search and limps down the stairs to see where they're coming from. I don't move, but I hope they weren't meant for Danny. I hear heavy steps on the front porch as they're leaving the house and leap up to look out the window.

You've got to be kidding me. Sal's uncle, Elio, is in plain sight. And up the hill, I watch as two other men scatter into the woods, unnoticed, at least for now. The one who doesn't know *anything*. *He'd never do anything like that.* More lies. It looks like Elio took a shot at Mr. Dennis but only grazed him. You picked the wrong dude, Uncle Elio.

He's completely surrounded now, and they're not waiting for a trial. In unison, they shoot him, pummeling him with bullets. Once he drops, they continue looking around the property and seem satisfied that Elio was the man they were looking for. They think he killed the wolf and left the message on the tree. I feel kind of bad knowing I dodged a literal bullet, but hey, better him than me. *There's that dark side again.* The clean-up crew moves in from nowhere and clears the area. The dogs are hunched down, still afraid, while Uncle Elio is probably headed for the incinerator.

When the property is quiet and clear again, my father calls out to Sonny and Cher. He crouches down to look less intimidating. With tails still between their legs, they come to him. He gives them both big strokes to sooth them, which seems to be working. He takes a seat on the patio retaining wall and looks it over, maybe flashing back to when he built it. He glances toward the end with the safe, gets up, and starts removing stones. *Yikes.* He exposes the safe, opens it, and flips through the cash. He glances at the note, but I have the gun. He looks around again, probably unsure what to make of it. There's no way he'd believe Jessica, or I for that matter, could figure out the combination.

My father looks at his watch, piles the stones back in place, and leads the dogs back inside. Since they forced their way in, the door is unstable, but he makes an effort to secure it to keep the dogs from getting out.

His ride pulls in the driveway. If I'm not mistaken, it's the same Rolls-Royce-driving Realtor we met when we first looked at the property. Thomas, I think. I shouldn't be surprised he's connected to this. My father glances over the property one more time and then he's off.

I'm ready to get off this rollercoaster ride but am afraid to move. It's 3:00 p.m. Where's Danny? He should be here by now. I think of Sal, and the temptation to call him is extreme, but I also know that I have the upper hand. I doubt he's aware of what I just witnessed. I'm sure he thinks I fell for his loveable Sal routine. He's probably at a hotel, plotting with some of his other family members. I imagine their faces when he tries to explain the ritual hunting arena. Even for a tough crime family like them, it will be disturbing as hell. As it should be. No one is more disturbed than me.

I take a mental check of myself. How am I handling this? Why do I feel so numb? I just watched a man I've known for many years executed. I feel nothing. I try Danny's number again and he picks up.

"Stop calling me. Just open the damn door."

I run downstairs and let him in. He's covered in mud and has twigs and debris in his hair, but I hug and cling to him. I finally lose it.

"It's okay, Jenny. It's okay."

We have a lot of catching up to do. Despite Jodi's mother's supposed sobriety, I spot a jug of Tito's and pour us both a shot. Then another. We sit down to exchange the details of the day. I go first.

Danny cannot believe his ears about the crematory, the architecturally extravagant and symbolic follies, my truce with Sal, his uncle's recent departure, but especially the occurrence and discovery of the Twenty-Fifth Acre.

"Now you go," I tell him.

"Well, I was pretty productive too."

Danny made it to the church, but it was completely surrounded, so he traced his way back to the cemetery we spotted the night before. It was small and meant to be hidden. He found Denise Brandt's headstone, then he pauses.

"What?"

He looks me in the eyes and tells me our names were engraved on headstones.

"Excuse me?"

"I know. It didn't sit well with me either. It must have been for show. Maybe the agency had them do it. But still. Creepy. I don't like it. Mom was there too."

"What about Dad? Why not add the whole family?"

"He wasn't there."

"Maybe he will be tonight."

Danny goes on to explain more about his venture. He wanted to know what the deal was with the Indian reservation. He went through thick brush to get as close to the area as possible.

"I heard growling and wasn't sure if there were wolves surrounding me or what. I could see a house not far off. It was a log cabin. Then I saw a small barn. I dodged trees, rocks and everything else until I was able to see in the window. It housed the wolves, Jenny. If I had to guess, a temporary station for them. But they have to be the ones you saw in the arena. I was able to count five and then got out of there and headed back toward the church."

I have my hand over my mouth as he describes everything. After a few hours, Danny took to technology again. He tapped into their security system and set off all of the alarms. Technically, he turned them all on and let them set them off. They darted out of the church with the Wheeler guy and shoved him in the van. "Then I heard like an eerie bomb threat warning go off."

"Yeah, me too. That was insane."

"All hell broke loose at that point, so I ran as fast as I could to the creek. I covered myself in mud because I heard dogs, and didn't want them picking up my scent."

"Where's the bag with our clothes?" He picks it up.

"Still clean. I left it pretty soon after I started. It was weighing me down. What do you say we have a few more shots, take some showers, and get ready?"

"I have to feed the animals, Danny."

"I thought you said you saw some men head into the woods behind the house. It's not safe."

"Yeah, but they're probably all off prepping for tonight by now. They just watched their uncle or brother-in-law get massacred. And not by me. I'm low on the hit list right now, but I'm sure they're plotting old-school revenge against their enemies. The hunting arena and execution has probably thrown a giant wrench into what they may have thought were soft targets. If Sal told them everything, I bet they're shitting their pants. They're not there."

"You're probably right. All right. Same deal. I watch, you feed and put them away." We circle the woods behind Jodi's house and come up on the property from behind. I get the feeling someone is watching us and remind Danny to look up at the stands. A sense of relief washes over me as I finish feeding and providing fresh water for the sheep and Miss Mable. I don't have time to muck, so I lock them up for the night.

The chicken coop is a mess. I never collected eggs yesterday, so they're piling up and some are on the ground. I turn my T-shirt into a bowl and collect the good ones. The chickens are starting to get leery of their own living space. It takes some coercing to get them inside. This time, I take the key. I need to keep track of all the keys I have at this point. I have a stash of them now. We head into the house and I put the eggs in a bowl. This is ridiculous. There must be five dozen by now.

The dogs are happy to see us, so we give them some much-needed attention while Danny double-checks the crawlspace. The dogs are stressed, and I want nothing more than to bring them with us to Jodi's, but they're better off here for now. I get the thumbs up, and we give them an extra big portion of food and shut the door as securely as we can. We're back at Jodi's house ready to head in through the back door when we're in for another surprise.

"You watching your parents' farm *and* the Bergers?" We turn around to see Ben Grover standing behind us.

43

BEN GROVER

Why can't anything be simple? Even for a minute. Ben is every bit as handsome as he is on TV, wearing an expensive suit and all cleaned up. No doubt, he's ready for the event. Danny and I look at each other and know what we have to do. We have to fall all over the guy. I scream, "No. Freaking. Way. Ben Grover? Are you in between seasons?" Then Danny starts in.

"Dude, tell me what's going to happen to Charlotte. I'm dying over here."

Ben looks annoyed, like he's not buying our act. But we persist, acting obnoxiously star-struck. I ask if we can get a selfie with him, but he isn't having any of that.

"Maybe some other time." He turns his attention to me. "You're the one who pulled a gun on me the other day. You slash my tires too?"

"Someone slashed your tires? In the country?" I look over at Danny. "Honey, I told you it wasn't safe here."

Danny pats my back and comforts me. I'm using my now-getting-better acting skills to confuse him. "Funny you should mention that though. I went to New Hope today with a friend and when I got back, it looked like someone forced their way into my parents' house. We were just contemplating calling the police. Is there something we need to worry about? There was a cop here the other night too. Christopher Brandt. Maybe we should call him, honey, I'm really getting scared. I need to call my Dad and tell him about this too."

"I don't think you need to worry," Grover says. I can't tell if he's playing along or actually means it.

"Are you the one with a Volvo?"

"Yes, I have a Volvo," Grover admits.

"I came out to collect eggs and there was a chicken laying in the coop with its head cut off. Then I saw your car and assumed you did it. Of course, had I known I was pointing a gun at Ben Grover, I would've been mortified. You didn't cut off the chicken's head, did you?" I look at him suspiciously. "Why were you there anyway?"

Now he looks caught, and a little defensive. "I noticed a car in the driveway I hadn't seen before. It's a small community. I was just being nosy, I suppose."

"Glad I didn't pull the trigger then. The country spooks me enough as it is, let alone finding one of my parents' chickens without a head. I've been carrying a gun everywhere ever since." I pat the one exposed and attached to my belt. "To answer your question, yes. Jodi, the intriguing neighbor over here, asked my boyfriend and me to look after the house while they're away. They're at the Jersey shore. What's one more house? We can watch yours too if you want?" Danny and I both fake laugh and I add a snort for special effect.

"Why the hell are you so full of mud?" he asks, looking at Danny. I smile at him and wait for a story.

"Let's just say, I'm a tad clumsy. I went fishing over there at Deep Creek and slipped. In fact, I'm off to shower. Damn car broke down over there too. I have to call AAA. You got this, babe? It was so nice meeting you, Mr. Grover, and I can't wait for the next episode. Can I call you Ben?" Ben nods with annoyance. "I sure as hell can't wait to tell all the guys I met you."

He doesn't look happy with that idea in the least.

"Absolutely, babe. I got this."

Danny gives me a big kiss on the lips and heads back to our old house. Now I'm awkwardly standing here alone staring at him. "Are you sure I can't get a selfie? I would love to put it on Facebook." That goes over as well as I figured.

"Is that your boyfriend's bike?"

"He doesn't have a bike. Why?"

"Okay. Jessica, is it?"

"How'd you know my name?"

"I called your father today. He told me you were staying here."

"You know my dad? He never mentioned you. That jerk! I like it here, but, honestly, I can't wait to get back to Boston. Can I ask you a question?"

"Sure."

"Are there wolves around here? I've been hearing howling, so I looked up wolves in Bucks County and found that there might be a hybrid species they're calling coywolves. Is there any truth to that?"

"That's what they say." He's finished. "Okay, Jessica. You have yourself a good night. Is your mother still coming home in time for the event?"

"Yes. She's on the road now, but she may be late. I promised to go with her, but I'm tired. I might just relax this evening. I haven't even had time to hit the pool. I think we may do some skinny dipping." I wink at him. He's way over me.

"Have fun. Nice to meet you."

"You too. I may come back here more often now that I know you're here."

I'm sure he hopes not. He gives me a fake smile and I watch him hike up the hill, back to his estate. All five symbolic blades on his windmill are turning around and around.

This isn't good. I stay in the house just long enough to grab the backpack with our wrinkled clothes in it. I inspect the front door. There's some damage, but the dead bolt goes back in enough to keep it stable. We came in through the back, so hopefully he's unaware that I know of a break-in here as well. *Jesus, this is complicated as hell.*

I casually walk back across the street. The dogs are wagging their tails. Danny's still standing there with them, full of filth.

"We're just gonna have to make do here and be on alert that's all," he says.

We agree this is now our best option for getting ready. Danny takes a shower and I put on one of Katie's bathing suits. I need to make it look good. I stroll out by the pool and start cleaning it of leaves, dead bugs, and debris. I hear a car and look down toward the road. It's Ben. He's off somewhere in the direction of the Brandt Estate. I enthusiastically wave at him. Once he's out of sight, I casually stroll back inside and tell Danny we need to hurry up. I have a bad feeling about this.

44

THE EVENT

We're showered and I'm in full makeup, looking more glamorous than I have in years. The little black number fits perfect. I borrow some of Katie's jewelry and give myself an up-do. I struggle with it a bit, which leaves us no time to spare. Plus, I had to steam my dress and Danny's suit to get the wrinkles out.

"Wow, Jenny! You look amazing. Holy crap."

"So do you! We look like the prom king and queen for heaven's sake."

"Yes, the king and queen of boarding school high!" he says, rolling his eyes.

"Brother, the Harley's out of the question. I'd look like Cousin It by the time we got there."

"Well, I wouldn't want that. We're quite the Addams Family as it is."

We decide to leave Jack's car in the driveway to make it look like we're still home and decide to abandon the clunker forever. It's in Antonio's name anyway, and he's literally as good as toast. Instead, we opt for an Uber driver.

As we wait for the driver, we consider our options for entering the country club. We can strap on a set and walk straight through the doors. Or we can take a more conservative approach and slip in through the pool entrance. We can't dismiss the possibility of needing to break in if we're turned away. Danny checks his apps.

"Okay, seriously. How do you have so many James Bond gadgets and resources?" It turns out my brother is in a serious relationship with a man he met in Rome. He gushes a little about how he's one of the brightest special op security techs in all of Italy, working publicly as well as undercover for the Swiss Army. Danny's face lights up as he talks about him.

"He's in charge of high-level security systems, coding, and decrypting. Just about everything around Vatican City." Danny met Fabrizio on a job, and they hit it off right away. I'm so glad that he's happy and give him a big hug. He's grateful for the sisterly support.

We take a deep breath together as we see lights coming up the driveway. Our Uber has arrived.

"You ready for this?" Danny asks.

I have our tickets and hope our first approach works. Most of them know our faces now, so we could be thrown out, or worse. Mr. Dennis, Grover, and even the police may have described us well enough for our father to know who we really are at this point. Not having a getaway car is rather risky, so we give the driver some cash to sit in the lot for however long it takes. We direct him to park at the far end. Danny and I notice security at the door, on the roof, and in random cars. They're probably not as noticeable to most of the guests, but they seem quite indiscreet to us.

"What's our plan?" The event started a good hour ago and so far, no mayhem.

"This journey's about to come to an end, Danny. Why don't we march right through the front door and see what happens?"

"Deal." We're both nervous but hold hands, and our heads high, as we walk toward the entrance. We're aware of the eyes on us, but security holds their positions. Two distinguished gentlemen welcome us and open the door. We look at each other like *this is too easy.* There's a woman behind the desk, the same woman who handed me my ticket the other day. She seems to know exactly who we are and doesn't even bother to ask for our tickets.

"Jessica? You, your mom, and boyfriend will be joining Mr. Brandt and his family at the head table."

"Oh no, no, no. That's not necessary."

A man emerges, holding out his arm for me to take. I loop mine around his and follow him in through the reception doors. I hear a familiar voice speaking at the podium and freeze. I ask my escort to give me a moment, telling him I don't want to interrupt the speaker. He obliges and takes a step back.

"As you all know, my brother Doug was taken from us when we were just kids. As a way of turning something tragic into something positive, my mother started the Douglas Brandt Foundation. I'm proud to say we're twenty years and going strong." There's applause. Ryan continues with his speech, giving facts about how many people they've helped but how much work still needs to be done. I'm getting lightheaded. How can this be? The man I basically professed my love to is Michael Brandt's oldest son? What if I never found that lapel pin? How long would this have gone on? I check my purse, which is oversized for such an event. I still have the pin with me.

I always suspected our families were connected in some way, but I never saw this coming. He's a wonderful speaker and has moved half the room to tears. My emotions are changing by the second. I feel betrayed, but I also have butterflies at the sight of him, and I'm getting misty to boot. Danny's watching me, confused.

"What is it?"

"It's Ryan."

"*The* Ryan?"

"Yes. He must be Michael Brandt Junior or the third or whatever he is."

"Oh shit, Jenny. I'm sorry."

My cheeks are burning. I don't like being this blindsided. The whole room suddenly stands to give him an ovation, and our usher starts pulling me toward the table. I look at the head table and see Mr. Brandt and his daughter, Jaqueline, I assume, plus Ben, Jill, Ryan's empty seat, which he's walking toward, and the three empty chairs waiting for us. Everything's in slow motion. Ryan sees me coming and loses composure for a moment but regains it, shaking off utter confusion. I have no idea what emotion to show so I put on a poker-face.

It's taking every ounce of control for Ryan not to make a scene. I know the look. I'm also about to lose it, but this is not the time or place. Ryan looks from me to my father, who I now see sitting in a dark corner with Mr. Dennis. My father looks like his head is going to explode. As he internally rages, I swear I can see a vein popping out of his forehead. My father appears to be even more blindsided than I am. I can't help but look at his belt and wonder if he's going to beat me with it later. Or worse, give me a high noon hunt tomorrow. He looks from me to Ryan, trying to gauge if Ryan was aware of this situation. The surprised look on his face must give my father some reassurance that he was oblivious. But my father now knows he's been covering for me, and I worry about the repercussions.

Turns out Danny and I are exceptionally good detectives and liars. Another woman takes to the podium, talking about a new initiative. The lights dim and a projector drops. She's got a PowerPoint presentation. This gives us all some time to continue speaking with our eyes. I'm directly across from the man I've known as Ryan forever. His jaw is clenched, and his eyes are wild and accusatory. My father isn't even pretending to pay attention to the speaker. He's concentrating, trying to put the pieces together. Mr. Brandt has put it together, but Ben and Jill are confused as hell. They're looking at the staring contest between the four of us, trying to make sense of it. They still seem to believe that we're Jessica and her boyfriend and were probably planning on giving us another shake-down later.

Danny and my father are locked in a stare. I check Danny's expression. There's so much hatred that it makes my father look uncomfortably down at his feet. I'm happy to see a sliver of shame. After everything he's done to us, he should be ashamed.

I snap out of it, remembering there's much more at stake. We have enemies among us. I start scanning the room for a Rossi or D'Angelo. Ryan follows my eyes and knows what I'm thinking. He knows Sal's here and that we're all in danger. I make eye contact with him and nod. It's the sign he needed. He excuses himself and asks me to join him. I ask Danny for visual permission and he nods. As I follow Ryan up the staircase, he's on his wrist talkie, putting his men on high alert.

We move to the back of the room, overlooking the reception area. Shane approaches us, giving me a look I'm glad can't actually kill me. "How many do you think, Jenny?"

I provide them with a rough estimate but remind them that they have the upper hand with the hunting arena and church prison. They look at me like I have six heads.

"What the hell are you talking about?" Ryan asks.

"Oh, come on! No more lies, please. I can't take it. Stop lying to me." My voice is louder than I intended it to be, and we can see a few heads looking around beneath us.

"Shh. Jesus. What hunting ground? In the woods or something?"

"Ryan. Or should I call you Michael. Or Mike. Or Mikey?"

He lets out a deep sigh and Shane takes a step back. "I'm sorry. I promised no more lies and I meant it. I still mean it. I'm fine with Mike or Michael." I don't even know how to make that adjustment, so I tell him I'm just going to continue calling him Ryan. He's irritated and not playing games. He's right. There's no time for this now, and he's not the only one with two identities.

"I'm talking about the Twenty-Fifth Acre and the wolves."

Shane moves in closer again, and they look at each other puzzled.

"What's that?" Shane asks. I look from Shane to Ryan multiple times while they wait for a fuller explanation.

"How's it possible that I've been here for four fucking days and I know more than you? You've lived here your whole life."

"You're wrong there! I was sent to boarding school just like you. Except when I finished my education, a high school education by the way, I was ordered to watch you. I didn't get a chance to piss away law degrees and get a job in pharmaceutical sales. Who fucking does that anyway? I also work for the foundation. If I didn't, I would've gone off the deep end by now. You make me crazy, Jenny. I lost my brother and mother and babysit you. And you don't even appreciate it. Jesus, you're causing a shitstorm here tonight. This was a special night for me."

Shane advises him to lower his voice.

Ryan just threw a lot of truth bombs at me, leaving me somewhat speechless.

The guilt-trip worked, and I suddenly feel terrible for his losses. But how was I supposed to know who he really was? I never would've come here if he had told me the truth. He had so many chances. I still feel bad and reach for his hand, but he pulls it away.

"The monitors at the far end of the operation at home. Are they for the foundation? Is that why you didn't want me to see them?"

"Yes. I work remotely from Baltimore, but some of the staff is at my father's estate. I didn't want to live in Brandtville. Plus, we have a huge operation and work with the government as well as dozens of local agencies. The overall team is scattered, but Jackie and I lead from Baltimore. We fucking followed you there and worked around your schedule. I bust my ass every day, Jenny, protecting you and trying to stay ahead of predators like the one who took my brother."

He's upset and worked up, which is bringing me really far down too. I pause to process what he's telling me and wonder if they've been using him to find some of the local bad guys, so they can take care of them. He's going to flip when I tell him everything I've found, especially that his brother is dead, not missing. They're both still staring at me waiting for answers.

"Listen, you can both continue persecuting me later, but you need to hear me out. What's happening in this town is criminal and really fucking disturbing. My father's enemies aren't the half of it. After this event, we need to get both of our fathers in a room for a little interrogation. Frankly ..." I'm mid-sentence when the power goes out.

45

SHANE

Shane hurries toward the staircase and Ryan grabs my hand, pulling me toward the stairwell. He turns on his flashlight app to give us a little light.

"Generator should've come on by now. They must've gotten the main one. I doubt they'll find the other one, but damn it!"

"Ryan, I'm not leaving without my brother."

"That's Danny?" He stops and looks at me. "Honest to God, Jenny, I thought your brother was dead. What the fuck!" I believe him. "Don't worry, they have an evacuation plan down there. He's safe with them." We hear someone over the speaker tell everyone to remain calm and exit carefully. The event will have to be rescheduled. Ryan sees the man before I do and pulls me out of the way as a bullet near-misses my chest. We scramble back up the stairs.

"Not the children!" I hear my father's voice. He's trying to control his men. We work our way back the way we came. It's dark and Ryan's dragging me aimlessly through places I don't remember as a kid. I thought I knew it inside and out. Someone grabs my leg as we're running, and I let out a shriek. We look down to find Shane laying on the ground holding his abdomen. He's been shot. I kneel down beside him and rub his hair. He's in pain.

"Oh no, Shane. Who did this to you?"

He grunts that he doesn't know for sure. He couldn't see but assumes it's one of Sal's guys. I don't know what to do. Shane tells us to go without him.

"No way. I'm not leaving my favorite cousin." Ryan picks him up and tosses him over his shoulder like a sack of potatoes, and we continue running down a hall. Shane moans in pain with every step.

Ryan tells me to grab the card in his pocket and swipe to unlock the door in front of us. It opens and we move in just as gunshots fire in our direction again. People are now full-on hysterical. Screams bellow inside and outside.

I hear my father yelling again. "Cease fire! Watch the children." He says it like I'm nine years old again, bringing back ghastly flashbacks.

We sprint to the far end of the room toward another door. This one is steel, but Ryan is able to use his thumbprint to unlock it. He flips a switch as we enter, and the area lights up. It's some kind of an apartment. There's a round dining room table and chairs, a small kitchen, sofa, love sofa and tables, and at least one bedroom. There are multiple other doors, and I'm praying no one barges through them. Ryan lies Shane down in a bedroom and opens an armoire beside it. I see a suitcase on the floor in the corner. "Who's is that? Is someone staying here?"

"Yes. Sean. Your father stays here when he's in town."

"Oh, that's just great!" He pulls out an impressive first aid bag. In the armoire, I also see a defibrillator, blood pressure cuff, and plastic bins full of other medical supplies and equipment.

"Why's all that stuff in here?"

"Dr. Braun uses the apartment a lot and keeps the place stocked. He's kind of a private doctor for some of the club members."

I remember the name. He was my doctor when I was in the

hospital after I fell down the stairs. I seriously doubt he's in it for the club members. More like the cult members.

"Where is he now? He can help Shane."

"He's not here tonight. When Sean comes, he goes."

Shane is moaning louder, so I lean in and attempt to sooth him. "Everything's going to be all right." Then I have to ask, "the two of you are cousins?" They look at each other and grin.

"Yes, but he's the closest thing I have to a brother," Ryan replies. Shane gives him a weak smile in return. Looking at them now, I can see the resemblance. Both blondes, great builds, and olive skin.

Turns out, Shane is Sergeant Christopher Brandt's son. Christopher is MJB's brother. He's the police officer who dropped in on Danny and me after we broke into Mission Church.

Shane begins to tremble, so I rub his arms to try and warm him. This is getting ugly quick. Ryan goes to work, using the scissors to cut away his clothes and get a better look at the wound.

"Damn it!"

"What?"

"It didn't hit an artery, but it might have gone through part of his intestines."

"That's John's territory, Ryan. Let me call him."

"He'll never get here in time."

"Maybe he can tell us what to do."

"Yeah, okay, okay. Do it. Hopefully Dr. Braun has everything we need in here." I tell Ryan to wash his hands and start lining things up on the dresser near the bed.

I'm in the middle of dialing John's number from a landline when we hear the door open. We're surrounded by Danny, Ryan's sister, Jackie, and all three of our fathers.

Christopher Brandt hurries to his son's side. "This is your fault," he snaps at me.

"Uncle Chris, Jenny's calling Dr. Keller." The whole room seems to know who he's talking about and nods in unison. Everyone's quiet and on the same team for the time being.

A woman politely answers, his fiancé I assume, and I'm about to make a bad first impression. "This is Tricia Keller. I need to speak to John! Please hurry. It's an emergency."

"What kind of an emergency?" she asks.

"Seriously? Please get my ex-husband now!" I hear her call to him and repeat what I said. I put the phone down and on speaker.

"What's going on, Trish?" I explain with as few details as possible that a friend's been shot and tell him approximately where.

"We can't get to a hospital right now, but we have some supplies. Please, Johnny. I need you."

"All right. Good God, Tricia. FaceTime my cell phone so I can get a look."

I recite Danny's number and they connect. I motion for everyone to get out of the room except Shane's dad, Ryan, and Danny. I don't need a crowd, especially not this one. I grab the blood pressure cuff, put it around his arm, and push the button. His blood pressure is low, and his pulse is high. John tells me to keep taking it. I give that job to his father.

"Show me the entrance wound." Danny points the phone toward it.

"How about an exit?"

Officer Brandt flips him gently on his side. "Do you see it? The entrance is at the lower right quadrant. Probably somewhere near the ascending colon and appendix," I direct him.

"I see it. Okay. That's not the worst spot. It missed vital organs and hopefully his colon, but I can't be certain. He may be leaking and toxic. Do you have any pain meds you can give him?"

"I have Ativan and an antibiotic." Ryan lifts up Aleve and Tylenol too.

"Which antibiotic?"

"It's the new broad spectrum one I told you about."

"Okay give him three Ativan, three Tylenol and one of the antibiotics for now."

"Will he be able to take all of that?"

"If he gets sick, you'll need to get him on his side and potentially suction somehow."

Ryan hustles to get some water and Shane's thankfully able to swallow.

"He's going to need IV antibiotics and real surgery soon though. You realize this right? Hopefully I can buy you a few hours for now. Can you get him here? I can be ready. Who is he?"

I look at Shane's father, who's shaking his head, no.

I tell him I can't move him right now. He lets out a stress sigh. "Who's going to be my hands?"

"Me." I walk over to the bathroom sink and wash my hands. Ryan hands me some latex gloves.

"Tricia, this is insane!"

"I can do this. Please. Just help me."

"You're going to need to increase the size of the incision carefully. Would you happen to have iodine, a scalpel, clamps, surgical cloth, and suture thread?" He asks sarcastically.

Ryan nods. I tell him we have all of that stuff.

"You do? Where the hell are you?"

"John, please."

For the next hour, I do everything he tells me while Danny holds the phone so John can see my hands while I work. Ryan helps me keep the incision open but tries not to look at the same time. I'm a little afraid he's going to puke and tell him to aim far away if he does. I focus solely on John's orders and am thankful I'm not terribly squeamish. His father's trying to keep him calm, but Shane is letting out screams that make it hard for me to keep steady.

John releases stressful sounds each time he hears Shane yell out. Finally, the Ativan kicks in and relaxes him a little. The bullet went through his pelvic bone on the way out, so no wonder he's in so much pain. I stitch up the only tear we see at the bottom of his appendix. It released enough toxicity to still make this an emergency situation, but not an immediate death sentence. Seeing the struggle, John calmly tells me the best technique to put everything back in place. It takes both of us. Ryan holds pressure, while I stitch up the entrance area. He tells me to leave the exit wound open to drain for now. My stitching is going to leave him with Frankenstein scars. I'm horrible at it, but they're closing.

"You did a good job, Trish."

"Thanks to you," I say with a whimper.

He's all orders again and urges me to get him straight to the hospital. I thank him and we disconnect both lines. I can't even imagine what he's thinking, but I'm now the most grateful person in the world for smartphone technology.

I pull a blanket over Shane. He's fading in and out of consciousness, but his vitals are stable. I sit beside him, stroke his hair, and give him a kiss on the cheek. He looks comfortable enough, so I go back into the bathroom and wash up. I'm in black, so I have no idea what kind of gore my dress is wearing. I wash my arms, hands, and face, and dry off with a clean towel. Part of me doesn't want to come out. But this is the moment I've been waiting for. Time for the talk with my father.

I open the door and Danny brings me in for a hug and tells me what a great job I did. Shane's father agrees and thanks me. They move into the other room to give Ryan and me a moment to ourselves. I fall into his arms, feeling safe and loved in his embrace.

"You did great, Jenny. I'm proud of you."

"So did you!"

He leans in and kisses me on the lips. Yeah, I'm in love with this man. "Now, what do you say we have that big family discussion?" Ryan suggests.

46

FAMILY

Ryan opens his hand, locks my fingers with his, and leads me into the dining area. I finally feel like we're a team, but it's bittersweet under the circumstances. The tension in the room, exuded by so many strong and mixed personalities, is thick, making it hard to breathe. Before we take a seat next to our fathers, Ryan shakes Danny's hand then introduces me to his sister, Jackie, who is the female spitting image of him. Jackie's eyes are red from crying, but she forces a polite smile. I wasn't sure what to make of her until now, but she seems as far removed from the truth as the rest of us. Before I attack my father, I want a plan for Shane.

"Shane needs to get to Hopkins as soon as possible."

"No. Braun can see him as early as tomorrow. You already fixed him anyway, right, Jenny? Really saved the day," my father says sarcastically.

"He'll die by tomorrow." I turn to Christopher Brandt. "Mr. Brandt, please. I'll make sure John doesn't say anything to the authorities."

The men look at each other. "I'll take him," Jackie offers and rises.

"It's too dangerous, dear," her father insists.

"No. It's too dangerous in here!" Ryan shouts.

"If you're sure Dr. Keller can keep it under wraps, maybe they should go," Christopher Brandt advocates. "Get them both away from here, Mike."

Without committing to an answer, MJB picks up the landline in the kitchen, looking for an update on whatever's happening. He's talking so low I can barely hear him, but I make out the words "Permission granted," followed by a "Well done." It doesn't sound very good for Sal's side. He catches me eavesdropping and walks to the far end of the room. When he returns, he approves Jackie to take Shane and allows me to call John to give him an ETA. John promises to defer police questioning for as long as possible, but insists he deserves the truth. I don't make any promises and hang up before he changes his mind.

We file back into the bedroom. Shane's awake enough to follow the plan. He grabs me by the hand and pulls me toward him.

"Thanks, Jenny. I owe you." Then he whispers to Ryan, "She's not as much of a bitch as I thought she was."

"What did he say? If you weren't injured, you'd be in big trouble, mister." Even Jackie and Danny manage a quick laugh. I'm happy for the short stress reprieve, but my father ruins it.

"That's enough!" He takes charge and belts out orders. Jackie and Danny grab pillows and blankets while the rest of the men grab a corner of the sheet. They carry Shane through the kitchen and out a door to the garage. I'm nosy and protective at this point, so I follow. I remember a garage located to the back and right side of the building. There are certainly places for Sal's family to hide on either side, and the golf course is wide open behind the building. Getting off the property will be the most dangerous part of this exit strategy.

In addition to golf carts, I'm pretty happy to see three cars in the garage. They lay Shane down on the pillows and blankets in the back seat of an SUV. Ryan slips him his pistol and puts one on the seat next to Jackie. He makes her promise to call along the way. Christopher announces that he'll be tracking the car all the way to Baltimore.

Mr. Brandt is back on a cell phone giving orders. The men are all locked and loaded and shuffle Danny and me back into the apartment for safety. They'll have to fight off anyone waiting for them. As the door opens, there's a barrage of seemingly endless gunfire. I can't take the suspense and lean into Danny. Selfishly, I'm most worried about Ryan getting back inside and start pacing the room.

Finally, we get the knock that it's safe to open the door, and all four men rejoin us unharmed. Ryan protectively resumes his position close to me and reassures me that they made it out and onto the main road.

There's a collective sigh of relief. My father opens a cabinet in the kitchen and pulls out a bottle of wine. He uncorks it and places it on the table. Christopher Brandt follows his lead and grabs enough glasses for all of us, but I'm not tempted to drink with these men and honestly don't trust what's in the bottle. Danny, Ryan, and I all pass.

"Suit yourselves." He pours glasses for the Brandt brothers and they all sip simultaneously. "Who'd like to go first? How about you, Jenny? You've been very fucking busy, haven't you?"

"I'm not finished yet," I snap back.

"Like hell you're not."

"Why don't you start, Dad. I think you've got some explaining to do, don't you think? Or are we just as dead to you as you made us on our headstones?" Danny lashes back. "The feeling is quite mutual in case you're wondering."

"Is that a fact?"

"Let's start with your real name, Sean Engel," I suggest. "Might be a good place."

My father stirs in his seat, hearing his biological name. The other two men don't flinch, so I guess his children are the only ones who don't know his secrets.

I volunteer to go first and pull the lapel pin out of my bag and push it toward Mr. Brandt. "This is how my journey home began. I found it in Deep Creek a few weeks ago and started doing some digging."

MJB takes it in his hand, smiles, and looks it over. "Been looking for this."

"What's the significance? Why was it at the bottom of Deep Creek?" I ask.

"First part is personal, thank you. But the rest is public knowledge. I'm a faith minister, and that's where I baptize the good people of our congregation who seek repentance and rebirth." Danny and I make a face at each other. "In fact, I believe I was baptizing a new member earlier this summer when I lost it." My father nods. "Jenny, I thank you for finding it." He looks at my father then back at me. "You've clearly gone to extreme trouble bringing it back to me," he snickers under his breath.

"Extreme trouble is right," my father angrily agrees. "You have no idea what kind of irresponsible damage you've done. Some of it can't be undone, but some of it can. You and your brother will be the ones to clean it up. Be prepared to get your hands dirty."

"Wait. Public knowledge? Since when are you a faith minister? A minister of what exactly?" Ryan interrupts.

"I've been an active minister for many years, Michael. You would know if you came home more often."

"Where? At that fucked up church where mom killed herself?"

Mr. Brandt stands up and points a finger in Ryan's face. "You watch your blasphemous tongue."

I squeeze Ryan's hand under the table.

"Blasphemous tongue? Dad, seriously, what exactly are you a part of? I'm not following. Does this have to do with Doug and Mom? While we've been hours away working hard, what have you been doing? Something very illegal it seems, and you brought us into it? You brought us all into it. You know what I think? I think you're the fucking enemy. That's what I think. What sick shit have you been using me for? And Shane and Jackie?"

Danny holds Ryan back before he can physically assault his father.

"Relax, Michael. Just listen for a minute," Christopher says.

"Oh, I'm all ears. This is just great. I'm busting my ass for a foundation that's just a decoy for your real business?" Michael Brandt stands up to answer.

"We're part of a divine fellowship, son. Mission Church is special. It won't be long before you follow in my footsteps. You'll be a strong legacy and help lead the congregation."

I can't even look at Ryan for fear I'll laugh out loud. I'm having a hard time imagining Ryan as a minister and just wait for it.

"Are you high? Not a chance, padre." Mr. Brandt's face flushes varying shades of red.

"You'll do as you're told when the time comes. This is not the ideal time to try and explain. It's very complex."

While this insane banter continues, I take a closer look at my father for the first time all night. He's got deep scars on his face and throat. I bet before he had a wolf, he was sent into the arena with one. Some of the scars look like teeth marks, and I can't help but wonder what he did to get there.

"Why don't the two of you continue this conversation alone. Mr. Brandt, I would probably start with the memorial part, so I don't have to do it." Mr. Brandt closes his eyes. "Danny and I would like a word with our father."

"What memorial?" I hear Ryan ask.

My father rises, takes his glass of wine, and leads us to another door. He uses his thumbprint, which leads to an office. I'm surprised to see it's where he stores all of his old law books and even one of the foxhunt paintings. He closes the door and gets behind his desk. He sits with his hands folded, wearing a smug, you're-not-going-to-win look on his face. He doesn't know me very well, because I'm already winning to some degree.

"Look, we've got a bit of a head start over Ryan, so it's time for us to catch up," I suggest.

"You will refer to him as Michael from this day forward."

"Anyway, the scars on your face and arms. What did *you* do to end up in the Twenty-Fifth Acre?"

"Where'd you hear that term?"

"From you. I heard it from you in the middle of the night. I was hiding in one of the stalls beneath you and your cult in the barn. Remember when I fell down the stairs? I fell because I was in shock by what I heard. And now I know where it is."

His eyes are serious, and he has a no-nonsense tone. "The property around here is sacred, Jenny. I made some mistakes. Let's just say I was given a second chance."

"I know what Billy's mistake was. He stole money from the D'Angelos and brought a dead Dominick back here in the middle of his trial. You helped bury him and then things went terribly wrong. You had to take care of his brother too."

"You're wrong. Billy stole things back. Those people stole things from us!"

"Like what?"

"Not important. And I didn't realize you were in the barn. That wasn't a conversation for a small child to hear. Our way of life is something that you must take in gradually."

"Answer the question. What did *you* do?" Danny asks.

"A man was killed on our property the night we fled town. I did the right thing and protected you. The man who died was a very important part of our congregation."

"Chuck?"

My father looks surprised again. "You got into the retaining wall, didn't you?"

"Yes, I did."

"You figured out the code and everything. You're gifted and you don't even know why."

"Enlighten me."

"You're ready now. I thought we'd have to wait. But you're ready."

"Ready for what?"

"For mastering your talents and for leadership."

"Can we get back to your punishment?" I ask. His gaze is paternal and strange, but he shifts back to the conversation.

"I broke sacred rules and accepted my day of punishment. I survived and proved myself to be worthy once again. I was reborn, thanks to our great Imperator."

I look at Danny for translation. He shrugs with a lack of knowledge. I would ask what my father's punishment was, but I already know. He was placed in the arena on a day at high noon. He passed through unharmed, or least not dead, and they pardoned and baptized him.

"About your congregation. If Mr. Brandt's leadership responsibilities involve something to do with the element of fire, yours involve the element of earth, correct?"

"Yes, Jenny, that is correct." My father looks too excited that I know this much.

"Why is *our* property considered to be the foundation of your inner circle? Are you its founder?" He raises an eyebrow.

"Hardly. None of us were. Our home is located on very sacred ground, and the traditions in our village go way back. I cannot stress to you how very, very secret and private our Order is."

"Don't you mean was? It's not our home anymore. And how far back?"

"Far enough," he says. "And, again, I warn you that our Divine Laws must remain safe and protected. Understand me? Our enemies out there—they must all die for what they know, and then we'll all pick up the pieces."

He's making my head hurt.

"I find it really hard to believe that this tradition of yours is something that goes very far back. Wouldn't the whole world know? If your idea of far back is when we moved here, that's not so long ago."

"Like any constitution, there are amendments. We are blessed beyond measure by the gifts God has bestowed upon us."

"Blessed?" Danny questions "What kind of order separates children from their parents? Sends them away? Lies to them? Destroys their lives?"

"All of that was unfortunate, and I've paid the price for it."

"We all have, apparently. How can you live with yourself? Tell me the truth, was this cult your father's creation? Your father, the serial killer?" I ask.

I've seen my father angry before, but I've never seen the look he has now. It could haunt a house. I triggered something wicked in him, and without warning, he stands up and slaps me hard across the face. The force tears at a muscle in my neck as it whips to the side. It probably shouldn't have shocked me, but it does. I get a few ugly flashbacks from the abusive days of my childhood. Danny springs to his feet and pulls his gun on him.

I'm rubbing my face and testing my jaw for damage. I could stop right here, but I want more answers. I tell Danny to put the gun down and force myself to give my father an apology. This is serious business he thinks he's doing here, and now I know to be prepared for the worst by bringing up his father.

I change the subject and redirect my line of questions. I ask him if his secret society has a name outside of Mission Church. I'm not sure why I want to know. Maybe I feel like it would make more sense or that I could research its history and try to understand.

"Our Order has a name, but only those initiated at the highest level are privy to it. The punishment ritual that you witnessed is a very small aspect. The light can only shine once darkness disappears. And that comes to us through the ritual with the tëme."

"Through the wolf. You've created an inner circle with people who symbolically represent each element to form some sort of elaborate system with nature? Why the Native American participation?"

"Well the land was theirs first, of course." He's simmered down and has a strange smile. "You're pretty far off, Jenny, but you do impress me with your instincts. You and Danny, and Michael and Jackie were all to be initiated in the near future. We've been overworked and preoccupied with missions lately, and the Rossi and D'Angelo families have halted your introduction and lessons. I couldn't risk bringing you here and having our sacred grounds desecrated again. I've wrongfully procrastinated to protect you and the village. I shouldn't have. You're ready. And now you'll need to be initiated sooner in case something happens to us. You'll be trained, taught respect and discipline while you learn the culture and witness the secrets that makes our society so incredibly special."

"All right. I've heard enough. We're not participating in any of this nonsense," Danny protests. "If you've been brainwashed or something, Dad, we can get you help. I think you need help." My father laughs at the idea.

"You'll come to understand, son. I'm quite healthy, really."

Danny may have had enough, but I'm trying to learn more.

"The older couple you purchased the farm from, Mr. Alex and Ms. Aada? Were they a part of the Order? Did you know all of this when we bought the house?" My father blinks and pauses, wondering how much to say.

"Yes, I did. And we'll leave it at that for now."

"Well, how did Billy fit in? Was he a leader?" I ask.

"Hardly. Billy didn't have the bloodline."

"Bloodline? You mean you have to come from a long line of serial killers to belong?" Oh no. Danny pushed the button. My father stands up ready to take Danny out, but he rises with him, quite able to counterattack if necessary.

"Stop. Hold on! Why didn't you just keep the property? It's been sitting empty forever."

"It went against the rules. I wasn't allowed to keep it after Chuck was killed on the premises. There are rules in place for purpose. More importantly, I needed to protect the two of you from our enemies. The same enemies who have lured you into friendship. We should have disposed of them sooner, but we tried to avoid attention for as long as possible. They've disturbed the grounds, and they'll all pay the ultimate price."

"Jack Dorcy isn't part of the group, is he?" I hit a nerve again. I can see it.

"No, and thanks to this little stunt, we'll need to drive him and his wife from the village."

"Please don't hurt them. They're both good people," I implore.

"We won't hurt them. But they can't come back here again. We'll fill the house with another legacy. We should have done that a long time ago."

"What other rules are in place? What are the repercussions? This is a pretty barbaric system, don't you think? I shot one of the wolves. Does that come with an automatic death sentence?" I was half-kidding as I asked, but I fear I just set myself up. My father's eyes get wide and manic.

"*You* killed that wolf? Well, then you'll have to enter the arena in order to be forgiven. There's no other way." Danny pulls the gun on him again.

"She's not getting into that thing. Say that again and I'll execute *you*."

"Don't mess with the process. I cannot protect you."

"You would let us die before giving up your role in this Order?"

"I have no other choice."

Danny and I look into each other's eyes. He looks afraid for me. "Sean, you're dismissed. You can join your real family in the other room. I want to talk to my sister for a moment." My father is itching to violently lash out again, but with the gun pointed at him, he's helpless to follow through.

Danny locks the door behind him. We're holding up, but very worried about the new details. In the end, none of it really matters. Assuming we can get out of here alive, we're taking them down. We decide to call Sal for some intel. I need to know what's happening on his side.

"Jen. Jesus Christ. What the fuck? I've been trying to call you."

"I know what's happening on my end, Sal. What's happening on yours?"

"I obviously can't tell you everything, but we're up your shit's creek over here. Half of our guys, my family, are dead or have been taken away. Where do they take them?"

"Where are you, Sal?"

"I'm in the woods behind your old house. Near the letter D you marked on the trees."

"How many of your guys are still at the country club?"

"Not many. We're scattered and honestly just trying to get our guys and get out. No one gambled on this shit."

"Good. You should run as fast as you can because my father and the others are going to come at you with a force you didn't know existed. None of you stand a chance."

"Damn it, Jen. I don't know what to do. My own father's missing at the moment. I can't leave him. None of us can leave. We won't do that. Family is family."

"Have you killed anyone, Sal? Did you shoot Shane?"

"I haven't shot anyone. I'm just doing most of the searching. It's dark and I don't know where I'm going. Give me something. Let me at least get my dad out of here. For my mom's sake." I advise him to follow the letters all the way to the memorial. I remind him of the stands where he can look out and tell him about the incinerator. There's also a holding cell there. That's all I can give him.

"If I were you Sal, I'd stay up in the tree stand all night and let me get you down in the morning."

"What about you?"

"Let's just say, I may be the next one in the hunting arena. My father is sadistic and delusional, and he's not very happy with me. If I don't see you before noon tomorrow, can you find your way back to the arena? If I'm captured and placed there, I'll run toward the gate where my father stands. Find the same trees. Shoot the wolf or my father. Do whatever it takes. Got it? And Sal, I know where your Uncle Elio is, do you?"

"He better be home in bed, why?"

"Elio knew everything." Sal's quietly letting it sink in.

"I'll be at the arena tomorrow at noon. I'm done with this."

"Stay hidden and safe tonight, okay Sal?" I hear him suppressing the urge to weep. He's scared.

He lets out a shaky "Okay" and hangs up. Danny and I aren't sure if it was such a great idea to reach out to him, but we come to the conclusion that we're better off having Sal as an enemy over our father. We decide to let the two groups go at it tonight and hope to settle down into the crawlspace then get up and assess the damage in the morning. We consider calling the agency but want as much of this to be over with as possible first. It's not that we want death and destruction, but selfishly, we'd like to whittle down the bad guys from each side to give us less to fear in the future. Maybe that's just as bad as doing the actual murdering.

Danny cracks the door and asks Ryan to join us in the office. They don't allow it. Ryan looks wiped out by everything he's been told while we were gone. I decide we'll have time to catch up later and don't push. I exit out of the office first and Danny backs me up with his gun drawn. Instead of pointing it at our father, he aims it at Michael Brandt. Christopher and my father react defensively. That's when Ryan notices the shiner on my cheek. He glares at my father and without saying anything, he looks to me for permission to beat his ass. I shake my head. It's not worth it. Christopher attempts to reach for his gun, but Danny tells him drop it, or he'll shoot his brother between the eyes.

"Or, I can pick up the phone right now and call my ex-husband and give him this whole sordid tale. Shane will live, but John will have the Feds, CNN, and Fox News all over your little pentacle within a few hours." All three elders give up the fight. Christopher kicks his gun across the room, while Ryan grabs the keys to one of the cars.

There's nothing funny about this moment, but my father suddenly begins laughing like a lunatic. "You think you're so smart, Jenny. I look forward to seeing how you do tomorrow. You're on your own. You're my daughter, but I will watch my own animal rip you to shreds for the trouble you've caused." Ryan moves in fast and punches him so hard that it rearranges his nose. Blood sprays both of the Brandt brothers.

"Michael Joseph Brandt, you've disgraced me. Kneel and repent, for your loyalties are here." Ryan looks at me and then back at his father.

"I kneel for no one. How dare you. You're the disgrace! Congratulations though, Pop, you've officially lost both of your sons."

47

A SAFE PLAN

It's time to get out of my dad's secret apartment hideout and to safety. Danny keeps his gun pointed at Michael Brandt, takes their phones, and permanently disables the landline while Ryan and I step into the garage and blow out the tires of a Jag. We opt for the remaining vehicle, a Jeep Wrangler. On the way out, Danny secures the door with one of his fancy apps. This time he erases the thumbprint coding system to enter or exit. They should be trapped long enough for us to reach our destination. If only we knew how many others we're up against. Ryan can't be sure since he was only aware of his own "department," and Shane was a big part of that.

The garage opens, and we duck down as Ryan floors it. There's no one in sight. In fact, it's eerily quiet. I double check to make sure our Uber driver isn't still sitting there. No trace.

"Not a monster, huh?" I can't help myself.

Ryan takes it back and gives me a full apology. "You win. This is way worse than I could've imagined. What's the plan?" Danny and I look at each other and tell him to head back to our old house. "That's the best you've got?"

"Trust us," we say at the same time. But we have to dump the car.

Danny and I decide parking anywhere within the pentacle is unsafe, including the borders. We're going to have to trudge through more unknown territory in the dark. We turn into a driveway about halfway down Red Rock Road. It leads to another beautifully restored farmhouse I've never seen before. I calculate that we're a good two miles from the farm. We can stick close to the road along the tree line to keep from getting lost. A thirty-something man barges out of the front door with a shotgun in hand, demanding to know what's going on. I explain that there's an FBI investigation occurring and ask him if he's heard gunshots. Danny whips out his military ID and tells him he needs to take immediate shelter away from the village. He puts the gun down.

"We've been hearing gunshots all goddamn night. We've lost our landline connection and we've been calling 911 for the past hour. No one answers." He looks at me and asks why I'm wearing an evening dress. I had forgotten how I was dressed and look down at what's left of my gown.

"Let's just say this isn't exactly what I had in mind tonight either. There's no time to explain everything. You're not safe."

I advise him to gather a few days of supplies and get out. Danny convinces him that the current situation is top secret and not to call the authorities, or it could derail the mission. We wait impatiently for he and his wife to pack. They finally emerge, and the man pushes his crying and trembling wife into their BMW SUV. I give her a gentle pat on her back and tell her it's going to be all right. "We're here to help. Our only concern is your safety." She nods and attempts to put on a brave face.

We have our guns drawn as they pull out of their garage. They give Ryan permission to replace their car with the Jeep for now. They just want out. We escort them to the end of the drive and give them the go-ahead when we feel the coast is clear. We hear the tires screech almost all the way up the hill. Back in the house, we shut off their lights and pull the Jeep inside the garage. I'm never going to make it down the hill in heels, so I raid the woman's closet. I find a pair of sweats and a T-shirt and take her sneakers. I shove Katie's dress in a ball and put it in my bag. Ryan tries to convince us to stay here instead of our house, but we both explain that we'll be safer in the house. He doesn't understand our rationale but trusts us.

We begin our downhill hike through the woods. It's rocky and overgrown with vines and broken tree limbs. I'm getting scratched by branches and sticker bushes with each step. With the exception of a little bit of light from the moon, we're pretty much going at this blind. We hold off using any light in fear of being seen. I'm doing pretty well, considering, but am taken off guard as I trip over a log. *Shit!*

I get back on my feet and call out for Danny and Ryan, fearing it may not have been a log. Danny looks around before shining his light. It's a body. The body of Sal's father, no less. I let out a big sigh. Even though I probably shouldn't care, I can't help but think of Sal and his mom. They're going to be crushed. I go in for a closer look, wanting to see the cause of death in case it's important. It's pretty obvious. There's an arrow sticking out of his chest. I'm surprised whoever did this left his body here. We have no choice but to press on. I cover Mr. Rossi with leaves and some brush and try to take note of the surroundings for Sal. Even though he may not deserve it, I want to make sure they can give him a proper burial. Even more cautiously, we continue hiking.

The farm is finally in sight. We spot about a half-dozen men wandering around the property. Ryan recognizes a few of them. They work for his dad. We discuss our options. Ryan has the contact info to one of the guys and calls. "What the fuck, Mike?" I can hear the man right through the line. Ryan lowers the volume, so it doesn't echo right back down to them.

"Listen, my father's in trouble and has called a meeting. It's mandatory. Can you and the guys be back at the house in ten minutes?"

The guard is quiet and asks where *he* is. "I just left the event. Shane's been shot. A lot has happened. I can explain when we get there."

Ryan's explanation is good enough for them. The men begin vacating the premises. I can hear the dogs barking inside and know they must be so scared. I purposefully left one window open. It faces the side of the road, but it's better than facing the barn or Jodi's house. I convince them to let me go first and to cover me. Just when I think I'm going to pull it off, I'm grabbed from behind.

"And where do you think you're going?" I can't see him, and his voice isn't familiar. He turns me around to face him and I gasp. It must be the Native American that Sal saw in the arena or someone else from the reservation. He's not in full headdress or anything, but there's no mistaking his ancestry. He looks at me waiting for an actual answer and, so far, hasn't taken any action to harm me. I'm expecting him to throw a sack over my head and carry me to punishment, but he's just staring at me. The silence is weird, so I break it.

"Trying to get to safety, sir. Who are you?" His eyes narrow and squint, trying to figure me out. Our stare-down is brief. Danny moves in and sucker punches him, knocking him out cold.

"You all right?" Ryan asks and holds me close.

"I'm fine. Any idea who that man is?" Ryan has no clue. He didn't even know the old Indian reservation was inhabited at all. Assuming that's where he came from.

"What should we do with him?"

Danny looks at me and says, "The safe."

"Will he have enough air?" I wonder.

"In that thing? Enough for days if necessary." I climb in the window and look for more enemies. The dogs are confused, torn between attacking us and looking for attention as Danny and Ryan drag the man through the window. They're spinning in circles, tails between their legs. I grab some duct tape from the utility room, and they tape the man's hands and feet and drag him into the basement. I check to make sure he's still breathing. I really want to slap him awake for an interrogation, but there's no time. Ryan's impressed with the size of the safe as they lay him gently on the ground.

They look him over one more time, lock the vault, and Danny

replaces the paneling as best he can. We make our way back to the main floor and try to calm the barking dogs. I can see that they've lost control of their bowels and bladders a few times in the house, so there's no use in worrying about potty breaks. I grab a few cans of food and their bowls, and Danny leads the way upstairs, calling for the dogs to follow. Ryan's curious as hell about where we're taking him.

Just as we reach the top of the stairs, we hear voices downstairs. They're in. Whoever "they" are. Danny tosses the ladder outside to make it look like we escaped and recites the password. I lock the door to my old room to buy us a few more minutes if needed. The door opens to the crawlspace and Ryan and I pile in with Sonny and Cher behind us. Danny quietly shuts the closet door, the hidden panel, and finally the door to our new safe room. The room lights up like magic, and Ryan and the dogs are in awe.

48

STORY TIME

S onny and Cher are pacing, not knowing what to make of the space. They take turns barking, which makes me terribly nervous. Maybe I should've left them downstairs. Danny reassures me that the room is almost completely soundproof. The only room we need to worry about is the bathroom where he split the ventilation. He covers it with a towel for now to muffle any sound just in case. I crack open their food, hoping it will help, and place it in their bowls. They sniff it, reject it at first, then finally give in to hunger. Danny pours them some water and they go to town making a mess.

They're finally at ease and settle into a far corner and lay down. They place themselves strategically where they can't be snuck up on and scan the room. They look up at the lights, take in their surroundings, and give in to exhaustion, probably feeling safer than they have all day within this den-like space. I think about the Dorcys. I need to warn Jack at some point tomorrow. He needs to prepare himself and Katie for their homecoming, but I don't know how to prepare anyone for something like this.

Ryan's sitting on the ground near me, watching me and shaking his head in disbelief. "Okay, what am I looking at here?" Danny and I both laugh. It's still so amazing even to me, and there's not another person in the world I feel more at ease allowing in our private safe place than Ryan. Before I begin to explain, I lean in and give him a kiss. He returns it and I realize how natural it feels. Like we're really a couple.

Danny reaches into one of the shelves and pulls out a bottle of wine.

"No way!" I tell him my first thought when I saw some of the supplies. He opens it and pours us each a cup. "Sorry, no wine glasses."

For the next half hour, while no doubt there are numerous people coming in and out of the house looking for us, Danny and I explain the room. Ryan is touched and captivated by the whole story. "This is by far one of the most incredible spaces I've ever seen in my life. I totally understand why you wanted to be in here now." Ryan backs up against the beanbag chair and says, "I think it's time you explained all of this hunting and pentacle talk now." Danny stands up and pulls out some markers.

"Wait. Is that a whiteboard?"

"Yes, it is, dear sister," he says in a childish tone.

"You're a creative genius."

"Well, I have to admit, when I painted them, I thought we'd reunite for a game of *Pictionary*." I smile remembering it being one of our favorite board games we'd bring in to play.

Now Danny's using it to draw the geographical pentacle. He catches Ryan up using diagrams with the skills he's developed as an architect. He's drawn the perfect depiction of everything from the pentacle to the church to the memorial. Ryan's eager to see the memorial and can't believe he's wasted so much energy trying to learn what happened to his brother, when the answer was here all along. He's eager to see everything. I'm kind of eager just to take the two men I love more than anyone else and get out of Brandtville. But

I know we're in for a battle at some point before we can wash our hands of our families and this town forever.

It's Ryan's turn. He starts by telling us about his childhood, which was fairly normal in the beginning. His father was, in fact, a huge legitimate real estate mogul and inherited millions from his grandfather and great grandfather. He said our fathers became close going to Mission Church together but otherwise, he had no idea they were into something as malicious as what we're describing. He's truly baffled.

"They began attending Mission Church together around the time of Doug's disappearance. My father told us that they had a lot in common because they both lost sons." He looks at Danny. "Guess that wasn't true. Nothing's been true. Who knows how long they've really known each other."

Ryan's mother belonged to Mission Church but didn't go very often, saying she didn't like what they were doing there, but she wouldn't say why. Guess we all know now. Instead, she devoted herself to the foundation. It gave her purpose. Ryan was young, just like us, when he and Jackie were sent to boarding school. They went to separate places in the Pacific Northwest not far from Danny and me. Danny's boarding school turned out to be only eighty miles away from mine in Idaho. If only we had known. Jackie and Ryan went to schools outside of Vancouver. They were told it had to be that way so the family could focus on Doug's disappearance. When Ryan graduated, he came home to a huge addition on the property with an entire team working around the clock. His father was elusive and private, so he avoided him and worked alongside his mother instead.

"One day, I overheard my parents yelling at each other. They didn't realize I was in the other room. My mother was demanding to know what was happening in the church. She said they were keeping secrets from a Grand Master or something. She said she watched them go down into a cellar with what looked like a prisoner. So, from what you're telling me, this adds up. My father told her she was crazy and that he would send her to a loony bin if she ever said anything like that again. She became withdrawn and would sneak out of the house. I'm guessing she discovered some of the things you found or the beginnings of it. Maybe that's why she chose to kill herself in the church. She wanted to taint it." He looks down solemnly, so I reach out and hold his hand. He takes it and smiles.

"Soon after, I was ordered to work remotely while watching you. To be honest, I was happy to take on the job to get out of this town. My sister moved out too. You'll never guess where?"

"Where?"

"She's in the townhouse next to mine. Shane stays with her often. They're very close, so I'm glad she's the one who took him to Hopkins."

"Are you serious? I don't remember ever seeing her."

"Speaking of, I almost forgot to tell you that I got a text. They just got there and everything's going well." I'm tremendously relieved to hear that. I know John will take good care of him. I'm not sure what to tell him when I get back. Will we get back? Ryan explains some more about his sister. "She's a workaholic and very passionate about the foundation. I'm worried about what all of this is going to do to her."

"Wow." I shake my head. "We'll all take care of each other. That's all."

"I like that plan. Anyway, I was about to abandon this life altogether. Join the military. Anything. But, one day I was eavesdropping on our fathers while they were talking." He moves me away so he can look at me while he speaks. "I heard your father tell mine that he would confine you if you continued to elude and disgrace him. That's when I started protecting you from him as well as for him. I covered for you. A lot! I was afraid of what he was capable of doing. I was told you were the only surviving member of your family and that you still had enemies, including Sal's family. I was told in no uncertain terms that it was my duty to protect you, and I accepted it as my role."

"And I was a real sport, wasn't I? Ryan, I wish you would have just told me everything. I would have behaved so much better."

"I couldn't. My father threatened me in the worst possible way. He threatened to remove and replace me with someone else."

"Why didn't you?"

He looks at me with great endearment. "Because I cared about you. I had feelings for you and was unwilling to trust anyone else with your life. Even though you made me nuts."

I'm so touched. I look at Danny who's tilted his head, loving this romantic story. I feel a tear run down my cheek. I reach in, hug him close, and thank him for protecting me. He squeezes me hard and plants a soft tender kiss on my lips.

"Aww. Now I wish Fabrizio was here."

Ryan breaks free and asks, "Who?"

Now it's Danny's turn. He fills us in about his time spent in boarding school. He was lonely and scared and had the same separation anxiety. It wasn't until he got to Rome and met Fabrizio that he felt happiness again. He confided in Fabrizio about our childhood. He's the one who gave Danny hope that I was still alive and that we had just been betrayed. So, they flew in together and created the room. Danny figured either way, it was cathartic and made him feel better. They had no idea we'd need it under circumstances such as these.

We break the news about our grandfather—the serial killer of cult leaders. Not surprisingly, it's hard to believe the extent of odd behavior and criminal activity. He comes up with a quick theory that maybe he was really some sort of hit man. For the whole group. Maybe they don't like competition. That's something I hadn't considered.

It's getting late. We decide to get cracking on an early morning plan. I admit, I want to stay in here just like I did when I was little until we're safe and under the protection of the agency again. Danny and Ryan try to talk me into staying, but I can't. I know the layout of the pentacle better than they do. We gather our thoughts and develop an action plan. Ryan's not happy with the contact we've made with

Sal, but tries to see the advantages, especially hearing the details of his extreme predicament.

Things get really serious as we discuss the lengths to which we may need to go to end this catastrophe. We agree our priority is to end the rituals played out by this Order. As tough as I've been, I vote to remain without blood on our hands. None of us wants to be the next generation, as my father put it. I'd rather be the first generation to cleanse these so-called sacred grounds and correct the course. We agree, but vow to protect each other no matter what.

I'm getting sleepy and smile to hear the dogs snoring. We eat some of the emergency food Danny planted for us. It isn't great, but it's necessary. We grab sleeping bags and pillows and spread out. Danny removes the towel he stuffed in the vent and reminds us to stay quiet. He listens for voices but hears none. We're sure our enemies are close and plotting away. Most are probably confused by our disappearing act, especially about how the dogs could have vanished.

Ryan sets the timer on his watch for 5:30 a.m. Maybe if we're lucky, we'll get a solid four hours. He pulls me in so that my head is lying on his chest. As I listen to his heart beat, I know it's the last thing I want to hear at the end of every day, possibly for the rest of my life.

49

THE LENAPE INDIAN

We all jump at the sound of the alarm. It jacks up my heart rate, and my hands start to tremble. I have no idea what lies ahead of us. I just want it all to be over. I'm starting to forget what normal is and wish I could just go back to my "terrible" life from just a few days ago in Baltimore. In hindsight, that was a picnic. My father's words echo in my head. They go against every natural parental instinct. He's willing to put his only daughter in an arena where she, I, will be torn to pieces.

Ryan sees my anguish and embraces me. "Everything's going to be okay, babe."

I smile, liking the sound of that.

Danny looks out through the peephole and doesn't see any movement. I look out next, as far toward the barn as possible. I'm worried about the animals, but the stalls still look locked.

Our first goal is to check on the Native American. Danny opens the safe room door and peeks out, then shuts it again. My old bedroom is completely torn apart. Jack's computer is gone. Great. I shake my head and think of Jack and Katie. I have every intention of telling them this whole demented story. I hope it makes them rich. I also hope they forgive me.

Danny opens the door again and lets the dogs out. I call for them to stay, not wanting them to venture too far. They obey and wait for me to come out of hiding.

The house is seemingly empty, but things are turned upside down. We're sure there are still eyes all around the property. Together, we make our way in a single file down to the basement. As Danny removes the wood paneling, I'm half expecting to find the safe empty, wondering if my father got to it first. But the man is still there, quite awake, and not at all happy. The dogs are growling at him and the hair rises on their backs. I sooth them and try to convince them that it's all right.

The man can't move, so Danny and Ryan help him up and drag him over to Jack's workout bench. He's cursing up a storm. We all shush him and tell him to lower his voice. Danny releases his legs and helps him shake them out to get the blood circulating again.

With the light on, I can see him better. He's older than I thought, with deep lines and wrinkles. He has a grey goatee, and his matching long hair is hanging in a messy braid. He's wearing a pair of jeans, work boots, and a black T-shirt, which is drenched in sweat. I find an unopened bag of plastic cups and pour the man a big cup of water. His hands are still duct taped, so I have to hold it up to his mouth for him. He's irritated but thirsty and accepts, polishing off the whole thing.

I'm not really sure where to start, so I introduce myself, figuring he probably knows who I am already anyway. Danny and Ryan do the same.

"I've never heard of the two of you, but I sure as hell know who the Brandts are ... I assume you're Michael's son."

Ryan confirms the assumption.

"You've never heard of our father? Sean O'Rourke?"

"Why the hell would I?" It surprises us all. We assumed this man was part of their inner circle, the one representing the symbol for spirit.

"Now you know who we are, who are you?" Danny questions. "Why did you grab my sister?"

"The name is David Rawtom. My wife's second cousin maintains the old reservation on Church Road. I came to visit my son who's been staying on the property this summer. They were supposed to be preparing a museum of some sort for school children to come and learn about the Delaware River Lenape Indians. I was in for a rude awakening. No sooner did I pull in, I heard yelling and screaming and gunfire. I followed the sounds, which led me to this house. I couldn't believe my eyes." He looks down, lost in the traumatic memory of last night.

"Did you recognize any of the men on the property?"

"I recognized Michael Brandt and Ben Grover, the actor. He was walking around looking like fucking Rambo. He had on camouflage and weapons, the whole nine yards. At first, I thought I stumbled upon the set of a new movie or something. I was about to get comfortable and watch. But it was no movie. I saw my own flesh and blood shoot a man right in the chest with a bow and arrow. I hid behind a tree for what felt like an eternity. Finally, I saw you crawling in the window. I was hoping for an explanation, not a night in a wall safe. I thought I was going to suffocate."

"Could you describe the man your son shot?"

He describes Sal's father. He must have survived long enough to run into the woods. That's why his body is still there. I ask him if he knows anything about Mission Church and if he's aware of the sacred grounds.

"I don't know anything about Mission Church, or even much about the town. I'm from Detroit, for God's sake. My wife told me it's been there a long time. It's true, though, about the grounds. The grounds above the church that lead to the reservation are sacred Indian grounds. That was all going to be part of the school trip lecture. At one time, the largest colony of Lenape Indians occupied it. My wife and her family are descendants."

"What makes it sacred?" Ryan asks.

"Our ancestors believe in being one with nature. We believe in living in harmony with all people, animals, and even plant life to some extent. We rely on the physical earth to cooperate with the supernatural to bring us balance. We have an obligation to the land. So, yes, the reservation is protected and designated as sacred ground. You don't want to disrupt it. It may sound superstitious, but we feel disrupting it will plague the village. Why do I get the feeling that's already happening?"

I ask him if he knows about the wolves on the reservation. He nods. They were granted permission many years ago by the local government to own them.

"Wolves are symbolic to our people. But they're also dangerous and only let out to roam each day around noon from what my son told me. He said they provided a gated pasture of some kind. I personally haven't seen it. I've seen the wolves though. Beautiful animals."

His story seems believable. I ask him more about his son. He has sadness in his eyes but attempts a smile as he talks.

"We sent my son off with his older cousins to give him new direction in life. To do something important. He struggles with drugs. Now he's killed a man. I'd say he's in serious trouble with the law. You need to take this damn tape off so I can find him and turn him in."

We agree, but Danny has a hand on his pistol.

"What are the three of you going to do? We need to get the Feds involved."

Danny agrees and tells him we're on it and not to worry, but that we need to go back to the Brandt Estate to try and talk to our fathers. Mr. Rawtom wants to head back to the reservation on his own, which is probably a good idea. Maybe he can straighten the mess out up there. We wish him good luck and open the door. Danny and Ryan cover him until he disappears into the woods.

"He's lying," Danny says.

"What makes you think so?" Ryan asks.

"When I removed the tape from his ankles, I saw a tattoo. It was pentacle with a wolf in the center. It looked a little like the one from the church."

"Why did we send him back to the reservation then?"

"To buy us time. By the time he tells his people that we're heading back to the Brandt Estate, hopefully most of the gang will wait for us there. The only place we haven't really explored yet is the windmill up there on the Grover's property. I say we give it a quick look and then work our way back through the woods toward the memorial." We agree.

The farm is quiet. Way too quiet. I let the dogs do their thing and put them back into the safe room. At least one of us has to be alive enough to get them out later.

50

THE WINDMILL

We begin our route to the windmill through the woods behind Jodi's house. Danny's ticked to find the Harley completely dismantled.

"Sons of bitches."

I can see the large windmill poking up through the trees. It's bigger than most windmills, and since it's been restored, I have to assume it's still being used. Most of the windmills in this area are rustically beautiful from a distance, but old and rotted up close. This one is unique, still functioning, with five blades, which could be symbolic. Normally, a mill like this would be used for crop irrigation. There's a large cornfield in the distance. The Grovers are the last couple I'd predict were farmers. A cover perhaps. I can't imagine Jill getting her hands dirty.

Again, we run into the obstacle of a fence. This one is also wrought iron, but without the barbs, and circles the entire property. The house is lovely, like all of the others, and has a barn with several horses grazing in a field. Jill riding horses—now that I can visualize.

Closer now, I can see that the windmill isn't running. It sits within the borders of their property but away from the cornfield. If the mill isn't powering the water supply, I have to assume the Grovers use it as another form of energy source. Maybe electricity?

We've reached the limits of the protection of the woods and will have to continue by ducking into the cornfield. I have a fear of being captured with some of our vital equipment, especially the keys that open the doors to the church prison as well as the holding cell by the memorial. I dart up the last tree before the cornfield and place the keys and a phone safely on a flat branch. I'm trying to think of every worst-case scenario and ways to get out of it. I hope Sal comes through if I end up in the arena.

Out of the tree and into the cornfield we go. It's late summer, so the stalks are taller than we are, thankfully. It would take us way too long to crawl. Danny points out that there are stairs leading up to the large stone base of the mill. There's definitely a big space inside, perhaps one that holds the mechanical and plumbing systems. This is Danny's territory, but we decide that it's safer for me to try and enter the windmill while Ryan and Danny cover me. We need to get over the fence, which is tricky. I get a leg-up from Danny and climb over. Ryan gives Danny the same leg-up maneuver but has to rely entirely on his arm strength for his own trip over the fence. He slips a few times but manages with only a few bloody scratches. He gives me a mini nervous breakdown worrying that he won't make it.

I'm ready to investigate and creep my way toward the mill. I climb up the short set of stairs and realize there's a combination to get in. Frustrated, I'm about to turn around and tell Danny, but see the door is damaged. It's loose so I give it a good yank. It gives. *Sweet!* I look back at Danny and Ryan and give them a thumbs-up before cautiously stepping inside. It's a mechanical room with a terrible stench. Spoiled water? I put my head in my shirt to keep from getting sick. I look up first and can see all the way up to the turbine blades. Then I notice splattered paint across the walls. Nope. It's blood. I take a closer look at the ground and see bone and body parts at the far end. The bloody walls feel like they're closing in on me. I can't get out fast enough.

I open the door, looking for the comfort I need from Ryan and Danny, but find that I'm alone. Through the fence, toward the house, I see they're being led to the Grover Estate by four men. They're coming for me too. Two men, as well as Jill, are sprinting in my direction. If it were just Jill, I'd take her on, but her bodyguards are enormous. I don't have the same upper body strength as Ryan and need to take a running leap at the fence. I get up far enough to grasp the top and pull myself over. There's no time to worry about my bloody scratches. I turn toward the cornfield and run for my life.

I know if I stay in a direct line, it'll take me into unfamiliar woods, and I risk getting lost or caught. They will also likely expect that approach, since it's the fastest and simplest. Instead, I take a diagonal route, but I have to move much more slowly to avoid shaking the stalks.

I come up on a dilapidated old stone building and rush in for cover. I bolt through the doors and up a ladder into a loft, pulling the ladder up behind me. Graffiti covers the walls and beer cans are littered throughout. This is obviously the local teenage party spot. Through a window, I see the stalks swaying. I duck into a corner with wood scraps and random debris. Spiders scurry. I try not to think about it, but my father taught us about black widows around the same time as copperheads. I'm quiet and peek out again. They're coming my way to check the building. I have no plan other than to hope not to be seen.

I look at my watch. It's 8:00 a.m. Danny and Ryan will be placed in the punishment arena by noon. I hold back tears and wish we would have just quit while we were ahead. This could have been over, but now I have to fix it. I lay down in a fetal position. They'll only spot me if they can get up into the loft. I hear shuffling as the men enter the building. I've got a hand on my gun and am tempted to get up and start shooting but remember the pact we're trying to keep. I'll shoot in self-defense, but I won't initiate violence.

Their search is over, but I stay still long enough to be sure they're really gone. As I lie here, I wonder whose blood and bones were in the windmill. I wonder if one of Sal's relatives accidentally crawled up the ladder and was killed by the motor. I doubt it. I think it was yet another cruel way to symbolically get rid of a so-called enemy. I look at my watch and decide twenty minutes is long enough. If they didn't find me, they'll head back to the Grover Estate.

I'm unsure how to make my way back to the pentacle without being seen, so I decide I'll have to take the long way around it some-how. There's another farmhouse on the other side of the cornfield, so I make a break for it. I see a big old Lincoln Navigator in the driveway with my name written all over it. I need to get back to the keys and the phone. It's nearing 9:00 a.m.

I make a run for the SUV, which is thankfully open, keys in the ignition. At least something is going my way. I start the engine and pull out of the driveway. As I'm reversing, I see blood again. Lots of blood splattered in the back. I try not to think about it, because I need to get out of here. I decide to investigate when I'm safer and back on a main road.

My foot shakes and I struggle to maintain pressure on the acceler-ator. Once I'm far enough away, I pull onto an unfamiliar dirt road, stop the car, and get out. With gun pulled, I open the liftgate and find three broken and battered bodies lying twisted together in the trunk. I throw up, look back, and throw up again.

I see stars and am beginning to feel faint. I sit down and put my head between my legs to avoid hyperventilating. As much as I don't want to, I need to go in for a closer look to see who they are. In their state they're tough to identify, but I'm fairly certain I don't recognize any of them. As far as I can tell, none of them are part of Sal's family or part of my father's group either. I'm about to make my way back on foot, because there's no way I'm driving around with a vehicle full of dead people, when I see a hand move.

I hold back a scream and try to overcome the terror. I look closer at him, trying to distinguish his body from the others, when his eyes fly open. I fall back on my ass, get up, and run, giving in to my fight or flight. Only a few yards down the road, though, I come to my senses, realizing I don't have it in me to leave the man.

I take a deep breath and slowly make my way back to the SUV for another look. The man is now alert and pleading for me to help him. I tug at a stiff arm of the body closest to me, which allows him enough room to move. He rubs his head, which has fresh blood flowing from a gash. Otherwise, he's in much better condition than his fellow passengers.

I shift the bodies aside and release him completely. "Where am I?" he asks. I give him a general idea and ask who he is. "I work for the Douglas Brandt Foundation. Technically, I work for the government, but occasionally we come to Brandtville. My friends and I were here to support Michael at the event last night" He's trying to get his bearings and remember the details of what happened. As he looks at the other two people with him in the trunk, he remembers. "Oh no. Oh no."

"Shh. I know this is hard. Try to tell me what happened. I need to know."

"It was Mr. Brandt. He rounded the three of us up. We were in some kind of church. We've been working with the foundation for years. Why would he do this?"

Oh, this poor man. I examine his head. He was lucky. It's a graze wound, but it's deep enough to have made him look terminal. Whoever piled the men in here must have a plan for later.

"For starters, you worked with a man who no one really knew up until now."

"He was a minister. He baptized my whole family," he recalls, confused.

"Where's your family? Are they here in Brandtville?"

"No. Our home is in D.C. Hopefully, they're safe."

I wonder how many other victims had no idea about Mr. Brandt's alternative belief system. He needs to be stopped. They're way off their platform of killing people who deserved it.

Even in his horror-movie condition, I ask the man if it's possible to gather enough strength to take the SUV and get help. I warn him that he can't go to the local police and advise him to aim for Doylestown. He's starting to get his wits about him and thinks he can do it. I help him back in the SUV and into the driver's seat. He looks traumatized but able to withstand the drive. *Maybe.*

"What about you, miss?"

"I'll be all right. Just get as far away as you can."

"You should come with me."

"I can't. I need to find my friends. You go and get help."

"Be safe."

He's weak but seems okay to drive. He thanks me and floors it, disappearing onto the backroads and out of the village.

I'm left alone again and have to make up time. I'm less than three hours from high noon, which is a phrase I'm becoming too familiar with. I jog around the perimeter. I know the general area and focus on heading southeast. I turn a corner and spot our old Catholic church. I carefully open the doors, look around, and light a candle. I kneel down and say a prayer to St. Christopher and every other Saint I can think of. It's do or die time, and I'm praying I have a guardian angel watching over me.

51

SHORT FUSE

I'm completely out of breath by the time I reach the far corner of the Grover Estate. I ran a good two miles to get back to where I left the keys. I have Katie's sneakers on and feel blisters forming. I climb up the tree and thankfully find everything where I left it. The tree is tall, so I take the opportunity to climb further up and look around. I'm higher than I've ever been in a tree except for the stands near the memorial. I have a full view of the Grover Estate. There's very little activity. I can only see one person standing guard at what looks like the only gated entrance to the house. I like the odds and start making my way toward it.

I hear the gate open and see a red pickup truck gaining access. Without overanalyzing, I race toward it and with a little luck make it before the gate closes. I kneel aside the truck with my back to the passenger's side. The driver and the security guard are engaging in a conversation.

"What do you mean you lost her? She saw the inside of the mill. If Sean or Mike find out how she killed them, we're all dead. She went against every rule and left the mill a bloody mess. We had no time to clean up."

"And Georgie said she took them guys from D.C. out of the cell and pulverized them too. What's worse, she wants me to clean everything up. How the fuck did they break the code so easily?"

"Door was busted. One of them put up a fight," the driver says. "Jill is out of control. We all know this ain't the way it's supposed to be. My parents must be rolling around in their graves." The main security guard agrees and sounds frantic.

"We have to keep it between us for now, but make no mistake, the Grovers will pay for this."

I pop up and point the gun at the security guard. "I won't tell if you give me more information about Jill."

The security guard puts his hands in the air, but the driver attempts to take off. I shoot and blow out two tires. He brakes and retreats. I tell them both to relax and ask them to open the door to the house. The guard is even more upset now.

"Lady, you have no idea what you're doing," he yells. We enter into a contemporary living space. Everything is very white. White marble floors, a white leather sectional, and white walls. Throw in a white straitjacket and you've got yourself a ward.

"You're right. I don't know exactly what I'm doing, so please enlighten me. I want more information about Jill Grover. But first, I want to know where my brother and Michael Brandt Jr. are now! And while you're at it, tell me who was slaughtered mercilessly in the mill."

They look at each other. The security guard says, "You're Sean's daughter?"

I nod.

"We were told your whole family was murdered. We've seen your headstones."

"Yeah well, surprise! Who'd you think I was, then?"

"They said you were the daughter of the people who own Red Rock Farm," the driver says. The looks on their faces seem true to their words.

"Well, lying seems to be the name of the game around here."

"Honestly, we're not high up enough to know much. Aside from keeping guard, our biggest job is to not ask questions. We thought we knew enough about the rules up until last night. Shit got real crazy then. People we thought were friends turned on each other. We still don't know who's friend or foe. We've both just tried staying alive by following orders and remaining loyal to the Grovers, Sean, and Mike. Our current mission is to find you, who we were told was Jessica Dorcy, and bring you to the Brandt Estate unharmed."

"Well, here I am. Maybe that's exactly what we should do. Is that where they took my brother and Michael? I would prefer it if we're all together anyway. But first, who was killed in the mill? And why?"

They need more encouragement.

"I'm not going to say a word. But you realize this whole town is going to implode by the end of the day, don't you? Neither of you will have jobs. Your loyalty means nothing. You're not protecting anyone. In fact, after you drop me off, I would take off and try and get yourselves a good old-fashioned alibi for not being here. The Feds, Secret Service, and every agency in between is going to have a literal field day over this."

They know I'm right and aren't sure what to do. "So, who's in the mill?"

The driver speaks. "Ben and Jill brought several people into the mill. They seemed to have a system. Like they've done it before. That mill is iconic, sacred even. Mike and Sean like this section of the ecosystem, if you will, to be sanitary. That's why everything's white. It's an area of purity, sustainability, and trust."

"Describe who they brought into the mill."

He describes Antonio to a T and said the other man worked for the foundation. "I knew him well," the driver says. "He was a good man. If they did that to him, they'd probably do it to us." They're scared, and I don't blame them.

I curse under my breath. I didn't like Antonio, but knowing I was stepping on his body parts in the mill makes me dry heave. The Grovers may be even bigger animals than my own father. "What's the deal with Jill Grover?" They look at each other. One rolls his eyes and the other shakes his head. "She's a loose cannon. She's from here, but her father took the family to Prague when she was a teen. Her father was a professor but was also working on some top-secret project or something. Jill was taken and held hostage by an enemy looking for information. For how long, Bobby?" He looks at the other man.

"Oh, like six months or something. They abused her mercilessly. Michael and Sean found the men and killed them. She came home with her mother, but later her father was found murdered too. Her mother was my aunt. May she rest in peace."

"So much death! How'd she hook up with Ben?"

"Well, she's hot, so ..." I shake my head, wishing I didn't know he was that shallow.

"So, what do you say you follow orders and take me over to the Brandt Estate?"

From a side door, Jill slips in. I'm not terribly surprised to find that she's been listening. Before I can blink, she shoots both men dead. My eyes are closed, waiting for the next shot to be mine.

"You can open your eyes, Jenny. As much as I'd love the honor of killing you, I have my own orders. Give me your gun and keep your mouth shut about the mill. If you say a word, I'll make sure Danny is chopped into pieces too." She has my gun and the phone I didn't get to use, but I still have the keys for whatever they're worth, stuffed in my bra.

I look back at the men. They've painted the room red. I think of the disturbing details I now know about her. "You know, Jill, karma is a real bitch. You're screwing up and it's going to come back to bite you. Literally." She laughs at me like I'm out of touch. Jill's in denial about her current situation.

"Yes, I must congratulate you for turning our Order upside down. But you're the one facing karma. I look forward to seeing you punished at the hands of your own father. I'm not sure if you'll have a hunt or an execution. Sean will decide." She looks at her watch. "He'll have to decide soon because we're running out of time."

"How did someone like you end up sitting on the corner of the pentacle which represents purity and trust?"

"That's for me to know and for you to never find out. But Sean and Mike trust us more than anyone in the world."

"Real trustworthy from what I just heard. The men who kidnapped you did a number on you, didn't they?"

"Shut up! You don't know me. But you, Sean's own daughter. Even if you pass through the arena unharmed today, you'll never have the privilege of being initiated into our way of life. Never. I'll make sure of it. To think of the plans they had for you. Ha!"

"Here's a little news flash for you, I'd rather be dead than be a part of your so-called way of life. And here's another tidbit, Mission Church and whatever cult you all claim to be part of will cease to exist after today. That's a promise."

With that proclamation, she clocks me in the same place my father hit me, splitting my lip open. I taste blood. I have no intention of killing anyone today, but I may have to give this maniac a beating if I get the chance.

"Mind your mouth. Let's go."

She leads me through the house and into the garage where Ben joins us. I smile at him with blood-stained teeth. "I'd still like that self-ie." He looks at me with disdain. I may as well remain defiant to the end. I take a seat in the back next to him while Jill drives. I assumed we were heading to the Brandt Estate, but we're definitely heading for the church. *Oh no.* I only have a key to the room, not the cells. We pull into a spot and Ben shoves me out of the car. They each have an arm on mine as we enter the church. The key players are standing in the front, along with some very angry-looking congregation members.

We bypass any jury system and head down the basement stairs. As predicted, I'm led into a cell. As I look around, I notice each has a different symbol consistent with Mr. Brandt's pin. They all contain Latin words for each element. I'm in "terra" for earth, my father's private holding cell. The rest of the walls are too difficult to decode. They're an extensive eyesore of symbolism. "I want to speak to my father. Now!" I order.

My father limps down the stairs and pulls up a chair in front of my cell. His eyes are black and blue from the broken nose he sustained on behalf of Ryan. While I'm eyeing up his face, he takes note of the fresh blood on my cheek and lip and calls for Jill. She comes down the stairs, looking smug and proud of herself.

"Yes, Sean?"

"Did you touch her? Why does she have a fresh bruise and a fat lip?" Now she looks nervous. "Did you lay a hand on my daughter?"

"I apologize, Sean. She was taunting me. She told me our society would cease to exist after today. It was a knee-jerk reaction."

"Trust, Jill. All you had to do was obey orders and bring her to me unharmed. You broke the trust and we both know it's not the first time." I can see the fear in Jill's eyes. My father goes from a calm sitting position to a standing position. He swings hard and punches her in the face, much harder than he's ever hit me. She goes down without the ability to break her fall and her head hits the concrete, making an awful sound. I can't help but think, *"the agony of defeat,"* like Danny sang to me after I fell off my bike. I'm warped and hope it's just because I'm exhausted.

I didn't even have to mention the mill to get that reaction out of my father. Ben is upstairs asking what's happening. My father tells him to return to his duties. I'm so stunned that I can't speak. He's annoyed and exhales loudly as he opens her own symbolic cell that says "aer" and drags her inside. Her mouth is hanging open, and I can definitely see she's down a few teeth. He's got a shorter fuse than even I remember.

He locks her cell and casually sits back down in front of me like he just handed her a cup of tea instead of a Mike Tyson left hook.

"So, here you are, Jenny. See where your rebellious nature has gotten you?"

"Where are Danny and Ryan? Please don't put them in that

arena. Just stop all of this." He grins at me, taking pleasure in my emotional stress.

"No, honey. Their punishment will be to watch *you* in it though. Is there anything you'd like to say to me before your trial? Everyone gets a chance for some last words."

I'm not half as brave as I had been. I'm thinking hard of how to play it. I could play into any fatherly affection, if he has any human feelings left, or remain defiant. It's a tough call, so I try a little bit of both.

"Well, I guess I'd like to remind you that you've drastically underestimated me thus far. You have no mercy, but if I get out of the arena alive, I'll show you as much mercy as I can. I'm not like you. I prefer to focus on the good and not all of this revenge. It's a terrible waste of time and energy. Imagine the good you could be doing with your talent and power." I'm staring into his eyes.

"What happened to you, Dad? What was so awful in your life that makes you justify doing these terrible things? You had it so good. We were a family. We all worshipped you." He almost looks apologetic. *Almost.* He's looking at me, searching for words. Perhaps recalling memories from his childhood. "What was your father like? I read about him you know. Before all of that, what kind of father was he? Just like you? Cruel? You'll no doubt top him in that department if that's been your goal."

"You have it all wrong. We do good work here. We do what our justice system is incapable of doing and make sure those who deserve it are punished. People like my father. I only wish I had the chance ..." He stops himself. "But we do it humanely, Jenny, through nature, and give people the chance to repent. If it was meant to be, they'll pass through unharmed. And this is such a small part of our culture."

He believes this. He truly believes it's his God-given mission to carry on with this work, which started in Brandtville a long time ago, or so he says. Maybe it started with the best of intentions. But my father and his crew of killers have taken it to a whole new level. They're nothing more than a sophisticated, very dark, cult of vigilantes. I don't know where the Kool-Aid is coming from, but they're drinking massive doses. He's looking at me like he's still hopeful that he can get through to me, that I will buy into this.

"You know, Dad, there's no hope for someone like me against a wolf."

"You're my daughter and you're strong and resourceful. We will make a great team someday. I fully expect you to survive."

I look over at a knocked-out Jill. "You really trust all the people you say you do? The people in your congregation?"

"Jill will get a slap on the wrist for touching you without my permission, but yes, I trust her. She's loyal. Better be after everything I've done for her."

I figure it's a good time to narc on Jill, hoping it will buy me out of the arena. I describe what I saw in the mill and tell him exactly who was murdered. I describe it so vividly that he has no choice but to believe me. "That can't be," he says, more like a question than a statement.

"Why would I lie?" He stands up and I can see the veins popping out of both sides of his temple. His temper is flaring again.

"I wish you luck, Jenny, hope you'll survive, repent, and work by my side." With that said, he limps back up the stairs. According to my watch, I have an hour left before noon.

52

GAME TIME

I sit in my cell trying to strategize. My father survived a hunt in the arena—maybe I can too. I wonder if playing dead is an option. The wolves like running after game and hunger for the chase. I consider it as a possibility to surviving. My true hope is that Sal will be waiting for me, and hope he isn't among the dead. I also hope he didn't chicken out and run home. That wouldn't surprise me either.

As I'm mentally going through my options, I hear Jill moan. She's coming to. I watch her in silence, waiting for her reaction to her own predicament. She manages to push herself into a sitting position, rubs her face, and realizes that she's missing teeth.

She looks mortified, and I can't help but get a devilish grin on my face. She's by far the most vain woman I've ever laid eyes on. She doesn't appreciate my expression and jumps to her feet. "This is all your fault."

"Technically, it's your fault, Jill. You had orders. So much for that trust thing." She's livid, screaming for Ben and the others to let her out. No one comes to her rescue. Grief-stricken, she sits back down on her bench.

"My father has one hell of a temper, doesn't he?" She throws me a dirty look.

"He's just teaching me a lesson. He won't punish me like he will you."

"You sure about that? I may have spilled a few details about the mill."

"Fuck you! No, you didn't!"

"Karma, Jill."

That does her in. There's no way out now, and she knows it. After what I saw in the meat mill earlier, I don't feel sorry for her at all. The clock is ticking and I'm getting more and more nervous. A woman comes down the stairs, carrying two grey prison uniforms. She hands one to me and tells me to get dressed. Then she hands the other one to Jill. I check her again for a reaction.

"What the fuck? You've got to be kidding me."

The woman looks shaky and apologizes to Jill. "Sean is going to put you both in the arena together." This news even catches *me* off guard.

"No. That's not a rule. Everyone would have to be in agreement."

"You can do this, Jill. You're strong. Then Michael will baptize you and you'll have all the same privileges. It'll be okay."

Jill loses it and starts crying We're left to change, and I suggest to Jill maybe it's a good idea to strategize together. "In all of your years putting people in that arena, how many have come out alive? Is there a particular strategy that works best?"

"Here's a news flash for *you*, Jenny. Virtually no one survives a hunt. I've only seen three people live. The wolves are trained to kill anyone in these fucking clothes. Your father survived because he literally overpowered his wolf. He managed to get the upper hand and struck the wolf with a rock. Now he's your father's wolf. If you do manage to overpower one, be sure it's still alive. That's the rule, or at least it was the rule. Margo up there will tell us all about it once we enter the arena. You already killed one, so you should've already gotten the death sentence."

"Well, I didn't know the rules when I did that. So ..."

Reality is kicking in and I start to tremble. I can't believe this is really happening. It's felt mostly like a bad nightmare up until this point. But it's real, and it's sick. I find a little hope in a new idea. The new information Jill gave me is interesting. I plan on stripping off my clothes as soon as I run.

"Jill, why don't you run toward your house, since that's your territory? Plus, isn't your husband without a wolf? If you run toward that gate, they'll have to release a dog further away." It's not like I care about her, I just don't want her running toward my father. That's where I'm going.

"That's what I'm planning on doing. What, do you think I'm stupid?"

"Not the sharpest tack." She throws me a dagger.

It's game time. I hear the door open again, and two men come to retrieve us. Jill is screaming profanity and vowing to punish them for doing this to her. I assume this must usually be her job. My heart is beating out of my chest. I'm shaking and feel a sense of doom. I can't help but let tears stream down my face. I just don't think I have a chance. Poor Ryan and Danny will have to witness me getting ripped apart and eaten.

Sacks are placed over our heads, and we're put in some sort of van. I can hear the wolves in the distance. I'm not sure I'm going to be able to move when the time comes.

The van stops, and we're ushered into the gothic folly fort. They close the door and remove our sacks temporarily. Danny and Ryan are tied up. Their eyes are red and they look like complete emotional wrecks. It breaks my heart to see them like this, but I have to stay focused. I tell them which way I'm running, not that they can do anything to help. But, just in case they can escape, they'll know I'll be heading back to the house. I look at Danny's hands and see how bloodied they are from trying to release himself from the zip ties. Even he looks hopeless. There's no app for this.

It's time. The sacks are placed back over our heads, and Ryan and

Danny yell at the top of their lungs for them to stop. We are ushered into the center of the arena and given our orders. We are to choose a gate. Each gate is an opportunity to survive and be reborn. Our destiny lies on the other side of each. As the woman continues explaining the rules of engagement, Jill tells her to shut up. She abides, but I'm annoyed that I didn't get to hear all the rules. Jill now has an advantage.

The sacks are removed. I look around and see all the main players. Ben looks visibly upset to see his wife in the arena but is indeed without a replacement wolf. I hear the drums, followed by a trumpet. It rouses the wolves. They look hungry and ready for a meal. The gates begin to open, and I take off before I'm supposed to, hoping it'll buy me some extra time. They should know by now that I'm not good at following orders, let alone partaking in this medieval bullshit. The leaders look at each other, not knowing what to do. Jill follows my lead and takes off in the direction of her husband.

I've got my shirt off and throw it near my father on the way out of the gate. My pants are off on the other side. It's just me and my panties and bra, out in nature. I look through the trees and spot Sal. I'm flooded with relief. He jumps down with gun in hand, but I tell him to be still. The wolf is coming, but it's confused without a chase or a scent. He stops and listens for the sound of his prey. I take the gun from Sal, trusting he's never shot a thing in his life, and aim. I get the wolf right between the eyes, and we run like hell in the direction of my old house.

Through the mass confusion, I hear Danny screaming to me, "There's more coming! Run, Jenny!" They must have released them all.

"Fuck me!" Sal yells. I ask him where the rest of his guys are, and he says they're down to two and waiting at the house. "They'll protect you if they can. This fight is between them and your father." I'm fine with that. We stop, hearing bloodcurdling screams, and know Jill has met her fate. It's chilling.

We're getting close to the creek, and my blisters are bleeding. I can feel the dampness around the pain. I turn around just in time to see the two remaining wolves coming at us. "Oh no, Sal." I stop and aim. They're coming at us fast and I'm only going to have time for one. I shoot and hear another shot simultaneously. Both wolves are down. Who shot the other one? I look around and see Jodi racing toward me.

I've never been so mad and happy to see anyone in my life. "Jodi!" There's no time for scolding. We embrace and keep moving. She confesses that she didn't want to lose me again and had to come back. She took her mom's car and left in the wee hours of the morning. *Good thing she didn't fall asleep.* We make it to the other side of the creek where Mr. Dennis is waiting. He's got his gun pulled. I tell Sal and Jodi to duck behind the trees. Sal and I make it, but Jodi takes a bullet to the leg. Sal drags her behind a bigger tree as she whimpers, holding her injury.

"Sal?" I yell. "I'm breaking my personal code."

"Do it," he agrees. I spot a stand a few trees away.

"Stay here with Jodi for a minute." I crawl toward the first one and run toward the next. I narrowly miss the next bullet meant to kill me. I climb up the stand as fast as I can. Mr. Dennis is gaining ground toward me. I take aim and fire, catching him in the shoulder. He stumbles back in disbelief, but it only motivates him more. He moves in quicker. Damn it! I don't want to have to do this. I have the gun pointed at his head, and if I pull the trigger, I'll kill him this time.

"Dennis, enough!" It's my father's voice. Mr. Dennis has his gun out still thinking about it. Why didn't my father let him take the shot? Mr. Dennis retreats as ordered and backs away. I climb down, and help Sal lift Jodi, each of us taking a leg. I'm suddenly glad she only weighs about ninety pounds.

We make it to the edge of the property, where my father is standing in the middle of the driveway. We're trapped with nowhere to go, and I realize I'm starting to lose the will to live. I can't handle another round of punishment. We're surrounded by my father's loyal followers. I have no choice but to drop my weapon.

My father throws my prison clothes back at me and tells me to get dressed. They have Sal in cuffs and drag him in the direction of the holding cell. I pat my bra as I get dressed. The keys are still in there. I wink at Sal, so he knows I have a plan. He nods. I'm mentally exhausted and need this to end now. One way or another, this is going to end.

Jodi looks pale and weak. She's got blood pulsing out with every heartbeat, streaming down her leg. I yell out to my father to help me make her a tourniquet. He looks around the yard and finds a stick, more like a branch. I tell him it's too big, but he keeps walking toward us. "What are you doing?" The men step back while I attempt to cover Jodi. "What are you doing, Dad?" I play the dad card hoping he'll snap out of it. "Dad, what are you doing?"

His eyes are fixated on Jodi. He pushes me aside like a rag doll, raises the branch, and practically splits Jodi's skull in half. I let out a scream so loud, it echoes several times from the surrounding rocks. I think of one of my father's favorite phrases. "This is going to hurt me more than you." Nothing could hurt me more than watching him do what he did to Jodi. A friend that risked her life to come back and help me. I see stars and stumble back. Then blackness. Then nothing.

53

HYSTERIA

I wake up in Danny's old room. My father is sitting on a chair beside me. Just the sight of him triggers tears that stream down my face. "You're a monster. Just kill me now and stop all of this. I don't want to live anymore."

"It's not that easy. But it's tempting." He's done talking and walks out of the room. I'm so close to the crawlspace, and I have one more phone in there. It's my last chance to call the agency.

I sit up and am joined by a Native American, the one who actually stands in the symbolic corner for *spirit*. He's in full headdress, and there are feathers sticking straight up out of a headband of some sort. His face is war-painted, and I lose it. I can't help but laugh. This is all too much. I'm bordering on hysteria. As hard as I try, I can't stop laughing. I know I must look insane, which makes me laugh even harder. He's less than amused by my disrespect. My father yells up the stairs and tells me to stop. It makes me laugh harder. I hear him limp up the stairs, and suddenly it's not so funny. He looks around the room and spots a fishing rod. Here we go! I'm in for it. But I don't really care.

I instinctively roll over, preferring an ass whooping to more shots to the face. He whacks me hard, over and over. I wince but don't scream. I realize the physical pain is easier to take then the mental anguish I feel. On the sixth or seventh blow, the rod breaks and he throws it across the room. I turn back over to look him in the eye. Something is changing. He's lost control, and he knows it. I may have been the one beaten, but he's the one who looks broken. With his head down, he walks out of the room and back downstairs.

The Native American shakes his head but is back at it. He's chanting. He's walking around the small room chanting something ritualistic. I make a run for it, but he traps me at the doorframe. With strength I can only describe as divine, I push him with all my might, and he falls down the stairs, taking my father out with him. I dart into my old room and recite the password. I'm in and the door is locked. The dogs are jumping all over me and barking. I need a break and lie on the floor and let it all out. I sob, my shoulders heaving. I remember the phone and grab it. There's only one area to get service—by the bathroom vent. I'm not getting anything. *Oh, come on!* I'm so desperate. I finally get a signal and call the agency, telling them everything I can in a short amount of time. The woman on the other end of the line sounds shaken but promises to have a task force there as soon as possible. They already have word from the man I sent to the hospital. I'm relieved and a little surprised to know he made it.

I'm trying to think straight and look out the peephole. I see Mr. Brandt—his head is bandaged. I hope that means Danny and Ryan got to him. Where are they? I hope they found a safe place. The now also-limping Native American, Mr. Dennis, and my father are walking in circles all around the house. They must have assumed I climbed out of the window again. My father is screaming orders to the other men. They split up and take off in different areas of the woods. My father remains on the grounds. I need to focus and commit to my next move. Unfortunately, with Danny, Ryan, and Sal out there, I can't in good conscience stay here. I'm still wearing the prison uniform, so I dig around for other clothes. I find some of Danny's camo gear and put it on. I take Katie's shoes off and examine my feet. They're a blistery mess. I apply some first aid cream and Band-Aids. Katie's hiking boots are still in here too. I put them on and gulp down a huge glass of water.

The men ran in every direction except toward the Brandt Estate where I know they have Sal. I need to get to him first. I look out the peephole again and my father is pacing and shaking his head. He can't believe that I've vanished.

I open the safe room door and peek out. The room is empty. The fire ladder is not in the window anymore, so they must have yanked it. I go back in the safe room with the realization that I'm going to have to go out the front door. How? I'm so exhausted.

I take another deep breath and slip out. I look cautiously down the vacant stairs. As quietly as I can, I descend. I hear people in the kitchen, so I can't go out that way. I hope Jack and Katie don't come home yet, or they'll be dead meat too.

I sneak around the corner and open the basement door. I've just begun to descend when someone grabs my leg. I manage to stifle a scream and try not to lose my balance but fall into a sitting position on the stairs. It's the man we put in the safe, David Rawtom. He sees it's me. "It's okay. It's okay. Shh," he says.

"What are you doing down here?"

"I got in through the doors. I saw the whole damn wolf thing. I was hoping to help you. I'm so sorry. I swear I knew nothing about any of this."

I ask him to lift his pant leg, so I can see his tattoo. He shows it to me, and I ask why he has one. "It's part traditional, part my son's idea. I see why now."

"I'm at a loss. I tried calling the police and no one answers. I've been hiding under the stairs and had no choice but to knock that guy out." I look and see a body. I get closer and see that it's Christopher Brandt.

"He is the police. You know that, right?"

"I know it now," he says.

"Any idea what ritual your cousin-in-law was about to perform on me?"

"I have no idea. Our people are peaceful people. So whatever ritual they were about to perform has been contrived."

"I figured. I'm going to need to get out of here to find my family." I grab Christopher's gun and hand it to him.

"I don't like guns. You take it and I'll take my chances."

"Okay. I'm going to run behind the house. If you see anyone on my trail, alert me somehow." I remind him the safe isn't a bad place to hide if he needs a place. He shakes his head.

"Not going back in there, dear. I hope you know what you're doing."

"Me too," I say. He leans in and gives me an awkward half-embrace. I need a full one and pull him all the way in. He's very paternal and I need the positive aura and energy that's radiating from him. He backs out of the embrace, looks at me, and smiles. "You got this, sweetheart."

"God, I hope so."

On three, we each open a side of the Bilco doors. I dodge behind the biggest tree on the property. I'm glad it's overgrown now and remember how annoyed I was the first day I saw it. I seem to be in the clear and run fast and furious, deep into the woods behind the house, then up a tree stand and wait to see who follows. My ass is throbbing where my dad beat me. I curse him under my breath. There are two men. They must have heard my footsteps and run in my direction. I start to feel hopeless and trapped again. I know I need to stay positive, but I can't help but think of Jodi. Of what my father did to her. I will never be able to un-see it.

Another thought occurs to me, to run for the Jeep, but the men are just feet away now. I can almost hear them breathing.

Then I hear the siren. The creepy military alert siren from yesterday. The men change course and run toward the Brandt Estate. I descend down the tree and run up the steep hill. I pass Mr. Rossi's body on the way up. It's starting to decay and smell. I hold my breath until I'm well beyond it and in view of the house. It looks empty. I open the back door, head in through the garage, and back the Jeep out and onto Red Rock Road. I'm not totally sure how to find the holding cell via any back routes, so I circle my way all the way around and come up on Deep Creek Road before the covered bridge. It's as far as I can go with the car. I climb out and channel my sense of direction. There's no room for error or time to get lost. I'm at the base of our meadow, which will lead me to our side of the memorial. I run. No time to think.

54

TRUST ISSUES

I'm out of breath from running and need to stop. My lungs hurt.
I take the moment to look around and listen. I'm not totally
sure where I am. There are no tree stands in sight, so I have to
go on gut instinct. I smell something burning. They must be firing up
the incinerator. Sal.

I have renewed energy and know I need to find him before it's too
late. I continue running in the most likely direction until I see smoke.
I'm getting close and hear voices. I freeze and look up trying to find a
stand but still don't see any. The voices are coming closer. Ryan
comes into full view, nonchalantly talking to another man. *What the
hell!* Where's my brother?

I'd call out to him, but I need to find Sal. Who is Ryan talking to?
He's joined by two other men and some hounds. I'm so confused. I
stay still and wait until they're out of sight. They're working their
way back to the farm. I take off again, dodging trees one at a time
until I'm behind the memorial. I can see the incinerator waiting to
ash its next guest.

I have Christopher Brandt's rifle ready to fire and move to the
front of the mysterious, pillared folly. I look in and see Sal. He's been

brutally beaten. I dig into my bra and find the key, unlock it, and go inside. He's tied to the chair and looks drugged.

I shake him. "Sal. Sal. Sal." He moans.

"Jen?"

"Sal, we have to get out of here."

I can't free him. I walk back out and spot one man at the incinerator. I have to take him on. I have no choice. With gun pointed, I move in fast. He didn't hear me coming.

"Let this man go or I'll shoot you and shove you in there."

He's taken way off guard and makes the mistake of disbelieving me. He takes a step toward me, and I fire. I catch him in the shin, no doubt permanently disabling him. He hollers and hands me the key. "What the fuck? I was going to give it to you." He's off and hobbling away to get help.

The sound of gunfire will reverse Ryan's course. He and his new buddies will be here soon. My adrenaline is working against me and I'm fumbling with the cuffs. The key is so tiny. Finally, I have him free and he's attempting to look at me through swollen eyes. I find a water bottle and make him drink. He's weak and dehydrated.

"Come on, Sal. Work with me. We need to go."

"You shouldn't have come back for me. I have nothing. This place has taken everything from me."

"I'm still here. It's still me and you against the world. And your mom, Sal. You need to get up and move for your mom's sake. She needs you." He thinks about it and knows I'm right.

"I'm sorry, Jen. I'm sorry I put you through so much."

"There's time for all of that later. Come on."

I get him on his feet, which are rubbery, but his morale is rising.

As predicted, Ryan is working his way toward us. Why didn't he let Sal out of the prison? I'm angry and confused again.

"Jenny. Baby, thank God." He rushes to my side but I'm cold and suddenly paranoid that Ryan may not be the man I thought he was. Maybe he is in cahoots with his old man. Maybe they even struck a new deal.

"Where's Danny?"

"He's making his way back to the farm from the other side. We split up hoping at least one of us would find you." The lack of trust in my expression along with the cold shoulder looks like it's cutting him deep.

"Come on, Jenny. You don't trust me?"

"Why did you leave Sal in here? I just shot a guy who was probably going to shove him in the incinerator alive."

"No, he wasn't." He moves in closer to me and I step back.

"Jenny. You're the only one with the key."

"Bullshit. He was put in here way after I took the key. Antonio was in here first, so someone else had a key and put Sal in here."

Sal speaks up. "He's right, Jen. I remember now. Ryan and several other people tried to get in but couldn't."

"The only other guy with a key is missing, Jenny. We did try to get him out. I swear," Ryan insists.

Sal holds my hand and gives it a squeeze. I let my guard down again and am flooded with emotion. I can't help but cry. I look at Ryan and apologize. "I'm sorry. I just don't know who to trust anymore."

He slowly steps toward me and I allow him to pull me in. I wince at the pain it causes me from my father's beating.

Ryan lifts up the back of my shirt and sees the marks. There's fire in his eyes.

"You can trust me. I promise."

"I know. I'm sorry."

He lifts my chin so we're eye-to-eye. He examines the bruises on my cheek and the rip in my lip. A tear goes down his cheek in empathy and guilt for being unable to protect me. "What did he do to you?" Sal wants to know too.

"It's not important. Let's find Danny."

Sal is fired up and looking like his old self, ready for battle. Ryan wants my father's head on a platter.

One of the men with Ryan breaks up the moment. "Okay, now what?"

"If my brother is on his way back to the farm, he's in trouble. It's a war-zone over there. I did manage to call the agency and they should be here soon. But Danny. I'm worried about him. If he's caught, my father will take his rage out on him."

I look at the men surrounding us. "Who are these guys, and where have you and Danny been until now?"

"The good guys. My guys. They got us out of a holding space in my dad's basement. All these years." He shakes his head. "Have you seen *my* father?" Ryan asks.

"Yes. And he looks injured. He had some kind of bandage around his head."

One of the men shifts around cocky looking for attention. "You can thank Bruce here for that." Ryan pats him on the back. "Gave him a good blow and got us out."

"Well, let's get moving back to the farm. Jack and Katie are going to be home any minute. They're not safe."

I feel a little better with the protection of these men and the hounds. We head back, even though I dread it.

55

PSALM 25

W e're a rough-looking bunch by the time we make it to the woods behind the barn. The hounds are going apeshit, so it's not like we're sneaking up on anyone at this point. We're going all-in confrontation.

I'm frustrated to see a dozen or so more men with my father and Mr. Brandt. It's like they come out of the woodwork. They're waiting for us. Waiting to punish us. The Native American who was hovering over me is now out of his garb and in jeans alongside Mr. Rawtom's son. Ben Grover is sitting on the retaining wall looking shell-shocked. He's going to need psychological help like the rest of us. I assume Jill is dead and didn't survive her hunt. It's hard to think about anyone dying in such a way. Ben's loyalty to this group must be deeper than the love for his wife. I don't understand it.

I notice Danny lying lifeless on the grass near the patio and give Sal my gun and permission to kill my father if he rushes me. I dash to Danny's side. Ryan and his guys also have guns drawn.

"Danny!" I shake him and check for a pulse. I find one and flip him over. There's fresh blood covering the front of his shirt. My assumption is that he's been shot. I lift it up and take a step back, unable to believe my eyes. They marked him. They carved out the symbol for *earth* on the front of his chest with a sharp instrument. It's deep enough to leave scars, but thankfully not deep enough to kill him. I look over at my father, who's smirking like he won a round. I look back at Danny's chest and dry heave.

Ryan makes his way over and sees what I'm seeing.

"*Please* let me kill him," he begs.

"No, don't. The agency will be here any minute. I want him locked up, so he can think about this for the rest of his life."

I look back at my father and he's waiting for my predictable defiance. I cover Danny's wounds and stroke his hair. "Danny. Wake up," I repeat. He reacts to my voice and opens his eyes, trying to remember what happened. He feels pain and puts a hand on his belly. He lifts up his shirt and sees it. Danny must have been out at least when they did it because he doesn't seem to remember.

"I know. I know. I saw." He tears up. "John knows ten good surgeons who can clean that shit up. It'll be okay." He makes an effort to smile and reaches for my hand. I tell him how much I love him and to just stay down.

I get up and walk over to my father. He isn't armed, but some of his buddies have guns aimed at me. He orders them to lower them.

"I want to hear what she has to say."

I'm thinking long and hard about it. I'm tempted to spit in his face. I'm tempted to throw a punch. But I stay in control.

"I know enough about your father, but what ever happened to your mother? You took her name because you loved her, didn't you?"

He's taken off guard by the question and looks from me to the rest of his group. They all take a few steps back.

"What happened? She didn't know her place? Was she abused? Is she still alive? Would she be proud of you?" My father is thinking, so I'm definitely striking a nerve. "Would she be proud that you turned out just like your father?"

"Enough! I'm nothing like my father." He slouches, and his eyes take to the ground. He's got a memory that I wish I could pull out of thin air and see for myself. Perhaps nightmarish memories. I push him.

"What did she look like?"

"Enough." He scolds and takes a step toward me like he's going to assault me. But he stops himself. I've gotten into his head, at least a little. The thought of his own abuse must be surfacing. I press on with my questioning.

"Do I look anything like her? My grandmother?"

He's back in a memory and gives in to the question. "Your eyes. You have her eyes." My father's anger shifts to sadness. Dark and deep sadness.

"Is she still alive?"

"No."

I don't push any further. Whatever happened to my grandmother ... it most likely doesn't say "natural causes" on her death certificate.

He looks at a loss for the next step. Then I hear it. The sound I've been waiting for. Sirens. Helicopters. He looks at me with surprise. "What have you done?"

His men prepare for more war. Ryan is calling for me to come back to him. And then I hear a gunshot. From where? I look in the direction where my father was standing and he's down. He's been shot. A sniper got to him already?

I look at Ryan and Sal and the other men, who are just as confused. Then another shot echoes through the chaos, and Mr. Brandt is down. We all take cover, not knowing who's firing and from where. Then I see her. It's Mrs. Rossi. Breast cancer or not, she looks strong as nails.

Sal screams, "Ma! No!" and covers me, worried she'll take a shot at me next, but she doesn't. She drops the gun and screams profanity in Italian. I can understand most of it, and it's actually quite appropriate at the moment.

The property is surrounded by a small army of men, some in SWAT gear, some state troopers, and some FBI. A helicopter lands in the meadow and K-9s on leashes gallop toward the scene with their masters trying to keep up. Despite my relief, I feel sad.

The remaining members are put in handcuffs. There's police tape being tied from one tree to the next. I look back at my father and he's eyeing me. I walk slowly to his side and kneel down.

He's been hit in the chest, but the opposite side from his heart, if he has one. He's going to live. The paramedics scramble to his side. I'm numb, not sure if I'm relieved or disappointed. I'm about to go back to Danny's side when he calls out to me. I kneel back down beside him.

"Jenny. I know you judge me, but you don't understand everything. All of this. All of this is to protect what our Order is really all about. This is nothing. We can still be a team someday. That's all I've ever wanted." I believe him, but I don't forgive him. And I'm not in the least bit curious to know what they're really about. It doesn't matter.

"While I'm in prison, study. Find the monographs. Study the ancient mysteries. Learn." He's delirious and drifting in and out of consciousness. He's still talking about his Order. But his Order is history.

He opens his eyes again. "I'll be out soon. Swim, Jenny. Channel your psychic abilities." He's not making any sense, and I can't take any more cult talk.

"Dad, you're not coming out of jail. You'll be tried and sentenced as a judge and jury see fit. You will not get the chance to go through a trial by wolf. You will not be reborn this time. You will have to pay for your sins."

I have a moment of clarity and remember Psalm 25. The verse that inspired his cult to create the Twenty-Fifth Acre. I recite it to my father.

"In you, LORD my God, I put my trust. I trust in you. Do not let me be put to shame, nor let my enemies triumph over me. No one who hopes in you will ever be put to shame, but shame will come on those who are treacherous without cause."

He smiles at me with a look of pride, which is not what I was going for.

"I can't comprehend how you thought all of this was okay. How you slipped so deep into madness. I can't imagine anything more shameful than what you've built. In what you've done. And I can't imagine anyone who's more treacherous without a true cause than you.

"Your enemies. The ones you created have triumphed over *you*. I have complete trust in God to take it from here."

He turns his head to the side and closes his eyes.

I hear my name being hollered, louder and louder.

"Tricia. Tricia. Tricia!"

Oh no. It's Katie running ahead of Jack. My father's head pops up to take a look at them, his eyes locked on Katie. They run up the hill toward me. A few FBI agents try to stop them, but I ask to let them through, telling them it's their house.

Ryan and Danny rush to my side. Sal is next to his mother who's now in handcuffs.

Katie is desperate to know what's happening. Jack has both hands covering his mouth in disbelief as he takes in the scene. "Kiddo?" he asks. I look at Jack through watery eyes.

"Jack." I pause, looking for the right words. "Jack, have I got a story for you."

ABOUT THE AUTHOR

Heather Slawecki lived in four towns in Upper and Central Bucks County, Pennsylvania. One of her favorite homes was an old farmhouse similar to her main character's. She enjoyed the best of everything: Swimming in streams, tubing down the Delaware River, and riding her horse almost every day with her best friend.

Heather is a proud graduate of Central Bucks High School East and of Widener University where she holds a Bachelor of Arts Degree in English Literature.

She began her writing career as a feature writer for the *Bucks County Courier Times* and has spent the last twenty-five years as an award-winning senior copywriter.

Heather currently lives in Delaware with her husband, daughter and two playful kittens who hop on her keyboard every time she starts to type! In her spare time, she loves gardening, cooking, and volunteering.

Follow Heather on social media to learn about events, read her free blog, and find out about new releases:

facebook.com/graylynpress

twitter.com/HeatherSlawecki

instagram.com/heather_slawecki

AUTHOR'S NOTE

Thank you so much for reading Book 1 of my debut trilogy, *Element of Secrecy*. It has been an incredible experience.

Because I'm a busy working mom, I don't have much time to read. I hear the same story from so many other people. Therefore, my goal was to create a fast-paced, fun, interesting, suspenseful series that simply makes you want to drop the remote, sit down, and binge away from the TV.

If I succeeded, I would be so grateful if you took a few minutes to write a review on Amazon. Good reviews mean a lot personally and professionally.

When you're ready, dive right into *Element of Danger*, Book II, for more mystery, adventure, and suspense.

ALSO BY HEATHER SLAWECKI

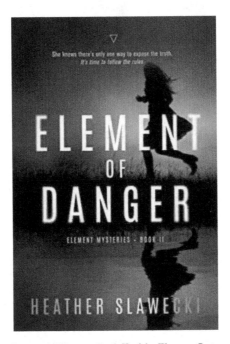

Element of Danger, Book II of the Element Series

A devastating murder brings Jenny O'Rourke back to her hometown. The reality is, it's not over. Not even close. This time she has a new strategy to put an end to it all—infiltrate her father's secret society. The question is, how? A chance meeting brings her face to face with a member of the inner circle, a boy she once knew. He has the intel she needs, and she has what he lustfully desires. It's a dangerous combination. Jenny finds herself swept away by the lure of adventure and the reveal of mysterious springs, sinkholes, submerged caverns, and elaborate underground dwellings. As she acquires a sliver of society knowledge, she's determined to understand the rest. But, there's only one barbaric way to get to it. Becoming one of them requires following their rules. Rules that could easily kill her. There's a lot at stake, but she's ready and willing to risk it all.

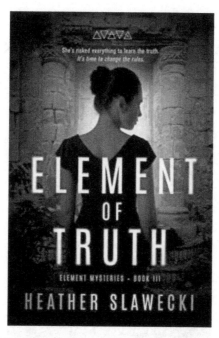

Element of Truth, Book III of the Element Series

As Jenny O'Rourke recovers from a near-death punishment ritual, she gains access to a world she didn't know existed. She discovers the secret order, which she sought to destroy, contains ancient mystical wisdom, untapped scientific breakthroughs, religious truths never known, natural wonders and more. As she tries to sort it out, she also tries to wiggle her way out of a love triangle. Will she choose the man she's destined to marry—the one who has always protected her—or the man she's forbidden to be with? More dramatic events halt her progress but, finally, she's given permission to initiate. Jenny delves through Five Days of Knowledge, each day enlightening her more and drawing her in. Now that she understands the marvel of each element, and the order's original path, she can't deny that she is privy to something special. Something worth protecting. In the end, she has to decide whether to destroy the secret society that nearly killed her ... or to take her rightful place in it.